LESSONS IN LETTING GO

A Study Abroad Novel

JESSICA PETERSON

ALSO BY JESSICA PETERSON

FOLLOW ME, Y'ALL!

- Join my Facebook reader group, The City Girls, and hang out in one of the coolest spots on the internet. I'm biased, but I'm also pretty thrilled by how awesome the people in my group are.
- Follow my not-so-glamorous life as a romance author on Instagram @JessicaPAuthor
- Follow me on Goodreads
- Follow me on Bookbub
- Like my Facebook Author Page

LESSONS IN LETTING GO
Study Abroad #3

Published by Peterson Paperbacks, LLC
Copyright 2016, Peterson Paperbacks, LLC
Cover by Najla Qamber of Qamber Designs

❀ Created with Vellum

Chapter One

RHYS

August
Madrid, Spain

It's just after nine A.M. and the air is thick with arid heat. The Spanish sun, a white-hot pinprick in a huge, cloudless sky, bears down on my face and shoulders. I'm only on my first lap around the football pitch and already I'm sweating bullets.

As if my recent performance—or lack thereof—hasn't made these training sessions brutal enough, now I've got this hellacious heat to contend with. When I was growing up, I couldn't wait to escape the near constant drizzle and shivery damp of Wales. But now that I've lived in Spain for a couple years, I'd give my left nut for one of those rainy Welsh days.

A drop of sweat lands in my eye. I wince, wiping it away with my shoulder. I wince again at the low throb of pain in my left leg. It radiates down my hamstring and settles in my knee. Mother*fucker.* It's been more than a year since the surgery. My knee should be feeling better. Much better.

It's not. It hurts. But then again, so does everything else.

1

My legs, my lungs. I feel sore. Tired. Worn out. Not an auspicious way to start the season that's supposed to save my career. My play has been absolute shite for months now, pretty much from the moment my surgeon cleared me to play again. I've got to do better.

I pick up my pace, trying to push through the pain. I don't care how much it hurts. I'm not going down. Everyone —fans, media, my teammates and managers, people back home—they keep waiting for me to follow in my infamous father's footsteps. *The apple doesn't fall far from the tree*, they whisper behind my back.

I can't end up like him. Not with so many people back home depending on me. He let them down, but I won't.

I pump my legs harder, faster. I'm the first one on the pitch this morning—training doesn't usually start until ten— in the hopes that some extra dedication will make up for my embarrassing performance as of late. I can't help but think that maybe *this* will be the practice where everything changes. Where I play like the superstar I want to be, the superstar everyone thought I'd mature into when Madrid first traded for me. Maybe today is the turning point.

But judging from the stringent burn in my quads, it's not looking good.

"Ah! Mon petit chou! My little cabbage, what is 'e doing all alone on ze pitch? So very early today!"

I start at the sound of a familiar voice. I close my eyes in an attempt not to roll them. The last person I want to see right now is Olivier Seydoux, our squad captain. Yes, he's my closest mate on the team, but he's also a pain in the ass. It doesn't help he's got the entire organization—managers, trainers, even the kit men—calling me "little cabbage." I honestly have no idea what it means, but I do know I hate it.

"It's not even nine thirty, and already you're busting my bollocks," I yell across the field, turning to face him. "Who

2

pissed on your croissant this morning, you smelly Frenchman?"

He stands by the goal, a shit-eating grin on his face as he tugs at the zipper of his jumper. The sun glints off his black skin and bald head. I get why half the women in the world want to bang Olivier's brains out. He's tall and has magazine-cover good looks, and is one of the best strikers in the league.

That doesn't mean I have to be nice to him, though. Not today.

"Ah, ze little cabbage, 'e is feeling very sensitive today, eh? Is it ze women troubles?" he asks, jogging over to meet me.

"Listen, mate, I live off boiled chicken and broccoli and go to bed at nine every night. What woman in her right mind would sign up for that?"

Olivier falls easily into step beside me. "You are a foot-baller! You 'ave a little blond man bun! From what ze womens tell me, zey love you and your 'airs very much."

"No time for girls," I grunt, trying to keep up as Olivier quickens his pace. He's a full head taller than I am, and his stride is enormous. "I've got to focus on my footy."

"Fo-*kus*. What a boring F word. I zink you should fo-*kus* on a better one. Like—"

"Frozen yogurt?" I almost jump when I see Fredrik Ohr's giant blond bulk trotting behind us. His German accent, usually quite slight, thickens when he's out of breath. "And is training starting early now? Where did everybody go?"

"No, our petit chou is fo-kusing on 'is footy, so 'e comes early to ze pitch," Olivier replies. "But I think 'e should fo-kus on other zings too."

"Frozen yogurt really does it for me," Fred says. "Some-times it's the only thing that gets me through that last hour of training—knowing I will have a giant cone of vanilla chocolate swirl on the way back to my flat. It's like my good luck charm."

I blink. "Seriously?"

"Seriously. You should try it."

"I'll do anything at this point to find a good luck charm. Do either of you know a shaman? Maybe a practitioner of voodoo?"

"Me, thinking of having ze naked fun with my lady is *very* motivating," Olivier says. He spins around to face us, still keeping pace even though he's running backward.

"I wish I could find a lady to have naked fun with," Fred says.

"You wish you could find a lady, period," I say.

"Ha bloody ha," he replies. "But it is true. You know I am fucking shit at talking to girls. They're just so . . . pretty. And they smell so good. I sniff their perfume, and poof! My brains spill out of my ears and I forget how to speak."

"Maybe you should give my pickup lines a try," I say, smiling.

"Thanks but no thanks, Cabbage," Fred huffs. "I think silence works better."

"Silence definitely works better," Olivier says.

We round a corner of the pitch. My legs feel like lead weights. Keeping up with the lads didn't used to feel so hard, I used to be one of the fastest blokes on the squad.

I *am* one of the fastest blokes on the squad. I just . . . I don't know. For a while I thought it was my knee that held me back. I mean, it definitely hurts. But I'm starting to think that the pain is part of a bigger problem.

I've got to keep pushing. Maggie's waiting on the education I promised her, and she and Mum are still living in Splott, the inner-city ward in Cardiff where I grew up. Mum refuses to leave until her sisters and all my cousins can leave too. No one else is going to get them out of there.

It's up to me. It's up to me to get the help Aunt Kate needs with her eleven-year-old daughter, Marie, who requires round-the-clock care. And then there's my cousin Will, who is too much like my father for his own good and really needs to go to rehab, but no one can afford to send him. My cousin Rachel is expecting her first kid, my other cousin Lydia just dropped out of school to help support the family but can't find work—

God, that's a lot. But considering my aunts helped to raise me after my dad left—considering how dirt poor they all are—taking care of them is the least I can do. We are one big, sometimes-happy-most-times-dysfunctional family.

"You all right, Cabbage?" Olivier asks.

"Stop showing off." I wave him and his backward running away. "I can outrun your ass any day, backward or forward."

Olivier smirks. "Not with zat bum knee of yours."

"I'm going to jam this bum knee into your bollocks. Then we'll see who's faster."

"I put my money on Cabbage. Meaning no offense, Olivier," Fred says.

"None taken." Olivier turns his attention back to me. The beautiful bastard, he hasn't even broken a sweat yet. "I know you 'ave worries about ze future, Cabbage. You 'ave much talent. You will get your rhythm back, I know it. Maybe ze womens, zey will 'elp you find it? I 'ave been in love before, and I played my best footy zen. Sometimes, ze love, it can fokus you. Remind you of ze love you felt for football before all ze moneys and ze crazy parties."

I shake my head. "Not worth the risk. You saw what happened with Alessandro—he fell head over heels for that Italian chick, what's-her-name, and now he can't pay a football club to take him."

"She *was* really hot," Fred says.

"Idiot, that Alessandro," Olivier says. "In my mind, it is up to ze man to decide whether 'e will be distracted by love or inspired by it. If you are with ze right woman, you will make ze right choice."

I glance over Olivier's shoulder at the mountains in the distance. Spain may be hot as Hades, but it is a beautiful place, especially if you're taking it in from the practice pitch of the most valuable sports franchise in the entire world. I used to dream about training here. When I was thirteen and skinny and living with my two aunts and five cousins in a tiny, run-down flat, I'd spend hours imagining what it would be like to play for Madrid's famously dominant squad. I remember wanting very, very badly to be a part of something so special.

Wanting to right the wrongs my father made on this very pitch.

Now I'm here. Building a career in professional football is so much harder than I ever imagined it would be, but I still don't want to lose my place—I don't want to leave. I have too much to lose.

And I am a very sore loser, if the number of red cards I have is any indication.

"Heads up, lads, gaffer's coming out," I say, nodding at the lean figure in smart trousers and a scarf making its way towards us.

"Oh, Christ," Fred says. "I wonder what William Wallace is going to bludgeon us with today."

I bite back a grin. Our manager's elegant outward appearance hides a very angry, very feisty Scotsman with a mouth that'll put hair on your grandmum's chest.

"Bring it in, ye tits, it's time to get goin'!" he shouts.

Olivier turns back around and starts to sprint. I take off two steps behind him, pumping my legs harder, harder, my lungs burning as I pass him just as we reach Coach at the top of the pitch.

Olivier arches a brow as we hustle to a stop. "See?" he

pants. "We just talk about ze womens, and already you run faster."

"Women?" Coach asks. "What fecking women are you two bawbags gettin' on about?"

"Bawbags?" Fred asks.

"Scrotums," Olivier replies.

"Oh," Fred says.

"It's nothing," I say, turning to Coach. "We weren't talking about anything. What's on the schedule today?"

A few hours later

Fred comes flying down the touchline, his bright orange singlet flapping against his beefy build as he dodges Matteo. He almost decks Ignacio before passing the ball to me, the shouts—most in Spanish, a few in incomprehensible Scots—of the lads and our coaches filling the air as I move toward the goal. My pulse throbs in time to the frantic refrain inside my head: *don't mess this up, don't mess this up, please God, don't mess this up.* We've got a big match in two days against our rival team in Madrid, and I'd like to prove to Coach that I'm worthy of quality playing time.

I see Olivier waiting from the corner of my eye. He darts across the pitch, trying to elbow aside two very big, very insistent defenders. Sweat drips into my eyes and makes them sting. The sun is so hot I feel like I'm being roasted inside an oven. I'm exhausted, waiting for the coaches to blow their whistles and end this interminable practice session, but so far, no dice.

I remember, vaguely, how much I used to love playing footy. Just playing for playing's sake, running around the muddy pitch in Splott with my mates and a half-deflated football. I lived and breathed the game because I loved it, almost

7

as much as I loved my mum and the little spice cakes she'd make. Football was an escape. When I was on that pitch, it didn't matter that I was poor and everyone thought I'd end up in the gutter, just like Dad. All that mattered was how I played. And because I played well, I felt important. Wanted. Strong. Some nights I couldn't go to sleep because I was so excited about playing football the next morning.

Now it's all I can do to drag myself out of bed when I have to play.

Panic electrifies my limbs as I dribble the ball closer to the goal. It's just so hard to focus. So hard to clear my mind and let my instincts take over. I'm trying, I really am, but I can't do it.

I bloody hate it.

Frustration blurs my vision before I'm even in the box. The voices of my mates and the managers press in on me, my feet stumbling beneath my unsteady stride. I try to forget the slight twinge in my knee and keep going.

It's getting harder and harder to just keep going.

In the split-second that Olivier manages to untangle himself from the defenders, I launch the ball across the pitch, aiming it a little in front of him. I watch, heart in my throat, as Olivier leaps into the air, scrunching his eyes shut as he anticipates nailing a solid header.

The ball soars more than two meters behind and four meters above his head and hits the sideboards with an audible *thwack*. My heart drops. My face burns.

Shit.

The pass wasn't even close. It was *awful*. Not worthy of an amateur, much less Madrid's Great Welsh Hope. (That's what the press called me when I first came to Madrid. *The Great Welsh Nope* has appeared in a headline or two over the past few months. I wish I could say it didn't rankle.)

Coach holds his hands behind his head and blows out his

8

cheeks. The lads look away. Fred claps me on the back, telling me to keep my head up. I feel like burying it in the grass.

I bungle one drill after the next. My passes are laughably inaccurate. My attempted goals soar above or past or way outside the net, so much so that our goalie, Alexsandr, yawns not once but twice as I work inside the box. My footwork is messy and my speed is nonexistent.

The whistles sound. Training ends. I hit a new low—this is the lowest I think I've ever felt on the pitch. I make a beeline for the showers and don't say a word to anyone in the locker room. I can't wait to hole up in my penthouse suite—my flat is currently being renovated—and lick my wounds in private.

I'm doing everything I'm supposed to. I've rehabbed my knee, I put hundreds of hours in at training, I take care of my body—all in the hope that my hard work will pay off, and my luck will change.

How bloody long do I have to wait for my luck to change?

It won't be long before I'm dropped from the first team, or worse. William Wallace's patience with me is wearing thin, and there are countless other lads on the reserve team rearing to take my place and prove their talent. My agent has gently warned me that if I don't show improvement in the next few matches, I may not have much of a future in football at all.

So much rides on me turning this thing around. And time is running out.

Chapter Two

LAURA

A Few Days Later
Madrid, Spain

Maybe it's the man bun.

Maybe it's the tattoos that cover his arms from neck to wrist and curl beyond the collar of his jersey.

Maybe it's his baby blue eyes. Or his ferocious, angry-Welshman style of play. Or the way his lips twitch into a confidently wicked smirk—oh, that smirk, it slays every vagina in a thousand-mile radius—after the ref makes a call that shouldn't go his way but does.

I don't know what it is about Rhys Maddox, studly soccer superstar, that's got me reaching inside my yoga pants while I watch the highlights from this afternoon's game. All I know is that he does it for me in a big, orgasmic, toe-curling way. Yeah, he's having a rough season, but that doesn't change the fact that he's smoking hot. I bet his skin audibly sizzles upon contact.

My hand slides lower, my middle finger dipping between the slippery lips of my sex. Jesus, I've been watching these highlights for, what, three minutes, and already I'm this hot and bothered? Rhys has to be my most potent celeb crush I've ever had. I love a good celebrity crush. It's pure, delicious fantasy.

Orgasms are the name of my game this semester, and fantasy Rhys is all too happy to help me out there. The hookup culture back at Meryton University bred this kind of sick double standard when it came to sex. I always got the guys I was with off, but they never, ever returned the favor. And I finally realized that I'd been so obsessed with what turned on my boyfriends, I had no idea what actually turned *me* on. So now I'm doing a little—okay, a lot—of masturbating to figure out what I do and don't like when it comes to fantasy, touch, and . . . well, pleasure.

I suck in a breath as the tip of my finger grazes the slick, swollen nub at the top of my sex. Sensation, tight and hot, bolts through me. My finger strokes my clit again and again, circling, slow, insistent caresses that have my back arching off the fluffy expanse of my giant hotel bed. My apartment for the semester won't be ready for another few days, so my parents put me up at this five-star spot in the meantime. It's ridiculous, I know, but I wasn't about to turn down two nights at Madrid's ritziest hotel.

I watch Rhys slide tackle a guy on TV, sweat pouring down his face as he rips off his shirt when the game ends. My eyes settle on Rhys's bare chest and torso. He's got a leanly chiseled body, broad shoulders that move into a sculpted chest and washboard abs, his smooth, tan skin slick with sweat. An athlete's body. A trail of dark blond hair arrows down the flat plane of his stomach, disappearing into the waistband of his shorts.

Yum.

Even in his anger he moves gracefully, forcefully, the muscles in his biceps bulging as he clasps his hands at the back of his head in defeat. Digging his teeth into his bottom lip, he yells something to no one in particular.

Something that looks a lot like *fuck*.

I almost come, the first stirrings of my orgasm slithering through my body, tightening the muscles in my legs.

Fuck me, I plead.

My eyes flutter shut and Rhys is there. Shirtless. Sweaty. Smirking his deadly smirk.

With pleasure, love, he murmurs in his gorgeous Welsh accent.

My orgasm hits me hard, a wave of potent, throbbing sensation.

I smile. I'm getting there—I'm figuring it out, my sexuality, my likes. I've come more in the past few weeks than I have in the past few *years* combined.

I've always had a boyfriend. I wouldn't say I'm boy crazy, and I don't intentionally seek out long-term relationships. But I dated a guy pretty much all through high school, and when we broke up my freshman year of college, I kinda fell into another relationship with the brooding music major down the hall. We split up sophomore year. A week later, the cute dude I'd flirted with at a fraternity mixer showed up at my door, and a week after that, we were exclusive.

I don't regret dating any of those guys. Well—maybe I regret the music major, he was pretty douchey. But now that I'm single for the first time in, like, forever, I recognize how much of myself I sacrificed while I was in those relationships. I'm a bit of a people-pleaser, so whatever I thought my boyfriend at the time wanted, I made sure to give it to him. I put aside my own needs—orgasmic and otherwise—to make sure he was happy.

My boyfriends never got me off like this. But delicious orgasms like the one I just had are, like, the best thing ever.

Way better than fumbling my way through a hookup in a frat house.

Speaking of orgasms, the one I just had was good. Really, really good.

I close my eyes, let out a sigh of contentment.

My semester of self-love and sexual awakening is off to an excellent start.

After a post-orgasm nap and shower, I settle down on the bed and make a quick call to my bestie for the restie, Emily. She's studying abroad too, but she'll be in London for a full year. Her classes don't start until late September, so she's still at home in the States.

While I wait for her to answer, I grab the hotel's magazine on the bedside table. There's a beautiful, curvy woman on the cover I recognize as Monica Cruz, Spain's most famous plus-size model. She looks fabulous.

"Why hello you world traveler," Em says. "I miss you already. How is Madrid?"

"I mean, I've only been here for a couple hours," I say, flipping to Monica's cover story. "But already I've had some awesome cheese at the airport and an orgasm, so I'd say Madrid is pretty great so far."

"An orgasm? Cheese? Holy shit, who are you? I don't think I've ever seen you touch a piece of cheese, much less eat it."

I laugh. "It just felt like the right thing to do. New semester, new city, new me. Or something like that."

"I approve of this new you. I still can't believe Mr. Frat Star never made you orgasm. I mean, you went *an entire year* without coming."

"And I mean to make up for lost time, believe me. I'm

going to come twelve times a day, and eat so much cheese I develop lactose intolerance."

I hear Em munching on something. I smile. She always eats when she's on the phone, usually something bizarre and condiment-oriented—oyster crackers, cornichons, mustard on a spoon, an oyster-cracker-and-cornichon sandwich *dipped* in mustard on a spoon.

"What about making a bucket list for your semester in Madrid?" she asks around a mouthful of her condiment of the day. "You know, writing down all the things this 'new you' wants to do. Come, eat cheese, go to all the museums in Madrid or whatever. Could be a fun thing for your newly-single self to do. Maybe keep you away from the boys for a bit. It's about time you started treating yourself better and getting healthy again."

I nod. Back at Meryton, my people-pleasing streak bled from boys to my body too. Part of being the perfect girlfriend is—*was,* it *was*—being perfectly pretty. Which of course meant having the perfect body. I do not jest when I say I lost my entire sophomore year to the treadmill. I think I lived off hard-boiled eggs from the dining hall salad bar and iced coffee that year. It was not fun, and it definitely wasn't healthy.

I quickly scan the first couple paragraphs of Monica Cruz article. I can't get over how happy she looks in these pictures, her smile wide, her eyes laughing. She's healthy. Confident. Fearless.

All things I want to be.

Maybe I *can* be those things. Maybe I can be like Monica. Why not? This semester *is* all about fresh starts.

"I like this bucket list idea, Em," I say. "I like it a lot. I don't know what else I want to do besides eat and come, but I'm sure I can think of a couple things."

"Awesome. Listen, I gotta run, Luke is calling me—"

"Say hello to him for me," I say. Luke is Emily's longtime boyfriend she met at freshman orientation and they have been inseparable ever since. Even if he is a little full of himself—his dad is a senator and Luke is confident he'll follow in his footsteps—I like him, mostly because he seems to make Em so happy. They have plans to take the world by storm after we graduate: Luke is going to run for office, and Em is going to be his economic policy advisor. I mean, how cool is that?

"Of course," Em says. "But I'm glad you got to Spain safely and that you're doing you, literally and figuratively. Keep it up. And call me! Love you."

She makes a kissing sound. In my head I can see the crumbs that always stick to the screen of her phone when she does this. A wave of homesickness washes over me.

"Love you too, Em."

I head down to the hotel bar for a bite to eat. Our program warned us Madrileños like to eat late, but I'm still surprised to find the bar empty at a quarter 'til eight.

The bar itself is swanky to the max. Dark lacquered furniture is scattered around the high-ceilinged space, and the walls are covered in antiqued mirrors that blur my reflection into a sexed-up version of my jet-lagged self. I feel seriously underdressed in jeans and a white top, but I'm too hungry to care.

The bartender politely pretends not to judge me for ordering a Midori sour. My mom, a bourbon drinker, says Midori sours are "stupid cocktails stupid teenage girls order with fake IDs" but my Auntie Janice and I respectfully disagree. It's the first drink I've (legally) ordered as the drinking age in Spain is eighteen. Fine by me; I turned twenty last February.

Glancing at the menu, I order what I *think* is some sort of ham sandwich. My Spanish is a little rusty, but I'm proud of myself for not taking up the bartender on his offer to speak English with me.

"No gracias," I tell him. *No thanks. I'd like to practice my Spanish.*

He grins. "Vale," he says, which he then explains is Spain's awesome mash up of "cool/okay/yes/let's do it."

"Vale," I reply, grinning back.

Maybe, in addition to coming and cheese, I should make it a point to learn to speak Spanish fluently this semester.

Sipping on my Midori sour—I know it's not cool but yikes is it good—I start to think about all the fun things I want to do while I'm here. I'm going to try octopus and maybe ride a moped and of course I want to learn flamenco guitar. I'd really like to do some community service (maybe with kids?) and I am going to masturbate twice a day to Rhys Maddox . . .

A list. Em was so right. I need to make a list—a bucket list, if you will—of Fun Things I Shall Do While in Spain.

A spark of excitement catches in my chest. I grab a cocktail napkin from the bar and dig a pen out of my tote bag. Holding the corners of the napkin between my thumb and pinkie, I begin to write.

MY SPAIN BUCKET LIST

- *Orgasms. Keep having them. Keep exploring what I like sexually.*
- *Go see Rhys Maddox play in real life.*
- *Learn to speak Spanish fluently.*
- *Eat carbs, cheese, and weird things like octopus.*
- *Buy jeans in a bigger size without wanting to die.*

I turn the napkin over.

- *Community service—tutor kids? Do literacy work?*

- *Tour of Madrid on a moped (preferably a pink one).*
- *Go see flamenco guitarist/learn how to play?*

I stare at that last bullet point for a while as I slurp the last of my cocktail. There are a million other things I want to do, I just can't think of them at the moment.

Another Midori sour will probably help. So will getting my food. I'm *starving*. It's been a while since I ordered—I wonder if service is usually so slow in Spain?

Setting my glass on the bar, I look up in the hopes of waving down the bartender. I jump when I see a guy standing next to me, so startled I knock my pen to the floor. He must've sidled up when I was lost in thought writing.

"Pardon me," he says, ducking to grab the pen. His British accent is crisp, cut-glass. It sends a shiver down my spine.

He stands, holding out the pen, and meets my eyes. His are blue, a shocking, urgent foil to his deeply tanned skin.

"Here you are," he says.

My stomach drops to the floor with a *squish*. A starry rush fills my head.

I know those eyes.

I know that face. I also know the tattoos that peek through his starched white shirt, unbuttoned at the neck.

Oh God.

Oh *God.*

Ohmigod, ohmigod I am going to scream don't scream don't pee yourself play it cool ohmigod this can't be happening don't pee please don't pee you are in public ohmigod.

It's the real Rhys Maddox. And in the space of three heartbeats I am more turned on by him than I ever was by his fantasy counterpart.

Chapter Three

LAURA

It's like something out of a dream. I reach out in slow motion and take the pen from his hand, my heart hammering inside my throat. This can't be happening. My first night in Madrid and I run into the super-hot footballer I've been crushing on all summer?

I mean, what are the chances?

"Thanks," I breathe. He smells delicious. The musky, clean scent of his cologne fills my head, surrounds me. A familiar heat tugs at the place between my legs. Whatever cologne he's wearing, I want to swim in it.

"Sorry to startle you," he says.

"It's all right," I say, my face burning.

A beat of silence passes between us as his eyes search mine. I'd like to think the silence is heated, filled with sudden, passionate longing, but I know that's just wishful thinking on my part. I've been getting off on this guy for a couple months—back home, I started watching Madrid matches after I was accepted to this study abroad program—so of course my brain is going to short-circuit to all things sex when I see him in real life.

But those baby blues . . . good*ness* they slay me. Their translucent color is warm liquid, less slate blue than warm Caribbean-Sea cerulean. They seem to glow in the low light of the bar.

My face is so hot I'm worried I might faint. Thankfully the bartender appears and Rhys clears his throat, turning to him.

While they chat, I check Rhys out from the corner of my eye. He runs a hand through his thick, dark blond hair. Tonight he's wearing it loose, and it falls with Prince Charming-like elegance away from his face, grazing the top of his collar. His jaw and neck are covered in golden-hued stubble; his profile is strong, handsome, marked by a boyish, pert nose and invitingly full lips. I watch his lips move as he talks, transfixed by their softness, bowled over by the curiosity to know what he tastes like, how he kisses, if he's as good with those lips as he is in my fantasies.

As if his face wasn't gorgeous enough, he's dressed to the nines. Nothing fancy—jeans, white button-down, navy blazer, sneakers—but the way he wears it all makes for a devastatingly perfect whole. The jeans hug his thick, muscled thighs in just the right places. His shirt and blazer fit him so well, so snugly, they must be custom-made. His woven red belt matches his pristine kicks, making him appear at once casual and sexily slick. A monogrammed Louis Vuitton roller suitcase is drawn up beside him.

And don't even get me started on the tattoos. I can only see them when he moves just so, peeking from underneath the sleeve of his blazer or the collar of shirt. A hint of script there, the bottom half of a star here. There's something tantalizing about only getting a glimpse of his tats. Like, even though I've seen him shirtless and I know what they look like, I'm turned on by the tease.

I also can't help but think his tattoos are somehow incongruous with his polished, almost preppy outfit. The tats say bad boy, but the custom blazer says well-to-do businessman who also happens to be super-hot.

So which one is Rhys—the bad boy or the businessman? Is he both? Neither?

I really, really want to find out the answer. Which is ridiculous, because—hello—he is Rhys Maddox and I am an American nobody.

I'll just have to settle for a little after-dinner sesh with fantasy Rhys. Not a bad gig, considering he makes me come, hard, every time I ask him to. I should actually thank real Rhys for providing such excellent inspiration for hours upon hours of orgasms.

Rhys orders a porterhouse steak I don't remember being on the to-go menu, and vodka on the rocks to sip on while he waits. No well liquor for this guy—he asks for Belvedere.

I watch him reach for his back pocket, pulling out a wallet that matches his suitcase.

I should thank real Rhys.

My pulse thumps, and the idea appears, fully formed and insistent, inside my head. I shouldn't—I mean, yeah, this is my chance, I'll never see him again, but it'd be weird, wouldn't it—I can't just come out and say—

"I got it," I blurt, reaching around my chair for my bag.

Their gazes—Rhys's and the bartender's—snap to my face.

"I'm sorry?" Rhys says.

"Your drink." I pop open my wallet and dig out my debit card. "Your dinner too. Everything. All of it. I want to pay for all of it."

I'm about to pass the bartender my card when Rhys holds up his hand.

"That's kind of you, but I can't let you do that."

I manage to wiggle around him, placing my card in the bartender's hand.

"Too late," I say. "Let me buy you a drink."

"For what?" he replies. "Winning? Because we didn't win today. I was complete shit out there, as a matter of fact."

His accent dips, softens, when he says *shit*. It comes out sounding more like *shite*. My heart skips a beat.

I like it.

"No," I say, swallowing. "Not for winning."

He looks at me, the skin around his eyes crinkling as he narrows them. Good God, he's gorgeous. "Are you a football fan?"

"Not particularly." My face is going up in flames again. I turn to the bartender. "Another drink for me too, please," I say. Eff, I forgot to use my Spanish.

"Then why do you insist on treating me?"

I watch the bartender scoop ice into a short, wide glass. "Because." *Because I want to thank you for all the orgasms.* "Um. It's a way of thanking you, I guess?"

"Thanking me?" He nods his thanks at the bartender as he grabs his vodka rocks. "For what?"

He's looking at me, I feel it. I resist the urge to pick up my bucket list napkin and fan myself with it.

The words are out of my mouth before I can stop them.

"For the good times," I say.

My eyes flick to his. Oh, he's definitely looking at me. But his eyes have changed. I could be imagining it—*who am I kidding, I'm definitely imagining it*—but they're alive in a way they weren't two minutes ago, the blue shaded with a spark of something warm. Interest, maybe? Amusement?

His perfectly kissable lips part, like he's about to say something. But our food arrives, and suddenly we're surrounded by a phalanx of waiters. His dinner is ready at the same time mine is, naturally, even though I ordered mine half an hour before.

I pick at the french fries on my plate and watch the waiters fawn over Rhys. *Would you like us to have this sent up to your room?* one of them asks, pointing to the tidy boxes of food on the bar. *I'll have all our sauces sent up as well*, another adds, snapping at a busboy.

"Actually," Rhys says. He sets his wallet on the counter pulls out the bar stool next to mine. "I think I'd like to eat here, if that's all right?"

I almost choke on a fry. Uneasy silence settles over the bar, and it hits me that Rhys is waiting for *my* response—not the waiters'.

"Um," I say. "Sure. Yeah. Yes, of course."

"Brilliant." Rhys sets his glass on the bar. His elbow brushes mine as he places a napkin on his lap. I think I'm going to have a heart attack. "But first, an Instagram."

"An Instagram?"

"Yes." He pulls his phone from his pocket and snaps a quick picture of his fancy steak and fancier drink. I notice he makes sure to include his designer wallet in the shot. "I get a lot of likes on food pictures. I've got eleven million followers, but I'm hoping to bump it up to twenty. Sponsors really love it when you have a big following like that."

"Oh," I say. "Right. Makes sense."

"So," he says, pocketing his phone again. "What good times are you talking about? I'd remember if we met."

"We haven't," I say.

"I know." He sets his knife down and crosses his right hand over his left, offering it to me. "I'm Rhys."

"I know," I say, trying not to smile. "I'm Laura."

I take his hand, noticing the fat gold Rolex on his wrist. I grip his hand firmly, trying not to squirm when I realize how clammy my palms are. He grips me firmly too. I appreciate that. I think it's a little patronizing when guys handle you like you're made of glass.

His skin is warm, his enormous hand swallowing my own. His touch is confident, sure.

I want you to touch me like that all over.

"Laura," he repeats, "tell me more about these good times. I'm intrigued."

"You shouldn't be. It's really not that great of a story, Rhys." *Reese*—it's pronounced like the candy. Saying his name out loud, in public, feels weird.

One side of his handsome mouth kicks up as he chews his steak. "Somehow I doubt that, *Laura*."

"Let's see how much liquid courage that'll give me," I say, nodding at my fresh green cocktail, "and then maybe I'll tell you."

He cocks a blond brow at my glass. "What is that? A sour apple martini?"

"Worse," I say. "It's a Midori sour."

"That *is* worse," he says, laughing.

The sound of his laugh—genuine, deep, pleased—makes me smile so hard I feel it in my eyeballs.

It makes me relax.

"Midori sours may not be cool," I say. "But they are delicious."

"As delicious as you?" he asks, his smile morphing into a devilish little smirk.

"Wow." I sip my cocktail. "Wow, Rhys, that was pretty terrible."

"It was, wasn't it?" He laughs again. "Sorry. I'm complete rubbish at pickup lines. Like, embarrassingly awful at them. I should probably put in some practice before I send another girl running from the building like it's on fire."

"You've sent girls running?"

"Well, no." He meets my eyes. "But it's only a matter of time. You were tempted to run, weren't you?"

I bite my lip. "If the bartender didn't have my credit card, I would've been out the door ten minutes ago."

"I wouldn't blame you."

"How about this?" I ask, straightening in my chair. "Practice your pickup lines with me. I promise not to judge."

"No you don't."

"You're right, I don't, I'm totally going to judge you and tell all my friends how terrible you are at getting laid. But I paid for your dinner, so I think that's fair."

"Agreed." Rhys sets down his knife and fork on his plate. He turns to me, resting one elbow on the bar and the other on the back of his chair. His blue eyes dance. "Ready?"

"Ready."

"And you promise not to laugh?"

"Promise."

"All right." He clears his throat. His face is a mask of mock-seriousness. "Hey girl, do you know karate? Because your body is kickin'."

I suck in my cheeks to keep from laughing. Not at the line, but at him, because Rhys is trying not to laugh too.

"Hey girl. Do you work at Starbucks? Because I like you a-latte." He leans in. "Get it? A-latte?"

"I do," I manage. "Keep going. The 'hey girl' part is amazing."

"I know. It never works." He takes a sip of his vodka. "Hey girl. Apart from being sexy, what do you do for a living?"

"Total winner right there."

"Isn't it though?" He wiggles his eyebrows. "Hey girl. I love every bone in your body, especially mine."

I bend over, clutching my waist.

"Hey girl. Is your mom a baker? Because you've got some nice buns."

That's it. I can't take it. I burst out laughing, and Rhys does too. He hands me a napkin to wipe the tears from my eyes.

"Thanks," I wheeze. "That was awesome."

"Awesomely awful, you mean," he says.

I blink the last of the tears away. Rhys's blurry face snaps into sudden, devastating focus. It's like I'm seeing him—the *real* him—for the first time all over again. He's so freaking hot it makes my stomach flip.

I look away. "Amazing or not, your pickup lines made me laugh harder than I have in a long time."

"Then it was worth the embarrassment," he replies. "You've got a beautiful laugh and even better smile. You should show them off more often."

I drain the rest of my drink. I can't meet his eyes.

I mean, seriously. If you look past the glitz and polish of Rhys the soccer star, there's a pretty charming dude to be found.

We talk, we laugh some more. I tell him that I'm studying here for a semester. He tells me about his favorite places in Madrid I should try out. Restaurants, cafés, shops.

When I finally check my phone, I'm surprised to find it's almost eleven.

"Yikes," I say, pushing back from the bar after I ask for the bill. My stool wobbles. "It's way past my bedtime. I should get going. I have a lot I need to get done before classes start this week, so . . ."

Rhys stands. He takes my elbow in his hand and gently helps me to my feet. Ribbons of warmth unfurl inside me from this place where skin meets skin. His fingertips linger on my bare arm.

I look up at him. Whatever was in his eyes before—the interest, the amusement—it's back, stronger now, and he makes no effort to hide it.

"I'll walk you up to your room," he says.

My pulse leaps. My hand shakes as I sign the bill.

"Why are you staying here? At a hotel, I mean." I nod at his suitcase. "You have a place in Madrid, right?"

Rhys pulls up the handle on his suitcase with a *snap*. "I do. But my flat is being renovated at the moment, so I come here when I need a break from the noise and the mess. Plus I've done a few commercials for this hotel chain. They comped me a suite."

"Ah," I say, starting to walk away from the bar. "Must be nice."

"Wait! Don't forget your napkin. Looks like you put a bit of work into it."

Shit. In my hot-soccer-player-stupor, I'd forgotten about my bucket list. I whirl around and grab the napkin, stuffing it into my purse before he can get a closer look. I don't know why, but I don't want Rhys to see it.

"Jotting down some thoughts?" he asks, cocking a brow again.

A tiny voice inside my head says *tell him. Tell him how you're determined to live a little this semester. Tell him the list is all about becoming the happy, healthy girl you want to be.*

But I don't. Rhys may be a charmer, but he's also a guy. A really rich, really good-looking guy who obviously cares a lot about appearances. The flashy Rolex and porterhouse steak and Instagram photo are all proof of that. I'd feel silly, telling him I'm trying to care less about superficial stuff like that, telling him I'm looking for *happy* and *healthy* and self-induced orgasms instead. I can imagine him rolling his beautiful blue eyes as he pumps the brakes on our fun, flirty conversation.

I also feel like I'd be passing judgment on Rhys's fabulous footballer lifestyle. I don't know him. I don't know what his story is, or where he comes from. I'm sure he has his reasons for living the way he does, just like I have my reasons for putting together a wine-and-cheese heavy bucket list.

Reasons I don't feel like sharing with Rhys Maddox at the moment.

"It's nothing," I say, zipping up my bag. "Just a little project I'm working on. C'mon, let's head up."

Rhys smirks again, a devilish, knowing little thing that sends a shiver down my spine. "Let's."

Chapter Four

LAURA

The smell of Rhys's cologne, woodsy, spicy, swoony, has me weaving on my feet as I step inside the elevator.

"What floor?" I ask, thumbing the button—sixth floor—for my room.

"Twelve, I think? Whichever is the top."

I glide my thumb to twelve. There's a brass plate below it, engraved in small, tidy script.

"You said you had a suite," I say. "Not the *penthouse* suite."

Rhy's mouth twitches. "I like my privacy."

"Of course you do, fancy pants."

The elevator doors close.

"Thanks again for the drink," Rhys says. "And for dinner. Lovely of you to treat me, especially after the disaster I was today during the match. If a Madrileño saw me at that bar, he'd probably wring my neck. I'd deserve it too."

I sneak a glance in his direction. His head is tilted back, eyes glued to the floor numbers above the door that light up as we ascend. The masculine beauty of his profile makes my chest contract. It's overwhelming, how handsome he is.

How much I want him. Him, the real Rhys Maddox.

I take a deep breath, let it out. I need to slow my roll. Rhys probably has a couple A-list actresses waiting for him in his Jacuzzi upstairs. There's no way he wants me like that. No freaking way.

"You're hard on yourself," I say.

He turns his head. Meets my eyes. "I am. Especially when I'm not playing well. You're not a fan of the team, so you may not know this—but my play hasn't exactly measured up to expectations lately."

"I actually do know about your injury," I say, my eyes flicking to his left knee. He blew it out last season, and had to have his ACL reconstructed a while back. "How's the recovery coming? Besides this supposedly shitty play, of course."

"Not well," he says. A muscle tightens along his jaw. "But I did have a good bit of down time a few months ago. You know, time for other things. Friends, family."

I can't resist. "Lady friends?" I ask, leaning against the handrail at the back of the elevator car.

His mouth twitches again. He leans back beside me, crossing one ankle over the other. Our shoulders brush. He smells so. Damn. Good. "You heard my pickup lines. No lady friends to be had with those, I'm afraid."

He's probably lying—I mean, the guy's gorgeous and charming as hell, he gets laid anytime he wants—but his modesty is super cute nonetheless.

The elevator dings, and the doors glide open.

"Welp," I say, pushing off the handrail. My face—my body —my entire being is on fire. "This is me. It was nice meeting you, Rhys. Good luck with your knee—and don't forget to keep practicing those lines. The karate one was my favorite, by the way."

His gaze moves over the length of my body. It's a slow, intentional perusal. He wants me to know he's looking.

From the hungry gleam in his eyes, I'd say he's appreciating too.

I bite the inside of my cheek. I'd be lying if I said I didn't like the way he's looking at me.

Tucking my hair behind my ear, I start to move toward the doors. His eyes follow me, gleaming with the kind of mischief that filled the romance novels I devoured in my angsty adolescent years.

"Buenas noches," I say. *Good night.*

The sound of my footsteps swishing against the carpet seems enormous in the silence that follows me out of the elevator. I can't breathe. I close my eyes. *Keep walking*—

"*This* is where you're staying?"

My heart trips to a halt. I glance over my shoulder to see Rhys's head poking out of the elevator. He's checking out the hallway, brow furrowed in disapproval.

"It's a bit shabby, don't you think?" he says.

"Listen, Rhys," I say, biting back a grin, "we can't all live the penthouse-and-porterhouse life. My room may not be a suite, but it's still pretty nice for a girl who's still in college."

"It's not as nice as my room, I can guarantee you that."

"Is that another attempt at a pickup line? Because if it is, it's even worse than your first."

"One more drink." He steps halfway into the hall, facing me, and holds the elevator doors open with his back. He crosses his arms, making his biceps bulge against the sleeves of his blazer. The way he moves—steadily, gracefully, with lethal intention—makes the heat between my legs blare louder. "Come up to my room for one more drink. If only so you can see what real luxury looks like."

I blink. That hungry gleam in his eye deepens. Taunts me.

I'm not an idiot. I know Rhys is asking me up to his room for more than a drink. He wants to have a pajama party. Sans, of course, the pajamas.

I shouldn't I shouldn't I shouldn't. This semester is all about self-love, remember? After having boyfriends for so long, I need a break from guys. I need to mind my own business and masturbate. If I don't, I risk settling back into old habits. Bad habits, like getting guys off without getting off myself.

"Shouldn't this be the other way around?" I ask. "I should be the one seducing you. I mean, I already bought you dinner and got you liquored up."

He smirks, a devastating quirk of those deliciously full lips. "Then let me repay the favor. I'm known for my generosity."

I swallow, hard. The desire spiking through me is so potent it electrifies my skin, my blood, the gathering tightness low in my belly. I feel raw and sexy and desired.

I wonder if Rhys Maddox would be a fucking un*real* lay. A trophy lay, one for the books, and not just because he's the super-hot footballer of my dreams. He'd be intense, athletic. Hard in all the right places.

For God's *sake,* he is smoking hot. He's an athlete, with an athlete's hard, delectable body. He's got an accent, and a British one at that, and he is charming as hell.

He is asking me up to his *penthouse suite*.

"Are you really so generous?" I ask, breathless.

He runs his tongue along the slick inseam of his bottom lip. "Why don't you come up to my room and find out?"

My heart skips a beat. "Liar," I say. "God, Rhys, you're such a liar."

"I am?"

"You said you weren't good at pickup lines."

He smirks. "I dropped the 'hey girl' this time. Is it working?"

I shouldn't.

But oh, I want to. And isn't that what that bucket list I just drew up is all about? Doing what I want, eating what I

31

want, *being* who I want without worrying about what anyone else thinks?

Tonight I want to be the girl who makes her footballer fantasies come true.

Tonight I'm going to do what I want.

And I *really* want Rhys.

———

By the time we get up to the penthouse, I'm so nervous I'm shaking. Rhys holds up his keycard to the lock on the door door. It beeps, a pleasant little chirp, and then he holds the door open with the flat of his palm and motions me inside.

"Are all British guys so polite?" I ask. My sandals clack on the marble floor as I enter the suite.

"I'm not British," he replies, following me in. "I'm Welsh."

"Oh. Right. Sorry."

"Don't be." He unloads his pockets—keys, phone, gum, valet ticket—onto a small table in the hall.

"So, like, excuse my ignorance. But don't Welsh people have their own language? Or their own accent? Your English sounds really . . . English, I guess."

"We do have our own language—people in the north mostly speak it, but I'm from the south. We have our own accent too. Mine was much thicker when I was young. But I haven't lived there in a while, so." Rhys shrugs, digging his hands into the pockets of his jeans. "Ready for that drink?"

"I am."

He tilts his head toward the suite. "Let's go, then. Vodka all right?"

"Vodka's fine."

"I've got the good stuff," he says.

Of course you do, I think.

"Wow." The breath leaves my lungs as I step out of the hall into the suite. "Just . . . wow, Rhys. This is beautiful."

The suite is enormous—seriously, it's two stories tall and as wide as a house—with a wall of steel windows that over-looks the city. Mod, cushy furniture in varying hues of grey occupies the airy space. The walls are upholstered and hung with several monumental pieces of art. A marble fireplace gleams in the light of a massive crystal chandelier that bathes the room in low, warm light. There are bowls and vases of fresh flowers everywhere, the perfumed scent of lilies filling my head.

"A bit better than your tiny box, isn't it?"

I scoff. "Just a bit."

My heart is working double. I feel like I just walked onto a James Bond set. This would be the room where he seduces a lethally attractive woman while simultaneously fending off a henchman or two.

Spectacular doesn't begin to describe it. It's sexy, it's luxe. It's perfect for a fancy-pants footballer like Rhys.

Outside the windows, the city is lit up, pulsing with energy. I watch a line of traffic snake down a wide avenue. The ornate facades of nearby buildings are illuminated in a rainbow of colors—purple, pink, blue. It hits me that I am in *Spain*, thousands and thousands of miles from home. It's exciting, but it's also a little daunting. I hope I feel less lost here than I did back at Meryton.

I hope I have the courage to actually do the things I put on my bucket list.

Starting with sex. Which is probably the most compli-cated line item on said list.

I've had sex before. Not a ton of it, but I'm not a prude either. No matter who I was having sex with, I was always so caught up in trying to be the "perfect" lay—enthusiastic but not *too* enthusiastic, willing but not slutty, giving without asking for anything in return—that I never really enjoyed it. In fact, a lot of times it made me feel like shit about myself. It seems like, as girls, we're always walking that fine line between sinner and saint. I wanted to get off with my boyfriends, but I wanted them to respect me too. I felt like I could only get one or the other, but I could never get both.

I was never in control of how I felt about sex—before, during, or after. I let the world tell me how to feel, what I should and shouldn't do, what I should like.

This semester, I'm determined to find out what I like. To take control of my sex life. To take control of how I feel about it.

I want to call the shots. I also want to stop being so self-conscious about my tiny boobs and tinier nipples—seriously, they're like the size of a pencil eraser.

Calling the shots sounds awesome in my head. For weeks I've been giving myself mental fist bumps, assured in the knowledge that I shall rule the (sexual) world now that I'm single and ready to mingle.

But here, staring down the barrel of my first encounter as this new, somewhat-sexually-empowered woman, it dawns on me that I have no idea what the fuck I'm doing. Where do I even start? I thought I had started by masturbating eleven times a day to my super hot celebrity crush, Rhys Maddox.

Yet here I am, shivering in the penthouse suite as the real Rhys Maddox pours me a drink. I never imagined in a million years my fantasy would become reality. I am *so* not prepared for this.

I am also so turned on.

"How do you like it?"

I start at the sound of his voice, turning to see Rhys set a gorgeous bottle of vodka on a nearby table, along with two cut-crystal glasses filled with ice.

"Like what?" I ask.

He smirks. "Your drink, love. How do you like your drink? There's soda in the fridge, tonic, juice . . ."

For a minute I'm too stunned by the fact he called me *love* to even blink. His accent dipped again as he said it, curled around the word to make it lusciously casual: *luv*.

Holy Jesus, it's so hot I might fall over and pass out right here on the plush silk carpet. It sounds so much hotter in real life than it did in my head.

"Um." I clear my throat. "However you take it is fine."

Damn it. That is not the answer my empowered self would make. But Rhys makes me too . . . too hot and bothered, too self-conscious to think empowered thoughts. He's too sexy. Confident. Overwhelming.

Hot.

He is unbelievably hot.

"On the rocks?" he asks, uncorking the bottle.

"Yeah. Yeah, that's fine."

My voice trembles. It's embarrassing. I gotta get it together, stat.

This is not my first rodeo. And this is not how I promised myself I would behave this semester.

I want to call the shots. Right now, I'm giving Rhys all the power, just like I gave my boyfriends back home control over me. I hated how it made me feel then, and I'm going to hate how I feel tomorrow—unless I make a change.

Unless I make my move *now*, and do what I want to do.

The only thing is, what *do* I want to do?

I look at Rhys, my gaze trailing down the masculine lines of his profile to land on his hands as he pours the vodka. He's got enormous hands, blunt-edged fingers.

Longing gathers between my legs, in my lips.

I want to fuck Rhys Maddox, that's what I want to do.

"Screw the drink," I say.

Rhys looks up from the glasses on the table, bottle poised

midair, and furrows his brow. "Screw the drink? Laura, please tell me you're not leaving. I'd really like you to stay."

"Screw the drink." My heart pounds as I move toward him. "I want to screw you instead."

The lines in his forehead disappear. His blue eyes flash as he smirks a smirk so potent it knocks the breath from my lungs. My whole body pings with the awareness of his scent, the way he moves.

Oh yeah. I definitely want to fuck this guy. Here. Now. All night, I want to claim him. Come a hundred times with him.

"That's awfully forward," he says, teasing.

"That's what I want."

"You really want me to screw you?"

"No," I say, moving closer. "*I* want to screw *you*."

I'm standing in front of him now, so close our noses almost touch. Rhys isn't much taller than I am—maybe a few inches—but he somehow manages to feel overwhelmingly huge. He surrounds me, blocking out everything else, the room and the night. It's a struggle not to fall into his eyes as they flicker with heat. Not to lose my grip on what I want.

And that is to *enjoy* having sex on my own terms. To let go of all my hang-ups and just have fun.

He sets down the bottle.

"We'll see who screws who," he says, his voice a low rumble.

And then he slides his hands onto my face and looks down at me. He searches my eyes, asking for permission. His gaze is wet with heat, soft and hungry all at once.

Like I could ever, ever say no to that gaze. That face.

"Yes," I say. "Please."

Smirking, Rhys dips his head and presses his lips to mine, opening my mouth like he owns it, sucking my bottom lip like he knows exactly what I want, curling me into the magnetic pull of his body like I am his for the taking.

In an instant, the kiss is messy, and deep, and possessive. I've never been kissed like this, I've never been taken captive by a kiss before. His fingers are in my hair now, and he's tilting my head, guiding me in time to his ardent caresses. He knows what he's doing, and it's driving me wild.

Oh God, I think, my pulse throbbing, my mind going blank as he kisses me, and keeps kissing me, an intense, relentless kiss that gets hotter and faster and better with each frantic heartbeat. *Oh, fuck me, two minutes in and already I'm losing grip.*

And I don't mind it one bit.

Chapter Five

RHYS

Laura's mouth is wet and warm and deliriously soft. I slide my tongue between her lips, begging entrance, and with a small moan she lets me in. She surrenders, her head falling back into my hands.

I take a step closer, nudging my body against hers. Laura isn't petite, but there's something small, almost vulnerable about her body. I hold her closer, letting the warmth of my skin seep into hers. She's covered in goosebumps.

"Are those good goosebumps?" I murmur, sliding my lips to her jaw. "Or bad goosebumps?"

Laura smiles against my mouth. "Good goosebumps. Really freaking good, Rhys."

My dick twitches inside my jeans, a hard, prickly rush of blood. I bite her bottom lip and she moans again; I go from half chub to full salute in two seconds flat. Laura must feel it too, because she presses her belly against my erection. The heat and pressure feel so fucking good I let out a growl.

I kiss her harder. She meets me stroke for stroke, her arms twining around my neck, pulling me close. She tastes sweet, a little fruity, like that Midori she was drinking at the bar. I like the way she tastes.

I like the way she feels even more. This girl—Christ, I needed this tonight.

I need to escape the pressure.

I am so fucking desperate to escape. For a little while, at least.

What I told Olivier at training the other day—I don't have time for girls—is and isn't true. My football career is (hopefully) just getting started and my current contract is puny compared to those given to the big guys. Those filthy rich bastards can make upwards of fifty *million* euros a season. I make way less than that. *Way* less.

Which is still a lot, granted. Growing up as poor as I did, I recognize I'm very well off. But by the time I pay taxes, an agent, a publicist, a manager, a financial manager, and an assistant, I don't have nearly enough money to support my family the way I want or need to. My sponsors make up for some of that. But to make the big bucks like the big guys, I need to up my game, and start playing like a superstar. I need to focus on footy, not on a serious relationship.

That doesn't mean I can't have a little fun with a girl every now and then—so long as it's the no-strings-attached sort of fun. I've beaten myself up for months now, my thoughts a constant refrain of *you're rubbish you're rubbish you're total rubbish*. I'm under a lot of pressure to make my career work. Sex is in some ways a mute button. It gets me out of my head and into my body. It allows me to live in the moment. Which is huge, considering I spend basically all my time sweating the future.

And who better to help me live in the moment than a gorgeous, whip-smart American who laughs at my pickup lines? Already my heartbeat is scrambling the well-worn rhythm of my thoughts, drowning out the negativity, the doubts, the fear.

It never happens this quickly with a girl. Usually it takes a solid chunk of time to unwind from my worries. But tonight —tonight it happens fast. Maybe because I'm all too eager to escape the crushing reality of where I am right now with my footy. Maybe because I'm so bloody attracted to Laura.

Maybe it's because I haven't had fun, just for fun's sake, in a long time. I had fun with Laura at the bar, and I hope to have even more fun with her, the naked kind, in the very near future. It's Sunday night—the night after a match—the only night of the week I can let loose. I'll never, ever be caught drinking the night before a match like my dad (that little stunt cost him his career), so I tend to be quite tame during the week. But tonight —tonight, I don't plan on wasting a single moment.

Laura slides her hands beneath the lapels of my blazer. I roll my shoulders back, helping her to take it off. Her palms whisper against the fabric of my shirt as she goes for the buttons. I laugh as she fumbles with the first one, and I cover her fingers with my own, guiding them as we unbutton it together.

"Sure you're all right, love?"

"Yes." She pulls back, just a little. She meets my eyes. "And. Um. No. I've never really hooked up with a celebrity before. The closest I ever got was my boyfriend in high school. He was the varsity lacrosse captain and was, like, this huge deal on campus. But that's seriously small beans compared to you. You're . . . *you,* you know? Eleven-million-Instagram-followers *you.*"

I laugh again. "Wait 'til I get to twenty."

"Good thing I nabbed you when I did," she says, biting her lip. Her hazel eyes, green in this light, dance. "I have a shot with Rhys Maddox the famous footballer. But I don't have a chance in hell with Rhys Maddox the *super* famous footballer-slash-Instagram-god."

I hook my arm around her tiny waist and crush her against me, nuzzling into the inviting curve of her neck. I inhale the smell of her perfume, something floral, a little sweet. She smells fucking delicious.

"I thought I was the one who nabbed you," I say.

She digs her fingers into the hair at the nape of my neck. My blood warms, tightens. "Not with those pickup lines, you didn't," she says.

"Hey. They weren't all bad."

She tilts her head, spearing me with a look.

"Fine," I say. "They were terrible. But I did make you laugh."

"You did." She smiles. "Hard."

Straightening, I take her face in my hand, run my thumb along her bottom lip. Her eyes darken. "You're gorgeous when you laugh. You're gorgeous, period. This body . . ." I look down, devouring the curve of her breasts. "It's ridiculous."

"You're ridiculous." She fingers another button on my shirt. "But thank you."

I pull at her lips with my mine, a long, slow, lingering kiss. My body feels plugged in, lit up with the need to bury myself in her cunt that's probably as sweet as her perfume. I glide my hand underneath her shirt, skimming the smooth skin at her hip before I grab the hem and begin drawing it up over her belly. Her head falls back and she lets out a pant when I trail my mouth over her neck, my hand making steady progress up her side. Her skin is warm and soft, silky almost, so silky it makes me fantasize about how silky and warm and soft she'll be between her legs.

My dick pulses, straining against the fly of my jeans. My

hand reaches her breast. I finger the lacy cup of her bra, and Laura arches into my touch.

"Rhys," she breathes.

"Hands up, love," I say, nipping at her earlobe.

Laura does as I tell her. I slip her top over her head, her long hair fanning out over her shoulders, covering her chest. I drop the shirt to the floor, ducking to kiss her, my hands roving over all this fucking *skin*. I circle my hands around her waist, my thumbs trailing over her belly button, the soft outline of her ribs. They come to rest at the waistband of her jeans, toying with the button of her fly. The throb between my legs heightens, starts to scream.

I begin to slowly back her up, toward the bedroom, our legs tangling as she works feverishly at the remaining buttons of my shirt. With a grunt of satisfaction she tugs it over my shoulders. I untangle my arms from the sleeves, and then I pull her close again, reveling in the feel of skin against skin, bare flesh against bare flesh. I bury my hands in her hair and cover her mouth with mine, swallowing it whole. Thrusting my hips into her groin—*gah*, the friction, it's killing me—I keep urging her backward. For the first time, I wish this suite wasn't quite as big; it's a bit of a hike from the living area to the bedroom, and I am bloody impatient to get this girl naked and in my bed.

Laura places her palms against my chest, like she's overwhelmed, like she's trying to shield herself from my onslaught. I hesitate, pull back. But then she's slowly moving those palms lower, exploring as she goes. She digs her fingertips into the ridges of my abs and teases her pinkies along the hard angles of my hips, dipping a questioning finger into the waistband of my jeans. I jump and she grins, making this perfect, throaty-grin-sound as her eyes flick to meet mine.

"I mean, seriously," she says, coming back to my abs. "This —these muscles—they're ridiculous. Who *are* you?"

"I'm a bloke about to go mad if I don't get you naked in the next fifteen seconds."

"Dude. Ditto." She pops open the button on my fly.

I reach around, pop open the hook on her bra.

"Whoa!" she says, clapping an arm across her chest in an attempt to catch her bra. She only half-succeeds, her bra dangling from underneath her forearm.

I hold up my hands. "I didn't hurt you, did I?"

Laura swallows and shakes her head, blonde waves falling across her chest. "No. No, I just—um . . ."

"Listen, Laura, if you don't want to . . . you know. We don't have to—"

"No," she says, more firmly this time. She closes her eyes, squares her shoulders. Still holding her arm across her chest, she looks up at me and hooks her finger back into my pants, working the zipper down one centimeter at a time as she slowly begins to back into the bedroom. "I want this. I want you, before you get those twenty million followers and become *completely* unattainable. I gotta strike while the iron is hot."

"Oh, this iron's hot, all right."

She rolls her eyes, playfully. "You and the lines."

"They keep getting worse, don't they?"

"They really do."

"Sorry."

"Don't be." Laura smiles. The gathering, stretching heat low in my belly throbs.

We cross the threshold into the bedroom at the same moment my jeans slip from my hips. I pluck at Laura's lips as I shimmy them to my knees. I toe out of my sneakers and kick off my jeans, leaving them at the door. It feels so good to press the head of my dick against her belly, separated from her skin by just the flimsy jersey of my boxer briefs, that I suck in a breath.

"Christ, Laura," I say. I tug down the zipper of her jeans, kissing her hard. Kissing her like I mean it, drinking her in, running my tongue along the slick, hot inseam of her willing mouth.

I slip my hand into her open fly, her lacy underwear warm against my palm as I cup her sex. I roll my hips, impatient, as I finger aside that maddeningly tiny underwear. My finger parts her folds and meets with—fuck, oh, God, *yes*—the center of her wet, swollen pussy.

It's Laura's turn to suck in a breath. I pull back from her mouth, and watch her eyes get hazy and dark as I press that questioning finger into her wet heat. She clenches around my finger, and for a second I think I'll blow my load. She's small and tight and so wet my hand is already drenched.

I close my eyes and blow a breath through my nose. I'm going to devour this girl.

"Am I—is it—all right?" Laura stutters.

I open my eyes and look at her. Her face is flushed, her eyes glitter, her lips swollen and very pink.

I dip my head, nose her throat, her jaw. I trail my finger up the length of her slit, pressing my fingertip to her clit. She cries out.

"All right?" I murmur against her skin. "Love, you're fucking gorgeous."

I slide my other hand to her hip and begin to guide her farther into the room.

"Wait," she breathes, pulling back. Her eyes flick to the door. "Hit the lights."

My eyes land on her chest and she's still clutching her bra, covering her breasts. I don't get why she'd be self-conscious about her body. I feel like I've told her ten times tonight how beautiful she is.

"What if I want to see you?" I ask. "All of you. I hate having sex in the dark."

Laura ducks out of my grasp, my hand falling from between her legs, and a second later the lights overhead go out, followed by the lamps on either side of the bed. It's dark, the only light coming from the faint glow of the city outside the windows at the far end of the room.

"I don't think you'll hate having sex with me," she says, turning back to me. "Even in the dark."

I grab her—I don't know how, I can't see shit, it must be instinct—but I grab her and pull her to me. Desire flashes like lightning, white-hot and loud, between our bodies. It's almost elemental, the attraction that my body feels for hers. We may only have known each other for a few hours, but the chemistry we have is insane, instinctive.

I am going to devour this girl.

I wrap my fingers around her arm. The faint, salty scent of her arousal fills the small space between us. "Drop it," I say, nodding at her bra. "If I can't see all of you, I'm going to feel you. Every inch of this fucking incredible body of yours, I want to feel it."

Her bra falls to the floor. Then she's circling my neck in her hands, her fingers tangling in my hair, and pulling me against her. My dick surges at the press of her hard nipples against my chest. Skin on skin on *skin.*

"Oh, love," I say, trailing my hands up her sides. I take her tits in my palms, thumbing her nipples. "Oh, Laura."

She moans into my mouth, her fingers tugging at my hair, her silky skin warm against my own. She rolls her hips against mine, begging, teasing.

I fucking lose it.

Our legs hit the bottom of the bed. I take Laura's face in my hands and give her lips one last, almost violent tug. Then I buck my hips, urging her onto the bed, as she falls onto the downy coverlet with a pleading sigh.

I can just barely see the outline of her body, the curve of

her breast gleaming in the light from the window. I take off her sandals. Then I grab her jeans, her underwear, and she lifts her hips to help me tug them off. The scrape of my palms against her legs sounds above our labored breathing.

And then she's naked. Gloriously, beautifully naked.

My heart dips. She's so beautiful. Sexy.

But Laura turns her head away from me on the bed and tries to cover herself, roping her arms around her chest.

"Don't," I say, taking both her wrists in my hand. She bends one knee and I straddle the other, tangling our legs as I lie on top of her. Holding myself up on one elbow, I guide her hands above her head with my free arm, baring her to me, exposing her body to my advances.

"Rhys," she pants.

"You're all right," I say, kissing my way down her neck. "We're all right."

Her hips roll beneath me as I kiss her breast. When I take her nipple in my mouth, biting the pebbled point, she cries out, her legs falling open. I feel the heat and the wet of her exposed pussy against my thigh. *Christ.*

I settle myself between her legs, spreading her wider, opening her wider, and I roll my erection against her pussy, sucking on her nipple as I roll harder, pressing my dick to her center, wanting so badly to be buried there. Her breath is sweet and short, stalling every so often in her throat when I hit just the right spot. I dry humped practically everything when I was a randy teenager. Now I know why. As much of a tease as it is, it heightens the anticipation. And sometimes the anticipation of the act, rather than the act itself, can, frustratingly enough, be the best part.

She keeps rolling against me, me against her, the friction making my cock pulse in agony. Her body is winding tighter too, her pants become moans. She's close. Painfully close.

I give her nipple one last flick with my tongue. Then I

move lower, pressing kisses into her ribs, her belly. I'm about to let go of her wrists so I can kiss her cunt when she grabs me by the hair.

I lift my head, confused. My eyes lock onto hers, shining in the darkness. She looks aroused, a little afraid.

"No," she says, breathless.

"Why not?" I cover the skin just beneath her navel with my mouth. I smell her, smell her arousal, and I want to get her there—I want to get her there before I'm inside her, because I don't think I'll be able to control my own orgasm, much less hers, once I sink into her tight warmth.

"Because. I want you. I'm ready." Her fingers tighten in my hair, pulling me back up her body. "Do you have a condom?"

"You're sure?"

She offers me a grin that fades when I bite her nipple and her face contracts with pleasure. "I'm—Jesus, Rhys, I'm sure."

I climb up the length of her body and place my hands on either side of her head, my hair dangling in her face as I bend my neck to press my mouth to hers, our tongues meeting in a frantic, fractured kiss. Then I lean back, I slip an arm around her waist and lift her a bit farther onto the bed. Her leg grazes my dick. My blood riots and I let out a hiss.

My hand falls heavily on the bedside table. I almost pull the drawer off its hinges as I open it and wrangle a condom from the mess of chargers and cords I've shoved inside it.

I rip open the condom with my teeth. Laura is tugging down my briefs, and then she reaches up and takes the condom from my mouth.

"Let me," she says.

I wiggle out of my underwear and hoist myself back onto my hands, lifting my hips for Laura. "I'm all yours, love."

"Love," she says, looking up at me. My arms almost buckle

when she takes my cock in her hand and gives it a solid tug. "Is that what you call all the girls you sleep with?"

"No," I grunt, managing a pained smile. "Only the pretty ones."

She swirls her thumb over the head of my dick, making it slick with precum. For a minute my vision goes dim.

"I'm not—" I pant. "I'm not going to last much longer if you keep touching me like that."

"Like what?" Laura rolls on the condom slowly, very, very slowly, her thumb all the while still making circles on the head. Her touch isn't as potent as it was before the condom was on, but my body has begun to shake with impatience.

"Like *that*," I say, and then I cover her hand with mine and settle my hips between her legs. I let my weight rest on her, just a little, and she lets out a satisfied sigh.

Together we guide my dick toward her center. She arches against me when I press myself against her clit, circling, provoking, just like she did. I'm sweating now, and so is she.

"You," she pants, "are such a tease."

I kiss her neck, her ear, her chin. "Payback's a bitch, isn't it?"

When I kiss her mouth, her lips curl into a smile.

We find her center. Even through the condom she is hot and wet.

"Christ, you'll be the death of me," I say. I push—a baby push, I don't want to hurt her—and she cries out, rolling her hips against me, asking for more.

"Is this okay?" I ask.

Her eyes are closed. "Is it okay for you?"

"Pffshhhh. It's better than okay. Much, much better."

"Then give me more."

"How much more?"

"Everything."

"Like this?"

I take her leg in my hand and hitch it over my shoulder, spreading her wider. I sink inside her a bit more and feel her stretching around me, pulsing with heat, with need.

"More, Rhys." Her free hand clutches at my chest, her nails biting into my skin. The sensation ricochets through my ribcage, my belly, landing in my cock.

I can't. I can't take it. I can't hold on anymore.

I roll back my hips and I take her mouth in mine in a bruising kiss. And then I surge forward, sinking to the hilt inside her in one swift, smooth motion.

Oh my *God.*

I see stars. She feels so bloody good I could die. She is hot and tight and wet, so tight it almost hurts.

I absorb Laura's cry with my mouth. She bites my lip; I nip at her cheek. For a minute I just stay there, filling her, holding her, possessing her. My mind is blank, my senses focused on the thrum of her pulse as I flutter my lips down her neck. Her heart is *pounding*.

So is mine.

Laura tilts her hips, looking for more friction. I grin. Sweet, sweet girl—it's like she knows what I want before I do.

"More," she whispers in my ear.

"More." I pull back, hammer forward. Our bodies make a lewd nose as mine meets with hers. "How much more can you handle?"

She opens her eyes, just a sliver. "As much as you wanna give me, fancy pants."

So I give her everything. I don't go fast, I just go hard, steady and intent and unrepentant—long, deep, gutting strokes. I circle my hips as I stroke, and she arches against me, her body rising to meet my rhythm. She loops her other leg over my other shoulder, seeking *more*, and I hold myself up on my hands and use the muscles in my lower back to go deeper. My mouth is on her mouth, my mouth is on her tits, teasing her nipples, her pussy grips me tight and wet. I don't know how, but she's getting wetter. I bloody adore it.

I close my eyes. My body goes and goes and goes. It's a workout, but one I'm really, *really* enjoying. I lose myself in the feel of Laura, the feel of taking, of having, of giving. My body is loud but my mind is quiet. I am totally present in this moment, and because I've been so distracted lately—because I've been so stressed—it's almost overwhelming, how much I *feel*. I feel her and I feel heat. I feel wound tight and I feel let go. I feel everything intensely, like I'm feeling it not only with my skin but with what's underneath it too. Marrow and bone. Blood, sinew.

Laura's hands glide up my back. I sputter at the first stirrings of my orgasm. I'm surprised I've lasted this long. My dick almost hurts from the barrage, from her tightness. I circle my hips again, hitting her *just* there. She gasps, throwing back her head. Ecstasy is written all over her features.

Yes. So much yes.

"I'm close," I say. "I want to come together, love. Are you ready? Come for me."

She nods her head, never opening her eyes. Her forehead and cheeks are damp with sweat. "I'm close too."

As if on cue, her cunt tightens around my dick.

This time, my arms do buckle.

I try to keep some of my weight on my elbows, but Laura drops her legs and pulls me down, pulls me against her.

"I like the feel of you," she says, then sucks in a breath, like she regrets saying it at all.

I laugh, kissing her. "I like the feel of you too. Come, love. I want you to come."

I hit her hard where she likes it. She's breathing hard, her breasts rising and falling against my chest. I'm going fast now, unable to slow my strokes, but Laura keeps up, offering up her hips, taking what I offer.

I'm wound so tight it hurts. I'm close, I don't know how much longer—

Laura's pussy contracts, once, twice, four times. I lose count, because I lose myself in her orgasm. I surrender to my own, gasping, fireworks bursting behind my closed lids as I empty myself inside her. Every muscle in my body tightens, twists. Then they unfurl and sing, my legs shaking at the violence of my release. I'm dizzy. My chest feels hollowed out. The uneven beating of my heart drowns out everything else, Laura's skin singeing my own. It's a good singe—a welcome one.

There is so much heat between us. Me and Laura.

Laura.

"*Laura.*"

Laura. Sweet, lovely, gorgeous girl.

I open my eyes. She's opened hers too. For several heart-beats we just look at each other. She looks . . . bewildered. A little scared.

"Holy fuck, Rhys," she says. She tucks an unruly curl behind my ear as I breathe above her, my nose two inches from hers.

"I know." I try to catch my breath. "That was good. It's never—it's not like that for me very often."

I watch the sinews of her throat as she swallows. "Me neither."

I nudge my nose against hers. "I'm glad you enjoyed it as much as I did."

"I did." She swallows again, turning her head away from me. "Yeah, definitely."

I pull back a little. I get the feeling something is off with Laura. But then she's grinning, rolling her hips against mine, teasing me about another a round.

I feel myself miraculously getting hard again.

Laura. Sweet, sweet girl.

We fuck again before we go to sleep, and again when we wake up (Laura insists we do it under the covers, where it's still dark). Each time is better and longer and more intense than the last.

I'll ask for Laura's number—it's just less awkward for everyone if I do, a way of ending the encounter on a pleasant note—but I won't call her. Yeah, it's a dick move, but really, I'm sparing us both a good bit of aggravation and heartache in the long run. Laura's a lovely girl. She deserves someone . . . better, I guess. Someone who can commit to her. I can't. The timing isn't right. I'm focusing on footy, remember? And I've made it a rule never to go back for seconds.

If I did though—if I could—I'd definitely go back for seconds with Laura.

Chapter Six

LAURA

The Next Morning

Rhys emerges from the bathroom, tugging a grey T-shirt over his head. I sigh from my vantage point on the edge of the bed as his tattoos disappear for the last time. He spears me with a blinding, boyish smile, running a hand through his bed-mussed hair. He's scruffier this morning. I like it.

"What?"

"Your tattoos." I run my sweaty palms over my jeans. He's so hot he makes me nervous. "I liked them."

Rhys's smile becomes a smirk. His hands still on his shirt, he says, "Shall I take it back off, then?"

"No," I say, laughing. "Did you get them back in Wales? Your tattoos, I mean."

His smirk tightens, then falls. "Some of them."

"I bet you miss it."

"Miss what?"

"Wales. Home. I've only been in Spain for twenty-four hours, and already I'm a little homesick."

He grabs his phone from the nightstand without looking at me. "No, not really."

I hesitate. Is he kidding around, being the smoking-hot charmer he was last night? Or is he just being rude? I can't tell.

"Oh," I say.

I wait for him to fill the awkward silence, but he just scrolls through his phone. The heat that crackled between us just minutes ago dissipates, leaving in its place a clammy kind of cold. Must be the air conditioning. I shiver.

"Well then." I stand up and tug at my jeans. I'm already sore between my legs. I guess that's what three times in one night will do. My poor (lucky?) vagina. "I should get going. Classes start on Wednesday, and I have a to-do list that's, like, a mile long to tackle before then . . ."

Rhys looks up from his phone. It could be my overactive imagination still reeling from endless hours of the best sex I've ever had, but his blue eyes blaze with heat as they meet mine. Heat and a little regret, maybe? Even as I shiver again, my face burns. Does he regret having sex with me? Do I look ugly? Fat? Worse for the wear?

His smirk returns. He looks so handsome when he does it, it's like a physical blow to the gut—I struggle to breathe.

"I had a lot of fun last night, Laura."

"I did too." I grin down at my feet. "It's not every day I get to bang a professional athlete."

"Just promise me that when you sell your story to the tabloids, you'll tell them how big my . . . ah, *heart* is."

I meet his gaze. Here he is again, the charmer. "I make no guarantees, fancy pants."

He steps closer. The scent of his cologne surrounds me. My groin pulses with a familiar heat.

"So," he says, thumb hovering over the screen of his phone, "may I get your number?"

My face burns hotter. I must be the color of a tomato. I look back down at my feet. "I thought you were after those twenty million Instagram followers. Where in the world are you going to find the time to get naked with me?"

When I look up, my heart stalls in my chest. Rhys is standing in front of me, his eyes locked onto mine, his perfect lips curled into the smirk I've come to know and crave. I feel lightheaded. God, he's hot. Overwhelmingly handsome. When he leans forward, tilting his head just a little, and plucks at my lips with his own, I just can't deal.

"You really think I'm not going to call you after sex like *that*?"

But he doesn't. Monday, Tuesday, Saturday. I don't get so much as a text from him.

"Listen, friend, appreciate it for what it was," Emily says when I call her, bummed out, on Saturday afternoon. "You got to bone Rhys Maddox. *Rhys Maddox!* He's, like, one of the hottest soccer players in the world. And you said the sex was great, so. Yeah. I think you win, whether he calls you or not."

The sex *was* great. The best I've ever had. The only thing I kinda regret is faking that orgasm. I was intent to come for real, but then Rhys was super into the idea of us coming together, so the people-pleaser in me—the perfectionist—caved and did some kegels when he asked me to. He seemed to enjoy it. A lot. Like a *lot* lot.

So I faked my orgasm again, when we had sex the second time, and again in the morning. It was just . . . easier, I guess. I didn't want to hold Rhys up, and I definitely didn't want him to go down on me. I have some, um, *complex* feelings about boys touching what's between my legs with their mouths. What if I smell? What if he's grossed out by me? What if he goes down on me and it takes forever for me to come so I just fake it anyways so I don't offend him?

"I know," I say. "And it's not like I *like* him or anything. We were together for, what, eight hours? Most of which was spent . . . you know. Not talking. But it still stings."

"Always does," Emily sighs. "You've been spoiled, chica. You're used to guys being all over you all the time."

I pout. "Not true."

"Oh really? When was the last time a guy turned you down?"

"Well," I say, after thinking for a minute, "there was this one guy, freshman year of high sch—"

"Please, you and I both know whatever you're about to say is a lie. You've never *not* been pursued by a guy you're into, Laur. So a super famous, super busy dude didn't call you back when he said he would. It was going to happen sooner or later. Might as well rip that Band-Aid off." She munches thoughtfully on her condiment of the day. Pickles, maybe? "I mean. Maybe this was meant to happen, so you could focus on your bucket list instead."

"The bucket list," I say. "Right. I've actually been thinking about that a lot this week. I already signed up to tutor kids at this after-school program here in Madrid."

"Awesome. Go do that, and forget about this footballer dude. Well, don't forget his magical skills in the sack. But you know what I mean. Move on to something better. Move on to you."

Emily is right. She's always right.

Sunday

Determined to "do me," as Em says, I decide to start tackling my bucket list ASAP. Starting with line item #2: *Go see Rhys Maddox play in real life.*

I know, I know, it's a total cop out—to tell the world

(read: Emily) that I'm pursuing an activity of empowerment and self-actualization when in reality I'm stalking my ridiculously hot crush—but hey, I put together my list before the whole Rhys/best-sex-of-my-life thing happened, so it still counts, right?

Right.

I gather a flask of whiskey and a couple girls I met this week through the Mertyon in Madrid program—Viv, Maddie, and Rachel—and head to the Sunday afternoon match at Madrid's famous football stadium.

The seats I nabbed online aren't all that bad. We're a few rows up from the field—or "pitch" as proper football fans call it—close enough to hopefully see the sweat on the players' faces, which Rachel especially appreciates.

"My type is hot and sweaty," she says. "The gym is my personal nirvana, and not because I like to workout."

It is hot, and it is *loud*. The noise is deafening. People shout and sing, a kind of chant that rises and falls throughout the match. From the nosebleeds, drums sound out a *Gladiator*-esque beat. The smells of cheap beer and cigar smoke fill the air as the sun beats down on our shoulders, making us sweat almost as much as the players on the field.

My stomach flips when Rhys and the rest of the team make their way onto the pitch. The crowd goes crazy, and I can't help it, I do too. The girls and I jump up and down like lunatics, screaming Rhys's name, waving our arms over our heads. The old dudes sitting next to us would totally hate us if they weren't doing the same thing. I guess hot footballers make fools of us all, young or old, man or woman. They are just that hot.

So hot I can hardly stand it. I've never been this close to the action. I've never been to a game, period. Watching Rhys jog out to play, his stride effortlessly limber, his handsome face a mask of deep concentration, makes me feel short of breath. He wears his blond waves loose, held back by a very Euro, and very thin, elastic headband.

Throw in the white Madrid uniform, and it's like I got hit by two-ton weight of *want*.

"The whiskey," I sputter. "Where is it?"

Maddie presses the flask into my hand, giving me a small pat. I've only just met the girls, so I haven't told them about my hookup with Rhys (yet). I can't decide if I'm embarrassed about the whole thing—about Rhys not calling me back—or if I want to keep the memory of that night for myself. It *was* pretty delicious.

"I'm gonna need a lot of this today," I say.

"We're all gonna need a lot of it," Viv murmurs, her eyes following Rhys as he moves down the pitch. "These guys are all so . . . fast."

"Sweaty," Rachel says, transfixed.

"Foreign," Maddie adds.

I take a long pull of whiskey. It burns my throat and riles my stomach, but it does nothing to quell the ache that swells just beneath my breastbone. Being up close and personal with Rhys's footy skills—with Rhys, period—is not for the faint-hearted.

I read up on all things football and Rhys related this morning. Apparently he is a winger, meaning he hangs in the "wings" or right and left sides of the pitch. He's an offensive player, one who either assists his strikers, the guys who score goals, or scores goals himself. A couple sources said he's one of the fastest players in the league. There's an urban legend floating around that he was clocked running 30-something kilometers per hour before he hurt his knee.

The match starts to the roar of the crowd. The energy in the stadium is insane—Spaniards take their football very, very seriously. It's so loud the concrete beneath our feet trembles, and I feel like I'm in the epicenter of football-induced earthquake. Across the field—sorry, *pitch*—a legion of photographers aim their giant lenses at the players as they dash up and down the sidelines.

Luckily for the girls and me, Rhys is playing on our side of the pitch today. He's so close at some points I can hear the not-safe-for-work things he shouts at his teammates. He is lethally fast, zig-zagging and ducking and turning with surgical precision. And he's got this cocky confidence about him that makes my heart skip a beat. He plays like he owns the pitch, broad shoulders square, his cleats (like most people from the UK, he probably calls them "boots") moving so quickly they're a neon green blur. He challenges the opposing defenders, mowing them down when they get in the way.

I freaking love watching him work. The ache inside my chest burns. God *damn* Rhys. Why didn't he call me back?

I hardly know him. But I'm nervous for him. I know he's trying to come back from his knee injury he was so obviously upset about the night we met at the bar. While reading about Rhys this morning, I found out his dad is kind of a washed-up footballer. The article didn't go into detail, but I wonder if that has anything to do with why Rhys is so hard on himself —or why Rhys totally shut me down when I asked him about Wales.

Not that I have any right to wonder. It's clear he's over me—

"Stop."

I look up at the sound of Maddie's voice. "What?"

"We may have only just met, but I recognize that look, Laura. Whatever death spiral your thoughts are leading you down, stop." She takes a sip from the flask, then passes it to me. "We're in Madrid, watching these stud-muffin-athletes slay it while getting drunk on a Sunday afternoon. Life is good. Chill out."

Chill out. Right.

I take another slug of whiskey.

The visiting team nabs the lead early in the match. By now Rhys's jersey is so soaked with sweat it's plastered to his torso. When he runs—and he's always running—the muscles in his shoulders and chest pop against the flimsy material. Never mind his enormous leg muscles that bulge and harden when he launches a pass across the pitch, or streaks up and down the touchline.

"I mean, seriously!" Rachel says. "I might need to excuse myself for a minute."

After a while my body starts to feel warm and buzzy from the whiskey. During a break in the action, Rhys stands a few feet away, his back to us, his hands on his hips as he surveys the pitch. My eyes rove over the strong, confident lines of his body, the ink scrawled on his wrists and arms. The longing inside me glows brighter. I remember tracing my fingers over those tattoos. How Rhys would make this sound, a masculine rumble-growl-thing in his chest, when I did.

I fan myself with the flask. I swear to God, I just might faint.

The match starts back up and he launches into a sprint again, and I marvel at his talent, his passion. I'm a little jealous. What I would give to be so confident, to find my belonging and be so ridiculously good at it. I'm trying to figure my life out, sure, but no matter how hard I try, I don't think I'll ever be part of something quite like this. I'll never be the brightest star in a crowded night sky.

The minutes pass, and the girls and I pass the flask as my nerves return with a vengeance. The other team is still in the lead at the sixty-five minute mark. Football matches last ninety minutes, plus injury time (thanks, Wikipedia), so there's plenty of time left. Still, the clock is winding down, and play is getting a little sloppy as the players tire.

Then, seemingly out of nowhere, Rhys manages to steal

the ball from a rival midfielder. He dashes up the sideline, moving with almost brutal speed and focus, and crushes a pass to Olivier Seydoux, who waits inside the goal box. Seydoux leaps into the air and heads the ball. A ripple of excruciating anticipation moves through the stadium as we watch the ball arc through the air. Half a heartbeat later, it soars just over the goalie's outstretched arms into the net, tying the match.

The crowd erupts into pandemonium. The old man besides me grabs my face and plants a wet kiss on my cheek. We both laugh like little kids, gleeful and uninhibited. On the pitch, Rhys leaps into Olivier's arms, and their teammates pile on. The giant stadium scoreboard shows a close up of Rhys's face. He looks bewildered, like he can't believe what just happened.

Like he's utterly shocked by this sudden, unexpected stroke of luck.

My pulse skips. *Keep it up*, I silently urge him. *You certainly could on Sunday night.*

The other team keeps possession of the ball for the next several minutes. The clock is ticking: seventy-two minutes, seventy-nine, eighty-four. I bounce on my toes, trying to keep my nerves at bay. The game is still tied, and the opposing team still has the ball. Things do not look promising for Madrid.

In the eighty-ninth minute, one of our defenders manages to deflect a pass intended for one of the other team's strikers. A Madrid midfielder grabs the ball and darts down the field. Halfway across, he passes the ball to Rhys, who's been waiting patiently on the side of the pitch.

And then he takes off like a bat out of hell. He's moving so fast my vision blurs as I watch him. His legs pump at manic speed as he outruns a rival defender. He guns down the pitch, making a beeline for the goal box. He bumps up against another defender, using his arms and the bulk of his body to hit back. It scares me, how fast he runs, how hard he hits and gets hit. Some of the guys he plays against are so big it must feel like being hit by an elephant.

I'm jumping up and down with the rest of the crowd as Rhys barrels into the box. He skids right, then left, and then he launches the ball past the goalie into the goal.

Goosebumps break out on my arms and legs. Holy fuck. Rhys just scored. He just scored the winning goal in the biggest game of the season so far.

The girls are screaming beside me, and then I'm screaming too. Rhys's epic goal electrifies the stadium. The old dudes beside us are saying, "He's back! The boy is back!" in garbled Spanish, while the young dudes in front of us are crying literal tears of joy (egged on, no doubt, by gallons upon gallons of beer).

Rhys turns to the crowd, that look of happy disbelief still on his face as his gaze roves over the eighty *thousand* people chanting his name.

It's the coolest thing ever. Some part of me—the drunk part—fantasizes that, high on victory, Rhys will finally call me, maybe thank me for providing the sexual mojo he needed to turn his game around.

I roll my eyes at my own ridiculousness. Rhys isn't going to call. Which is a good thing, because I have more big plans for my bucket list this week, and none of them have anything to do with Rhys Maddox.

Well, except the masturbating thing. I might need to, er, utilize him for that.

Chapter Seven

RHYS

That Night

"Zat, it was fucking awesome, mate!" Olivier says, pounding me on the back. "Where did it come from? For so many months, you play like a terrible child. But today? Today you play like a champion."

"Thanks, dickhead," I say, laughing as I tug on my trousers. The familiar scents of the locker room—sweat, soap, antiseptic—surround me. For the first time in forever, they fill me with hope. Happiness. I'm actually glad to be here. "Nice goal, by the way."

"Not as nice as ze assist."

"That's it, Cabbage!" William Wallace—I don't think anyone knows his real name anymore—appears at my elbow, clapping loudly. "Whatever girl you and your dobber mates were chattin' about at training, I want you to see more of her! I haven't seen ye play like this since before ye balls dropped."

"Thanks," I say.

"I mean it," he says, looking me in the eye. "Ye're comin' back, lad. Keep it up, yeah?"

I fight back a smile. The relief that floods me—the disbelief that my luck might actually be turning—is overwhelming. I finally played like the legend I hope to be. In this sport, legends get paid very, *very* well. And heaven knows I could do a lot of things for a lot of people with that money.

My sponsors lit up my mobile tonight. I even got a new one—a giant diamond company—that promised to pay me twenty thousand euros if I showed up at their event tomorrow night.

Needless to say, I cleared my schedule and accepted the invitation. Relationships with sponsors are fragile, so I always make an effort to put my best foot forward and attend every event they invite me to.

I shake hands, slap backs, smile as the squad compliments me on the pass. But all the while I'm thinking of only one thing.

One girl.

I admit I'm superstitious—what athlete isn't—but even I'm not daft enough to think my legendary performance today has anything to do with Laura, or the ridiculously intense orgasms we had together. Orgasms are magical, sure, but they don't have magical powers.

Do they?

Because that feeling I got when I gunned down the pitch, the way my instincts took over, and guided me—it came from the same deeply buried place inside me that came alive when I fucked Laura, her eyes wet and lucid, her hair wild, her silky skin flushed.

Maybe coach is right. Maybe Laura *did* make me play better today. It makes sense—sort of. Nothing else about my life has changed in the past week. I ate the same food, trained the same way, slept my customary nine hours a night.

Hanging out with Laura was the only deviation from my

carefully scripted schedule. It was the only time I had fun, cut loose. I spend so much time doing the things I *should* or need to do, but I rarely do what I want. I wanted to get naked with Laura, so I did. There was something so . . . liberating about it.

Sure, I've thought about Laura this week. I haven't called her, though, because that's my rule. But I have to admit that even my training sessions were better—every single one of them.

I suppose playing so well in the match today just confirms that there's something at work here.

That I finally played really, really well for the first time since blowing out my knee after I slept with Laura could be purely coincidental. It could be a not-so-funny joke, engineered by the big guy in the sky. The connection between my performance and Laura could mean nothing.

Then again, it could mean everything. It could mean the difference between being demoted from first team or making all my dreams come true. If I keep playing like I did tonight, there's a seriously exciting future ahead of me. A future where I can do right by my family, and prove to the world I'm not going to wash up like my deadbeat dad. A future with the biggest sponsors and the biggest paychecks and the best bet to live the life I've always wanted for myself, and for Mum, and for Maggie.

The kind of life Dad promised us, but never delivered on.

I'm certainly not alone in my superstitions. Alexandr swore it was wearing the bright yellow boots his wife "blessed" with a kiss every morning that made his performance in last year's Euro Cup so astounding. Fred's got his ice cream. Sergio bangs on the brick wall outside the locker room exactly six times before every match. If he doesn't, his play will be rotten (so he says). As athletes, so much of our professional lives—our successes, our failures—depends on *chance*. To touch the divine and play like the gods we want to be, the timing's got to be just right, and the stars have to align. That ever-elusive shadow called luck must be on our side.

No one knows what it is, exactly, that keeps that shadow in our corner, or lures it away. I'd sell my soul to know the nebulous math that solves the equation in my favor. But as much as I believe in the power chance, I also believe in my own power—my own agency. I can't control luck, but I can run after it as hard and as fast as I can.

Tonight, I ran pretty damn fast.

Shrugging into my suit jacket, I know what I have to do. I have too much at risk to underestimate this Laura thing. Maybe it's real, maybe it's not, but I will do anything—bloody *anything*—to keep my stars aligned.

Lucky for me, that "anything" is a gorgeous girl with an even more gorgeous body. Just thinking about that body, the way her pussy clenched around me again and again, has me adjusting the crotch of my trousers.

I've got to run like hell after Laura, and convince her, somehow, to let me see her again. Tomorrow, perhaps. I'll apologize for not calling sooner, tell her I've been busy with training. The diamond guys want me to bring a date to the event, and Laura *would* look really hot in heels and a tight little dress.

With the most important season of my career on the line, I have to see her. Perhaps make her laugh with more awful pickup lines, or give her another orgasm, or five. God, the look in her eyes when I slammed inside her . . .

I swallow, hard.

It's not serious. It can't be. But I've got to see her.

I think I just stumbled upon the good luck charm I've been looking for.

Laura

Monday

Today is my first day at the Santa Caterina After School Program (bucket list item #6: *Community service—tutor kids, literacy work*). Considering I've spent the past hour in a classroom with twenty-three five- and six-year-olds I've only just met, it's going pretty well. Only one little boy peed his pants, and the kids seem to be enjoying my terrible Spanish renditions of some of my favorite picture books (*The Giving Tree* gets me every. Damn. Time. even in a different language).

I've always been a big reader—I began sneaking romance novels from my mom's bookshelf when I was eleven, and now my massive collection of pink- and purple-spined paperbacks is the thing I treasure most in this world—so I knew when I got to college I wanted to do some kind of literacy work. My dirty book habit aside, I hoped to work with underprivileged kids. I remember what a proud, magical moment it was when I learned to read, and I wanted to relive that feeling with the children I volunteered with.

The kids and I are seated in a circle on the floor. They're a little fidgety—being asked to sit quietly after a full day of school is not easy when you're six—but they return my smile when I close *The Giving Tree* and settle it in my lap.

So, I ask in embarrassingly stilted Spanish, *the giving tree was very kind and generous with the little boy. Is there anyone in your life who is kind and generous with you? Someone who gave you something special?*

A few small hands shoot up. I point to a little girl who is missing her front teeth.

My dad says Rhys Maddox is going to give us a title this year, but only if he doesn't play like garbage.

I blink. Seriously? I can't get away from this guy. Less than twenty-four hours ago, I swore to dedicate myself to my bucket list. And yet here Rhys is, invading my carefully guarded personal space once again. Damn him and his ridiculous, delicious, rock-hard body. Oh, that body . . .

Yeah, another girl in pigtails says. *My dad says Rhys Maddox can be the best player in the world if he just gets his head out of his ass.*

"Whoa!" I say, before remembering to use Spanish. *Celeste, excuse me, but you cannot use that word here.*

Rhys Maddox would be kind and generous if he played as well as he did last night so we could win the war against Barcelona, a little boy named Miguel says.

Well, it's not a real war, I say. The rivalry between the football clubs in Madrid and Barcelona is intense. Some Spaniards —older generations, mostly—see that rivalry as a continuation of the Spanish Civil War, or at least a reenactment of it.

My grandpa says it is, he replies. *We've been fighting it for a thousand years, and only Rhys Maddox can win it with a league title.*

I bite back a grin. I can't resist. *Do you think Rhys Maddox is kind, like the giving tree?*

Maybe, a little boy says when I call on him. *My mom says he is very handsome. It makes her happy when he takes his shirt off. So maybe that means he is kind?*

Hmmm, I say. My belly aches from trying not to laugh. *I'm not so sure about that one.*

When we finish up reading hour, I take the kids outside to play on the playground. I jump when my phone, tucked into the back pocket of my jeans, begins to ring.

Are you all right, Miss Bennet? Miguel looks up at me, holding a hand to his forehead against the fading sun.

I grin at him and nod, even though my heart weirdly begins to pound as I dig my phone out of my pocket. The girls I went to the soccer game with usually text me, as do my friends back home. The only people who actually call me are Em and my parents. And considering both—well, all three of those people know I'm working right now, they wouldn't be calling me unless it was an emergency.

I glance at the screen. It's a number I don't recognize—a European number. My heart pounds faster. For one stupid, heady heartbeat, I think it might be Rhys, finally making good on his promise to call.

I look around, quickly. I'm not supposed to use my phone while I'm with the kids, but this could be an emergency. Ducking into the shade of a nearby bench, I slide my thumb across the bottom of the screen.

"Hello?"

"Laura?"

My stomach plummets at the familiar rumble of the voice that greets me.

Holy *shit*. It can't be. No way. *No freaking way.* I bite the inside of my lip, just to make sure I'm awake and alive and that this *is really happening*.

"Uh. Yes?"

"It's Rhys. Rhys Maddox."

I take a deep breath, let it out. "Oh, hey, uh, Rhys. What's, um. What's up?"

Barf. Why do I have to be so awkward?

"I want to see you," he says.

"See me?"

"Yeah. Where are you?"

"Where am I? Like, physically?"

"Yes." He laughs. "Where on the earth are you located?"

"Right now?"

"Yes. Where are you right now?" There's a loud noise in the background, like he's vacuuming or something. Only Rhys wouldn't vacuum because he's, well, Rhys Maddox.

What the hell?

"Um." I glance at the playground. "I'm volunteering at Santa Caterina. It's this after school program in—God, I actually forget what the neighborhood is called. It's not in the best area in the city . . ."

"You're at Santa Caterina?"

My stomach drops again. "Do you know it?"

"No. But I've got Google maps. I'll be there in twenty."

Now I really feel like I'm going to barf. "Wait, Rhys—no. No, don't . . . please, you don't have to—"

He already hung up.

I drop my phone on the bench, my hands shaking as I smooth my hair back from my face. I feel like I just got electrocuted. *Be cool*, I tell myself. *Stay calm.*

But how in the world am I supposed to stay calm when Rhys Maddox is on his way here? After calling me? And inexplicably telling me he wants to see me?

I don't get why he's in such a rush. Did he just find out he has a horrible, non-curable STD he passed on to me? Is he just in a good mood after his win last night? Does he want to get naked again?

I mean, what the *frick* is going on?

I stand up and survey my outfit. Of course Rhys would pick the day I'm dressed like a sweaty hippie hobo to drop into my life. I was more than a little hung over this morning after yesterday's shenanigans at the football stadium, so I only had time for cruddy jeans and a little mascara before I had to leave for class. And after hanging outside in this heat, I probably smell just *lovely*.

I run my hands through my hair, giving my tired waves a bit of a boost. I adjust my shirt and discreetly check for any signs of BO. The situation isn't great, but it isn't terrible either.

I take another deep breath. *Be cool. Be calm.*

And then I laugh at the absurdity of trying to be either of those things when the hottest, sexiest human on the planet just called to say he wants to see me this very minute. I am *so* out of my depth here. And I can't tell if that excites or terrifies me.

Chapter Eight

LAURA

When the throaty rumble of an exotic sports car fills the playground, I feel like I'm going to faint. On cue, the kids drop whatever they were doing and hurry toward the fence. They let out little gasps of surprise as a black convertible Lamborghini pulls up to the curb.

I bared myself to Rhys in every sense of the word last week. I felt relatively brave then. But now? Not so much. I feel embarrassed. Some small, mean part of me thinks he came here just to make fun of me for my hairy vagina or awful, pretend O-face.

I remind myself I have nothing to lose, that I'm focusing on me, myself, and my bucket list this semester, but that doesn't do much to slow my racing pulse.

I look down at a tug on my hand. It's the little girl with the missing front teeth.

It's all right, Miss Bennet, she says. *That's Batman. He is kind and generous, just like the giving tree. Although sometimes he kills people too.*

Rhys revs the engine one last time—boys and their toys, so ridiculous—before he turns off the car and climbs out, tucking his sunglasses into the front pocket of his tuxedo jacket.

That's right. As if this whole scenario wasn't ridiculous enough, Rhys is wearing a goddamn *tuxedo*. I feel like I'm in a commercial, one of those ads that's trying to sell probiotic yogurt to middle-aged women. Rhys is one tall class of yogurt —water—whatever—in his dapper duds. I didn't know feeling weak in the knees was actually a thing until this very moment. I grab onto the fence to steady myself.

"You all right there, love?" he asks, lips twitching.

I try not to appear too bewildered as I lean in to accept the kisses he presses into my cheeks. His stubble scrapes against my skin, and a wave of goosebumps (the good kind) breaks out on my arms and legs.

Oh. *Oh.* He smells delicious.

"I'm good," I say. "Great. I'm great. How are you? And, um. What's up with the tux? Not that I mind it. I don't mind it one bit, actually, you fill it out . . . uh . . . nicely? You make it look nice?"

Rhys laughs. I cringe.

"Have you got any plans this evening?" he asks.

"Plans?"

"Do you always answer questions with more questions?"

"No-o?"

He laughs again, toeing at the gravel that edges the sidewalk. "I'm wearing a tux because I have an event tonight—and I'd like you to come with me."

My heart trips a stop. "Wow. An event. Um . . ."

The kids take advantage of my temporary stupor to start screaming Rhys's name. *Mister Maddox, your car is so cool! Rhys Maddox, please take off your shirt for my mom! Mr. Maddox! Rhys! Hello, I love you!*

Rhys blinks, as if he's just noticing the twenty-some-odd kids who surround me for the first time. He shrinks back.

You'd think the kids were waving scythes à la *Children of the Corn* instead of their hands. His buoyant expression dims, becomes unreadable. I recognize this look, this coldness, from the morning after our naked marathon, when I tried to ask him about his past.

Mr. Maddox, Miguel says, producing a soccer ball from out of nowhere. *Would you please play football with us?*

"Maybe another time," Rhys says, looking away before he remembers to translate his response into Spanish. "Lo siento, no puedo jugar hoy."

Miguel's face falls. The kids go quiet. I'm embarrassed— for them or for Rhys, I don't know.

"Um. Okay. Vale," I say, and with a promise of snacks, usher the kids back onto the playground.

"My tux," Rhys says, by way of an explanation. "The label is one of my sponsors, and they gave this to me to wear tonight. I doubt they'd be pleased if I showed up with dirt on the hem."

I buy the tux excuse. But that's not the only thing that's keeping Rhys off the muddy patch of grass that passes for a soccer field here at Santa Caterina. There's something else at work—something that clearly makes him uncomfortable being around all these kids. I mean, he can hardly even *look* at them without squirming.

I'm starting to get the feeling that Rhys is a man of many faces. One he wears for his fans. One he wears for me. And one he keeps for himself. Maybe the faces he shows to the world are just masks he hides behind.

I don't know why I want to dig deeper, and uncover what it is those masks hide. He pretty much blew me off after the best sex of my life—the pretend-orgasm incident notwithstanding—and then all the sudden he appears a week later in a tuxedo and shiny shoes, asking me out on a date. (I mean, is a sponsored event really considered a *date?*) The whole thing makes no sense. I shouldn't care.

But I do. I care a lot. I always care. I'm trying to care more about my self-fulfillment and my health and less about everyone else's. But it's a hard habit to break.

"So what do you say?" he asks. "It's going to be quite the party. This big diamond company is celebrating the launch of their new line of diamond earrings. The theme is 'everything comes best in pairs'—so of course I've got to bring along a date. A hot date. You, Laura. I want to bring you."

My face gets hot at his compliment. I hold the fence between my fingers in a death grip. "That sounds, like, ridiculously awesome Rhys, really, it does. And I hate to say no, but I, um . . . already have plans, unfortunately."

Rhys cocks a blond brow. "Plans?"

"Yeah." Oh, God, now I'm really sweating. "It sounds stupid, but, yeah. I signed up for guitar lessons with this guy who plays flamenco. It's part of this bucket list thing I'm doing, trying to do some, you know, self-improvement or whatever. Anyway. My first lesson is tonight, so . . ."

His eyes flash with panic. "So you can't reschedule it?"

"I mean, maybe I could. But it's my first one, and I'd kinda like to be there for it."

Rhys ducks his head, stepping forward. "I didn't think my lucky charm would abandon me to walk the red carpet all by myself."

"Lucky charm?" My pulse leaps.

He puts his hands over mine on the fence and meets my eyes. "Yes. I don't know if you saw the match last night—"

"I did," I say, swallowing. My mouth is suddenly dry.

"But something happened to my game that completely turned it around. And I think that something is you."

For several seconds I just look at him, blinking stupidly, my head starting to hurt as it tries to wrap around the enormity of what Rhys is saying. I'm his *lucky charm*? I'm the one to thank for his wicked performance in last night's game?

"That's ridiculous," I say.

"Is it?" His fingers feel strong and sure as they tangle with mine. "I think it's real. And I'm not going to stop pestering you until you believe it."

"I think your performance has nothing to do with luck," I practically stammer. "I think it's about all the work you've put in. All the practice and the rehab. That's what made you play so great. Not me."

"Maybe. Maybe not. But I had a lot of fun with you last weekend. I haven't laughed like that in a long time, and the se —" He glances over my shoulder at the kids. "The, uh, *dancing*, it was really something special. Got me out of my head for a bit, yeah? Cleared my mind. I don't know if it was that, or your smile, or what have you, but after we met, whatever was broken inside me became whole again. You fixed it."

Now I'm blushing *and* sweating. "I'd insert a di—a dancing joke here, but with the kids so close . . ."

"Right." He smiles. "Look, Laura. Whether or not you believe you're my good luck charm, my career is on the line. I've got to cover all my bases. So come out with me tonight. My team—all of Madrid—they'll thank you when we win on Saturday. *I'll* thank you."

I scoff, staring at him in disbelief. "You're really going to put the outcome of that match on my shoulders?"

His gaze softens. "If it means you'll say yes. C'mon, love. You can't let me down. Not when things are finally going my way."

"God, you're shameless."

"I am," he says, lips twitching.

"And that doesn't bother you? That you're guilting me into . . . whatever this is?"

"Who said anything about guilt? This is about you and me

76

enjoying a lovely evening together in Madrid. I promise it will be a good time. We had fun together last time, didn't we? Please, Laura. Please be by my side tonight."

Even as his smirk deepens, he looks at me, eyes soft and pleading, and I feel myself softening too, my fingers twining more tightly around his. My insides go squishy. Beneath his bravado, he's scared, I can tell. He's afraid of losing. I would be too if I had worked as hard as he has to build his fledgling career. Rhys is trying to turn his life around. And no small part of me yearns to help him do that.

I promised myself I'd tackle this bucket list thing, that I'd stop being such a people-pleaser all the time. But what kind of person would I be if I didn't extend a hand to someone who's desperate? Someone who apparently believes he needs me to make his dreams happen?

It doesn't hurt that I had a *very* good time with that someone last weekend.

As we look at one another, my resolve to make it to my guitar lesson dissipates. I mean. I'd be an idiot to pass up a night out on the red carpet with Rhys Maddox, football superstar, right? Maybe we'll make out. Maybe I'll get some diamonds. Maybe he'll slay it again on the pitch next weekend.

Who knows what's in store for Rhys's future? All I know is I won't be the one to let him down. He needs me, and I need to be there for him. My guitar instructor can wait. But Rhys's career—his future—can't.

"Okay," I say, letting out a breath. "I'll go."

His handsome face—God, he's so handsome—breaks out into a smile so big and so happy it makes my heart contract. He gives my hands a squeeze. "I knew you'd come through. Thank you, Laura. I really do appreciate it."

"One problem." I glance down at my clothes. I look like a peasant compared to Rhys in his shiny shoes and shinier tux.

"I'm not sure I have anything, er, appropriate to wear to a red carpet event."

He laughs again. "Love, I've got you covered. I took the liberty of doing a bit of shopping for you this afternoon. Dress, shoes, naughty underthings—I've seen to it all. There's a hairdresser and makeup artist waiting for you at my suite in the hotel. But we've got to hurry—the event starts in less than two hours."

"Oh," I say, glancing at my watch. "Oh my. Okay. Um. I'm not supposed to be done here until six, so let me run and find someone to cover for me. I'll meet you at your car. That thing is ridiculous, by the way."

"Another sponsor," he says with a shrug. "They pay me to drive it around and be photographed in it every now and again. Speaking of, I should Instagram it—then the paparazzi will know I'm out . . ."

I think it's kinda weird that Rhys wants the paparazzi to follow him around, but I have too much on my mind to give that any further thought. I dash across the playground, my entire being lit up with the heady knowledge that I am *walking the red carpet tonight with Rhys Maddox.*

Me. Laura Bennet. Ten minutes ago, I was just an American student studying abroad. But now? Now I'm a professional soccer player's muse. His good luck charm.

As cool as that guitar lesson sounded, I gotta admit this is way, way cooler.

Chapter Nine

RHYS

That Night

When Laura makes her debut on the red carpet, the press goes nuts.

Wow, you're beautiful, one photographer shouts in Spanish, crouching to get a better angle.

Rhys, you lucky bastard, another says.

Yet another begs her for more time in front of his lens. *Show me your face, honey, the camera loves it.*

I make no effort to hide my pride, beaming at Laura as the cameras click. I'm not at all surprised they're eating her up. Hell, I am too. I've been fighting an erection for the past half hour. Laura looks fucking *ridiculous* in the tight dress and five-inch heels I bought for her at one of my favorite designer stores on Calle Serrano earlier today. Her long blonde hair is styled and sprayed into tight waves that fall over her shoulders, and the makeup artist really made her hazel eyes pop with thick liner and fake lashes. She looks like a model.

Laura's done up, sure, but she rocks the look with increasing confidence. She was a bit wobbly—literally and figuratively—when we first stepped onto the red carpet.

"You're gorgeous," I murmured in her ear, hoping to put her nerves at ease.

"Not as gorgeous as you are," she replied.

I ran my finger over the strong slope of her shoulder. She drew a small, tight breath through her teeth. "Hardly. How bloody lucky am I, that my lucky charm is so easy on the eyes?"

"You are a lucky bastard," she said, eyes teasing as they met mine. "Your lucky charm could've been . . . I don't know. A wart. Or a mangy cat. Maybe a stinky pair of socks you'd have to wear every game without washing them."

I laughed. So did she. Her shoulders fell back from her ears, just a little.

I knew Laura would get a lot of attention. Not only because she's hot as hell, but also because I rarely, if ever, bring a girl with me onto the red carpet.

I didn't expect she'd get *this* much attention, however. The photographers and reporters ask her for her name, where she's from, how long she's known me. She looks to me before answering, her gaze flashing with uncertainty, but I just nod my head, keeping my palm firmly on the small of her back as she responds to their questions. After a bit of a slow start, she handles the attention with aplomb, composed and classy, until the questions get a bit more personal.

"Is your relationship with Rhys serious?" a reporter, American by the sound of her accent, asks.

Laura looks at me again.

"Um," she says, rolling her glossed lips between her teeth.

"We met recently," I say, swooping in. "But I already know she's my good luck charm. Lovely, isn't she?"

Laura smiles. The cameras keep clicking.

I'm a lucky bastard indeed. Before things like social media and multi-million dollar sponsorship deals, it was enough to be just a really great footy player. You won games, wowed the crowd, and got paid decently enough. But in the age of the Kardashians and reality TV, it's all about *attention*. Attention is where the money is. And heaven knows I need that money.

My family needs it, badly. Seeing those kids today at the rundown playground at Santa Caterina was an unwelcome reminder of my people back home and what they still need—what I still haven't been able to give them, despite my best efforts. My cousins and I used to play at a playground like that, some of us running from fathers with a mean left hook, others because there was no other place for them to go.

They still have nowhere to go. That's what I want to give them. I want to give Mags Oxford. I want to give Aunt Kate's daughter all the therapy she needs, the tuition to special schools, and access to the best doctors. I want to give Mum and my aunts homes, real homes with more than one bathroom for eight people and a roof that doesn't leak.

So, yeah. I court attention, because attention equals huge bucks if you do it right. And big bucks equal saving my family from squalor.

It works like dominoes: I get attention by being photographed at events like this, or being photographed on a yacht, or by posting pictures of myself driving a car worth half a million euros. The flashier and more aspirational the picture, the better. The more attention I get—the more people know who I am—the more Instagram and Twitter and Facebook followers I get. And the more followers I get, the more paid sponsorships I get too.

Like I told Laura, sponsors want celebrities with big followings. It makes sense if I have a lot of followers, a lot of people are exposed to sponsors' brands or products when I do a sponsored post. A lot of people recognize me in a commercial or on a billboard. The more followers I have, the more I get paid to do those posts too.

On the surface, it doesn't make sense why being

photographed by the paparazzi coming out of Harrod's, or driving a Lamborghini, pays off. But all that glitz and flash is worth its weight in gold. There are millions of people on Instagram who post selfies with their dogs, but only a few post selfies with supermodels on private jets. "Aspirational marketing" as my publicist calls it. People want a glimpse of the glamorous lives of the rich and famous. They want to *own* a piece of that life, whether it's the shaving cream I hawked from a bathroom on a yacht or the silk bow tie I'm wearing tonight.

A couple of players on my squad make more from sponsorships than they do from their contracts with the team. I'm not there yet—not even close—but one day I hope to be. I've got to stay in the press's good graces to do that. The second they turn against me—the second they catch me doing something unworthy of Madrid's most promising player, something uncool—there's a very good chance this golden spigot gets turned off.

A good performance out on the pitch always garners attention and pleases the press too, especially here in Spain, where fans and the media alike take what happens on the pitch personally.

All the more reason to keep Laura close.

The cameras click. We smile.

Laura

Later That Night

"Oh my *God*," I say, leaning over my lap in an attempt to quiet my wildly beating heart. "Oh my God, that was ridiculous! Amazing, but ridiculous."

Rhys revs the Lambo's engine once, twice, three times,

and with the squeal of tires we dart into the night. My hair flies into my face, tugged upward in a sudden surge of wind. I let out a giggle.

"You all right?" Rhys half-shouts above the scream of the engine.

"When I'm with you?" I straighten in my seat, holding my hair back, and grin. "Never."

"They loved you," he says, shifting into second gear with an authoritative thrust. He took off his jacket so he's just in his white tuxedo shirt, the loose ends of his bow tie flapping in the breeze. "And you handled them like a pro."

"Thanks," I say, tugging at the hem of my dress. It's so short that when I sit down, you can practically see my junk. "I'm sure this very tiny dress had absolutely nothing to do with all that attention."

Rhys turns his head to look at me. His eyes flick over my body, a palpable perusal. The heat that's been simmering between my legs flares to new, white-hot life. This car isn't helping. The engine is so powerful and so loud it makes everything vibrate, including my seat.

He smirks, reaches over and grabs my hand. "Don't touch that dress," he says, gaze moving to the tops of my thighs. "The view is quite lovely from here."

Rhys drops my hand to shift again. Then he sets his hand back on my thigh. The gesture is familiar. Intimate. My pulse spikes.

"You have fun?" he asks.

"I did. I mean. It was overwhelming. A little weird I got so much attention when all I really did was stand there and look pretty in a really expensive dress."

"The heels cost more than the dress, actually."

I roll my eyes, still grinning. "Of course they did. The shoes might actually be bigger than the dress, so that makes sense."

Rhys glances in the rearview mirror and smiles.

"What?" I ask.

"Looks like we have an audience."

I glance in the side mirror. A moped or two emerge from the darkness. A second later a bright flash reflects off the mirror, blinding me.

"Paparazzi," I say. "Did you tip them off?"

"They knew we were at that event. They probably hung out behind the building, waiting for us to leave."

"And then they saw this car and knew it was you."

He looks at me, swiping his thumb gently across my thigh. "Smart girl. Yes."

"Do they always follow you around? Or does it only happen when you want it to?"

"I'd like to think I have some control over it, but . . ." Rhys shrugs. "I don't really know, to be honest with you. For the past couple years I've been trying to establish my career, build my brand, that sort of thing. So any press has been good press, you know? I feel lucky they're paying any attention to me at all."

I nod my head. "I get it. Although I've heard the press here can be pretty intense."

"It can be," he says. "I don't really know how the media works in America. But Europeans—Spaniards and the British especially—are mental about their football. The appetite for news is voracious. And I'm not just talking about coverage of the matches or trades or whatever. I'm talking everything and anything about the players. Our families, our holidays, our sex lives. *Especially* our sex lives. I'm sure you've heard the term *WAG*?"

"You mean the super hot 'wives and girlfriends' of super hot footballers like you?"

"Yes." He grins. "We all get a lot of press when it comes to our WAGs. Most of it is harmless. The lads like a good brag every now and then, showing off pictures of their girls in magazines wearing nothing but lingerie or whatever. Some of it, though, can be quite awful. The press is powerful here. They can make or break your name, depending on how they feel about you. One guy—he stopped playing football a couple years ago, but he was big, really big here in Madrid—wasn't very friendly with some reporters during an interview. He basically told them to piss off. So they went and printed a story alleging he had an affair with some shop girl. I don't know if it was true or not, but it destroyed his marriage. Almost destroyed him too. He lost quite a few sponsors and a good bit of his income."

"Wow." I blink. "Rhys, that's actually kinda scary."

"Doesn't happen often. But it pays to stay in the press's good graces. I scratch their back, and they scratch mine."

I unstick a lock of stray hair from my lip gloss and tuck it behind my ear. "Right. They scratch your back by getting your name out there. They make you famous, get you more followers and sponsors."

"Exactly. I've got to be seen on a regular basis. I've got to stay visible."

I close my eyes at another pop of bright light in the rearview mirror. My eyes smart, blinking back neon dots that blur my vision.

"I'll give them this—they're persistent," I say.

Rhys turns his head. His lips twitch as his hand moves farther up my thigh, his pinkie toying with the hem of my dress. "Shall we give them a show? Something worth photographing?"

My mouth falls open. For half a heartbeat I just look at him, my mind racing to come up with a witty yet firm way of saying *no fucking way do I want the world seeing pictures of you fingerbanging me in your car.*

"Don't worry," he says, laughing. "They really can't see much—the windows are tinted."

"Oh," I say. "Oh, okay—"

I gasp when Rhys's questioning pinkie slips inside my (seriously undersized) thong. He rotates his hand and hooks his index finger around the strap and tugs, hard, snapping it. As if by command, my legs fall apart, and Rhys glides the fingertips of his first two fingers around the top of my sex.

His eyes go wide. "Holy shit, love, you're wet. So bloody soft."

"What do you expect"—I slam my hand on the dashboard, searching for something to hold on to as sensation spikes through me—"when you're dressed like *that*? Rhys, you looked so hot in that tuxedo I thought I was going to soak through my dress at the party."

"Christ." His Adam's apple bobs as he swallows, hard. "If I had known, I would've commandeered a bathroom and seen to you sooner."

Rhys presses a finger inside me. My head falls back onto the seat, my eyes rolling up to the night sky. *Who the fuck am I?* I ask the stars. The city lights dim their brightness, but I can still make them out against a purple velvet background.

Who is this girl getting fingered in a Lamborghini while trolling around Madrid with a famous footballer?

It's too delicious to be real.

But it is. The things I'm feeling right now are *very* real. Potent. Terrifyingly real and potent.

My hair swirls around me, the night air a warm rush against my skin. I feel the rumble of the car in my breastbone as Rhys revs the engine, drowning out the sound of the wind, the sound of my breath coming and going in shallow gasps. His fingers work over and around and inside me. My legs start to shake.

I know we're putting on a show. Two car lengths behind

us, a growing swarm of paparazzi gathers, eager to catch a glimpse of Rhys Maddox and the mystery blonde who appeared at his side tonight, seemingly out of nowhere. Part of me is put off by it—put off by everything, the press and the party and this inane piece of stretchy fabric that some wackadoo designer called a *dress*.

But another part of me is totally, overwhelmingly, irrevocably dazzled by it all.

I tighten around Rhys's fingers. The pressure between my legs closes in on me. It's unbearable. It's sweet.

It will be the first time I've ever come with a guy.

Who am I?

I close my eyes, ready to surrender to my orgasm, when a white light flashes across the backs of my eyelids. Rhys curses and jerks his hand away, cursing again when he downshifts and the car veers sharply to the left.

I grab onto the seat and open my eyes to see us zooming into oncoming traffic. My stomach seizes, and a wave of fear moves through me that's somehow both ice cold and so hot I break into a sweat.

"Oh my God, Rhys—"

"Hold on!"

I glance to the right. I see a pair of paparazzi taking up the right hand lane, where we should be.

"Assholes," I say. "They ran you off the road, didn't they?"

"They did," he grinds out. "They're not usually this aggressive, but now that you're in the picture . . ."

Rhys shifts and slams on the gas pedal, the engine throbbing as he tries to pass the photographers. The force of the acceleration sucks me into my seat, making my stomach flip. I glance at the dashboard in front of Rhys, the illuminated needles all jump to the red. We must be going well over one hundred. If Rhys loses control right now, or we ram head-on into another car, we are so, *so* dead.

The oncoming traffic approaches and we have to get back into our lane, *now*.

"Oh my God," I say again, squeezing my eyes shut. This is too much, it's overwhelming, I can't *breathe*—

The car jerks to the right, tires roaring, and I open my eyes to see that we're back in our lane, decelerating to a nice, easy fifty kilometers per hour. A couple cars—the ones we would've taken out head-on—honk as they pass us in the opposite direction. One guy gives Rhys the finger. Rhys just smirks, smoothing back his hair as he checks his rearview mirror. The paparazzi are now keeping an unsafe but doable distance of one car length behind us.

"Sorry about that, love," he says, putting his hand back on my thigh. "I suppose I'm not the only one you've got all hot and bothered this evening."

I let out a sputtering breath. I feel dizzy.

"Are you all right?" His brow creases. "I really am sorry, but there was nowhere else I could go. I had to pass them, and it was either the wrong side of the road or the sidewalk where loads of people were walking. Talk to me, love. I hate the idea that I scared you."

I glance at Rhys. His blue eyes are translucent in the darkness, hopeful. The fear that gripped my heart two seconds ago loosens. He is unbelievably handsome, his strong, masculine profile outlined by the glow of the dashboard. He's tied his hair up at the crown of his head, the breeze loosening stray tendrils at his temples and neck. The remnants of his smirk make him appear deliciously reckless.

He *is* reckless, but he makes it look good. He handled this car with cocky assuredness, just like he handled the ball on the pitch last Sunday night.

Just like he's handling me.

He's looking at me—really *looking*—the kind of soft, sorry, interested look that turns me on and turns me inside out.

This was supposed to be the semester where I avoided that look at all costs. This was supposed to be the semester of self-love and various Spanish cheeses. But here I am, wallowing in that look, soaking it up, the heady beat of longing between my legs too loud and insistent to ignore.

I don't know if I've ever wanted anyone as much as I want Rhys. He's a lethal combination of athleticism and hotness and charm and oh *dear* those eyes. I've never met anyone like him. He was so kind and attentive on the red carpet. Even now I shiver at the memory of his hand on my back, his touch firm and gentle and reassuring all at once. I adored the way he beamed at me as I faced the press for the first time, like he was proud of me, pleasantly surprised by my poise and my patience with their questions. They loved us together.

I love us together.

As I look back at him, it hits me that I *am* scared. I know, in this instant I just know, I want more from him, of him, and I'm scared he doesn't want more of me. I mean, come on— he's practically a god, and I am all too human, especially now that I'm eating that cheese. Why would he ever be seriously interested in someone like me, even if I am his good luck charm? It's only a matter of time before he realizes that little theory is bogus, before some hot supermodel, or maybe a pop star, catches his eye and he moves on (and up) to a better, luckier, and all around more perfect *charm*.

My crush on him was doomed from the start. It was sort of funny before, when I masturbated to him on TV. But now it just hurts.

I turn away, swallowing my heart. "Keep your eyes on the road, cowboy."

"I did scare you."

"No you didn't," I lie. "I'm fine."

"Let me make it up to you."

"I'm fine."

"You're not."

"It's the dress," I say after a beat. "It's tight. Makes it kinda hard to breathe."

"Then let's take it off." He draws his hand up my leg, pushing the dress up around my waist.

I grab him by the wrist. "Wait," I breathe. "Wait, Rhys."

I feel sweaty and sticky between my legs.

I feel overwhelmed. By what just happened. By the way he wants to touch me.

By the way I want him to want me.

I want him to want me. I want him to make what I feel real by acknowledging it. I want him to feel it too—this wave of desire, of complete and utter awe.

I remember how my body felt when I was in his arms that night at the hotel. How my heart exploded watching him play on Sunday. I remember my bucket list. Rhys would be really great at helping me with line item #1 (*exploring what I like sexually*). Now that I've had Rhys, I don't want anyone else. No one's going to do it for me the way this smoking hot footballer does. Masturbating's *especially* not going to do it.

Orgasms are great. But Rhys Maddox is better. And who's to say the two are mutually exclusive? Once I learn to loosen up a little—surely I can learn to stop being so afraid of my own vagina—I have no doubt Rhys will make me come all over the place.

In the meantime, I'm going to make *him* come. Even gods have needs, and I want to be the human who tends to his. Plus I am really sweaty and probably smelly, and I don't want to risk turning Rhys off with my grossness. I don't want to mess this up.

I am going to do anything I can to make him want me the way I want him.

I meet Rhys's eyes. A beat of heated silence stretches between us.

I drop his wrist and creep my fingers across the center console and onto his crotch. His blue eyes flash with something dark as I pop the button on his tuxedo pants.

"Laura—Christ!" He jumps when I slip my hand inside his underwear and wrap my hand around his dick—he's already hard and hot to the touch—but, giving him a good tug, I put my other hand on the center of his chest and push him back into his seat.

"Keep." I lean forward. "Your eyes." I unzip his fly. "On the goddamn road, Rhys."

And then I go down on him.

He growls, his head falling back onto the headrest as I press my tongue into the sensitive seam that runs up the underside of the tip of his dick.

"Oh, love." Rhys digs his hand into my hair. He lifts his hips, thrusts gently into my mouth. "Oh, *love*."

Chapter Ten

RHYS

I almost crash the car when I come. The feel of Laura's mouth on my cock, coupled with the surprise of such an unexpected treat, has me seeing stars when my orgasm hits me. The muscles in my legs tighten and burn, the rush coming over me in a single, almost blinding instant. Laura swallows me whole, her tongue working the head of my dick as I empty myself into her mouth. Sweet girl is very, very good at this.

"Jesus Christ," I sputter, blinking back the bright dots that threaten my vision. "That was nothing short of spectacular."

Laura sits up in her seat, offering me a sly little smile as she discreetly wipes at her mouth with her thumb. "Thought you might enjoy that."

"You didn't have—"

"I wanted to," she says.

I turn my head to look at her. "Well thank you for that. I enjoyed it very much, if you couldn't tell."

"I'm glad you did."

I take her chin in my palm and quickly pull her to me. I kiss her lips, but two seconds later she pulls back, eyes wide.

"You're really going to kiss me after . . ."

"After what?"

"You know," she says. "After having you in my mouth."

"Of course I'm going to kiss you," I say. "That was the best bloody blow job I've ever had in my life. It's the least I can do."

"Really?"

"Really," I say. I kiss her again, opening her to me. I taste the salt of my arousal on her tongue. "I don't get it when blokes won't kiss their girl afterward. It's rude, for one thing. And I happen to think it's sexy as hell to taste it, for another."

Laura furrows her brow. "You're in the minority then."

"Would you kiss me after I went down on you?"

"Um. I guess?"

I make a sharp right, taking us up a wide, pretty street. I glide into the first parking spot I see and put the car in park.

"You guess?" I say, turning to her. "Well, darling, you'd better. I bet you've got a raging case of blue balls. Or would it be blue ovaries?"

Laura smiles. "Blue clitoris?"

"Blue labias, I'd say."

"Isn't the plural of labia . . . well, labia without the *s*?" she asks, laughing.

I unbuckle my seatbelt and lean toward her. "Let's ask the labia . . . s what they think, shall we?"

I'm about to reach between her legs when she catches me by the wrist again. She did the same thing when I tried to touch her before.

I look up, but she won't meet my eyes.

"Do your labias not like me?"

She laughs a second time. "No. They lo—they like you a

lot. But I'm kinda tired, to be honest with you. And, um. Really, really sweaty."

"I don't care."

"Why don't we go back to your place so I can get cleaned up first? I could really use a shower."

I fall back into my seat and tug a hand through my hair. "Actually, love, I was going to drop you off at your place tonight. As fun as a shower together would be, I've got to behave myself during the week. Especially tonight—we've got our first training session of the week tomorrow morning. I want to go in fresh. You know, get a solid night's sleep, have a bit of quiet time with my coffee in the morning. I keep a pretty strict schedule during the season, and it doesn't allow a lot of time for . . . er, fun and such, sad as that sounds."

"Oh." Laura tries to catch her face before it falls. "Oh, okay. Yeah, sure, that's fine. I definitely don't want to mess with your mojo after last night's game."

"Thanks for understanding," I say, meeting her eyes.

"No problem," she says. "Really. I get it."

"I'd love for you to stay over next Wednesday, though. We've got a game that night, which means no training the next day. We can sleep in, perhaps you can rub some of that luck off onto me—then maybe some breakfast and little quality time together?"

She offers me a smile. "Yeah. Yeah, I'd like that. You know, I've been wanting to do a moped tour of Madrid. Could be fun?"

"A moped tour?" I arch a brow. "Is that a thing now?"

"I don't know," she says, looking away. "Just something I thought sounded fun. Funny. I don't know."

"We can play it by ear, all right?"

"Sounds good to me."

"You sure you don't want me to . . ." I nod at her lap.

Laura pulls at her dress, tugging it as best she can over her thighs. "I'm sure. I think I've had enough excitement for one night. Thanks, though."

I put my seatbelt back on and coax the car into gear. I hate to disappoint her, especially after that fantastic performance a minute ago. But being a professional athlete isn't all Lamborghinis and glamorous parties. There's loads of hard work involved, tens of hours of training each week including brutal conditioning drills, weight lifting, intense scrimmages, and endless amounts of running. My body has to be in the best shape possible to make it through those sessions and then the matches, which means I've got to get the proper amount of sleep and rest. I've got to eat really, really well too —no alcohol (except on nights I don't have training or a game the next day), no dairy or sugar or eating out, really.

Yeah, I may be a bit anal about keeping such a strict schedule. But with so much on the line, I can't afford to let loose or make a mistake. My father let loose, started drinking a couple nights a week to cope with the stress of his career. It wasn't long before he was drinking so much and doing so many drugs he'd get sick at training. In the span of a single season, he went from being one of the most talented players in the league to an emaciated alcoholic who brought down an entire team.

He brought down our entire family too.

People don't talk about James Maddox around me. But I know what they're thinking—I'm just like him, I'm going to fall short and screw everything up for everyone.

They've got another thing coming. I'm not my father. I didn't inherit that defective gene that led him down a dark path, and I am willing to go to any length to prove it. My father may have been photographed pissed out of his mind, bottle of gin in his hand. But I make sure I'm photographed enjoying the glamorous spoils of a promising football career. Cars, girls, shopping sprees—not only do I get a lot of mileage out of these things when it comes to endorsements and goodwill with the press, I also get to show the world, and the naysayers back home, that I'm my own man. That I'm making something of myself.

As restrictive as my schedule is, I've got to stick to it. My game depends on it. So does my reputation, and my family.

Thursday Morning

"Thank you," I gasp. "Thank you. *Thank you.*"

I thrust my hips with each *thank you*, burying myself deeper and deeper inside the soft, sweet grip of Laura's cunt. She begins to contract around me. Delirious with need and relief and excitement, I come too.

I fall back onto the bed, blinking against the darkness of the room. Sunlight, strong and white, peeks through the gap in the curtains. As usual, Laura wanted to have sex in the dark.

"I'd say you're welcome," Laura replies, covering herself with the sheets despite the darkness. "But I'm telling you—I think you killed it last night for the same reason you killed it last weekend. You're super talented. You work hard. So you played great. Those goals had nothing to do with me."

I glide my mouth up the slope of her shoulder. "I beg to differ, love. Those things helped. But you're the one who tipped luck in my favor. You're the one who made the difference. I mean, I scored three goals in two matches. I've never done that before."

Laura laughs. I do too. I'm just so damn gleeful. I killed it on the pitch last night. Absolutely *killed* it. I played the entire match and scored two of our three goals. Any fears I had of last week's performance being a fluke disappeared, replaced by the heady euphoria of belief. Belief that this is really happening. Belief that I'm back, that I'm not going to drown.

Belief that Laura truly is my good luck charm.

I've got to keep her close.

"I'm going to go clean up," she says, scurrying to the bathroom before I have a chance to glimpse her hot little body.

"Give me a moment and I'll join you!" I call after her.

I take care of the condom and grab my mobile off the bedside table. I scroll through a couple headlines—BLOND AMBITION: RHYS MADDOX TEARS IT UP ON THE PITCH—and the 182 texts (literally) I've received overnight. I pick up Olivier's first.

Need to celebrate come over for pool time and drinks today my woman is here you should bring one for you and one for Fred see you soon mate

I grin. The lads and I were too knackered to do much celebrating last night after the match, so it makes sense Olivier wants to make up for lost time. His flat is ridiculous— as it should be, bloke makes twenty million euros a season— complete with waterfalls in both his bathroom *and* his rooftop pool.

I've got to admit, I don't hate the idea of catching some sun while ogling Laura in an itty bitty bikini at Olivier's extravagant place. Even better, the press knows where he lives, and they often camp out outside his building to catch photos of the celebs attending his infamous pool parties. We always make sure to put on a show for them.

The last thing I want to do is disappoint our captain. Olivier and I are mates, but that doesn't mean I've got a free pass to blow him off.

I'll be there with my plus one, I text back. I head for the bathroom.

Laura is still wrapped in a sheet, brushing her teeth, when I walk in.

"So, about today—"

"You still up for that moped tour?" she asks, brightening even as toothpaste spills from her mouth.

"The moped tour. Shit! I forgot about that."

"Oh," Laura says. She turns back to the mirror. "I mean, I don't think it's too late to rent some—"

"How about a bit of pool time instead? Olivier—one of my mates on the squad—he's having a few people over to his flat this afternoon to celebrate our win. It's always a good time. And I'd love to show you off to the lads."

"Oh," Laura repeats. "Olivier has a pool at his apartment?"

"Yes. It's the most ridiculous thing you'll ever see. Definitely worth the price of admission. He'll have food, drinks, a DJ, the whole thing."

She holds back her hair with one hand as she rinses out her mouth.

"Sounds like you really want to go," she says.

"I'm not sure I have a choice," I reply, scoffing. "When the captain of the squad invites you over, you don't say no."

"Even if you were the star of the game last night?"

"Even if I was the star of the game, I've got to pay my dues." I sidle up behind her, pressing a kiss to the crown of her head. I put my hands on her hips and meet her gaze in the mirror. "C'mon, love, I promise it will be fun. I want you there with me. And most importantly, I want to see this hot little body in a bikini."

Laura looks at me for a long minute, her hazel eyes trailing over my hair, my face, my groin. I'm naked as the day I was born, and I can tell she appreciates that fact. I step a little to the side, so she can see more of me.

"God, you're totally shameless," she says, fighting a grin. "Totally shameless and totally hot."

"You'll go with me, then?"

She lets out a huff. "Yes, I'll go with you. Although I'm

not sure how I feel about chilling in a bikini with all your footballer friends and their hot WAGs around. I don't think I'll measure up."

"Trust me, you'll slay the competition." I kiss her cheek. "We'll do the moped thing another day, I promise. All right?"

"All right," she says.

Laura

Later that week

MADDOX'S HOT STREAK: *Rhys dominating on and off the pitch*, the headline screams. I scrunch my eyes at the grainy photo of me. In it, I'm biting my lip as I adjust my bikini top. The fact that the picture isn't so great actually works in my favor, my edges are thankfully blurred, making me look thinner and tanner and more well-endowed than I actually am.

Still, I put down the sandwich I'd been eating and don't pick it back up again. Yeah, I wanted to eat cheese and paella this semester, but that was before I knew pictures of me in a bathing suit would be in newspapers all over Europe. I'll probably stick to salads, at least for the foreseeable future. Rhys is hot, and he deserves a hot girlfriend.

I want to be that girlfriend. I want to be his, any way he'll have me.

Rhys is beside me in the photo, his hand resting possessively on my ass. He looks face-meltingly sexy in short, Euro-style swim trunks, the muscles in his abs and legs on full display. My heart contracts. *I want.* I need. It's only been two days since I saw him, and already I miss him. Pathetic, I know, but now that I've glimpsed his world, felt and tasted and enjoyed it, I want, more than anything, to be a part of it.

We just . . . we get along so well. And he's so hot. So talented too.

I still don't buy the idea that I'm his good luck charm or whatever. But it's a thrill nonetheless to think that I'm a part of his life now—somehow I help fuel or inspire that talent.

My phone rings. I pick it up and see that it's Rhys.

"Hey!" I say.

"Hello, love," he replies. "How are you feeling? Everything still all right?"

Rhys called yesterday before the pictures were printed to give me a head-up they'd be in the papers today. Not gonna lie, I was a little freaked out at first. But he assured me his publicist Cristina wouldn't let any unflattering photos make the news, and told me he liked the idea of us being seen together.

I mean. How the hell do I say no to that?

"Yes," I reply. "I still think I look a little chubby—"

"I think you look hot," he says. "I love those photos of you. As a matter of fact, I might ask for a few copies for . . . uh, *personal* use."

"Thanks," I say, my heart swelling as his compliment fills it to the brim. My face is hot. I feel dizzy.

I swear, Rhys brings me to my knees in a way no other guy ever has.

"We still on for Sunday?"

"Yes," I say, a little too quickly. I clear my throat, try again —this time with more dignity (I hope). "Yes. I'd like that."

Sunday is five days away. Five very long days. But Rhys has a big match against Madrid's rival, Barcelona, that afternoon, and he'll be preparing for it all week long—meaning he won't have time to see me. Of course I'm bummed, and I kinda wish he didn't have such an insane schedule. I'm not the biggest sports fan, granted, but no one really talks about the unsexy side of professional athletics. The daily grind of practice and PT and interviews and meetings. Rhys is hella talented, but he also works really, *really* hard. So hard he says he usually passes out by nine every night. In my college student bubble, I never really considered that Rhys's rock hard abs and his dominance on the field came at a price.

A price I admit I am willing to pay. Especially when Rhys invited me to a "sleepover" at the penthouse after the game on Sunday, promising to make up for lost time.

I'll just have to gird my loins and be patient, maybe use the free time to work on my bucket list.

"See you Sunday, then," he says.

"Yes," I say. "Can't wait."

Chapter Eleven

LAURA

September

Rhys keeps scoring. I keep falling. I can't stop wanting to be close to him. Even though I still haven't had an orgasm with him, he still turns me on, our white-hot chemistry in the bedroom mellowing to a heady, fuzzy warmth in the morning. It's like Rhys is the sun and I spin in his orbit, basking in his warmth when we're together, yearning in the cold when we're not. He is the center of everything, and I gave up the struggle against his gravitational pull long ago. I surrendered, foolishly, not knowing where we are going or what we even are.

"Yeah," Em asks one Thursday afternoon in late September, "what *are* you guys? Like, are you just hooking up? Are you two talking? Exclusive? Dating? I'm a little confused."

"I honestly don't know," I say. I'm supposed to be working on the charity auction I'm putting together for Santa Caterina in December—I already searched for three hours this morning for the perfect venue without much luck—but instead I'm scrolling through the lingerie on a high-end department store's website. I hover my mouse over a sheer lace bra and thong set. €68 is ridiculously steep for something that's as big as a sock, but I know Rhys would love it. I glance at my bowl of gazpacho as I put the lingerie set in my cart. If I'm going to look good in this tiny thing, I *have* to watch what I eat. What's that saying? Nothing tastes as good as skinny feels? I need to live by those words.

Speaking of, I gotta make it to the gym by six for that spin class . . .

"So? Why don't you find out?" Em munches on the marinated olives she picked up at Borough Market in London—she finally made it across the pond to join me in Europe. "I mean. Aren't you curious?"

"I am. But things are so great between us right now, and I'm having so much fun with him . . ." I sigh. "I guess I just don't want to rock the boat, you know?"

"Are you scared of what he'd say if you asked him?"

"No," I say. "Well. Maybe a little. He keeps saying I'm his good luck charm, but he's really busy all the time, so I don't see him a lot. We *do* keep having great sex—"

"Have you freaking come with him yet? A real orgasm, not something you faked."

"—so I'm not worried that he's hanging out with other girls. I just don't see the need to put a label on it. Us. Whatever we are."

"It sounds like you want to, though," Em says. "It sounds like you're really into this guy."

"I'm not *really* into him. I'm just, uh, having fun," I reply.

It's Em's turn to sigh. "Whatever you say. I just don't want to see you get hurt. I also don't want you to give up your bucket list. You were doing so well for a minute there."

"I'm still doing well," I say, a little defensively. "I'm at Santa Caterina twice a week. And . . . and I'm working on the other stuff too."

Only I'm not. Not really. Don't get me wrong, I had every

intention of checking off more line items on the list during the week, when I wasn't with Rhys. But between classes and homework and hitting up the gym and shopping for cute outfits to wear when I *do* hang with Rhys, I just can't seem to find the time. It's like Rhys has somehow taken over my life, even though I only see him for a day or two each week. It's exhausting and exciting all at once.

We've settled into a little routine, Rhys and I. With his schedule as crazy as it is, I don't have much control over when and where our time together happens. He lets me know when he's available—usually the night and day after a match —and I'll meet him at the penthouse, where we'll hang out (read: bang until our private parts hurt), make some food, and watch some TV. Occasionally, Rhys will take me to a publicity event, and every so often he'll text me when he finishes up early at the training facility and we'll grab a quick cup of coffee and a quicker fuck.

For the most part, though, we spend more time apart than we do together. It's a bummer, but it comes with the territory. As Rhys's *good luck charm* I don't want to disappoint him, and I don't want to bug him with annoying questions. Questions like "What are we?" and "Why don't you want to see me more often because I want to see you all the time?" I mean, every guy hates being asked those questions. I am *not* going to be the kind of girl who asks them.

Rhys needs to focus on his football—the guy practically came back from the dead, he pulled a miracle—and I don't want to distract him from that.

For the most part, I'm happy to just go with the flow and hang out with him. I'm happy not knowing what we are, or what I mean to him. Sometimes, when I fall asleep in his arms, or when he makes me laugh, I think he means enough to me for the both of us. Like I care enough about him to make up for any indifference he may feel about me.

A couple days after my conversation with Emily, though, my curiosity gets the better of me. I guess she planted the seed, and now that it's here, I can't stop thinking about it.

Rhys and I are hanging out in the penthouse suite, sipping coffee on the couch while we read through the Sunday papers. A picture from the life and style section of a British newspaper catches my eye. It's Rhys and me, emerging hand in hand from a gala we attended last week for his watch sponsor. He looks dapper in a navy blue suit and slicked back hair; I look skinny—*yes!*—if a bit pale. I'll have to wear more bronzer next time.

Rhys Maddox and his girlfriend, Laura Bennet, a student, out and about in Madrid on Sept. 21, the caption reads.

I blink. Then I venture a glance at Rhys. He's absorbed in the sports section of the same paper, head bent, messy hair tucked behind his ears. I think this Rhys—the unshowered, unshaven one—is my favorite Rhys. Maybe because I'm the only one who gets to see him like this. The world gets the guy in the tux and the Madrid uniform. But I get this guy. This sexy, bed-mussed, scruffy man.

I want this man, badly. I want to be his in every sense of the word.

I want to be his girlfriend. I want what this caption says to be true.

Am I Rhys's girlfriend? Are we exclusive? All I know is that I want to be.

My heart begins to pound. If there ever were a time to bring this up, now would be it. And if it goes sideways—if Rhys is clearly not interested in having this conversation—I can always bail and make it sound like a joke, like the writers at this paper are the idiots, not me.

"Hmm," I say. "That's interesting. You think they'd fact check this sort of thing."

Rhys looks up and scratches his scruff. "What sort of thing?"

"This." I hold up the picture so he can see it. He's sitting close enough to see the caption too. "The caption is wrong. I mean. I'm not your girlfriend," I say, waiting for him to correct me.

Waiting for him to swoop in and hold me in his arms and say *no, Laura, you absolutely* are *my girlfriend, I adore you and want you and hope you'll accept me as your ever faithful boyfriend, flawed through I may be.*

Instead, Rhys looks away, a distinctly uncomfortable expression overtaking his features. He sighs.

My heart falls. Was I really that obvious?

"Listen, Laura . . ."

I put the paper in my lap and reach for my coffee, hiding behind it lest I be unable to control the tears that have begun to prickle at the backs of my eyes. *Goddamn it*, I think. *How could I be so stupid?*

"Yeah?" I hope my voice sounds less high and thin to him than it does to me.

"You're a really great girl"—*ugh, the dreaded great girl lead in* —"and I really do believe meeting you has done wonders for my career. You're the best good luck charm a lad could ask for."

He pauses, still not looking at me. A faint flush of color crawls up his throat.

"Thanks," I say after a beat. "I'm happy for you. You know, that everything is going so great with your career."

"But that's just it, love—my career is very demanding right now, and after where I've been the past season and a half, I've got to give it my all. Prove to the coaches and the owners and the fans that I deserve my spot here. I'm afraid I haven't got time to do that *and* a relationship properly. I like you, Laura, I do. A lot. But . . ." Rhys sighs, tugging a hand through his hair. "But would you hate me if I said I wanted to keep things casual for the time being? I'm having loads of fun with you, and I can't very well let my good luck charm go. What do you say to keeping things as they are now?"

"As they are now?" My hands have started to shake, so I put down my coffee cup. "Like—"

"Like . . . like no strings attached. We see each other when we want to, we have fun, we have fantastically amazing sex . . ."

And then what? I want to say. People who have fun and great sex together usually end up dating. Will we eventually end up together? Or will December roll around and I'll leave Spain for good and he'll go off on his merry footballer way and we'll never talk again?

The thought of that happening devastates me. But what can I do? I'm not going to beg Rhys to date me when it's clear he doesn't want to. When he *can't*. What in the world did I expect when I became involved with a super-hot professional athlete? He's not a normal guy. And I adore him for that— hello, rock-hard body and ridiculous parties and penthouse suites—but it also means I can't expect to have a normal relationship with him.

Yeah, I want that normal relationship. The boyfriend-girl-friend, dinner-and-a-movie thing. But Rhys's doesn't, so that leaves me with two options. I can tell him the truth, that I want *more*, and I won't settle for anything less.

Or I can take him up on his offer. This is the only way I can have Rhys—on his terms, and on his turf—and I've got to decide if that's enough.

I want all of Rhys. But that's not on the table. So would I rather have a piece of him, or none at all?

He meets my eyes. My stomach contracts. God they're beautiful, full and pleading and kind.

"Please, Laura, don't leave me hanging." He grabs my hand. "I need you. I need you to be there for me. Please. This is too good to let go."

He lets me search his eyes. The thought of never looking at them again—of never being looked at *by* them again—makes me feel like dying.

He needs me. I can't tell him no, not when he's looking at me like this. Not when there's so much on the line for him.

Maybe there's a way to make this work in my favor. Yeah, I'm not getting what I want. Not exactly. But part of my bucket list *is* about figuring sex out. And who better to figure sex out with than the guy who rocks my world in bed? I haven't had the big O yet with him. But surely I'll get more comfortable with him the longer we're together. If I'm comfortable, maybe I'll finally have the courage to ask for that orgasm. Hell, maybe I'll even let him go down on me.

Rhys needs me. And in some weird way, I need him too.

"Okay," I say. "Sure. Yes. Casual works for me. Yeah, it definitely works. I've got a lot going on with school anyway, and I really want to get to know Madrid, so . . . yeah."

"Thank you," Rhys says, releasing a relieved breath. "I just don't want to disappoint you, love. This career—this sport—it's not for the faint-hearted. It requires a lot of sacrifice, and I hate the idea of giving you all these expectations and then falling down on them."

"I know," I say. And I do. I hate disappointing people. I would especially hate disappointing Rhys. I'm in too deep and care too much about his career and his dreams for the future. I'm not going to fall down on him either.

I square my shoulders, determination taking root inside my chest that still feels a little sore from Rhys's rejection.

I'm going to be the most perfect, most supportive good luck charm Rhys has ever had a casual relationship with. I can do that. I *will* do it.

The rest, orgasmic and otherwise, will fall into place. Hopefully.

Chapter Twelve

LAURA

Three Months Later—Late November
Madrid, Spain

The private jet is like all the others we've been on this semester. "Posh" as Rhys says, decked out in plush leather and burled wood and shiny gold accents that give his Rolex a run for its money.

It used to excite me, traveling in style like this with Rhys. Joining the mile high club. It used to turn me on.

But fast-forward a couple months from our first flight together, and now flying on a private jet makes me feel the way I do lately when I'm with Rhys.

Depressed. Anxious. A little angry.

It makes me feel like crying.

I huddle into one of the giant, cushy bucket seats and look out the window, hoping Rhys doesn't see me blinking back tears. *How did it come to this?* What a coward I've been, letting it—us—go so far.

I'm supposed to be trolling around Madrid on a pink moped right now. I *finally* rented us some mopeds for this weekend, and I drew up a route for us to follow through the city. I've been excited to do what I wanted for once, to pay some attention to my neglected bucket list. I usually cave to Rhys's requests for quiet nights in, or dinner at one of the two restaurants he'll eat at in Madrid (he pretty much eats only grilled chicken and kale, things that are tough to come by on menus in a country known for salty, cheesy tapas and carb-heavy paella).

But then Rhys's sponsorship appearance in London got moved up—another celebrity spokesperson had a scheduling conflict with a movie he's filming—which meant the event was happening *this* weekend. The same weekend I blocked off for our Madrileño moped adventure.

"Come on," I'd said to Rhys. "I know I told you I'd go with you to this thing, but I've been looking forward to my moped tour for, like, ever. I've had it planned for weeks now."

"But you promised you'd come with me," Rhys pleaded. "The champagne people were thrilled to hear you'd be attending. They love you. Everyone loves you."

Everyone but you, I thought.

"And really," he continued, "you want to blow off an all-expenses-paid trip to London—we'll be staying in a five-star hotel, by the way—to ride around Madrid on a tiny motorbike?"

"I do," I said. "It's on my bucket list."

"Your bucket list. Right. Aren't we checking off things on our own unofficial bucket list, though? Aren't we traveling around Europe, living in style, meeting fabulous people? Aren't you doing things you'd never in a million years dreamed you'd do?"

"Yes. Yes, definitely. But this is *my* bucket list I'm talking about. Things *I* planned to do while I'm in Spain. The moped tour is important to me, Rhys."

"I know it is, darling." He pressed a kiss onto my forehead. "And we'll get it to it, I promise."

"You keep saying that."

"And I mean it. You know how busy I've been. I'll make it happen. Just come with me to London, and then we can figure it out. I need you there, love. I need my good luck charm with me. You've been such a fabulous date—I don't think I'd know what to do with myself on the red carpet if you weren't there. Imagine what all the photographers and the journalists will think if I showed up without you. They'll hound me. How in the world do I explain to them— how will I explain it to my sponsor—that you blew me off to ride around on a bloody *moped*? I'll look like a massive fool."

Even as I rolled my eyes, I felt my resolve wavering. The last thing I want to do is embarrass Rhys in front of the press or his sponsor. I know how important his relationship with them is.

So here I am, on a plane to London, miserable and exhausted and mad at myself for letting Rhys sweet talk me out of my plans and into his yet again.

Don't get me wrong, I appreciate the luxury that surrounds me. But I know, deep down, that this stuff isn't making me any happier. Not the way it seems to make Rhys happy, anyway.

He falls into the seat beside me with a long, satisfied sigh. I watch his reflection in the window as he spears a hand through his hair—he's growing it out, and it brushes his shoulders—and leans back against the chair.

Even now, more than three months after our first fateful tryst at that hotel, his gorgeousness makes my stomach flip. I love his pert little nose and his piercing blue eyes. I still love that smirk of his especially.

But somewhere along the line, I got caught up in Rhys's

life—it was so easy, he is so persuasive—and stopped living my own.

I started the semester off on the right foot with Emily's suggestion of putting together a bucket list. But the ink wasn't even dry on that napkin when Rhys walked into my life and turned my plans upside down. I wanted to eat anything and everything, but then Rhys really loved that picture of me in a bikini, and he was always complimenting me on my looks and my "hot little body."

So I didn't. I didn't eat the cheese and paella and octopus that were on my bucket list. I've been eating the way I did back at Meryton, because I thought I needed to be skinny enough and pretty enough to deserve a spot in Rhys's stratosphere.

Which is to say, I'm not really eating much at all. The headaches I used to get from being constantly hungry are back. So are the shin splints that come from logging too many miles on the treadmill. The pressure I've put on myself to fit into Rhys's ridiculous world is just . . . it's overwhelming.

I also haven't gotten any more comfortable, sexually speaking, with Rhys. In fact, I feel more self-conscious in bed than ever. I still turn out the lights when we bone. I *still* haven't come with him. He's intimidatingly perfect, and even though I'm trying to be, I'm far from it.

In short, I haven't changed a damn thing about my life. I felt a good deal of self-hatred before, when I couldn't live up to the impossible standards I set for myself—being perfect, being thin, making everyone happy. But now I hate myself even more for not making any attempt to shed those standards. Change them.

Rhys and I are still keeping things *casual*. I wanted, so badly, to be his girlfriend before. But now I'm starting to realize that the connection we have—as glamorous as it may seem—is superficial. There's something weirdly transactional about our relationship. Like Rhys keeping me around is some sort of good business decision on his part, one his accountant would approve of. His head's in it, but his heart is locked away, hardly involved at all.

I've become an object, some*thing* pretty and pleasing, meant to be consumed by the media and Rhys's fans, ignoring all along that I am some*one* who needs to get healthy, and have fun, and let perfect go.

All things I can't do if I'm with Rhys. His obsession with appearances makes me feel more insecure and insufficient than ever.

I am skinnier and blonder than I've ever been. I am the perfect, low-key girl who takes up as little space as possible in Rhys's life.

And I have never been unhappier.

I've got a little less than four weeks left in Madrid. For a while now—maybe a month or two—Rhys has been asking me to stay in Spain for another semester. "I need my good luck charm to stick around," he says. I've dragged my feet on filling out the application without really knowing why.

But now I get it. I'm so glad I haven't. I can't keep doing this.

Is it too late to change, to start my bucket list?

Am I already out of time?

I almost jump when Rhys clasps my hand in his. He rolls his head on the headrest, lips parting in a grin as he meets my eyes.

He is ebullient, relaxed, in his element, taking a private jet to London for an extravagant party hosted by his sponsor, the champagne company. They hired Rhys to be in their new advertising campaign. All across Europe you can see giant billboards of him, wearing nothing but a strategically placed bottle of champagne and that trademark smirk of his.

Picturing the billboard in my head, my anger and sadness and self-loathing crash through me with renewed strength. As hot as Rhys looks in it, that billboard represents all the reasons I shouldn't be with him.

It represents everything I said I'd leave behind at Meryton.

"You happy?" Rhys asks.

I blink. *Don't cry, don't you dare cry.*

I'm not happy. That's become clear to me in the past few months. If my constant, obsessive dieting didn't tip me off to that fact, the meltdown I had a couple weeks ago on the scale when I discovered I gained one pound—*one freaking pound*—after starving myself for most of a long weekend in Mallorca really drove the point home.

For so long I had fooled myself into thinking I was happy with Rhys. Now I understand I mistook the *appearance* of happiness for happiness itself. Our relationship may look perfect from the outside, especially if you read the papers and the gossip sites. But it's not. Being with him has made me miserable. Letting him sweet talk me into all this ridiculousness has robbed me of my self-respect.

I'm scared to tell him. I'm scared for a lot of reasons, but most of all because he's still convinced I'm his good luck charm. I hate to think what will happen if—when—I leave him.

And how do I explain *why* I'm bailing? He'll ask why I didn't confide in him sooner about how unhealthy I was back in Meryton and how I'm unhealthy like that now—again—and I don't have an answer to that question. Why didn't I? Because I'm an idiot? A people-pleasing coward? Both?

My intentions were always good. But it's time I owned up to my mistakes and started chasing my dreams and looking after my health before it's too late.

I just have to figure out how to tell him.

I glance at our joined hands, offering Rhys a watery smile. "Sure. Yeah. Yes, very happy."

Rhys

Laura says that a lot—*yes*. "Yes, I'm happy" or "yes, I like that" or "yes, this is fun." But with each "yes" I believe her less and less.

Tonight I don't believe her at all. She looks as beautiful as she always does, dressed to the nines in tight jeans and heeled boots, her dark blonde waves loose about her shoulders. But there's something off about her hazel eyes. They're glassy, unsure.

"Hey," I say, giving her hand a squeeze. "Are you feeling all right?"

She looks away, out the window. "Yes. Just a little nervous about the flight—the weather in London is supposed to be bad."

I believe that "yes" even less than the one she gave me a minute ago. But what the hell am I supposed to do? There's only so many times I can ask her how she's feeling.

I go to the ends of the earth to keep a smile on her face. Shopping sprees, trips to Rome and Paris and the Spanish coast and wherever else she wants to go, jewelry, dinner at Michelin-starred restaurants—I've done it all for her, every-thing I'm supposed to, and still I feel her slipping through my fingers.

I need Laura to stay. I'm hoping to convince her to extend her study abroad adventure in Madrid another semester, but she has yet to commit to it. I won't see her go, not when I'm playing as well as I am. Not when the squad is making our way toward a league title, not when my career and my contract are at risk. Right now, our tentative plan is for each of us to head home for Christmas in a month or so. Laura's already bought her ticket to Philadelphia, and I'll be going to Wales to see my family. I hope—I sincerely hope—Laura will meet me back in Spain in January.

The moment Laura came into my life, I started playing like the superstar I've always wanted to be. The superstar I *need* to be if I want to get paid enough to look after the people I love back home. I run harder after we spend a weekend together. I play smarter after we fuck. I've scored more goals and made more assists in the three months since I've met her than I did all of the season I had before I hurt my knee.

Call me superstitious, but I take that as a sign that I need to be with Laura. When you want to play footy better than anyone else in the world, you take these things very seriously. And I take my good luck charm seriously indeed.

As far as I could tell—and I know men tend to be thick as boards about this sort of thing, so perhaps I missed something—Laura was as happy as I was back in August, when we began seeing one another. We had sex a lot and laughed even more. But then she started changing, and I started worrying. She smiles less, enjoys the things I bought her less.

Now, when I catch her looking in the mirror as we brush our teeth in the morning, or after we get out of the shower at night, she looks . . . lost, I suppose. Like she doesn't recognize the girl staring back at her.

I'm worried about Laura, but I don't know what to do.

Still, I've got to try.

"Here's something that might lift your spirits," I say, tapping our joined hands on her armrest. The high-pitched wail of the airplane intensifies as we move onto the runway. "How about we make a quick stop at Harrod's on the way to the hotel? Pick up something completely inappropriate for you to wear tonight? A dress with a slit, perhaps. Thigh-high, of course, to show off those glorious legs of yours."

Laura gives me that tight smile again. It doesn't reach her eyes. "Good thing I shaved this morning."

"Did you now?" I ask, wagging my brows.

But just as I'm leaning in, Laura turns back to the window. "I'm going to try to get some sleep, if you don't mind. It's been a long week."

"Of course I don't mind," I say, even as my pulse thuds.

"Thanks," she says, and pulls her hand from mine.

Later that night

I'm so blinded by camera flashes on the red carpet that for a minute I can't see a fucking thing. Blinking back the strobe lights that pulse behind my closed lids, I tug at the sleeves of my tux. I've got a whole closet of tuxedos back at home, but I'm especially proud of this one: white jacket, smartly cut, worn with black trousers, a perfectly pressed shirt, black silk bow tie, and emerald cufflinks. All custom, all exquisitely expensive. Not that I had to pay for any of it, as a matter of fact, this fashion house pays *me* to wear their clothes. Not a bad deal.

Growing up in Wales, I'd fantasize about wearing ridiculous clothes to even more ridiculous parties. Clothes like this jacket, which probably costs several times what my mum made in a month.

I wonder how many more Instagram followers the tux, and this event, will get me. Between the fashion house and the champagne company, I'm being paid quite a lot to be seen here tonight. Thank God, because Mum called yesterday to tell me Mags is ready to apply to Oxford, and Aunt Katie needs a specially equipped van to get her daughter to her new therapist's office. Dad's turned up again, and he and my alcoholic cousin Will are worse than ever, drinking and disappearing together for days at a time. The bills keep mounting, and I've got to keep earning to pay them.

I feel a tap on my shoulder and turn to look Laura. She looks—Jesus. My pulse roars just like it did earlier tonight, when I saw her for the first time all dressed up. She's wearing the tight red sheath dress and sky-high black heels we picked out at Harrod's together. It's a fuck-me outfit if there ever was one, and my God is it working. Her curves are on full, delicious display. I reach down and tug my jacket over my crotch, willing my dick to behave itself for once.

Laura fingers the bottom of my jaw and lifts it back into place, a wicked little smile playing at her lips. "Rhys, you're staring."

"You're hot. Beautiful. Lovely . . . God." I dig a hand through my hair. "You've reduced me to a blubbering mess, love. Well done."

Her smile fades. Shit, was it something I said? Should I not have stared at her, not complimented her? I feel like I'm always walking on eggshells around her these days.

"We should head for the ballroom," she says. "They're waiting for you. It's a packed house. I don't think I've ever seen so many champagne bottles in my life."

I hold out my arm. "After you, love."

I follow her down the hall. I catch several men try—and fail—to hide their ogling as Laura passes. Righting my cufflinks, I bite back a grin while shooting said gents the deadliest glare I can muster. I shouldn't get off on their jealousy, but I do. I really, really do. Laura is a fucking knockout, and she is mine.

"I can't wait to get back to the hotel," I murmur in her ear, hooking a finger in the back of her dress. "I'm going to rip this thing off you. The heels, though—I believe I'd like you to keep those on."

She turns her head. "We can go back now. To the hotel, I mean. We can just skip this whole thing and get right down to business."

"You know I can't do that." I kiss her bare shoulder. "This won't go late, I promise. I don't want to hang out with these people any more than you do."

"That's just it, though." She meets my eyes. "I think you really do. I think you love the attention."

I blink. "I told you how important all this attention is, love. For me. For my career."

"But you're getting tons of attention already for how you're killing it on the field," she says. "Why do you need to keep doing stuff like this if your football is speaking for itself?"

"Because," I say. *Because I have eleven—no, twelve, Rachel had her baby—twelve people back home depending on me, most of them dysfunctional and needy and expensive as hell to look after.* "Every little bit helps. It's practically free money. They flew us out here on a private jet, they'll feed us lobster and champagne. They're paying for our weekend in London. Really, Laura, why wouldn't I keep doing stuff like this?"

Laura searches my face. I can't decipher the strange look in her eyes. We're standing close, so close I can smell the floral scent of her perfume, but she feels miles away. Miles from my reach.

I open my mouth, determined to find out what's bugging her, but at that moment we're ushered inside the ballroom and the mania begins. I shake hands, I smile for selfies, I schmooze. Laura stands dutifully by my side. Even though she tries to hide it, offering a grin here, a hello there, I sense her intense discomfort. I feel at home in front of the camera, and once upon a time, Laura did too.

But now—now I think she'd rather have her fingernails pulled out than be here with me. I keep smiling, keep signing autographs, but all the while there's a hand gripping my heart and squeezing, making it difficult to breathe. Whatever is wrong with Laura, I want to fix it. I want to see her face light up with that deadly beautiful smile of hers. I want her to be happy again.

I need her to stay, now more than ever.

We sit at the head table at the front of the room. I hold out Laura's chair, and she murmurs her thanks as I slide it under the table. I take my seat beside her.

"A glass of champagne?" I hold one out to her. "This is the reserve—less than fifty cases produced every year. Apparently it's the most expensive champagne in the world."

Laura takes the champagne with a tight smile. "Sounds like your kind of champagne. You should Instagram it."

I can't tell if that's a dig or a compliment. "You like it?"

"It's good," she says, smacking her lips after taking a sip. "Really good. Wow."

"It's delicious, isn't it?" I hold up my glass. I actually think the stuff is quite sweet, but perhaps it's an acquired taste. Everyone else seems to be enjoying it, so I suppose I've got to just keep drinking it until I do too. "I want to have a great weekend here with you, Laura. London's my city, and I can't wait to show you my favorite parts."

Her eyes, green in the low light of the ballroom, glimmer. "Are you going to show me all the spots you and your friends would hang out at? You know, when you were playing for that youth team here and you were broke as a joke? Because I'd really like to see—"

"No," I scoff. "Why in the world would you want to visit shabby pubs and even shabbier neighborhoods? Trust me, I've got better places to show you now."

The glimmer in her eyes dims. "Right. Of course."

I did it again. I said something she didn't like. But what? No one wants to go to the dreary parts of London when there are five-star hotels to stay at in Kensington, and private tours of the city to be had in Rolls Royce Phantoms. I don't get it. I don't want to revisit my past. Not with Laura. Not with anyone, really.

The salad course arrives, then the main course—surf and turf, my favorite treat I love to eat on off weeks like this one, when I don't have a match—followed by a series of speeches. The CEO, an actor, a few others. I'm getting buzzed off the champagne, having a good time. But when I look back at Laura, I catch her staring at a girl across the table. It's that girl—Monica, we've met a few times before—the one who is famous for being the first plus-sized model to make a splash in Spain. She's been in the headlines recently for her work with teens recovering from drug abuse. Apparently she's quite the saint, generous, full of life, sociable, so much so that she's become a bit of a darling in Madrid. Everyone adores her.

It doesn't hurt that she's beautiful. She's smiling as she chats with the man beside her, a giant, genuine, red-lipped thing that, strangely, makes me feel a bit hollow inside.

I turn back to Laura. She's watching Monica. A beat later she swallows, hard, her gaze flicking to her plate. She looks like she's about to hyperventilate. She pokes at her steak with her fork. She's hardly eaten a bite.

"You really do look lovely tonight," I say.

"Rhys." Her fork lands with a *ping* on her plate. "Rhys, I can't do this."

"What?" I ask, swallowing a bite of lobster. It's bloody delicious. "You don't like your steak? Here, we'll send it back. I know you like it a bit rare—"

"No." The forcefulness of her reply makes my heart skip a beat. "This. Us. You and me. Whatever we are. I can't do it anymore."

I blink. "Wait a moment, Laura. Wait. You don't mean—"

"I do. I can't—I don't—I can't be with you anymore, Rhys." She meets my eyes. "I'm sorry."

And then she drops her napkin on the table and pushes back her chair and walks out of the ballroom.

I leap out of my chair and dart after her. People stare as I rush past, but I don't give a shit. Damn it, I've lost sight of her—

I can't let Laura walk out on me like this. I need her to stay.

I need this girl to fucking stay.

The doorman sees me stalking toward him. Without a word he swings open the door and that's when I see her on the sidewalk outside, my eyes trailing up the thick gold zipper that runs the length of the back of her dress. Her shoulders are hunched forward, arms tucked across her chest against the cold. A few feet beyond the sidewalk, buckets of rain slide off the hotel awning and pummel the road. The sound is almost deafening.

"Laura."

She turns. Her eyes are wide and very full.

Chapter Thirteen

LAURA

"I'm sorry. I just c-couldn't—" I draw a sharp breath between my teeth as a tremor racks my body. I've been freezing my ass of all night in this ridiculous dress.

"Jesus Christ, Laura," Rhys says, tugging off his jacket. "It's bloody cold out here. Come back inside, please, and talk to me."

"Thanks," I say as he drapes his jacket across my shoulders. He coaxes it tighter around my body. The familiarity of the gesture, its tenderness, makes my heart fold in on itself. "But I'm not going to stay. I've already texted Emily—she doesn't live far—"

"You're not going anywhere until you tell me what's going on." He moves to stand in front of me, close enough that his chest bumps against my crossed arms every time he draws a breath.

I stare at an invisible spot on his perfectly tailored shirt. I blink, hard. I feel horrible that I have to do this—that I have to leave him. Rhys has been selfish, sure, but he's also been kind and generous to me. He is trying. Trying, in his own way, to take care of me. And I appreciate his effort, I do.

But being face-to-face with Monica Cruz tonight put the nail in the coffin. I remember that magazine I read the first night I was in Madrid. Monica *looked* happy on the cover. Tonight, I discovered she *is* happy. Genuinely, infectiously happy, so at home in her own skin. She is fearless and confident and pursuing her dreams without a second thought about other people's opinions.

Seeing her laugh and chat and *eat* with abandon made me ache. She is everything I aspire to be, everything I thought I'd become when I walked off the plane in August, determined to take advantage of my fresh start. Everything I set aside when I started hanging out with Rhys.

I sat at that table and stared at her, wondering where the hell I went wrong. I wanted to be her. In that moment I wanted it so bad I couldn't breathe. How did she do it?

How can I do it?

I need to escape Rhys's gravitational pull, for starters.

"What? Did you think I was just going to let you walk out on me without an explanation? What's going on, Laura? Why are you running from me?"

He reaches out. Takes my face in his hand, thumbs my bottom lip. Oh, *oh,* the confident, possessive way he touches me. I'm going to miss it.

"Talk to me, love," he says.

I turn my head away from his touch. I can't bear it. I look at him from the corner of my eye. "I'm sorry, Rhys."

"Sorry about what?"

"This isn't working for me anymore."

"Why?" he asks. He reaches out again, like he wants to touch me again. But then he thinks better of it and shoves his hands in his pockets instead. "Why isn't it working?"

"Because. A lot of reasons." I roll my lips between my teeth to keep a sob from escaping.

"Tell me so I can fix them and we can go back to being us."

"See, that's just it. You can't fix it. You can't fix *you*. You are who you are, and I'm—well. I'm different. Or I want to be."

"Different?" He furrows his brow and leans forward. "But that doesn't make sense. If you're so different, why have we gotten on so well? You like the travel, and the shopping, and —and everything else I do. We like the same things, Laura. I like being with you. I like treating you. We go well together, you and I."

I let out a sigh. How to explain this to him? "Look," I say. "You remember the night I met you, at the bar—"

"Of course I remember. How could I forget?"

"Rhys, please. Let me finish. That night I sat at the bar and started writing down everything I wanted to do during my semester in Spain—the bucket list I've been telling you about. I wrote it all down on a napkin."

"The napkin." He catches my gaze. "The one with the marker on it that you said meant nothing. That was your bucket list."

"Yeah," I say. "It was. I had big plans for this semester."

"Big plans? Like flying on a private jet all over Europe? Watching every Madrid home game from the players' box?"

"No." I shake my head. "No, the list wasn't about that stuff at all. The flashy stuff. The list was about reinventing myself, Rhys. I wasn't exactly a very happy person back at Meryton. I definitely wasn't healthy. I was wasting my college experience trying to be this—I don't know. This perfect Barbie doll, I guess. And it was making me pretty miserable. I hated who I was becoming. So when I had the chance to start over in Madrid—new city, new university, new classmates—I took it. Or I wanted take it, anyway. That's what my bucket list was about. It was about enjoying my time here. Forgetting perfect and seeking out the real instead."

I look down at my feet and rock back on my heels. *I hate this.* "But then I met you, and you're distracting to say the least. I can't count the number of times you talked me out of doing stuff on the list. We always end up doing what *you* want to do—I've wrapped my life around your schedule and your sponsors and your social media stuff. Now the semester is almost over, and I have barely done a damn thing on my bucket list. I've given it up so I can be with you, even though we're not really *together* together."

A couple passes us. Rhys catches them staring. He moves closer to me, shielding me from their intrusive interest.

My heart feels like it's going to burst.

"I get it," he says. "I get wanting to enjoy your time in Spain. Believe me, I understand wanting to reinvent yourself too. What I don't understand is why you can't tackle this bucket list while you're with me. I've told you we'll rent those mopeds—"

"But you won't. You've been saying for months now that you'll do the tour with me, and it still hasn't happened. And you know what? It never will. I'll never do it as long as I'm with you because you'll talk me out of it—you'll convince me to go to London instead, to some party, or to *your* favorite restaurant. Or you'll have back to back practice days, and the tour will be a distraction you can't handle. It's clear I can't be with you and do the things I want to, Rhys. I can't be with you and *be* who I want."

"Jesus Christ, Laura," he says. "We'll do the moped tour tomorrow, all right? Problem solved."

I squeeze my eyes shut. I don't want to hurt Rhys, but I have to be honest. He deserves an explanation.

"No," I say. "No. This—us—it's too far gone. A moped tour isn't going to change the fact that I don't like myself when I'm with you. I'm obsessed with all the wrong things—being skinny, looking good, wearing the right things, saying the right things. You inhabit this . . . this perfect world filled with perfect people. It's impossible for me to let perfect go when I see how much you like it. How you practically worship it. I can't be around it—you—and be who I want. I'm done, Rhys. We're done."

Rhys

Panic flutters inside my chest. This is more than just a misunderstanding. This is about Laura and what she wants and how she can't get it if she's with me.

I love treating Laura, I adore having her with me even more. But now she's telling me she wants something else, something *I can't give her*. I hate—*hate*—feeling so powerless. I felt this way for the first eighteen years of my life, and I swore I'd never feel that way again.

But here I am, hands balled into fists inside my pockets, wondering how the hell I can make this girl stay. Why *don't* the cars and trips and clothes I buy make her happy? They've made me decently happy, I guess. I hope one day they'll make me rich too, so I can finally get my family out of Splott and into a decent house in a decent neighborhood.

"I've only ever wanted you to be yourself, love," I try. "I never asked you to be perfect. I just want you to be happy."

Laura meets my eyes. Swallows. "I know, Rhys. But I just don't think I can be happy with you. Not right now, anyway."

My heart works double as I scramble to think of something to say. The rain is really coming down, a thunderous roar on the awning above our heads. Somewhere behind me cars slosh through the mess. The smell of wet pavement fills my head.

Maybe I'm being a superstitious tit, maybe I'm not. But the season is going so well and I'm finally feeling like I'm back on my feet, like I'm getting my life back together after the clusterfuck that was last year. I was so close to losing everything, but I'm still convinced meeting Laura brought me back from the brink. She's the one who knocked my stars into alignment.

"So let's try it," I blurt. "Your list—let's check off everything you want to do. The moped tour and whatever else is on there. Tell me where and when, and I'll be there. I'll help you. Let me help you, Laura. Let's try and make you happy."

Laura rolls her eyes, glancing toward the cars passing the line of taxis waiting beyond the bell stand. "There aren't very many Instagram-worthy things on the list. And it's not just about the list itself. It's about . . ." Her words trail off, and her mouth pinches shut.

I don't know this Laura. *This* Laura actually looks like she's angry with me.

She's never been angry with me. Ever. I'm not quite sure what to do with myself.

"Give me another chance," I stammer. "Please. I didn't realize how big this list was for you before. Now I do."

She's shaking her head, eyes still on the taxis. "No."

"Look at me." Before I know what I'm doing I'm taking her chin in my palm, tilting her face up. "Laura, love, look at me. This girl you want to be—the authentic one—I can't help but think she'd give a helpless chap another chance to prove himself."

She scoffs, running her tongue along her bottom lip. It's a struggle not to duck my head, take that tongue between my teeth. "You're hardly a helpless chap, Rhys."

I look her in the eye. My heart is pounding, pounding so loudly it drowns out the rain. "When it comes to you, I am."

For a beat she searches my gaze. She's breathing hard, her breath warm on my hand. The look in her eyes—she doesn't appear lost anymore. She looks determined.

"We'll see," she says at last.

"I can work with that." I meet her eyes. "I meant it when I said I want to see you happy."

"You know what would make me happy right now?"

"Whatever it is, I'll do it."

She nods at the taxis. "I want to take a cab to a pub—not a fancy one—a real pub where real people hang out. I want to drink a lot—like, a *lot* a lot—of good beer. And after that I want to eat so much street meat I pass out in a blissful meaty haze and wake up tomorrow at noon. That's my plan tonight with Emily, anyway."

I draw back, curling my lip. "Street meat doesn't sound appetizing."

"When you're drunk, it's the best stuff on the planet. Maybe we could even find a falafel stand. I freaking *love* falafel."

I don't. What would my champagne sponsor think if I was caught blowing off their million-pound party to eat street meat outside of a pub? I need to maintain solid relationships with all the companies I endorse if I ever want to stop living on the knife edge of not having enough money to pay my bills and my family's. It's incredibly stressful, having to choose which ones to pay every month. Stressful, and sad.

Then again, I have been busier than usual lately. Maybe Laura just wants some attention. Maybe she just wants to see me make a fool of myself for her. Olivier's girl pulls this sort of thing all the time. She'll have a fit, but it always blows over by the next morning.

I suppose I just need to indulge Laura's fancies until then.

"That's really what you want?" I ask.

"Yes," she replies. "Right now I want to eat falafel and drink beer with Emily."

"I've never seen you drink beer. Ever. I didn't know you liked it."

"I love it. I just never drank it because I worried it would make me fat."

"Fat?" I wrinkle my brow. "But you're not—"

"I'm done worrying about it. Thinking I'm fat, I mean. Being a size two."

I look at her. I have no idea what to say. I've never heard her talk like this before. I know she's conscious about her weight, but I didn't know she worried so much about it.

"Look," she says. "I have, like, four weeks left in Europe, and I'm not going to waste another minute trying to fit into these ridiculous dresses you buy me. I want to drink beer and eat some carbs, goddamnit."

I glance over her head at the hotel. Five hundred people wait for me inside. So does that delicious lobster and all the thousand-dollar-a-bottle champagne I can drink. I really shouldn't leave. I *am* the face of the company, and while the paparazzi are better behaved here in the UK than they are in Spain, there's still a chance they could catch me sneaking out early. If that happens, I can kiss this endorsement deal, my biggest yet, goodbye.

But this girl—this maddening, determined girl—wants to go out in the rain and drink beer and eat street meat.

Everything depends on this girl.

The pictures I took on the red carpet will be all over the gossip magazines and websites next week. The people who follow me will see (and hopefully purchase) the bow tie and shoes I'm wearing—I made sure to post a picture of me and Laura to my Facebook and Twitter pages. My work here can probably be done.

I just hope we don't get caught.

"All right," I say. "Let me ring my driver. The Phantom's waiting—with the tinted windows no one will know—"

She raises her hand, flagging the taxi driver at the head of the line. Her heels clack against the sidewalk as the cab drives up to meet her. She opens the door and slides inside. She begins pulling the door shut behind her.

"Fuck," I mutter under my breath. I step forward, kicking aside a stray cigarette butt, and grab the door before she can close it all the way.

Laura looks at me as I slide in next to her. "I didn't think you had it in you, fancy pants."

"Neither did I."

Chapter Fourteen

RHYS

The driver drops us at a little pub tucked away in a corner of Soho. Beside me on the sidewalk, Laura titters as she reads the clean, gold script marching across the faux-Tudor façade: THE SPREAD EAGLE.

"Really?" I ask, glancing over my shoulder. So far, so good —no sign that we were followed.

"Sorry," she says, hopping through the front door I hold open. "I'm just tickled. You'd never get away with this shit in the States."

I'm pleasantly surprised at how nice it is inside—much nicer than the pubs I used to frequent when I lived in London. It's clean, for one thing, and doesn't reek of stale cigarettes for another. Good looking twenty-somethings crowd the bar, and decent music pumps through the speakers hanging from high ceilings. The lighting is warm, low. My mood begins to thaw, just the tiniest bit, but I make sure to keep my head down. I would kill for a hat.

We've sidled up to a little side counter by a window that looks out onto the street. Laura is busy typing away on her phone.

"Emily says she'll be here in twenty minutes," she says. "This is her favorite pub in London. Probably because the name is so ridiculous."

"Emily," I say. "Your best friend back at Meryton, correct? The one with the serious boyfriend. Liam? Lionel?"

"Luke. Yup, that's Em." She sets her mobile on the counter and looks at me. "You remembered."

"She's the one who has a crush on the TA she keeps butting heads with in her section but won't admit it. Isn't he an Earl or something? A Duke?"

"A Prince, as a matter of fact. But close enough."

"I think it's safe to say I know Emily quite well by now, even though I've never met her."

Laura glances at the bar. Awkward silence stretches between us.

"So." I dig my wallet out of my pocket and nod at the bar. "You said you wanted to drink some beer. How about I get us a couple pints?"

"Sure," she says, not meeting my eyes.

I order us each a pint of bitter—by some stroke of luck, the bartender only asks for a quick autograph on a pint glass (no selfie requests yet, thank God, people seem to notice me but I haven't been approached)—and set them on the counter beside Laura.

"That looks delicious," she says. "You know, now that I'm thinking about it, I've never seen you drink beer, either."

"Well," I say, "getting pissed off beer isn't exactly conducive to winning a league title. Or worming my way back into Madrid's good graces. I could get away with drinking during the season when I was younger, but now that I'm staring down twenty-three, I've really started to feel it—my age. I only drink when I don't have training or a match the next day."

I don't mention that I keep my drinking in check for other reasons too. Reasons having to do with my father.

"I know. You're crazy about your routine." From the way she says it, I can't help but feel that's a dig. But why? She knows I have to be strict about my regimen to play well.

She touches her glass to mine and smiles, a bright, clear thing I've never seen before. "Cheers."

I watch her take a long, slow pull from her glass. My cock twitches at the sight of her sinewy throat working as she swallows, hard. I've been inside that mouth more times than I can count, and holy hell do I want to be inside it now. It's been fucking fantastic, the oral. The only thing that would make it better is if Laura ever let me return the favor, and go down on *her*. But she keeps saying she doesn't like it; sometimes she'll say she hasn't shaved down there anyway so could we please just get on with the sex?

Like I'd care whether or not Laura shaved. Her cunt is perfect because it belongs to her. I want her to enjoy sex as much as I do. I made attempts to eat her out after that first time, but she kept saying no. After a while, I just stopped trying.

"Is it good?" I ask.

"Really good," she says, still smiling. "Thank you."

"Looks like pissed off Laura left the building," I say. "Your smile is brilliant, love."

She shrugs, nodding at the pub around us. "Yeah, I'd definitely say I'm a bit happier here than I was at that fancy hotel. I don't know, I feel like I can finally breathe or something here."

I sip from my own glass. The smooth, malty flavor of the bitter has me closing my eyes for a moment. It's clean, the taste, a bit earthy, just a smattering of carbonation. I don't want to like it, but I do. I still wish I was back at the hotel drinking champagne, but this stuff—it's refreshing.

Weirdly enough, it's relaxing too, drinking this bitter, being at this pub. I know what Laura's talking about when she says she can finally breathe. I don't feel the need to be *on* the way I did at the champagne party. There are no cameras to pose for, no CEOs to impress. I don't have to be Rhys Maddox the footballer. Here I can just be me, a bloke having a pint with his girl on a Friday night. There's something very freeing about that.

I'm bringing my pint to my lips when a girl with long, bright orange hair dashes past me and launches herself into Laura's arms.

"Oooohhh myyyyyy *gaaaaahhhd*!" the red head cries. She's hugging Laura so hard they sway in time to their cries of joy. "You're here!"

"I know!"

"I can't believe you're *here*! With me! In London!"

"I know!"

"You smell so good it's nuts!"

"Thank you!"

The redhead's gaze moves to me. Her smile falls. "Oh. You're here."

"I am indeed," I say, feeling more unwelcome than ever. It's clear Emily does not like me.

She turns to Laura. "Jeez, Laur, you got skinny. Like. Really skinny." She looks at me. "Have you been feeding her? Like, at all?"

Her accusatory tone takes me off guard. Heat rushes to my face.

"I try my best," I say tightly. I hold out my hand. "You must be Emily. Nice to meet you."

She looks at my hand, then looks away. I quickly pocket the offending appendage. Emily *really* doesn't like me.

"So." I clear my throat. "What can I get you to drink, Emily?"

"Hm." Emily falls back, her red hair glittering with droplets of rain. "How about some shots?"

"Shots?" I ask.

"Shots," she replies, unspooling a plaid scarf from around her neck. "I'm in the mood to celebrate. Plus, chances are I'll run into Kit later—all of the sudden this is *his* favorite pub too, so annoying!—so I need a good buzz to deal with him."

I arch a brow. "Is Kit the Baron or whatever?"

"Prince," Laura and Emily reply in unison.

"Right. The Prince."

I've never been much of a royal watcher myself, but like most of the world during the nineties, my mum was a huge fan of Princess Diana. I believe I've heard of this Kit fellow— one of the Queen's grandsons, I think?—a member of the lucky sperm club for sure. He probably lives in his parents' posh palace here in London while partying away his days like the playboy he was born to be. I'd be jealous if I wasn't, well . . . me.

"So, these shots," I say. "Are we talking whiskey, vodka . . .?"

Laura and Emily exchange a glance. An evil little grin breaks out on Em's face; a second later, it appears on Laura's too.

"I think something a *tad* more ridiculous than that," Emily says, rubbing her hands together.

"Hm." Laura taps a finger against her lips as she pretends to mull this suggestion over. "What about . . . buttery nipples?"

"Buttery nipples?" Heat returns to my face with a vengeance. "You can't be serious."

Emily glowers at me. "It's buttery nipples or bust, Manbun."

I look at her. She looks back, defiant as ever. It's clear to me this is some kind of punishment. What sort of tosser orders butter nipples, and at a *pub* no less? For a minute I consider fighting it, but the longer I lock eyes with Emily, the more I realize I don't have a choice.

I've got to buy these girls buttery nipples.

Laura settles onto a stool beside Emily, their arms looped, and joins in on our staring contest.

"Come on," Emily says. "What's the point of being so rich and famous if you can't buy your lady and her friend a buttery nipple?"

I drain what's left of my pint. Lord help me, this is *not* how I imagined my Friday night in London would go. But I've got to appease Laura. Just for tonight, and then tomorrow everything will be back to normal.

"Buttery nipples," I say. "All right then."

"Thank you," Laura says.

Her face glows, her color high. The purple smudges beneath her eyes have disappeared. I didn't realize how drawn she's looked until now. How pale. Now—now she looks happy. Giddy, even.

She looks so damn sexy when she's being mean to me.

I grin. "You won't be thanking me later when that buttery nipple comes back up."

"Good thing I have you to hold my hair back for me."

"What a lucky man I am," I say.

The girls talk to each other as I belly up to the bar. The back of my neck burns. I know they're talking about me—Emily is capable of many things, I'm sure, but whispering is not one of them—and it's making me self-conscious. A little nervous too. Is Laura telling Emily about the bucket list, I wonder? Is she telling her that we're done, Laura and I, that I can't possibly help her with that list, that she's leaving me when we land in Madrid on Sunday?

I'll be without my good luck charm. I don't believe in

karma, not really, but I can't help but feel the good energy I've gotten this season will abandon me if Laura does.

And then who will I be? Another unemployed, washed up Maddox, just like my father. And just like my father, I won't be able to take care of Mum and Mags and all my loving, dysfunctional, hilarious aunts and cousins. I've got practically nothing saved—not the way I've been spending to keep both my career and my family afloat. I abandoned my education at sixteen. I have no diplomas, no technical skills. I'll be a loser, a nobody, and I've fought too hard and too long to see Mum's sacrifices, Maggie's too, go unrewarded. I've got too much momentum to mess up now.

"You all right, mate?" the bartender asks.

I blink. "Yes. Sorry."

He looks me in the eye. "Looks like you need another pint."

"Yes, I'll have another bitter, please." I set a fifty pound note on the counter. "I apologize in advance, good sir, for the request I'm about to make. But have you ever heard of a buttery nipple?"

His withering glare is all the answer I need.

Sighing, I place another fifty on the counter.

Plus—I'd never admit this aloud—but I'm having a good time. Sort of. Yes, I should be at the champagne party, putting pictures of the lobster I didn't get to finish on TikTok. I should be more responsible, because my father certainly wasn't. I should be thinking of everything and everyone that depends on those paychecks I get from sponsors like the champagne company.

But I'm not. I'm thinking about me, and Laura, and how lit up she is tonight, despite this new mean streak of hers.

I leave the bartender an eighty-five pound tip and gather the girls' shots between my fingers.

Chapter Fifteen

RHYS

A few hours later, and the girls are finally gathering their things to go. Kit the Prince never showed, but he did reply to Emily's text about the location of nearby falafel stands.

"How great is this? The falafel's right across the street," Emily is saying. She sways on her feet, and I hold her steady as I help her into her coat.

"Per-rr-fect," Laura slurs in reply.

"We gotta"—burp—"get you some fried shit to fatten you up, Laur. I thought you were supposed to finally *eat* in Madrid."

I blink. I guess she's been struggling with this weight issue for a while. I can't believe I didn't notice it before. I mean, I have hassled Laura about not eating enough—really, she eats like a bird—but she's always sworn she's full.

"I was," Laura says. "I am, I mean. I'm gon-nnn-a start rinow. Eating, I mean. I am so-*oo* hungry."

"It's pouring outside," I say, glancing down at my tux. The fashion house that made it is paying me ten grand to be seen in it tonight. They'll be none too pleased if I'm seen ruining it in the rain. "You girls really want to stand in line for falafel when it's this wet?"

"Yes," Laura says. "In the rain. Kit says the falafel is the best in London."

"We could go back to the hotel, order up some room service—"

But Emily is already out the door, and Laura is weaving her way toward it.

A thumb another fifty from my money clip. I offer it to one of the lads standing at the bar with a black umbrella tucked beneath his arm. It's not terribly cold outside, but the rain will soak through the girls' jackets in two minutes flat. I don't want Laura to catch a chill, especially not after seeing her so bright and lit up tonight. And I have to make an attempt to save this tuxedo.

Umbrella in hand, I chase after them.

Despite the rain, the line for the falafel stand is long. Swelled, no doubt, by the tipsy people stumbling out of nearby pubs.

Or, in the case of Emily and Laura, the absolutely *obliterated* people stumbling out of nearby pubs.

The umbrella is tiny. *Fuck*. It's not going to cover all three of us. I glance around, my gaze catching on a couple guys in black coats across the street who stand beneath an awning, smoking. They're looking at me. My pulse picks up. After a beat, they stub out their cigarettes and head down the street, away from us.

I let out a sigh of relief. Then I look down at my tux.

God I loved it. Maybe a good dry clean could save it? I guess we'll see. In the meantime, the girls need shelter from the rain far more than I do.

"Aren't you"—another burp—"a gentleman," Emily says as I sidle up behind them, holding the umbrella over their heads.

"So," I say when the girls get their giant falafel pitas. I watch Laura lick a stray bit of tahini from her finger, her tongue darting between her lips. A sudden, potent warmth sharpens between my legs, and not for the first time tonight I wish my pants weren't *quite* so tailored. Who knew watching Laura eat street meat would be such a turn on?

I clear my throat. "Sorry to duck out, but I'm knackered. If you're ready, Laura, I'll call the driver."

"You can call him whenever," she says around a mouthful of food.

"We can drop Emily off too if that works for you?" I glance at Emily.

Emily, in turn, glances at Laura. I dig my phone out of my pocket. I hope it's not soaked beyond repair, like my tux.

"We're not going with you," Laura says.

"What?" I look up from my phone. The half-chub I'm sporting suddenly disappears. "Not coming with me? What does that mean? Is this about the car again? Because we can take a—"

"It means I'm staying at Em's tonight. Her flat's just up the street from here."

My pulse thuds, panicked, in my ears. Good God, is she serious? Fat drops of rain drip from the umbrella spindles and land on my nose. I stare at Laura, my thoughts rioting with confusion. I thought for sure Laura's sudden change in mood didn't mean anything. I thought it wasn't serious.

Now I'm not so sure.

I want—need—her to stay. Watching her smile and eat and *enjoy* herself tonight has spurred my desire to new heights. I want to see more of that smile, hear that throaty, genuine laughter again and again as I make her come. I feel so . . . free, I suppose, and I don't want that feeling to end.

I meet her eyes. She's determined, that much I can tell. I

know no matter what I say or offer her, she's going to stay with Emily tonight.

I just hope that she plans to say with me in the long run.

"All right," I say. "You promise to call?"

She nods. "Sure. Yeah. We'll talk in the morning."

I kiss her mouth, lingering there longer than I should. She tastes like Laura, but different. Sweeter.

When I let her go, something inside me tears, and begins to bleed.

Chapter Sixteen

LAURA

The Next Morning

I glide my knife through a perfect pillow of poached egg, my stomach rumbling as the silky yolk seeps across my plate of eggs Benedict.

"Hell. *Yes*," I say, sawing off a giant bite.

Emily looks up from her own Benedict—she ordered the smoked salmon, I did the Florentine—and meets my eyes. "When was the last time you ate, Laur? Like. Really ate real food. You look even thinner than you did back at Meryton."

"I ate that falafel last night," I reply around a mouthful of egg, spinach, and the best damn English muffin on the planet.

"Yeah, but eating crap when you're drunk doesn't really count," she says. "This—you ordering eggs Benedict for breakfast—this is progress, but it's not enough. I've been worried about you, Laur."

"I know," I say. "I'm going to start working on it. Me, I mean. My weight. Being around Rhys and all the beautiful people he hangs out with hasn't exactly done wonders for my body image."

I set down my silverware and wash down that bite with a

long, slow sip of latte. I didn't even ask for skim milk. I just let the restaurant make it with whatever they usually do. Whole milk, maybe? It's freaking delicious.

When Emily suggested we grab a bite at her favorite, *awesomely bougie* breakfast place in Piccadilly, I jumped. I gotta say it's an amazing spot, a former bank with black tiled walls and a beautiful, buzzy clientele. It feels very . . . British, I guess. Utterly charming and cute.

"Yeah, I imagine that's a total mind fuck," Emily says, setting her wrists on the edge of the table, fork and knife still in her hands. "I'm obviously not Rhys's biggest fan, but he was kind of a gentleman last night. I remember him even holding an umbrella over our heads. *I think*. My memory's a little fuzzy after that third—fifth—shot."

"It was the sixth, I think. We stopped at six."

Em swallows, slowly, like she's deciding whether or not that bite of Benedict is going down or coming back up. "Never again," she says.

"Until tonight." I grin. "It's Kit's birthday, right?"

"Yeah," Em says. I can tell she's fighting a grin of her own. "I don't know why he invited me—I'm probably not gonna go. Who throws themselves a birthday party anyway? It's at this ridiculous restaurant in Marylebone, definitely not my scene. Gah, he's the *worst*."

"You keep saying that."

"Well I mean it. Every time I say it, I one hundred percent mean it."

I narrow my eyes at her. "You sure you don't have a secret crush on this guy?"

"Ew. No. He's totally gross," Em says, hiding her face behind a giant cup of English breakfast tea.

"If by totally gross, you mean a total babe, yeah. I googled him. He's one handsome ginger."

"Who cares? I think Luke is handsomer."

"You think Luke hung the moon."

"Whatever. I'm done talking about Kit and how terrible he is. Back to Rhys. I know you two were never really *together* together. But how do things stand now that you've . . . had it, I guess?"

I shrug. "You know, I started this semester thinking I was going to become this whole new person. I loved your idea of putting together the bucket list as a way to ditch some bad habits, and learn how to be okay with being . . . well, just okay. Okay instead of perfect, I mean. But then I bumped into Rhys, literally, and the bucket list went right out the window. I was *so* into him when we first met. Like, head over heels. I guess I kind of forgot about everything else."

"I know." Emily picks up her tea. "You liked him. A lot. Do you still like him?"

"Honestly? No. Not anymore." I pull hand across my face. "So, like, at dinner last night, we sat next to this model—not one of those super skinny models, she actually looked healthy. She was unbelievably cool, you would've loved her."

"Monica Cruz?"

"Yes!"

"I *do* freaking love her. I just read her essay on teenage drug abuse in British *Vogue*. I laughed. I cried. It was seriously amazeballs."

"She's funny and she's nice, and she's really interesting to talk to. What struck me most, though, was her attitude. It was very much 'I don't give a fuck.' Not in a bad way—she wasn't rude or anything—but more like she doesn't give a fuck what anybody thinks."

"Easy enough to do when you're that gorgeous and that rich."

"Well, yeah. But I just got the feeling that she wasn't trying to impress anyone. She's pursuing her passion fearlessly. I admire that. I want to do that. I want to be that girl."

Em offers me a lopsided grin. "So our little people pleaser was inspired by the girl who made a lot of money saying 'I don't give a fuck what you think, I like me and that's all that matters.'"

"Yes," I say. "Something like that. She's the kind of girl I set out to be at the beginning of the semester."

Emily chews thoughtfully on the last of her English muffin. "I want that for you, Laur. I do. And I agree with you that your current relationship with Rhys is standing in the way of you becoming that girl. You're really sure don't have any feelings for him?"

"I'm really sure. He's terrible for me."

"But he *has* helped you with the sex part of your bucket list, though, hasn't he? You've been bragging about his prowess in the bedroom since day one."

I look down at my cup. I feel like I'm going to be sick.

"Yeah, about that . . ."

Emily's eyes go wide. "Oh no. Don't tell me—"

"Yeah." My face burns. "Yeah, I've been faking it. The orgasms."

"All of them?"

"All of them."

"Wow." Emily lets out a low whistle. "I thought you were done doing that. You gave all your boyfriends the biggest egos ever because they thought they could make you come just by looking at you."

"I was done doing that—faking it," I say. "Or I was going to be. But then things got hot and heavy between me and Rhys pretty fast, and he was so . . . good-looking. And famous. And I liked him so much, and I wanted him to like me too. So I didn't want to risk turning him off with my yucky you-know-what."

"Did he ever say or do anything that would make you think you're yucky?"

I shake my head. "No. Definitely not. If anything, he kept offering to go down on me. He loves it when I come. Or when he thinks I come."

"*I* love a guy who loves to make a girl come." Emily looks at me. Her eyes narrow, like she's got an idea brewing. "I know you don't want to be with Rhys—"

"I'm done with him," I say. "I'm putting all my focus on next semester. I've already signed up for spring classes back at Meryton, and I'm thinking of whipping up a whole new bucket list to tackle there."

Emily sets down her knife and fork. She's started to eat like a British person, holding both at once as she cuts a bite, eats it, then proceeds to cut another. It's annoyingly cute.

"That's awesome," she says, making a steeple with her fingers. "However. I don't think you should give up on this semester's bucket list quite yet. As your best friend, I want you to have the best bucket list experience possible. And the sexual exploration thing—that's something I know you really, *really* want to do."

"It is. But I don't think I have the time—or the energy—to find a new guy to do said exploration with in the next few weeks."

"What if you don't find a new guy? What if you explore with Rhys?"

I shoot her a skeptical look. "Explore with Rhys? Didn't you just say my relationship with him is keeping me from becoming my own Monica Cruz?"

"I said your *current* relationship with him is keeping you from becoming Monica. But what if you changed the terms of that relationship? It's clear you don't *like* him like him, which means you're not in danger of getting hurt by him. Rhys wants to keep things casual, and now you want to keep things casual too—I mean, why wouldn't you try to cross off that bucket list item with him? Tell him what you want. Demand it. If he doesn't want to give it to you, then so what? Kick his ass to the curb. But if he does, think about all the orgasms you can have between now and the end of December. You wouldn't need to go through the whole rigmarole of finding a new guy, getting comfortable with him, getting STD tests . . ." She shrugs. "If you're never going to see Rhys again, what the hell do you have to lose? Let him make you come."

"That isn't on the list—coming with a guy," I sniff.

"Yeah it is," Em says. "Listen, I'm all for masturbating your clit off. But I think this new and improved I-don't-give-a-fuck Laura would also like to get off with a guy. She'd like to loosen up and let a studly soccer player do what he does best."

"What's that?"

She grins. "Scoring. On said clit."

"You're ridiculous."

Even so, I know she's right. Maybe I can take charge of my non-relationship with Rhys. Maybe I can make this fucked-up situation work in my favor.

I sigh in resignation. Emily smiles. She's a genius, and she knows it. Which makes the idea that she can't see how seriously hard she's crushing on Kit the Prince all the more baffling.

Of course it's a harmless crush, she's been head over heels in love with Luke for years now. It kinda worries me, actually, how invested she is in him, considering how young we are. I mean, Luke is literally her *everything*—not only her boyfriend but also her future. If things go bad between them, Em will be left with nothing.

Luke does seem to make Em happy, but there's something . . . I don't know, a little off about their relationship. He's a nice enough guy, but he can also be a little controlling. They hit a rough patch about a year or so ago. I don't know the whole story about what happened—Em can be pretty private about the inner workings of their relationship—but they seemed to have fixed whatever the problem was.

Then again, who I am to judge? I've obviously made less than stellar decisions about my own love life. Maybe I'm just projecting my fears and insecurities onto Em and Luke's relationship. Who knows?

"God," I say. "Why are you always right? Fine. Yes. I'll give Rhys a chance to . . . you know. I'll try, at least."

I laugh, but the knot that has suddenly appeared in my stomach tightens. Not giving a fuck and taking ownership of my sexual destiny sounds all great and empowering. But now that I'm staring down the barrel of actually *doing* it, I'm kinda terrified.

Chapter Seventeen

LAURA

Madrid
A Few Days Later

I shut my laptop—I was doing a little last minute research on florists for Santa Caterina's upcoming auction—and survey my dorm room. My giant suitcase lies half-opened on the floor, my clothes strewn around it like it projectile vomited them all over the place. I still haven't unpacked from London.

I have to say it's good to be back, to have a little space. After Rhys and I landed in Madrid on Sunday night, I needed some time to think.

I needed to get going on the promise I made to myself (and to Em) that I'd give coming with Rhys an honest try.

I'm still scared out of my mind. But I figure if I can get up on stage with a Flamenco band at a seedy bar tonight—I'm checking off another bucket list line item, "*Go see flamenco guitarist/learn how*" thanks to Maddie, who dates a pretty famous (and pretty hot) Spanish guitarist—I can probably try to have a real orgasm with another human being present.

I grab my phone from my desk. For several beats I just

stare at it. My plan is this: get a good buzz going at the bar, go on stage, and then meet up with Rhys for some orgasmic good times afterward. You'd think this was a good plan, but really, it's not. Mostly because it's Thursday night, and Rhys never does anything on Thursdays, least of all me.

But I've got to try while I still have the courage.

I type out the text. Taking a deep breath, I hit send and close my eyes.

Hey, it says. *I know this is a weirdly timed request. But do you wanna bone tonite?*

It takes him all of three seconds to reply.

Haha. Would love to. I could maybe sneak something into my schedule. What are you doing right now?

My heart skips a beat. He's trying. He's actually considering my proposal.

I'm actually going to play with Javier's band in Chueca. You know, Maddie's boyfriend? And I'm gonna need an outlet for all that adrenaline afterward. You free later, maybe around 10?

Three dots appear at the bottom of my screen. They stay there for several beats, as if Rhys is typing a text, erasing it, then retyping it. My heart is in my throat. I have to put the phone down and curl my fingers into fists to keep from tapping out a quick, spineless apology—*never mind, just kidding, know how busy and tired you are, bye forever.*

Sorry love, he replies. *That's a little late for me. Going to pass this time. But your friends will be there, right? You won't be out alone?*

My heart falls. That's a bummer.

Whatever. Tonight is going to be fun, and I won't let Rhys piss on my parade.

The Madrileñas will be there, I say, my fingers shaking as I type. *Not sure who else.*

The "Madrileñas" are the girls who went to that first football match with me—Rachel, Vivian, and Maddie. The four of us have become pretty close over the course of the semester. I didn't know any of them very well back in the States, but we've bonded over the challenges and triumphs of living in a foreign country. We meet for glasses of vinto tinto de la casa (house red wine) and tapas at a cute little restaurant every Wednesday night.

Yeah, Rhys may not be coming tonight, but I'm lucky my girls will be there. I need all the moral support I can get.

Have fun, Rhys replies. *Tell them I said hello.*

Later that night

I'm sitting at the bar, nursing a deliciously frosty Spanish beer, when I sense someone standing behind me.

"Hey girl," a familiar, rumbling voice murmurs in my ear. "If I could rearrange the alphabet, I'd put U and I next to each other."

My heart skips a beat. *There's no way*. It can't be . . .

I spin around on my stool to see Rhys standing half a step behind me, hands shoved into the pockets of his jeans. The clean, masculine scent of his cologne makes my blood jump.

"Holy shit!" I say, feeling a bit lightheaded with shock. "You came. How did you—I mean—the bar, how did you find it? How did you know I was here?"

"I googled it. The band, I mean. Javier's band. He's sort of famous, you know, so it wasn't difficult to figure out where he was playing." He lifts one shoulder. "I wanted to surprise you. I was serious when I said I want to make my good luck charm happy."

"That's sweet," I say, unable to meet his eyes.

"I want to convince you to stay in Madrid next semester," he says. "I want you to be happy, Laura. I'll do anything to make those things happen."

I roll my lips between my teeth. "Well."

"Just think about it," he says. He looks away, like he's not quite sure what to do next. His eyes flick around the bar, landing on a discarded cocktail on the counter beside me, sweating in its grimy glass. I know it makes him uncomfortable, the dinginess of this place. It's a dive bar, and Rhys doesn't do dive bars.

But he's here. He came. I'm not quite sure what to make of it. There's a fluttering in my chest, just beneath my breastbone. I can't tell if it's nerves or something else.

Something better.

Rhys is wearing what he usually does when he's trying to fly under the radar: jeans, a white button-down, heavy scruff, and a white baseball hat embroidered with the logo of his favorite rugby club from back home.

It always takes me by surprise, how lethally handsome he is, especially after not seeing him for a few days. Even though he's trying to fade into the crowd, he stands out. He's just . . . he's *more* than the other guys here. More handsome. More magnetic. More blond and tan and fit.

"You know the 'hey girl' still isn't working," I say.

He shrugs, a grin tugging at the edges of his lips. "Law of averages. The more I try, the better chance I have. Or something like that."

I turn around to grab my beer. "I still can't believe you actually came. I know a trip to a place like this isn't on your schedule today. Or any day, for that matter."

"I told you I'd help you with your bucket list, didn't I?" He doesn't smile, but the skin at the edges of his eyes crinkles as he looks down at me. "Plus, you've never propositioned me before. I admit I am excited about the 'boning' part of the night."

I bite my lip. "I am too. Thank you for coming."

"Of course. Wouldn't miss it."

A beat of awkward silence settles between us. What is he thinking? What am *I* thinking?

What the hell are we even doing?

"So, uh. I'd better get going," I say, pointing my thumb over my shoulder. The bar is getting crowded, and I'm getting nervous. "Javi's going to give me a quick lesson before we go on."

"Of course," he says. "Good luck, love."

Even after everything that's gone down between us, my heart still skips a beat when he calls me that.

Rhys

I watch Laura as she makes her way through the crowd, my pulse thudding in my ears. I take a quick glance around the bar, making sure no one recognizes me. I really, *really* shouldn't be here. If I'm caught at a bar two days before a match . . . well, suffice it to say I'd rather be dead. The team would go apeshit. So would my sponsors. And the parallels to my father's love affair with pubs like this would be too juicy for the press to ignore.

But none of that would even matter if I lost my good luck charm. I knew if I turned down Laura's invitation tonight, there was a good chance I'd never hear from her again. I'm skating on thin ice. I'm lucky she's giving me another shot, but that's all I've got—one shot to make this right. Considering I have no idea what "this" even is, I feel like I'm walking on eggshells. Which is why I offered to come see her play—I want her to know that I meant it when I said I'd try.

I want Laura to see that I'd go the extra mile for her.

I can't stop thinking about her. After that night at the Spread Eagle, I've felt a little . . . tired, to be honest. Not physically. This exhaustion feels more mental. It's almost like those I hours I spent with her and Emily, laughing and drinking and not giving a shit about anything but having a good time, were so bloody fun and free that the rest of my life now feels restrictive in comparison. Repressive almost. Training is a slog. The bland food I usually eat is more flavorless than ever. The boredom and monotony of my routine are getting to me in a way they haven't in a long time, not since I met Laura.

It used to motivate me, working hard for my family and my fans. Everything I do is for them. When you come from a place like Splott, you grow up fantasizing about saving everyone you love, giving them opportunities they'd never even dreamed of. I'm doing that now—I'm working very, very hard to make that fantasy come true—but I'm starting to think it isn't enough. That taking care of everyone else's needs at the expensive of my own doesn't fuel my competitive fire like it used to.

These days, it exhausts me. And it seems like laughing with Laura is the only cure—the only time when I feel excited about something. So when she texted me tonight, I jumped at the chance. I just have to keep praying that no one recognizes me.

I look up at a nudge on my arm.

"Hey," Maddie says, grinning. "I didn't know you were going to be here."

"Hey, Maddie," I reply, pressing kisses into her cheeks. "Yeah, I didn't want to miss it—she's really making this bucket list thing happen."

Maddie grins. "Isn't it so inspiring? How was London, by the way? Javier was telling me that jet you guys took was super luxe."

"We saw you guys at the airport on Saturday. That's right," I say, just now remembering it. I've been so preoccupied with training and chasing down Laura it's a wonder I remember to brush my teeth. "London was . . . well. It was all right, I guess."

Maddie and Javier have recently started dating after what Laura called "a lot of drama and dirty sex." Javier has a pilot's license and keeps a small plane at the same airport I use when I'm flying private (which is ninety-nine percent of the time). He and Maddie were just coming back from a little joy ride on his plane when they ran into Laura and me boarding the jet to London.

I like Maddie. She's a lot of fun, especially now that she's with Javier. You can tell how much he lights her up. How happy he makes her.

I wonder what his secret is.

"So how's the band?" I ask, motioning to the stage.

"They're awesome. Javi is ridiculously talented, and so is his guitarist, Leo. Though he's got, like, this errant pelvis thing that's a little intense. Oh, wait, it's Viv and Rafa—guys! Hey guys, we're over here!"

I say hello Viv and Rafa, another couple that met and fell for each other in Madrid. Vivian is Laura's friend from Meryton, and Rafa was—still is, I think—her Spanish tutor. Even now, months after they became a couple, they still look at each other like . . . like I don't know what. Like they can't get enough.

It kinda makes me uncomfortable. Or jealous? No, definitely not jealous. That wouldn't make sense.

Everyone grabs a beer at the bar—well, everyone except me, I don't drink on school nights, remember—and when Javier murmurs a greeting into his microphone, we all turn toward the stage. He introduces the band in Spanish, but then he gestures to the girl waiting in the wings and switches to English, his gaze focused on our little group at the back of the bar.

"We have a very special guest joining us on stage. Please welcome our good friend Laura Bennet, who will be helping us with some—uh—percussion stuff tonight. Please welcome Laura!"

The crowd erupts in whistles and claps as Laura appears on stage. Her long hair, straight tonight, is tucked behind her ears. She's wearing jeans and a loose black shirt, a far cry from the slinky red dress I bought her in London. But it's sexier somehow, this casualness. Maybe because she wears it with confidence. She's not tugging at it the way she does when she gets dressed up for my events.

I can tell she's nervous—her eyes are wet, and she moves stiffly—but when Javier hands her a tambourine, laughing, and she laughs too, her nervousness seems to melt into bubbly joy.

"I'm the tambourine girl?" I hear her say. She's just close enough to Javier's microphone that it picks up her voice, just barely. "Really?"

"Hell yes you are," he replies. "Time to get your Stevie Nicks on, mujer!"

Mujer. It's a word that men in Spain use to refer to their significant others in a possessive way. Literally translated as "woman" they say "mi mujer" or "my woman" when talking about their wives or serious girlfriends.

My relationship with Laura definitely isn't serious. And I know Javier doesn't mean anything by it. Still, hearing him, a good-looking Spanish guy, call Laura "mujer" makes my pulse spike. My hand tightens around my water, the plastic bottle crunching as the top pops off and rolls across the floor.

Up on stage, Laura is looking at the tambourine in her hand like it's a grenade.

"What do I do with it?" she asks.

"You play it!" Javier replies.

A shorter guy with pale, close cropped hair and a guitar

hanging low on his hips steps forward. He wraps his hand around Laura's on the tambourine.

"Yes!" he says. "Shake it! Shake it with the passions of your heart!"

He starts shaking it while thrusting his hips, guitar and all, against Laura's backside.

I hear the crunch of the water bottle in my hand again before I realize I've completely flattened it.

"That's the guy with the errant pelvis," I grind out.

"Yep," Maddie says, sipping her beer. "That'd be him. His name is Leo. He's really harmless once you get past the horny Elvis moves."

"He looks like an epileptic monkey," I say.

"Yep," Maddie repeats. "It's kind of endearing, actually."

"Is it?"

Javier counts out a beat, and then the band bursts into a loud, throbbing, up-tempo song. The bass vibrates through the floorboards, reverberating through my sternum as Javier starts singing, his voice clear and strong and perfectly suited to the pop-rock-flamenco vibe of his music.

At first Laura looks a little lost. Her eyes are glued to Javier as he nods in time to the beat, encouraging her. She raises the tambourine and taps it against the heel of her palm, once, twice, three times, totally off beat.

My heart clenches. I hope she doesn't get upset—

She laughs, a giant smile spreading across her face as she keeps trying to catch the beat. She starts shimmying her hips, just a bit, and Javier and that guy Leo shimmy along with her, all of them smiling as the music rises to a deafening crescendo. Even the crowd has started to help Laura. They clap, several people holding their hands above their heads.

Beside me, Maddie and Rafa start to clap too.

I glance around. I don't dance. The last thing I need is a random fan catching me clapping and dancing at a shit pub two days before my match with their camera phone and posting it all over the internet.

But then I catch Laura's gaze. She's still smiling, a wide, toothy thing that makes her eyes glitter. Only now she's smiling at *me*. My breath catches.

She's so bloody beautiful when she smiles like that. I don't realize I'm smiling back until my face starts to hurt. It's like we're the only two people in the room. A sense of freedom washes over me. *Who cares what day it is?* a voice says inside my head. *Who cares what everyone else thinks?* All that matters is Laura, and her smile, and the way it makes me feel. That's all that exists in this moment, and it fills me up.

I feel like I could fly.

Laura is still looking at me. Still smiling that heart-shattering smile. It's been way too long since she's smiled like this. *Let go with me*, it seems to say. *Let everything else go*.

I clap, once, totally off beat. Maddie looks at me and laughs.

We all laugh. I can't tell if I lose myself in it because I *want* to—because I've been so bored and lost this week—or because it's exhilarating, like leaping off the edge of a cliff without knowing where you're going to land.

I hold my hands up so Laura can see me clapping. She bites her lip, wiggling her hips a little harder in acknowledgement.

As I watch her, I feel my heart grow bigger with every beat. I like this liberated Laura. I like her a lot. She is fearless and sexy and *fuck* there it is again—that weird twinge inside my chest, between my legs. The scary need I felt for her after seeing her so lit up that night in London.

I should be thinking about tomorrow's training, about William Wallace's sharp-edged suggestions after my less-than-stellar performance on the pitch this morning.

But Laura keeps distracting me with her tambourine

black magic. She's having so much fun up there, and I'm having so much fun down here.

For the most part, I enjoy all the cool shit that comes with being famous. The parties, the free clothes, the toys. Getting lost in a moment like this though—doing what I *want* to do instead of worrying what it looks like or who it might offend or hurt—I honestly might enjoy this more.

After the fourth or fifth song, Laura hangs up the tambourine. Javier leads the crowd in a thunderous round of applause. People even stomp their feet, making the floor jump. Leo takes her hand—seriously, he needs to stop—and together they bow.

I have a fresh pint ready for her when she finds us at the back of the bar.

"Thank you!" she breathes. She's practically vibrating with adrenaline.

"You were brilliant up there, love." I offer her a smile. God, I want to touch her. Would she let me touch her? Would someone see us? "Absolutely brilliant. You make the tambourine look easy."

"Yeah, well. That's because it is easy," she says, laughing. She takes a long gulp of beer. "Holy shit, that was such a rush! I'm, like, shaking."

Viv touches her pint glass to Laura's. "Congrats, chica. I'm so proud of you."

"So am I," Maddie says. "You fucking rocked it."

"You seriously did," I say.

Laura looks up at me and smiles. "Did I see you clapping back here? Or was that some other hot blond guy in a white hat?"

"You think I'm hot?" I ask.

She gives me a once over, her hazel eyes sparking with mischief. "I do."

Before I can think better of it, I loop an arm over her

shoulders, pulling her close. For a minute she freezes. She's just as surprised by this sudden burst of PDA as I am.

I can't help it. The serious-minded footballer in me—the one with the weight of the world on his shoulders—knows this is a bad idea. But the *man* in me wants to touch the girl he's been eye fucking all night.

Just this once, I let the man win.

I reach for her and pull her to me, curling my arm around her waist. She opens her eyes, meets mine. Smiles, a devastating flash of confidence. Of happiness.

Holding her against me, I start to dance. Little movements at first. I watch Rafa and try to do what he's doing, sending up a silent plea that no one recognizes me because I *definitely* look like an ass right now.

Laura turns in the circle of my arms to face me. Thrusting her body into the waiting curve of my own, she meets my eyes, a wicked smirk on her lips. She slides a hand into my hair and gives it a quick, hard tug.

Holy. *Shit*.

The desire that flashes through me is so white-hot—I'm burning up, I'm on fire—for a second I can't see or feel or hear anything except *her*. In the space of a single heartbeat, it's just us again, the world and all its cares and obligations melting away, letting us just *be* together. I'm not thinking about how late it is, or how much sleep I'm missing out on, or what could happen if I'm caught. I'm not thinking about anything, and it's bloody lovely.

I'm practically shaking when I take her face in my hands and bring my mouth down on hers. She rises to meet my kiss, giving my bottom lip a bite. She kisses me harder, messier, making the kiss hers. She takes over, telling me with her tongue what she wants. For a minute I'm lost. She's never done this before. She's never been aggressive.

It's a total, obliterating, unwelcomed mind fuck.

"Ready for that bone?" Laura murmurs in my ear. "I'm so turned on I could wring out my undies."

I don't waste time thinking about the eighty-seven very good reasons why I should say no—I should go home, get some stretching in, study some play books, rest up for training tomorrow. Instead I grab her hand and spin her around and we are out of the bar and in a taxi in sixty seconds flat. I hate taking cabs, but there's no bloody way I could wait for my driver to come pick us up. The situation in my pants is a code red emergency.

I start to give the cabbie my address when Laura interrupts.

"I want to go to my place."

I blink. "Your place? As in your dorm room?"

"Yes. I want you to come with me tonight."

"Really?" I ask. "Isn't your bed quite . . . small?"

"Really," she replies.

"Love, I want to be with you, but I am worried—"

"No one's going to photograph us," she says. "I promise. We'll sneak in through the back, all right?"

She doesn't wait for me to answer her question. Instead she turns to the cabbie with her address.

Her tone—decisive, confident—signals the end of the conversation. As much as I hate the idea of going to her dorm room, I really like that she's finally being up front with me about what she wants.

I sigh, pulling my hat lower over my eyes. The chance of being photographed tonight *is* quite low. I suppose, considering Laura's request to get naughty, it's worth the risk.

"All right," I say. I put my hand on her thigh, my littlest finger toying with the crotch of her jeans as we speed through the nighttime swirl of Madrid.

Chapter Eighteen

LAURA

I'm still high from my Stevie Nicks moment when Rhys and I tumble into my dorm room. High and horny as hell.

A little nervous too. Because the time has come to . . . er, *come*.

I want to come with Rhys. A real, toe-curling orgasm *he* gives *me*.

I am going to ask for an orgasm. I am going to tell Rhys what I want.

I am so turned on from that dancing I could scream.

My dorm room feels a lot smaller with Rhys in it. He's never really stayed here before. Usually he prefers hanging out at his swank flat, where he can Instagram pictures of his swank shit. I'm kinda shocked, actually, that he agreed to come to my place at all. Almost as shocked as I was when he showed up at the bar.

I glance over my shoulder at Rhys, just to make sure it's *him*. Because this guy—the one who agreed to do anything at all tonight—I'm not sure I recognize him.

He closes the door behind us, sliding the bolt home with an impatient *bang*. My heart is racing. I take off my jacket and throw it over the chair, clicking on the tiny reading lamp. I should've made my bed. I should've picked up a little, maybe grabbed some air freshener—

Stop. I have to stop worrying what Rhys thinks about me, about my life, my world. The only thing that matters is what I think. And I think this dorm room rocks because it's in motherfucking Madrid.

Rhys takes off his coat and hat and runs a hand through his rumpled hair. The low light from the lamp catches on the angles of his face. He looks more like Prince Charming than ever: square jaw, perfect nose, long golden hair. Full, sensual lips that are still a little swollen from our dance floor make-out sesh.

My heart races faster, my resolve wavering in the face of his overwhelming handsomeness. I still can't get over that he's Rhys Maddox and that he's here with me, on a Thursday night, his blue eyes fiery with want.

He catches me looking at him. A slow, lazy smile spreads across his face.

"Come here, you." He hooks his first two fingers into the waistband of my jeans. The heat between my legs liquefies. I wasn't kidding when I said I could wring out my underwear.

He brushes his nose against my neck. "You were so great up there tonight, love. It was fun watching *you* have fun. Fun, and a huge fucking turn-on. I've been sporting wood since you picked up that tambourine."

"Really?" I breathe. He's nicking my earlobe with his teeth, fingers working at the fly of my jeans. *Tell him what you want.*

Why is it so damn hard to tell him what I want?

"I've got a raging case of blue balls to prove it," he says, dipping a single finger past my waistband into my underwear. My sex leaps in anticipation. I close my eyes.

Rhys is just so . . . overwhelming. Convincing. He makes

it too easy to melt into him, into where he wants this—us —to go.

But I'm done with easy. Easy got me nowhere and no orgasms. With a little extra effort and courage on my part, an orgasm could be in my very near future.

"Wait." I press my palm against his chest. He feels warm and solid. Alive, his heart beating against my hand. "Rhys, wait."

He goes still, eyes flicking to meet mine.

"Celibacy isn't a line item on your bucket list, is it?" he asks, half-jokingly.

I scoff. "No. No, definitely not. But coming is."

Confusion dims the heat in his gaze. "Laura, you always come with me."

I bite my lip. *Fuuuuck* this is not going to be fun to say. But I have to if I want to genuinely enjoy sex with him, instead of just pretending to. If I ever want to get out of my own way.

I owe him the truth. I haven't not come from his lack of trying. Rhys *does* try. He does want me to enjoy sex. I'm the one who was too cowardly to tell him what I wanted. I'm the to blame here.

The only way to fix this is to tell Rhys the truth.

"Um. Well. Actually I haven't come with you."

His hand falls from my fly. "You don't come with me? But I feel it, every time I make sure—"

"Rhys, I've been faking it."

The words hang between us like a ticking time bomb I fully expect to blow up in my face. He searches my eyes, and keeps searching, his nostrils flaring. His anger makes him feel huge. We're both breathing hard, my boobs bumping against his sternum.

"You're very good at faking." The words are clipped, his voice gravelly.

"I'm scary good at it. So good that for a minute there I even convinced myself I was the perfect girl I'd been trying so hard to be."

"And being that girl made you unhappy."

"Yes. Exactly. I can't fake it anymore. I can't keep pretending that a fake orgasm is as satisfying as a real one."

"Of course it isn't!" Rhys digs a hand through his hair and looks away. "Fuck, Laura. Why didn't you tell me? Why all this faking bullshit in the first place?"

"Because." I take a deep breath, let it out. "Because I was an idiot, for one thing. For another, I thought part of playing your *perfect* girl was being as chill and low-maintenance as possible. Like, not asking anything of you that you might not want to give, or that might gross you out. That probably makes, like, no sense at all to you, but I want you to know how sorry I am, Rhys. Really, really sorry."

I don't tell him how much I liked him—how much I wanted our *casual* relationship to be something more serious —and how afraid I was back then of messing things up *because* of that. I just . . . I don't want to go there tonight. I don't want things to move beyond *casual* with Rhys anyway. I can't ever truly accept myself, and love myself, with his perfection in my face all the time. I won't be able to see past it to more important things. Things that are more fulfilling than having a perfect body, or being the perfect girlfriend.

He looks at me from the corner of his eye. "Is that why you'll never let me go down on you? Because you think it might gross me out?"

I roll my lips between my teeth. "Yes. I just assumed that, um . . . like most guys you were just offering to do it without really wanting to. You know, to be polite or whatever."

He's searching my eyes again, the heat in his gaze returning with a vengeance. "Laura, when I say I want to eat your pussy, I fucking want to eat your pussy. I'm not being polite. I'm not playing some twisted game, trying to get out of something that's *gross*. Nothing, absolutely nothing, is gross about you or your body. I want to lick your cunt and make you come—that's what I mean when I say 'I want to go down on you.' Nothing more. Nothing less." His accent is dipping now, becoming less cut glass, more rough and round. *Fucking* curls into *fecking*. "Got it?"

A shiver darts up my spine. "Got it."

I love when he loses it. When he drops the fancy pants accent and morphs into an angry, passionate Welshman.

I love it when he says dirty words like pussy and fuck and cunt. Hearing those words come out of his Prince Charming mouth almost makes me come on the spot. I'm turned on, I'm dizzy with desire, I don't know what to do or say next.

"I-I'm s-sorry," I stutter. "I never meant to lie to you. I understand if you want to leave."

He takes a step toward me. "Don't think I'm not tampin' fumin' ragin' about this—"

"Tampin' fumin' ragin'?" I grin. "I've never heard you use that one before."

"It's a Welsh expression. Means pissing mad." He waves it off. "Anyway. I'm pissing mad you lied to me. But you've got another thing coming, love, if you think I'm not going to pick up the gauntlet you just threw down."

I draw back. "What gauntlet?"

"I've never made you come before. I fully intend to fix that sad fact tonight. You gave to me without ever taking anything in return." Rhys takes another step forward, surrounding me, challenging me, and holds out his arms. "So take. Fucking take what you want, Laura. Tell me what you want, and I'll give it to you."

I freeze. I wasn't expecting such an enthusiastic response.

He leans forward, lips brushing my ear as he murmurs, "And don't you dare ask me if I mean it."

Another shiver moves through me, this one potent enough to have me sucking a breath through my teeth.

Okay. The ball is in my court. Okay.

My hand is still on his chest. I rake my gaze from that spot down the length of his body, drinking him in as my thoughts riot. The ball's in my court, so what do I do next? I'm used to giving, giving guys what I believed they wanted. I've given so much and so often that now that it's my time to take, I have no idea where to start.

Rhys must sense my hesitation. He runs his thumb along the exposed ridge of my collarbone, his touch soft, teasing. "Take your time, love. I assume you've come on your own? Masturbated?"

"Yes." I swallow. "I masturbated to you, as a matter of fact. Before I knew you. You were, like, my ultimate fantasy crush."

His mouth twitches. "So tell me what I did in your fantasy to make you come."

A spike of heat impales the growing throb between my legs.

Okay.

"Okay," I say. I'm really going to do this. I'm going to say what I want, and I'm going to take it.

I lift my palm from his chest, put it back down. "This—your shirt—take it off."

He jabs his tongue against his bottom lip, still smirking. With deft fingers he works at the row of buttons down the front of his shirt, never breaking eye contact with me. More of his tan, muscled chest is revealed with each button he works through its hole, a smattering of dark blond hair peeking through the widening *V.* Ornate script is scrawled in black ink across his pecs and beside that, there's a cross, a bleeding heart in faded red, and a flag. There's something sinister about Rhys's tats. Something dangerously, tauntingly masculine.

After he unbuttons the last button, Rhys rolls back his broad shoulders and pulls off the shirt, tossing it onto the chair.

Looking at his bare torso, the tight, thick skin rippling with sinew and muscle, I can't help it. I lick my lips in appreciation.

"You are abso-fucking-lutely delicious," I say. My eyes rove over his ink. "How old were you when you got all these?"

He hesitates. I'm not surprised; whenever I ask him about his past, he coldly shuts me down.

He doesn't this time, but he doesn't answer my question either.

"You know you can look *and* touch," he says.

"I know," I say, reaching for him. "I know."

The sound of my palm scraping against his chest fills the small space between us. His breath catches when I thumb his nipple, my fingers digging into the rock-hard ridges that define his abdominal muscles.

Oh. Oh, yes, there are definite perks to dating an athlete. Those muscles are one of them.

I trace a finger over the tattooed clouds that cover the rounded bulge of his right shoulder, the looping script that trails along the inside of his bicep. I stop at the tattoo just above his elbow—another heart, this one with *mum* written in the center.

"This one's my favorite," I say.

Rhys looks down. "Mine too."

I move my hand to his torso, tucking my pinkie and fourth finger into the thick black waistband of his underwear that rides above his jeans. The muscles here are flat and hard as a rock, thick, sinewy veins snaking across his taut skin. My pinkie slips into Rhys's "porkchop"— that's what I call the delicious slice of bone and muscle just above his hip—and his whole body tenses, the muscles hardening beneath my touch.

He is so freaking perfect. This body, these muscles, his skin—there's not a single flaw to be found.

I, in comparison, fall far short in the area of physical perfection. Especially now that I'm eating real people food. You know, things other than nuts and lettuce. Carby things.

I swallow. Close my eyes. Steel myself against the doubt that worms its way through me. *What would Monica Cruz do?*

Monica would say it's time to fucking come already.

She'd say that I have nothing to lose.

I open my eyes and meet Rhys's.

"Take off my shirt," I say, my voice trembling.

He smiles. "I'll get the light."

"No," I say. It comes out more sharply than I mean it to. I close my eyes again and shake my head. "I want—I want to do this with the light on."

Rhys is quiet for a beat, then another.

"You're gorgeous, Laura. I'm glad you don't want to hide in the dark anymore."

"Trust me," I say, "I still want to hide."

"But?"

But I have nothing to lose, I say to myself.

"But I'm trying to be brave," I say to him.

If my heart was racing before, it's taken off at a sprint now.

"I like this brave new Laura," Rhys says. "Hold up your arms."

I do as he tells me. I sense him moving closer, the clean, warm scent of his skin surrounding me. And then he's pulling my shirt over my head and it falls to the floor with an almost silent *whoosh*.

He sucks in a breath.

"What next?"

"Um. Uh. My bra, I guess—take that off too."

His gentle touch sends a wave of longing through my body as he reaches around and unhooks my bra. With my eyes still closed, I begin to unbutton my jeans. I so badly want to do the opposite, to put my clothes back on, put the focus back on Rhys and his ridiculous footballer bod. It'd be easy and quick, and I wouldn't have to face this horrible fear that I'm ugly or undesirable.

That I'm unlovable, because I'm not perfect anymore. I'm just me. Or trying to be, anyway.

But just when my fingers hesitate on my zipper, Rhys is covering my hand with his and tugging that zipper all the way down.

"Don't stop," he murmurs, cupping my bare breast with his free hand. "You're doing very well, love."

My nipple hardens against his palm. My breath stalls in my throat. I am hugely nervous, hugely aroused too. I try to focus on the feeling of his hands on me instead of what he might be thinking about my half-handful boobs.

"Off," I stammer. "Take my—it, my jeans—take it all off, please."

My eyes are still closed, but I can tell by the satisfyingly masculine sound he makes that he's smiling.

"This too?" he asks, running a thick finger inside the lace band of my underwear.

"Yes."

He makes that sound again. He slides both palms inside my underwear. In a single, urgent motion, he coaxes my jeans and undies down to my knees. I raise one leg, then the other, helping him take them all the way off.

And just like that, I am completely, utterly naked in front of Rhys Maddox.

I let him see me like he never has before—I'm always hiding in the dark or diving under the covers when we hook up. I struggle not to flinch as heated silence stretches between us. This is horrid—he's probably thinking how small my boobs are, how hairy my crotch is, he's thinking I'm not up to snuff—

Why do I care what he thinks? We're over anyway, Rhys and I. We were over the moment we met. He's a super-famous, super-hot footballer chasing after titles, and I'm a student with five months in Madrid. He lives to impress the world with his playthings, and I don't want to be a plaything anymore. I want to be me, freely, without shame.

I'm going back to Meryton next semester. And Rhys definitely isn't coming with me.

I have nothing to lose.

Rhys sucks in a breath. I steel myself for the rejection that's coming.

When he finally speaks, his voice is different. Lower. A bit hoarse. "Jesus Christ, love, I can't believe you didn't want to turn on the lights sooner."

My heart skips a beat. "So it's not bad?"

"Bad?" he scoffs. "Are you fucking kidding? Quite the opposite, love. Open your eyes and see for yourself."

I pry open one eye, then the other. Rhys is looking at me, his gaze hard and focused—it's the face he wears when he's in the thick of a match—an enormous erection straining unabashedly against the fly of his jeans. His chest rises and falls with each hot, fast breath he takes.

He looks like a man possessed.

My body goes up in flames.

He takes my hand and spins me against him, my back to his front. He takes a couple steps to the side, bringing me with him, until I can see our reflection in the mirror above the bathroom sink.

My eyes go right to my boobs, and the pale bit of flab that sticks out on my stomach. What the hell is that shit? I ran hundreds of miles to get rid of that flab, and it's already back five days after I start eating carbs?

I knew learning to love my body wasn't going to happen overnight. But at the very least I thought I'd loathe myself a *little* less now that I'm making a real effort to love me for me.

That loathing, it seems, is worse than ever. The only things I seem to notice about my body are its flaws.

I swallow, meeting his eyes in the mirror so I don't have to look at myself anymore. "I don't see it."

Rhys holds up a hand. "May I?"

I nod.

He takes a step closer, plastering his bare chest against my back. His skin is warm and smooth, his nipples hard against my shoulder blades. My pulse flutters. I love the feel of him against me, love the safety of being curled into his body like this.

He puts his hand on my waist.

"You're beautiful," he murmurs in my ear, his fingers tickling their way across my stomach.

Something about him telling me that—that I'm beautiful—makes me feel exactly the opposite. There's already too much focus on my body as it is right now. It's overwhelming, and not in a good way.

"Stop," I say.

His hand goes still against my skin. "You all right?"

"Yeah." I squeeze my eyes shut. "Sorry. I didn't mean stop touching me. I meant stop . . . um. Complimenting my body, I guess? I don't mean to sound like a douche, but it's making me feel, uh, a little self-conscious. Um?"

"Okay," Rhys says slowly. "All right. Might I compliment you on something else then?"

I laugh. "If you want. But you know I'm a sure thing at this point, right? You don't need to get all Shakespeare on me to get in my pants."

"I know," he says. "But it might help you relax, no?"

"Maybe." I sigh. "Probably not."

"It's at least worth a try."

I watch in the mirror as his broad, thickly veined hand makes its way lower, oh, he's going lower—

"You're brave."

My breath catches when his middle finger slips between my legs.

"You're ambitious."

With his other hand he reaches up and brushes my hair off my shoulder, planting a kiss there.

"You're not afraid to forgive."

His middle finger parts my folds.

"You're *free*." He says it with such reverence, such longing, my heart skips a beat. I don't even know what that means— I'm free? free to do what? free *from* what?—but the way he says it makes me believe it's true.

I'm really wet—like, really—and Rhys grunts in appreciation, his breath hot on my neck.

"I don't know if you've ever been so wet for me," he says. "Tell me what you want me to do, Laura—tell me what feels good. Or better yet, show me."

He glides his finger back and forth, back and forth, catching on my clit each time.

"There." I grab his hand. "Stay right . . . oh, God, *right* there."

He puts his mouth on my shoulder as his finger works a lazy circle around the front of my pussy. My whole body seems to tighten and throb in time to his movements, my lips parting as I watch him touch me. He begins to rub his erection against my ass, slowly, baby thrusts that incite the heady beat between my legs.

I grab his other hand and bring it to my breast. "Here. Touch me here too."

His teeth are in my shoulder now, and he's circling his thumb against my nipple in tandem with the circles he draws against my clit. Sensation ripples from the hard point of my nipple down to my sex, making me clench around his finger. He slips another finger in, both fingertips swirling, teasing, pressing.

"That okay?" he asks softly.

"Yeah," I breathe. "Fuck, Rhys, that's better than okay."

His lips twitch. "Good." He curls one finger inside me. "And this? Is this better than okay?"

I can't even speak as he glides his finger against the front wall of my vagina. For a minute I think my knees are going to buckle.

"Good," Rhys repeats.

He presses me tightly against him, using his forearm to roll my body in time to his increasing thrusts. His skin is damp with sweat as his smirk disappears, a mask of pained concentration taking its place. I can tell he's trying to hold back. He's never had to wait like this, not with me. I was always quick to fake my orgasm so we could just get to his.

"Look," he says. "Look at yourself, Laura, in the mirror. Watch what your body can do."

I close my eyes, turning my head. "I don't want to. I can't."

"Try it," he says. "I think it will make you come harder, love. You're so fucking se—I mean you're so fucking *smart*."

I laugh and so does he, and I love the feel of his rumbling chest against my back.

His hand moves to my other breast, cupping it, working the nipple to a hard point. My eyes fly open at the searing pulse of need that tears through me and lands on the mirror. I'm flushed, my cheeks and chest pink, my bottom lip caught between my teeth. My hair is everywhere. Rhys is looking at me over my shoulder, his glacier blue eyes clouding with lust as my body responds to his touch. One of his thick forearms is strapped across my hips, the other rests between my breasts, holding me in place. He's so much stronger than I am, so much bigger, and yet I'm the one calling the shots.

This—watching us, watching my body come alive—*is* kinda hot.

I cry out when Rhys runs both of his fingers up the length of my slit. He presses his dick against my ass, he keeps pressing, keeps touching.

Screw this. Dry humping is for high school.

My eyes glue to the mirror, I watch Rhys's face as I reach behind me. With impatient fingers I unbutton his jeans and make quick work of his fly. His mouth falls open, his eyes dark and a little unfocused. I reach through the fall of his boxer-briefs and grab his dick. He's huge, and hot; he fills my hand, pulsing with frustration.

Rhys literally growls as I guide him out of his underwear, placing the tip of his dick at the small cleft where my butt cheeks meet, just beneath my tailbone.

"Stop," he says through gritted teeth. "Stop touching me. Tonight is about turning *you* on."

"This." I press my ass against him, his dick sliding up and down that cleft. His precum makes him slide a little easier, a little faster along my butt crack. "This is turning me on, Rhys."

He growls again, pressing the tips of his fingers hard against my clit. "I think it might be turning me on more."

I see stars. My legs begin to shake. "I'm coming," I breathe. "Holy shit, Rhys, I'm actually coming."

He slips one of those probing fingers back inside me. "I want to feel it. Don't rush, love. Take all the time you need. Just take, Laura."

He squeezes my nipple between his thumb and forefinger and circles his hips, wincing as he presses the head of his cock harder against me, the veins and muscles in his arms popping against his skin. I watch him in the mirror, my gaze roving from my body to his, his body to mine, the two of us writhing against each other, our skin glistening with sweat in the low light of the desk lamp.

I forget about my flab, and my tiny tits. My self-consciousness melts away in the face of the overwhelming sexiness in front of me. I can't stop watching us, watching me, my nakedness only making the tightness between my legs spiral higher, harder. This is so dirty, watching ourselves like this, telling him to touch me like this, and I like it.

Rhys is relentless, enveloping me in the heat of his body, the smell of his skin. I am drawn tight in his arms, the painfully sweet throb of my impending orgasm filling me up, making me feel weak with the need for relief.

His finger is frantically stroking my clit now, the other curled inside me.

"Oh my God," I say, my hair falling in my eyes. I shake it away. "Oh my God, Rhys."

He ducks his chin into the crook of my neck, and my head falls to the side as he digs his teeth into the skin there.

I come with a strangled cry, my eyes flying shut as wave after wave of release moves through me. The orgasm is so potent it leaves me boneless, but Rhys holds me tight against him, supporting my weight as it keeps coming, and coming, holy *fuck* I am coming harder and longer than I ever have. I feel myself clench around his finger, the tremors quick and tight.

"Christ, love," he pants. "You're coming hard. Keep coming."

And I do, the shockwaves strong enough that they're almost painful. My heart is popping around in my chest, the scent of my arousal surrounding us. I finally relax against Rhys, breathing hard. I open my eyes.

Rhys looks—I can't describe the look on his face. Ferocious hunger? Pain?

He meets my eyes in the mirror. "Are you able to stand up?"

"Um," I say, settling my weight back onto my feet. "Yeah. Yes. I'm okay."

"Good. That was the sexiest thing I've ever seen—felt. You coming. I am so fucking turned on it hurts, Laura. I'm sorry, but I've got to take care of this."

"Take care of—?" I turn around and see him take his dick in his hand, giving it one, two vicious tugs. He turns toward me.

"I'm sorry," he repeats. "And no, I don't need help. Lie down. You'd probably like to rest after coming like that."

"Oh—oh, okay," I say, my gaze moving over him as I crawl into bed. Maybe I'm still floating in the afterglow of my giant O, but watching Rhys masturbate—knowing *I* turned him on, *I'm* the one who's got him strung out like this—is making my body begin to throb again.

It's lewd, how hard he's stroking himself, sweat rolling down the plane of his chest, his handsome face tight and flushed. Lewd and very sexy.

"Laura." He's breathless, focusing his eyes on me. They flick down my body, flick back up, lingering on my shoulders, then my neck, then my face.

I offer him a small grin. "You gonna make it?"

He slams his palm on the desk in reply, grunting. He bends over, supporting himself on one arm. He winces.

And then he comes, pumping one last time before he cups the head of his dick in his hand. The orgasm hits him hard, the muscles in his shoulders and neck bunching.

A beat passes, then another. Rhys is breathing hard, his head tucked against his arm as his body rises and falls, rises and falls.

"Laura," he says again.

He raises his head and meets my eyes. His are so blue, so soft. The intensity is still there, the hunger. But that hunger is different, somehow, from the sharp-edged lust I saw in his eyes two minutes ago.

My stomach flips, a funny lightness taking shape inside my chest.

I don't think Rhys has ever looked at me like this before.

I tell myself that it's just the magical orgasm talking. The post-O endorphins or whatever making the world take on a rosy, romantic glow.

I've been naked with Rhys hundreds of times. Sure, I never actually *came* with him before. But there's no way a single orgasm could change anything between us. Could make me feel so much more raw and vulnerable and turned on than I ever have in my life.

I swallow, hard. Rhys made me feel like I was cherished, important, irresistible. It's a heady sensation, being in someone's arms and knowing they'll take care of you. Knowing they care as much about your pleasure as they do about their own.

"I did," I say. "Thank you, Rhys. For letting me, um . . . do the taking, I guess."

He shakes his head. "You should do the taking more often. I like it. I like making you come."

I like when he makes he come too. I like the way I feel when he says these things, when he looks at me like I'm the only thing he sees. And it's suddenly starting to scare the hell out of me.

Rhys and I were over before we began. I'm leaving, I'm going back home—

"I know you're exhausted," I say, reaching for my shirt. "You should probably get going, huh? Rest up for practice tomorrow?"

The wounded look Rhys gives me makes my heart contract. But he can't stay. Not after what just happened. The way he's looking at me, the way it's making me feel . . .

It's one thing to use this super delicious, super intense orgasm/hookup thing as a means of learning to accept or even love myself as part of my bucket list experiment. It's quite another to start feeling something deeper, something *more*, for Rhys Maddox. That would be just plain stupid. I'm leaving Madrid soon. I've already started brainstorming a whole new bucket list for my semester back at Meryton. I want a fresh start there, a new beginning that definitely won't happen if I start pining away for Rhys again.

Tonight was great. But it was also a fluke. An exception. Tomorrow he'll go back to being a slave to his schedule, and I'll be on my own again. Only this time, I'm not going over to his apartment after his match on Sunday. I'm done with that. I'm done with his ridiculous cars and clothes, his incessant need to show his Instagram followers how sick his life his. My bucket list is all about giving that superficial stuff up, including our *relationship*. I want no part of it anymore.

I want to tackle this list with everything I've got. If he's down to help me with that in the next few weeks like he did tonight, great. Anything else—anything more—I'm not interested. I can't be.

Chapter Nineteen

RHYS

Sunday – A Few Days Later

I collapse into my customary spot—second aisle, window seat all the way to the left—and close my eyes. God I'm tired. My legs feel like jelly, and my knee is throbbing. It's late, almost midnight, and like the rest of the lads, I just want this flight to go quickly so I can go home and go to bed.

We tied tonight, 2-2. The squad from Las Palmas isn't a strong one, but they fought hard and gave us quite a bit of trouble on the pitch. I played well, even though I didn't score (Olivier and Sergio took that honor). I thought my late night on Thursday might fuck with my body—I only got five hours of sleep—but I felt pretty good out on the pitch today. I felt great, actually.

Mostly because I was thinking of Laura the whole time. Well, not exactly. On the flight here I thought about her and her body and that first real, earth-shattering orgasm she had with me. I think I'll treasure that memory forever. But then I started thinking about how different she seems now that she's putting real effort into her bucket list. She tripped me up a little on Thursday when she asked me to stop complimenting her on her body. I had no idea that it made her self-conscious. I was hoping it would do the opposite.

But once I started complimenting her on other things—once I started thinking about all the things I saw in her when she was up on stage at that bar—I couldn't stop. There was so much to compliment. She's fun and she's brave and she's confident in a way she wasn't before. I remember telling her, right before she came, that she was free.

I'm not sure what I meant by that. It's just this feeling I got being with her that night. She wanted to play with a flamenco band, so she did. She told me what she wanted, and she took it. I'm sure at some point she might've felt embarrassed or unsure about what she was doing. But it was clear she was making an effort to not give a shit about anyone or anything else except *herself*. She was free from her baggage from the past and her worries for the future, and she was living purely in the moment. She was totally, enthusiastically present. And she seemed so much happier because of it.

So I tried to do the same thing on the pitch today. I hoped it might make the match feel less . . . I don't know, less like something to get through and more like something to be enjoyed. Usually I obsess over what my sponsors and my managers and my family back home will think of my play. I suppose in a way I've always played for them. Because of them.

But today—today I attempted to play just for me. Just because I love football (or I did, once upon a time), and because playing it used to make me so bloody happy. I wanted to be that kid I was back in Splott, who loved playing footy so much it kept him up at night. I wanted to play because I loved it.

So I tried just being present. It wasn't easy, and most of the time I caught myself slipping up, thinking about what the papers might say about this assist, wondering if the new boots my sponsor is paying me three grand to wear are getting photographed enough. Those were the moments when the match felt interminable, like I couldn't wait for it to end.

But when I was able to stop thinking about everything and everyone and just *play*—when I focused on the feel of air in my lungs and the catch of the grass beneath my cleats—I felt this surge of joy inside me. I had nothing to prove and no one to please except myself. Granted, it only happened once or twice in the seventy-six minutes I played. But still, I tried. And it sort of worked.

I've got to keep trying. I don't want to go back to the way I felt about football during the dark days of my recovery. I've been catching glimpses of that blackness lately, and it scares me. It scares me because my family is depending on me.

It scares me because I'm not sure if living that way, living to correct past sins and pay future bills, will be enough anymore. I was able to bully my way through it for a while. But now, knowing what I know, seeing what I've seen, meeting this new Laura, I don't think I can.

I don't think I want to.

I turn off the overhead light and settle farther into my seat, digging my mobile out of my pocket. I pull up my chat with Laura. My thumbs hover over the keyboard as I struggle to think of something to say. If this were pre-London Laura, she'd be waiting for me back at my flat, probably wearing one of those little lingerie sets I love so much.

As great as that sounds—I mean, it sounds pretty fucking great—I honestly would prefer to see post-London Laura. The Laura who has the courage to ask for something that scares the shit out of her, who is honest and a little wild. The Laura who lives in the moment. I admire her.

I want to be more like her.

Too bad I'm not sure I'll be seeing either Laura anytime

soon. She gave me a pretty strong "go away forever please" vibe when she kicked me out of her dorm room at one A.M. on Thursday. I haven't reached out to her—I got the feeling she needed some space—but right now I'm dying to tell her how she inspired my play today.

I wonder if she even watched the match. My pulse does this weird little hiccup thing when I think that maybe she hasn't.

I glance up from my mobile. People are still boarding. The lads are all around. As much as I'd like to call Laura, now is not a great time.

But I have to talk to her. I feel like we've been apart too long, and I want some of that liberated Laura to rub off on me again. It was so fun last time. So a text it is.

I don't suppose you're still awake?

Air blasts from a nozzle above as the engines come to life. I blink, my eyes watering, and reach up to turn it down.

I almost leap out of my seat with a *huzzah!* when my phone dings with her reply.

I am, the text says. *I know a tie isn't a win, but congrats anyway*.

Olivier's head appears over the seat in front of me.

"Doing ze sex-zing on ze phone wiz your lady friend, Cabbage?" he asks, cocking a suggestive brow. "You are a bit impatient, non?"

"Non. *No*. I mean no, I am not sexting with Laura. We're in public, for Christ's sake. What sort of animal do you think I am?"

He glances down at my mobile. I clutch it to my chest.

"I am very jealous," Olivier says. "You have much of the energies tonight."

I spear him with a glare.

"Fine," he says. "Okay, I leave you to be wiz your woman.

Do not worry, I bring ear plugs so I will not hear your sex noises."

He turns back around. I look down at my phone.

Thx. You stayed up to watch me? I text.

I did. You looked great.

I grin. *Pls stop complimenting my looks, it makes me self-conscious.*

You are naked on billboards across this continent, she types back. *You are a hot footballer. Aren't your looks all you have?* [winky face emoji]

God I hate emojis. Except when Laura uses them. Then I think they're sort of cute.

Fair point, I reply. *I thought of you when I was playing tonite.*

The usual good luck charm stuff?

No, I say. *I wanted to feel on the pitch what you felt on the stage. Not worried about anything, just being in the moment. Hard to explain.*

It takes a moment for her to reply.

The plane lurches away from the gate.

Really? she replies. *What do you think I felt?*

Now it's my turn to hesitate.

I don't know. But I like it. I'd like to make you feel more of it. Can I see you tmrw?

I am busy tmrw, sorry. Exam prep in my classes.

I lean back in my seat. I'm at a loss for words. She's never been busy the day after a match. She's never turned me down point-blank before.

She's also never mentioned she has class on Mondays. It makes sense that she would, now that I'm thinking about it. I admit I don't know much about university, but I imagine you'd have class most days, right?

Have you always had class on Mondays? I ask.

Yes, she replies. *Always. I have friends who take notes for me when I skip, but I don't want to miss anymore class, esp w exams coming up. Tmrw I have Psychology of Fascism and the Economics of Brexit. Cool subjects. Both count toward my major so I have to do well.*

I stare at my phone. It hits me that I don't even know what Laura's major is. All this time she's blown off important classes so she can be with me, and I haven't had the bloody decency to ask her what she's studying, or what she's interested in.

What is your major? I ask.

Political science, she replies. *Not sure what I want to do w it yet. But I think it's pretty interesting. Love studying it.*

Fuck me. I've really become a selfish son of a bitch. I've asked her, time and time again, to blow off her classes, her interests, and her bucket list, so that I can prove to the world I'm successful, stable too, unlike my father.

I dig a hand through my hair. No wonder the poor girl is fed up with me. No wonder she's trying so hard to put herself back in the driver's seat of her own life. For the first time, I get it.

I feel horrible. Granted, Laura never really opened up to me before—she never told me she had class on Mondays until now. But I also never asked her. We're both at fault, but at least Laura is trying to fix her mistakes.

She makes me want to fix mine.

"Cabbage?"

I open my eyes. Olivier is peeking through the space between the seats in front of me again.

"You all right?" he asks.

I shake my head. I'd be all right if I knew I could give Laura back her semester. If I could make up for all the times I was a dick, all the times I talked her out of doing the things on her bucket list.

It used to scare me, the thought of letting anyone close enough to mess with my focus or my footy. But now—now

I'm more scared of *not* having Laura close. I didn't realize how heavy the burden of everyone's expectations was until she inadvertently helped lift it from my shoulders. I like living in the moment with Laura. It's the only thing keeping me afloat. Her smile—I want to fall into it, to swim in it, soak it up like sunshine.

I'm scared. Really, really scared that I'm too late and going to lose Laura, and if I don't lose her, I'll lose everything else I've fought so hard for. But I've got to make this right. We're going to check every damn item off on her bucket list if it's the last thing I do.

The captain comes over the loudspeaker, telling us to stow our larger electronics, put our seats in the upright position . . .

Sorry, I text her, because I don't know what else to say.

Sorry? For what?

Everything. For being blind. For not asking you about your major. For being a selfish prick.

It takes a moment for her to reply.

Everything ok?

My mind fast-forwards to this week. Lots of training, lots more rehab, a couple interviews, more appearances, meetings with my agent, manager, and publicist . . . William Wallace is having the lads over for dinner one night . . . I'm shooting a commercial, and I'm way behind on my sleep . . .

Shit, I'm busy. I haven't got an hour to spare.

But I have to see Laura. I have to make this right.

Tuesday, I text her. *You free then?*

Ive got a really busy week Rhys.

I understand. But I want to see you. Can we do more bucket list stuff?

I'll be at Santa Caterina Tuesday @ 3.

It's all I can do not to groan. Santa Caterina is not my favorite place, for a lot of reasons.

But I am going to make this right.

I'll be there. Sweet dreams love, I text back.

I turn off my mobile. I could barely keep my eyes open ten minutes ago, but now I'm wide awake. I spend the rest of the flight with my heart in my throat.

This—breaking all the rules I've set for myself—it's a thrill. Life is suddenly fun. I hop out of bed in the morning and struggle to go to sleep at night because I'm so bloody excited about the next day. I'm like a kid on Christmas Eve. And it's all thanks to Laura.

But breaking the rules is also really, really dangerous. I keep waiting for the lack of proper rest to catch up to me on the pitch. I keep waiting to be caught doing something I shouldn't or for my sponsors to call me out on slacking on my endorsements. I haven't posted an Instagram in, God, five days now?

I keep waiting for my luck to run out. That can't happen. Not with my family depending on me. No matter how I feel or what I want, I have to pay the bills. I have to be the man my father never was.

I also have to see Laura again. When I don't, I feel like I can't breathe.

My luck has finally changed. Now I just hope it doesn't run out.

Chapter Twenty

RHYS

Tuesday
Madrid

I pull up to the curb and put the car in park. Glancing out the window, I see loads of little kids running about the playground at Santa Caterina, bundled up in tattered coats that are clearly hand-me-downs. I remember the powder blue coat I wore when I was six, maybe seven. It was my cousin Hannah's, clearly a girl's jacket, with pink and purple butterflies on the front. I hated it, but Mum couldn't afford to buy me a new one and the winter that year was terrible, so I had to wear it. I think I'm still a little scarred from being teased on the playground about those butterflies.

I take a deep breath, let it out. My heart is pounding like it was years and years ago when I had to wear that coat. Christ, this place cuts too close to home. There's still so much work I have to do if I want to make sure my cousins and their kids don't end up being mercilessly teased at a place like this for wearing a shitty jacket. There's still so much I want to give them. The educations, the doctors, the homes and that van for Aunt Kate's daughter Marie . . .

My thoughts begin to spiral out of control. *I shouldn't be here. I should just cut a check to Santa Caterina and go back to the pitch and practice my footwork. There's a reason I'm not very hands-on with the charities I support. I don't have time for this. My sports-drink sponsor isn't thrilled that I moved the commercial shoot to next week, and if I lose them I lose the fifteen grand—*

I blink, and realize I've been staring out the window right at Laura. When our eyes meet her face breaks out in a massive, glowing smile. It's like a bullet to the chest. I can't breathe. I can't think.

I can only stare at her and wonder how the hell I got so lucky that I can make a girl as excellent as Laura smile like that.

Her arms are crossed over her chest. She loosens one and waves at me, the late afternoon sun catching on her long hair as she does. I wave back, stupidly, and in that moment everything—my discomfort and my stress and my past—it all falls away.

I'm not that kid in the butterfly jacket on the playground anymore. I'm the guy who's looking at girl he's crushing on, hard, the guy with nothing to prove except his adoration for that girl. I don't notice the tattered jackets or the broken down playground, and I don't feel like my father is going to suddenly appear on the sidewalk, drunk and angry and ready for a fight.

I only want to hang out with Laura. Maybe try to shamelessly impress her and her kids with my footy skills. She's done so much for me, it's the least I can do for her. Plus I know now it's fun to play just for play's sake, to make the kids laugh. It's fun to play when I have no one to impress and nothing to prove.

I turn off the car, get out, and pop the trunk. I dig a stray football out of my training bag.

Flashing Laura a grin, I head her way.

Laura

My breath leaves my lungs when I'm hit with that *grin*.

For a minute the world spins around me, my heart drumming in my ears. My armor seems to fall away all at once, making the bones inside my skin rattle, making the skin around my bones burn with the knowledge of his attention.

Fuck. I am fucked. I want to fuck him. I don't know why I caved and told him I'd be here today—you don't invite your booty call to the school where you volunteer—but man, am I glad I did.

Rhys is dressed in jeans and a grey hoodie, nothing fancy, but somehow he manages to make it look face-meltingly sexy. It's the way he fills out the hoodie, maybe, the masculine breadth of his pecs and arms on full display. Or it could be the way his jeans hang juuuuuuust right on his narrow, athletic hips. And the messy man bun at the crown of his head—*yum*.

The kids are screaming, jumping up and down as Rhys approaches. He smiles, a boyish, happy thing, and waves hello to his little fans.

I blink. Who *is* this guy? Last time, he avoided the kids like they literally had the plague. He'd hardly look at them. Now he's smiling, waving at them like he's actually happy to be here. I don't get it.

When I mentioned in my text that I'd be at Santa Caterina today, I thought for sure Rhys wouldn't come. He says he's into helping me with my bucket list, but I didn't believe him.

Until this very moment, I don't think I believed him.

Rhys looks up at me. My heart skips a beat.

"Hola, Laura," he says.

I grin. I don't know why, but I'm grinning. "That's Miss Bennet to you, Mister Maddox."

"Oh. Right. You're the teacher here, aren't you? Well." He looks back down at the kids. *Do you think Miss Bennet might let us play some football together this afternoon? I need to practice before the match on Saturday,* he says in easy, smooth Spanish.

Then the kids are suddenly surrounding me, bouncing on their toes as they beg me to let them play with Rhys Maddox, football superstar and supposed war hero.

"Hmmm," I say, tapping a finger against my chin as I pretend to think about it.

Please please please, the kids say, frantic to be set loose.

Rhys opens the gate and steps inside the playground.

How about this, he says in Spanish, and squats beside the kids so he's at eye level with them. *If you promise Miss Bennet that you will behave and do everything she tells you to for the rest of the week, I think she just might let you play football with me.*

Yes! the kids shout.

Do you promise? he asks.

Yes! Yes, we promise! Now can we play?

He meets my eyes.

"Well, Miss Bennet?" he asks. "Can we?"

I tug my bottom lip between my teeth as I look down at him. It's like he's a whole new Rhys, stripped down to the bare essentials: laughing blue eyes, tons of charm, affable patience. *Where did you come from?* I wonder. *Where have you been hiding all this time?*

"Yes," I say. "Oh. Wait, I meant to say sí. Sí, por supuesto!" *Yes, of course!*

The kids take off running toward the muddy patch of dead grass at the far end of the playground. Rhys stands and hangs back for a minute, propping the ball between his hip and forearm.

"So, like, when did you become a child whisperer?"

"Child whisperer—that sounds a little murdery, doesn't it?" he says, and we both laugh. He shrugs. "I don't know. I grew up on a playground like this. There were always lots of little kids around. Lots of babies."

I cross my arms. "The fancy pants footballer—he grew up on a playground like this?"

"Yeah," he says. "I did. But mine wasn't nearly as nice. Maggie actually broke her arm on the slide—it was really rusted, and when she went to use it, it fell. So did she."

"Oh. Oh, I'm really sorry." I blink. He's actually talking about his past—his family.

He's never done this before. Not with me, anyway.

He isn't giving me much—just a hint, really—but even so, it makes my heart twist. It makes me feel soft toward him in a way I don't think I have before.

"C'mon, love," he says, nodding at the makeshift field. "Let's go play some footy."

"Yeah, about that. You know I was more of a mathlete growing up, right? Like the opposite of a world-class athlete like you."

Rhys smirks. "You're still scarred from that one week at soccer camp, aren't you?"

"Hell yes I am," I reply. "I was eight. Soccer was the cool sport that year, so I begged my mom to let me go. I cried through the whole thing."

"Laura." Rhys looks at me. "We're playing with a bunch of kids. I think you'll be all right."

"You don't know how hard I cried."

He grins. "Fine. But you're missing out."

Rhys drops the ball to the ground and dribbles his way onto the field. Even though he's barely jogging, his feet move around the ball with knowledgeable ease and confident control. I've always loved watching him play, but this—seeing him up close and personal, surrounded by kids that are no taller than his waist—takes it to a whole new level.

He shows the kids how to dribble the ball, how to pass it. He makes them squeal with delight when he bounces the ball on his head like a seal, and they go nuts when he traps the ball between his feet and flicks it behind his back and over his head, catching it with the front of his foot.

He tells the girls they can play as fast and as well as the boys. He tells the boys they'd better watch out for the girls because they're going to be really, really good.

Who knew Fancy Pants was 1: a feminist and 2: so amazing with kids?

I mean. I'm dying a little in the best possible way.

I watch him laugh with my students, I watch him be patient and kind. I smile so hard my face hurts. My heart dips inside my chest, just like it did last night.

The other teachers, having heard the commotion, come outside with their classes to watch us play with unabashed interest. A few of the other kids join in.

I want to join in. Rhys is genuinely having fun out there. So are the kids. It's infectious, the giggling, the happiness.

Before I know what I'm doing, I'm jogging onto the makeshift field. A couple of wide-eyed teachers try to stop me to ask what's going on, but I wave them off, breathlessly telling them I'll explain later. One of the little boys, Miguel, screams with pleasure when he sees me.

"Well look who it is," Rhys says, grinning. "Our star mathlete."

"Go easy on me, would you?"

"Absolutely not," he says.

He whooshes past me with the ball, and I just stand there with my hands on my hips and watch him dribble down the field and score in the pretend goal. His feet move so fast I can hardly make them out in the fading twilight. He's fast, and he's confident, running circles around everyone who gets in his way.

He's such a stud athlete. Jesus H. Christ, I don't even know what to do with myself.

"Showoff!" I call after him.

He just shrugs, that grin still curling at his lips.

Rhys lifts up his hoodie to wipe his face, revealing the chiseled edge of a hip and abs you could scrub laundry on. I catch a glimpse of a happy trail, a line of dark blond hair arrowing down taut muscle toward his groin. I'd very much like to follow that trail down his jeans.

I swallow, hard, and turn to help little Pedro tie his shoes.

We start to scrimmage, boys against girls. Somehow I end up defending Rhys, and I actually do a pretty sweet job of it at first. I taunt him, he taunts me back, inadvertently plastering myself against his body, my back to his front. I move against him and he moves against me, our arms and legs tangling. Laughter seizes my belly as we slap each other away.

"I'm going to kick your you-know-what," I say, deflecting Rhys's attempted pass.

He swoops to the side, and I swoop after him. "I would let you do anything you wanted to my you-know-what."

"Ugh. Perv."

"You like it."

"You wish."

"I do." He grins at me. Oh, that grin.

Rhys takes advantage of my momentary distraction and plows past me. He passes the ball to Miguel, and Miguel takes off running, a huge smile on his face.

Along with the rest of the girls, I chase Miguel and Rhys down the length of the field, breathless with laughter.

That's it! Rhys says to Miguel. *That's it, you're almost there!*

His arms shoot over his head when Miguel kicks the ball toward the playground, as far from the imaginary goal as possible.

"Goooooooaaaallll!" Rhys cries out, jumping in the air. The boys go wild.

I, in the meantime, can't stop the forward momentum of my body. I'm about to crash head on into Rhys when he catches me by the waist and turns, playfully whirling me off the ground.

"That," I breathe, struggling against a fit of laughter, "was *so* not fair! Using your superior skills against us."

"What?" he asks innocently. He dangles me above the ground. "Is it my you-know-what? Was it distracting you?"

I wiggle against his grasp, but he holds me tight against him. This dressed-down Rhys—he's so touchy-feely, I'd be lying if I said I didn't like it, if it didn't feel good. My whole body is one big goosebump.

By now we're both laughing. I manage to reach around and slap the you-know-what in question. I would bite it if I could. We're sweaty, we're breathless, and we're having fun.

Somewhere in the back of my mind I know I should stop. This is more than a friendly bit of trash talking. This is flirting. I don't want to flirt with Rhys, not here, not now. But this laughter between us—it keeps happening this week. It feels natural, and easy in a way it never has before.

I wish it wasn't so easy with him. I'm supposed to be putting all my focus on my classes and my bucket list right now. I'm running out of time. I have less than three weeks left in Spain, and I shouldn't be wasting it flirting with a guy who can't give me what I'm looking for.

Then again . . . Rhys did come to Santa Caterina today. I

know he had to blow off something important to be here, he probably didn't want to come at all. But here he is, playing soccer with my kids, flirting with me, laughing and being silly like he couldn't care less what the world thinks. And he actually talked about his family.

Maybe he isn't just trying anymore.

Maybe he's actually *changing*. I'd be lying if I said that didn't thrill me.

Rhys sets me down, the two of us gasping to catch our breath. For a minute we linger close to one another, our bodies still touching. It's so hard to step away. The attraction between us is magnetic, a struggle to resist. My non-sexual feelings are supposed to move in the opposite direction, away from Rhys. But they're sliding toward him, the feelings as potent and tingly as ever. I'm fighting them, I am, but looking into Rhys's eyes, wet with laughter, I know it's a losing battle.

Chapter Twenty-One

RHYS

It's dark by the time the last little lad and his mum leave Santa Caterina. Once word spread that I'd come to visit, parents and teachers and students appeared in droves. I must've signed hundreds of autographs, and taken even more pictures. My eyes sting from the bright white flashes of camera phones. My knee's begun to ache. Considering the day I've had, I should be exhausted.

I'm not, though. I actually feel the opposite—exhilarated. It could be leftover adrenaline from practice this morning. But the joy I felt laughing and playing with a field full of six-year-olds—and a very, very cute twenty-year-old—is the more likely culprit.

Not to sound like a dick, but when I agreed to meet Laura here after the match on Sunday night, I didn't have high expectations. I thought it'd be boring, frankly, and an unpleasant reminder of my past to boot. I thought I'd be counting the minutes until I could have Laura to myself. But I'm shocked at how *fun* this afternoon was. It seemed to go by in the blink of an eye. I guess that's what happens when you're fully in the moment. When you're present and acting like an idiot and not giving a damn who sees you. My ribs hurt from laughing so much.

"Thank you again for coming to help us today." Nuria, Santa Caterina's program director, wraps both her hands around my own. "It is very much appreciated. These children, they do not have very much, and it is so good for them to have a special surprise like this."

"Thank you for having me," I say, and I mean it.

"I hope you'll consider coming to our fundraiser," Nuria continues, giving my hand a squeeze. "We're hosting an auction to raise money for our makeshift library—it's currently in a closet by the bathrooms. The children love their books, and we don't have nearly enough of them. It's on the nineteenth of December." Her eyes move to Laura. Nuria smiles. "Laura has been a big help putting it together for us. It's going to be spectacular, largely because of all the work she's done. We are very proud to have her on the staff."

I glance at Laura. She's looking at her feet, blushing.

I dig a hand through my hair, giving it a solid tug. Laura's clearly put a good bit of effort into this auction, but I didn't even know it was happening. What else don't I know about her? What else did I miss out on while I was busy being the self-absorbed tosser I am?

Christ, I'm a tit. I feel horrible.

I've got to make it up to Laura.

"I'll be there," I blurt, turning to Nuria. "I'm happy to donate money, and anything from the team you'd like—autographs, equipment, whatever you think will raise the most money."

"Rhys," Laura says, a grin toying with the edges of her mouth. "You don't have to do that."

I meet her eyes. "I want to."

"Thank you," she says. "Really, Rhys. That's very generous of you."

"My pleasure," I say.

But the real pleasure was hanging out with Laura all afternoon, poking fun at her, helping her and the girls set up some goals and pull out a decisive victory against me and the boys.

The real pleasure was getting to *know* her. I want to know more. I want to know everything.

We walk from the school to my car in silence. Energy crackles between us, my body very much aware of hers. We both move to talk at once.

"Rhys—"

"Laura—"

I grin. "Sorry. You first."

"It's all right." She slows her pace, digs her hands into her pockets. "Thanks again for today. That was really awesome of you to come—I had no idea you were interested in this sort of thing. You're so great with the kids."

"You're really great with them too," I reply. "I know it's also got to feel great to be doing something you really want to do—crossing off another item on your bucket list."

"It does," she says. She turns her head to the side, coyly, and meets my eyes. "Thanks for doing it with me. You're a lot of fun all the sudden."

I take a step toward her. "*This* is a lot of fun all the sudden. Us. You and me."

"It is." Laura bites the corner of her mouth. "I didn't think it would be. I didn't think it'd be so fun, I mean. Were we really so boring before?"

"I was," I say.

She grins, scoffs. Her breath is a white cloud against the darkness. "Yeah, you were."

My heart turns over in my chest at the sound of her laugh.

"Why didn't you tell me?" I ask. "About the auction. It sounds like you've spent a lot of time on it."

Laura shrugs, a small, almost imperceptible thing. "Same reason I didn't tell you about my major. I didn't think you were interested."

"I am," I say, more urgently than I intended. "I'm interested in everything you do. I'm sorry I didn't ask sooner."

She looks at me, her eyes gleaming in the light of a nearby streetlamp. "I'm really, really glad you're coming to the auction, Rhys. It means a lot to me."

I offer her a grin. We've started to slow our stride. "Least I can do."

The thought of leaving her now, of her leaving me to spend the night alone in my flat with only my Instagram for company, fills me with inexplicable dread. I need to catch up on some sleep. I probably should call my sponsor again and do a bit more groveling for moving the shoot.

There are a million other things I should be doing, and none of them include hanging out with Laura.

I just can't help myself.

"Let's go for a walk in the city," I say. "All the Christmas lights will be up—it's quite lovely."

"A walk? Really?" Laura pulls her hand out of her pocket and checks her watch. "It's almost your bedtime."

"Fuck my bedtime," I say. "Let's go."

We walk for hours.

I only meant to take Laura for a quick stroll through a square or two to see the incredible displays of Christmas lights that decorate Madrid this time of year. My knee's still bothering me, and I have to get up early for training tomorrow, like always.

But Laura and I keep talking, and we keep laughing, the minutes slipping by as we walk one block, then another, the city unfolding in all its festive glory around us. We start at Retiro, Madrid's largest park, and make our way through my neighborhood, Salamanca, stopping to admire the intricate holiday window displays at the posh shops that line Calle Serrano.

"So, like, I don't mean to be rude," Laura says. "But why the about face? With the kids, I mean. Last time you came to Santa Caterina, you definitely didn't want to hang out. Now you're, like, everyone's best soccer friend forever."

I bury my hands in my pockets. "I wish I had a better excuse. But the playground, and the kids . . . it all cuts close to home, you know?"

"Actually," Laura says, flashing me a look, "I don't know. You never talk about home. Not to me, anyway."

I look away. My heart has started to pound. "I don't talk about it to anyone, really."

Laura scoffs, smiling. "Thanks for making me feel special, Rhys."

"It's not that," I say. "I just don't like going there. It makes me feel—I don't know how it makes me feel. Except not great. I don't like talking about my family."

"I've noticed." She must see the discomfort in my expression, because she adds, "But you don't have to talk about it if you don't want to."

I look at her. My every instinct tells me to change the subject, maybe crack a joke. This is a can of worms I do not want to open.

But how can I expect Laura to open up to me—how can I expect her to let me in—when I refuse to return the favor? My family is such a huge part of my life, whether I like it or not. I love them. But I am ashamed of them too. I'm ashamed of where, and who, I come from.

And then I'm ashamed I'm ashamed. My family is a sob story, yeah, but it's not a *total* sob story. There's still some good parts. Good stories. Good sides to everyone. Well, maybe Dad doesn't have a good side, but everyone else does. For the most part, I'm lucky to have them. It's just a lot of work, giving them what I want them to have. Trying to save them.

A familiar weariness comes over me. It's a heavy burden to carry, and I've been carrying it alone for a long time.

Maybe it's time I let someone help.

I look at Laura. She looks back. Her eyes are kind.

"I do," I say, slowing my stride. "I do need to talk about them."

She nods at a café across the street. "Want to grab a seat?"

"Yeah," I say. I grab her hand. "Let's."

Laura

I meet Rhys's eyes across the table. They're a little glassy, mostly pained, but I also see some relief there, like he just rolled a two-ton weight off his chest.

"Wow," I say. "Wow, Rhys. That's a *lot*. Like. A lot lot."

He fiddles with the cappuccino he hasn't touched since we sat down more than an hour ago. He hasn't had time to take a sip. He's been talking, talking, telling me about Splott, about his sister Maggie and her fantastic grades in the private school he pays for. He tells me about her dreams of going to Oxford and about his wonderful mum and his deadbeat dad. He shares that his aunt has an eleven-year-old daughter with cerebal palsy.

Mister Manbun Prince Charming really is a prince charming. All this time, I thought his toys and his Instagram and his general ridiculousness showed that Rhys was this vain, superficial Ken doll.

But now—now I see he courts attention and sponsors because he's trying to support a pretty giant family back home.

I'm stunned.

I'm stunned because he's so fucking wonderful.

I'm stunned because the guy who never told me anything just told me *everything*.

"I know," he says, scoffing. "Sorry for the long-winded saga."

"No. No, I don't mean your story was a lot. Long. Your story wasn't long—I mean it was, but what I'm trying to say is that taking all that on by yourself is a lot."

He reaches across the table and takes my hand in his. He keeps his gaze trained on our joined fingers. "What choice do I have?" he says slowly. Quietly. "I love them, Laura."

"I don't doubt you love them, not one bit. But it's a lot of work for one person, trying to fix everyone and save everyone and be everything your dad wasn't. That's a lot of work, Rhys, and it's crushing you. Anyone else would've been crushed years ago."

Rhys swallows, an audible sound.

"It *was* crushing me," he says. His eyes flick to meet mine. "But then I met you. I stopped thinking about them so much —my family. I don't mean that in a bad way. I just mean I stopped thinking about them first, before I thought about anything else."

"Before you thought about yourself."

"Yeah. Yeah, I suppose so. But really I meant you, love. I started thinking about you. I think about you all the time." He gives my hand a squeeze. Looks away. "I don't suppose you think about me too?"

It's my turn to swallow. "I do. I do, Rhys, but—"

"But." The skin at the edges of his eyes crinkles as he pulls his lips into a tight smile. "I hate that word."

I love this new Rhys, the prince charming charging through Splott to save a family in distress. I just wish I'd known this guy four months ago. Of course he'd pop into my life when I have mere weeks left in Madrid and I can't, under pain of death, start to like him again.

Of course he'd make me feel all mushy and happy and at home when our time together is about to end.

"I'm sorry," he says.

"Sorry for what?"

"For not asking you about *your* past all this time."

I offer him a playful smile. "Rhys, you just asked me about my freaking *major* two days ago. I didn't expect you to ask about my family."

"I'm really sorry about that," he says. "I want to make it up to you."

"I know," I say.

"Do you?"

I meet his eyes. There's this look there, this warmth I haven't seen before. They gleam with interest, arousal, intent. I see nothing proud, nothing possessive. Just softness and vulnerability and hope.

Hope that I won't crush him for confessing how he feels. Because that's what this look is—a confession. A question I never thought Rhys of the "let's keep things casual" school of relationships would ask.

Meeting his eyes head on like this—having nowhere to hide—is terrifying. Terrifying, and joyous.

Who the fuck are *you?* I want to ask. *Can I kiss you until you die?*

But I can't. We can't. I'm leaving. I *need* to leave, because staying here another semester in hopes that this new Rhys is real is just another way of putting my life on hold. I don't want to feel . . . whatever it is I'm starting to feel right now, because it's pointless. I gave into these feelings once, and Rhys totally burned me.

I am not going to let myself get burned again by falling for a guy I'm going to leave in two weeks' time. My plane ticket is paid for, as is my tuition for next semester at Meryton.

I push back from the table. "It's getting late. We should go."

I don't look at Rhys as we make our way through the café and back out onto the street. I'm about to start walking in search of a cab when Rhys grabs my hand, drawing me to a stop in front of him.

"Happy Christmas, Laura," he says.

He tucks a strand of hair behind my ear. A tingly warmth moves through my body.

I look away. "Do you think I could get away with saying 'Happy Christmas' instead of 'Merry Christmas' back home in the States? Or would I just sound like a total douche?" I ask.

"You'd definitely sound like a douche," he says, smiling. He steps forward, our bodies touching, and noses my hair. My stomach flips. It's overwhelming, how much I want this man. How much he's making me feel.

I can't.

"Rhys," I say, pulling back. "I'm leaving at the end of December. I'm not staying with you in Madrid."

His eyes blaze as they lock onto mine. I can't tell if he's angry, or sad, or both. I struggle to meet his gaze for several agonized heartbeats. Part of me wants him to take me in his arms just so I can push him away. Just so I can hurt him for doing this to me, for turning into this wonderful, wondrous, communicative guy just before I have to leave. Just when I'm sure I'm ready to be alone for once in my life, when I'm *excited* to be alone.

"Is that set in stone?" he asks, carefully.

I nod. "It is. Look, I'm having an awesome time with you lately. You're, like, turning into this whole new guy I really, really like. But I've been planning to go back to the States for a while now. I already registered for next semester's classes, and I'm coming up with a new bucket list of things I want to do at Meryton. I have a life there, friends and family and interests, one I'd very much like to get back to. You and I, and this keeping-things-casual thing . . . I don't, like, want to offend you, but I can't keep putting my life on hold for that. For you."

He draws a breath, lets it out. "What if we don't keep things casual? What if we become more than that?"

"It's too late." I close my eyes against the pain that arrows through my chest. Fuck, I'm in too deep, this has already gone too far. "Going back to the States is the right decision for me. I think we both know that."

"Do we?"

"I do."

"Okay," Rhys says after a beat.

"Yeah," I say.

I'm leaving. Rhys may have changed, but my plans haven't.

Chapter Twenty-Two

LAURA

Sunday Night
The Usual Madrileña Spot

Rachel tips back her wine glass and drains the last drop. "Shall we? It's almost time. Laur, I still can't believe you passed up box seats. What in the world were you thinking?"

I grab my coat and scarf from the back of my barstool. I know I'm asking a lot of the girls to sit outside at the match tonight—a cold front just hit Madrid—but it felt like the right thing to do. I want our last time at the stadium to be as ridiculous and electrifying as the first.

I also want to put a little distance between Rhys and me. Despite my declaration that I'm leaving Spain, we've been talking and texting and hanging out nonstop. Last night we talked on the phone for *hours*. We talked about nothing and everything, and when I hung up I had to resist the urge to call him back and talk more. Now that we've opened up to each other—now that we're learning each other—it seems neither of us can get enough.

It's gotta stop. I've made my decision, and I am sticking

to it. I don't want to leave Spain totally, completely heartbroken. I can't have the fresh start I'm looking for at Meryton if that happens.

"I mean, the box *is* great," I say. "But you're kinda cut off from all the energy and excitement up there. I want to actually watch the game, sing the songs, hear the drums, just like we did back in August."

"Do you also want to freeze your ass off?" Viv zips up her giant puffer coat. "It's, like, negative ten degrees outside. I *know* that box is heated."

Maddie snickers. "Your box is heated."

I shrug, wrapping my scarf a little tighter around my neck. "I brought our flask. We'll be fine."

You'll be fine, I tell myself.

But there's still a knot in my stomach. This is the last time I'll see Rhys play in Madrid. It's a bittersweet moment. As ready as I am to move on, and to tackle my stateside bucket list, I'm going to miss all the hoopla surrounding football season.

I'm going to miss Rhys.

The game is a close one, close enough to keep the girls and me too invested in the match to notice how freaking cold it is. We bounce on our toes to keep warm, our eyes locked on the field as Rhys and the rest of the guys try to dig out a victory.

A little after halftime, the crowd comes alive when Olivier charges up the field and passes the ball to Fred. Dogged by a pair of rival defenders, Fred passes the ball to Rhys.

Rhys doesn't hesitate. He dodges a midfielder, then ducks past another; my heart is in my throat as he manages to launch the ball at the goal just as a dude tries to slide tackle him. I watch, not daring to breathe, as the ball rockets past the goalie and into the net.

"Holy. Moly!" Rachel screams above the earth-shattering roar of the crowd.

"Holy shit!" I say, dizzy with relief.

People start chanting, they start singing. It's so loud that when Maddie looks at me and shouts something, I can't hear her. The ground trembles beneath our feet.

I start to laugh. This is fucking amazing.

When Rhys turns to face our side of the stadium, my heart skips a beat. He's laughing too, a giant smile plastered on his sweaty face.

I've never seen him smile on the pitch. Even when he scores—and he scores plenty—he'll usually run around like a lunatic for a minute and embrace a teammate or two. But he never, ever smiles.

Not until now.

Oh, that smile. It's handsome and happy and so very much him. I know he loves football, and I know it's been his dream to play it professionally. But I never considered until now that he hasn't been having much fun playing it. Tonight, though, he's having the time of his life—that much is apparent in his smile and the joyful way he clings to his teammates as they celebrate.

Rhys turns back to the crowd, holding up his arms. His eyes move over the stands, almost like he's looking for something.

Vivian nudges me in the ribs. "He's looking for you!" she yells.

I blink, a tingle moving up my spine. "No way," I reply. "He doesn't even know where I'm sitting. I didn't tell—"

But then his eyes catch on mine, and an even bigger smile splits his face. He brings his hands to his lips, and in a ridiculously dramatic, and ridiculously adorable, gesture, he blows me a kiss.

"Ohmigod," Rachel says. "Ohmigod, I am going to faint, that is the cutest thing I have *ever* seen."

Viv nudges me again. "C'mon, Laur, you gotta blow a kiss back!"

I smile. It's stupid, but I don't care. I do it, I blow him a kiss. At that moment Olivier appears at Rhys's elbow. Smiling his wicked, only-a-French-guy-could-get-away-with-it smile, Olivier pretends to grab my kiss just before it hits Rhys's mouth. Laughing, Rhys shoves him aside and trots down the pitch. On the sidelines, the photographers and the announcers are on their feet, pointing their lenses at me.

The only thing that would make this moment more magical would be if Rhys took off his shirt. Which, coincidentally, he does just as I'm thinking that dirty-old-lady thought. The crowd goes ape shit, the ref holds up a yellow card, and Rachel literally sways on her feet.

I keep smiling. I'm so happy for Rhys, and so proud of him, I could burst. I know how much winning a game like this means to him. It means a lot to me too.

I almost wish it didn't. Leaving Madrid—leaving Rhys—is really going to rip my fucking heart out.

Rhys

The lads hang about in the locker room, high on victory and buzzing with adrenaline. Apparently Olivier is having a bit of a celebratory soiree at his flat, but I'm not interested. There's only one person I want to see tonight, and what I want to do with her requires a more—er—private setting.

I've already done my requisite post-game interviews,

although tonight the media is going absolutely insane over "the kiss seen 'round the world" as they're calling it.

We've never seen you like this, one reporter said. *You seem very . . . elated. And your play was animated tonight. It's like we are watching a whole new player.*

I'm having fun, I replied in Spanish. *I think that is making a big difference in my game.*

Another reporter pressed me for details about "the lucky woman" who was the recipient of said kiss. *Are you in love, Rhys?* he asked.

I laughed into the microphone to hide the fact that I was blushing. I didn't answer the question, but I have a good idea of what I'd say if I did. I can't stop thinking about Laura. I can't stop wanting to be with her, wanting to live in the moment with her.

I can't stop feeling like *my* life—away from my family, my father, and my career—is finally starting. I didn't realize that by allowing so many people to have a say over my life, I was always trying to live up to their expectations. I was living to prove something to them. I was trying to prove to the press that I wasn't my dad. I was trying to prove to my family that I could provide for them in a way Dad couldn't. I was trying to prove to sponsors I was successful enough and popular enough and far enough away from the poor kid growing up in Splott to merit endorsement money.

Everything I did was for somebody else. I see now that my life hasn't been my own, not really. I thought I wanted to flaunt my footballer life in everyone's faces. I thought I wanted to make my family proud. But pursuing Laura's bucket list with her has made me realize that maybe what I really want is the freedom to be myself. To own my past and forge my future by enjoying the present.

My life is finally starting because of Laura. I know she has plans to head back to the States for good at the end of the month. But I can't let her leave. I'll be damned if I let the girl who gave me back my life go.

I've showered and iced my legs and packed my bag. My fingers shake with impatience as I button my trousers. Just a few more minutes and I'll be able to meet up with Laura. I smile at the memory of the way *she* smiled when I blew her that kiss. I felt . . . I felt fucking everything. Gratitude. Lightness. Freedom.

It hit me in the wild, ferocious seconds before and after my goal that I really was having fun. Honest-to-goodness fun. I was totally present in the moment. I wasn't thinking about what this goal meant for my career or how it would change my stats or how it showed the world I am a *very* different player than my dad. It was just me, and the ball, and the thunder of my heart.

"Petit chou!" Olivier shouts over the din. "What iz our little cabbage smiling about? You are not leaving, I 'ope?"

"Sorry, mates," I say, slinging my bag over my shoulder. "I'm absolutely shattered."

It's true. Every bloody muscle in my body hurts, and I'm going to be sore as hell tomorrow. But that certainly isn't going to stop me from fucking Laura's brains out tonight. After, of course, I go down on her for an hour. Maybe two. I have a feeling bucket-list Laura will finally let me.

"Bah! Petit chou, you are a very bad liar. You go to see your beautiful woman. I do not blame you, she is very sexy, yes?"

"Keep going." I level him with a glare. "Keep going so I can knock your teeth out."

"Come on, Cabbage!" Fred says. "You won the game for us tonight. You can't *not* come to Olivier's party."

"Yes." Olivier nods his agreement. "You must come. If only to bring your sexy woman and zat free champagne you get."

"So you're using me for my pretty girlfriend and my booze hookup?"

Fred blinks. "Well, yeah."

I roll my eyes. "Laura's waiting. G'night, lads. Great m—"

"Bring 'er!" Olivier replies. "Your little sardine. Bring 'er, the lady Laura iz always welcome at my 'ome."

"Tell Laura to bring her friends too," Fred adds. "*All* her friends. At least maybe five of them? One in five isn't bad odds, right?"

"Yes." Olivier wags his eyebrows. "All of zem. Come, Cabbage, do not disappoint your dear friend Fred. 'e did make ze assist zat 'elped you score ze goal of your dreams, no?"

Tongue in my cheek, I dig a hand through my wet hair. I really, really want to have quality alone time with Laura right now. I'm getting some pretty intense pants feelings just thinking about it.

Fred *did* do me a solid, though, helping me make the most epic goal of my career so far. I guess the least I can do is introduce him to some of Laura's girlfriends. I'll only stay for an hour, hopefully less. Just long enough to make sure Fred doesn't end up drunk crying alone in the loo. Then Laura and I can sneak out and finally get naked.

"Fine," I grind out. "How many bottles should I bring?"

Chapter Twenty-Three

RHYS

Later that night

Olivier's flat is packed with the usuals: the lads, our managers, WAGs. A few Spanish celebrities are sprinkled in, and rumor has it Olivier's favorite pop star is on her way from London in his private jet. I'd be jealous if I didn't have Laura here with me. Screw the singers and the supermodels. I have Laura, and I am hands down the luckiest man in this room.

I sip on a glass of the champagne I brought—the stuff is bloody sweet, why did I ever pretend to like it—my eyes glued to Laura across the flat. She's standing in a little circle with her friends, all of them smiling, drinking. She looks fucking amazing, relaxed and happy and a little tipsy.

God, this girl. She turns her head, just a little, and meets my eyes. One side of her pretty mouth curves into a grin.

I can't breathe. I love seeing her so happy, so joyfully in her element even when she's surrounded by all the ridiculous people who inhabit my world. *You are so lovely,* I want to tell her. *You mean everything to me.*

I give the crotch of my slacks a discreet tug. I have got to eat that cunt, stat, or I am literally going to explode. Best get the introductions over with so I can find a room with a lock on the door where Laura and I can take care of business.

Beside me, Fred nervously leans back on his heels. Poor chap. You'd think being a professional footballer—and one of the best in the world at that—would cure him of his terror of the female sex. He doesn't talk about it much, but from what I understand, he grew up a bit chubby, a bit awkward, and was teased relentlessly because of it. I think he's still traumatized by it all. Olivier and I also think he's still a virgin, but neither of us has the stones to ask him outright. No self-respecting twenty-two-year-old guy wants to be called out for that.

I clap him on the shoulder. "Ready to go say hello? Laura's friends are lovely girls."

"They are pretty." Fred takes a deep breath. "Really, really pretty. Forget it. I changed my mind. I can't go talk to them, not right now."

He tries to step away, but I use the hand on his shoulder to steer him back on course. "Listen, mate, if you can't talk to girls after winning our most epic match yet, there's something seriously wrong with you. C'mon."

I drag Fred across the flat. When we reach the girls, Laura stands on her tiptoes and presses a kiss onto my cheek.

"Hi," she says.

I smile. "Feeling all right?"

"Yes." She smiles too, turning to Fred. "Fred! I'm so glad you came over. The girls have been dying to meet you. This is my friend Vivian, and this is Rachel, she really loves, uh, sports . . ."

I watch Laura work our little circle. She's radiating this friendly, kind, confident energy. I can't get enough of it. I can't get enough of her. I reach down, twine my fingers with hers. She moves closer, filling the small space between us with the girly scent of her shampoo. The wash of heat between my legs burns hotter.

I am going to fucking lose my mind if I don't have her in the next five minutes.

Fred and Rachel are talking now—hallelujah—and Vivian and Maddie have disappeared onto the terrace off the kitchen.

I don't waste another second.

"Come on," I say, giving her hand a tug.

"You think Rachel's okay with him?" she asks, nodding at Fred.

"Fred may be a bit awkward, but he is a gentleman. They look like they're hitting it off."

"How amazing would that be, the two of them ending up together?" Laura murmurs, eyes still on Fred and Rachel. Fred is blushing, hard, and Rachel smiles up at him, eyes twinkling with interest.

"Not as amazing as the things I'm about to do to you," I say.

"Nice line. And by nice, I mean awful." She giggles as she trips into line behind me.

"I think it will do the trick."

"Where are we going?" she whispers conspiratorially as I cut a path through the crush of people. The crowd thins as we make our way to the back of the flat, where the bedrooms are. It's much quieter back here.

I push through the door at far end of the hall—I think this is Olivier's bedroom—and I move past the bed into the bathroom.

Yes. Finally.

I lock the door behind us. Laura marvels at bathroom-slash-rainforest-slash-spa-retreat that we're standing in. To our right, a thin sheet of water courses down a black marble slab, filling the tall-ceilinged room with the sound of splashing water.

"I feel like I'm in *Scarface*," Laura says.

"Told you it was ridiculous."

"Yeah, but until you see a bathroom waterfall in the flesh . . ." She shakes her head, turning to me. "Congrats on your win tonight, Rhys. You looked like you were having fun out there."

"You looked like you were having fun too."

"I was." She grins. "How did you find out where I was sitting? I bought those tickets online."

I shrug. "I have my ways. Did you like it better than the box?"

"I did. It was freaking cold though. And loud. So, *so* loud, especially when they were cheering for you." She meets my eyes. "I'm happy for you, Rhys."

A beat of heated silence passes between us. There is so much I want to say. So much I have to tell her, and ask her. Where the hell do I start? I'm nervous, suddenly, more nervous than I was a few hours ago, when the lads and I were waiting to come out onto the pitch before the match.

"Laura," I say, taking a step closer.

"Yeah?" She falls back against the vanity, oblivious to my distress, and clutches the edge of the marble countertop.

I clear my throat, try again. "Laura." My heart is pounding. My palms are clammy and I'm starting to sweat. Fuck me for life. I've got to grow a pair.

I've got to tell her.

I meet her eyes. "I want you to stay. Laura, I want you to stay with me in Madrid for another semester. I know I've asked you before, but this time, it's different. You're different. I am too. I don't want to keep this—us—casual anymore. You mean so much more to me than that. Laura, I think I'm in lo—"

"Don't." The heat in her eyes has morphed into panic. She turns her head away from me. "Please, Rhys, don't."

Her voice breaks, and in that moment I think my heart will too.

"I won't say it if you tell me you don't feel it too," I say. My own voice is shaking now. I slide my hands onto her neck. Her pulse jumps against my palm, skittish and hard. "Tell me you don't feel for me what you know I feel for you, and I'll leave you alone. The girl you were trying to be before—the perfect one—I'll be honest, I didn't fall for her. But I am falling for *you*, the real you, love. And isn't that what you want? To be adored for who you really are?"

Her face contracts. She starts to cry, her throat working against my hands as she swallows.

"Fuck." I catch a few tears with my thumb. "I didn't mean to upset you."

"I'm leaving." She closes her eyes. "Rhys, in less than two weeks, I'm leaving, and I'm not coming back to Spain. I have all of next semester planned out at Meryton. I'm finally doing so well with my bucket list here, and I put together a whole new one for next semester. I'm taking on a new minor, I have an awesome TA position with this really famous professor . . . I've got a lot I want to do on my own, Rhys. This—the timing—it isn't going to work. I'm not ready—"

"You're doing it again."

She opens her eyes. "Doing what?"

"Trying to be perfect. You're waiting for the perfect time to fall for the perfect guy when you're perfectly ready." I lean in. "The timing sucks for me too, love. *I'm* certainly not perfect, and Christ knows if I'll ever be ready to take on something as big and breakable as this. I'm risking every-thing, Laura. But you're fucking delusional if you think I'll let you go without a fight."

Laura touches her forehead to mine. "Rhys."

"I like who I am with you, Laura. I'm spontaneous, I'm fun, I'm happy."

"I'm all those things with you too," she whispers. "It's just —you, us—you're overwhelming, Rhys. The things I feel for you are completely overwhelming. And I kinda love it, which scares me to death."

I press my lips to her mouth. She rises to meet my caress, her body coming alive beneath my hands. The need that floods the space between my skin and bones is sharp, enormous. I pull her to me. She can never be close enough, I can never have enough of her. The more she gives me, the more of her I want.

I will do anything, anything, to keep Laura in my arms.

"Tell me what you want." I trail my mouth down the slope of her jaw. "Ask me for anything, Laura, and you'll get it, as long as you stay. Please, please stay."

Stay forever, I plead silently.

Laura pulls back. She opens her eyes. They are wet and clear, very green in the soft light, and they burn. They burn right through me. My dick hardens in one, two heartbeats.

"I want you to fuck me," she says, gaze flicking over my suit. "Mess up your hair and your fancy clothes. I want it messy, Rhys. I want it to leave a mark."

I don't think. I don't hesitate. I grab her hair and spin her around so her ass is pressed against my dick and bend her over the vanity.

We fucked this way once, on the night we met. I thought it was good for her then, but now I know it wasn't.

I'm going to make it good for her tonight if it's the last bloody thing I do.

Chapter Twenty-Four

LAURA

It all happens so quickly I don't have time to catch my breath. One second I'm in Rhys's arms, totally vulnerable, totally aroused, and the next I'm bent over Olivier Seydoux's sink and Rhys is pushing my shirt up my back and grinding his dick against my ass.

I don't want to feel the things I do for Rhys, but it's happening, we're happening, and I can't help but feel I'll regret it if I don't give us—this, whatever *this* is—a chance to bloom. He makes me *feel*. And isn't that the whole point of my bucket list/self-compassion exercise? To eat and experience and feel? To be totally present in each and every moment, and feel everything, the joy and the hurt?

Not so long ago, I used to think Rhys and his bougie ways were bad for me. But now that he's allowed me to see past all that bullshit—now that we're both digging a little deeper into ourselves, and into each other—I'm starting to think he's a big part of why I've been feeling so great about myself lately. He's sacrificed his sense of pride to tackle my bucket list with me. He makes me feel important, and wanted. He makes me feel beautiful, despite the fact that I'm not a size two anymore.

Without Rhys, there's no way I'd be so far along, and in so short a time, on the way to treating myself better. To *feeling* better.

I want to be happy, healthy. Rhys wants to win. It's unbearably sweet to think we could both get what we're looking for together.

Tears, the happy kind, well behind my closed eyes. He almost said the L word. And I was tempted to say it back.

My body throbs. I'm wound tight, confused and bursting with equal parts happiness and angst. I need relief, the kind only Rhys and his rock-hard footballer body can give me.

He reaches around and cups the crotch of my jeans.

"Christ," he grunts, his middle finger sliding along the raised center seam. "You're already warm. Hot."

"I may not be into your cars and your watches and all that stuff," I pant. "But that doesn't mean I don't get all hot and bothered watching you play. When you took your shirt off . . ."

His stubble scrapes against the nape of my neck as his lips move into a grin. "I thought you might like that."

"Like it?" My breath catches when he thumbs open the button on my jeans. "I almost came on the spot, just like every other red-blooded woman in Spain."

He grunts again when he unzips my fly and digs two fingers inside my underwear. I'm soaking wet. I've been turned on like this for hours now. So turned on it almost hurts when the pad of his finger grazes my slick center.

"Rhys," I say.

"Naked," he says. "I need you naked. Now."

I glance up at the lights above the vanity. A beat of apprehension moves through me. While the lights themselves are low, there are mirrors everywhere in this ridiculous drug-lord fantasy of a bathroom. Rhys will be able to see me from literally every angle.

But then he's drawing my sweater over my head and trailing kisses down my naked back and working the fingers of his other hand underneath my bra cup, wiggling them playfully against my nipple. He surrounds me, the warmth from his body seeping into mine. He holds me gently, tightly; he's struggling to hold back, I can tell by the pained sounds he makes and the quiet desperation of his touch. There is an urgency, a tenderness I've never picked up on before. He touches me adoringly, like I am a real, precious person.

He touches me like he loves me.

The apprehension retreats. Warmth and desire and confidence flood through me in its place. I am beautiful, and I am going to look fucking great in those mirrors, just like I did that night in my dorm room.

I'm holding myself up with my arms, my palms planted on the counter. They start to tremble, I don't know why, I was feeling so strong two seconds ago, but Rhys is there to catch me, curling an enormous arm around my waist.

"You all right?" he asks, nipping at the edge of my shoulder. He pays a lot of attention to my shoulders. It's the one part of my body I've always liked. I guess he likes it too.

"You're always asking me that," I say.

"I want to know what you're feeling," he says. His breath is warm on my skin. "You kept so much of yourself from me before. I want to know you, Laura. All of you."

I swallow. Close my eyes.

And then I toe off my booties and stand up, leaning against Rhys. I start to pull off my jeans. He covers my hands with his, then helps me pull them off my feet. The jeans take my socks with them.

I don't wait for Rhys to take my bra off. I reach around

and unhook it. It lands with a small, metallic *ping* in the bowl of the sink.

Behind me, Rhys draws a pained breath.

"Laura." He brushes my hair over my shoulder and uses his hands to tilt my head, pressing his lips to my bared neck. "Oh, Laura."

I lean forward over the vanity, crying out when my nipples meet with the cold marble. The searing heat between my legs sharpens.

I hear a small flutter—Rhys taking off his shirt—and then he's pressing his naked front to my back, skin on skin. I shiver. His mouth is working its way along my jaw. I turn my head and he covers my mouth with his. He drinks me in deeply, kissing me, *kissing* me, kissing me so well and so hard I feel myself coming apart beneath his ardent caresses.

Rhys slips a finger beneath the lacy strap of my thong. I press my ass against his crotch, egging him on, asking him to go further. He does. That finger moves lower on my ass, tracing the curve of my butt cheek.

He hooks his finger around the strap and tugs it aside. My pussy clenches in anticipation. He guides my legs apart, gently, slowly, with his knee, and I bite my lip at the rush of cold air that meets with my swollen sex.

And then that finger slips between the lips of my pussy from the back, coming to a stop right where he knows I like it.

Oh my *God*. He strokes my clit once, just a small, quick circle, and my entire body spasms against his hold on me. He slips his finger a bit farther back, and it sinks into my core.

"You're close," Rhys says. His voice is gravelly, strained. "Hold yourself up, love."

I lean my weight back onto my palms. *What the hell*—

I glance at a mirror across the room and watch as Rhys grasps the backs of my thighs in his hands and spreads them farther apart and sinks onto his knees. Placing his palm on the small of my back, he presses me down. My arms are shaking again.

I know what he's doing. And despite all my bucket list blunder about self-love and acceptance, I still feel incredibly self-conscious about his mouth on my vagina.

"Rhys," I pant. "Rhys, wait, please *wait*—"

"You smell so fucking lovely." Rhys presses a kiss onto the very inside of my thigh, gliding his hands down the length of my torso to rest on my hips. "Relax, love. I want to make you come. Let me."

I take a deep breath. I try to ignore the impulse that rises up in me whenever this happens with a guy—the impulse to close my legs and pretend I'm not interested and change the focus to *him* and *his* orgasm.

It felt so good last time, coming with Rhys. Letting him make me come.

I want to come with him again. It could be the last time.

So I close my eyes and I take another deep breath and I arch my back, curling my ass closer to his face.

He noses the lips of my pussy apart, gliding up my slit as he inhales. I feel like I'm going to faint.

"You're delicious," he murmurs. "So. Bloody. Delicious."

He presses the flat of his tongue to my clit. Sensation bolts through me. He licks, strokes, taking his time, taking all the time in the world.

My nipples prickle to renewed life against the cold marble, a searing contrast to the heat that pulses between my legs.

I lean farther over the sink, seeking relief. But there's only more tightness, more need.

Rhys circles the tip of his tongue around my clit. He slides a hand lower, slips two fingers inside me. A familiar swell gathers inside me, making my legs tremble, clearing my head of any coherent thought except *more*. I need more or I am going to . . . I don't even know what. Explode. Die. Melt into a puddle of goo.

He kisses the top of my pussy, an ardent tongue kiss, and I come apart, a burst of painful relief. My orgasm pounds through me. I think I'm dying, it's so good, it hurts so damn much. Rhys pulls his fingers out of me but keeps them pressed against my slit, his breath hot and noisy as I come, and keep coming, holy *fuck* I am coming.

I sputter and shout. Rhys bolts to his feet and covers my mouth with his hand, holding me against him. His abs contract against my back as he breathes, hard, his mouth on my shoulder, biting, teasing.

I finally relax against him. I'm breathing harder than he is.

Is it always like this?, I wonder. Coming with a guy. Will it always be so obliteratingly good? Or is it only this good because it's with Rhys?

We stand there for several beats, our bodies smushed together, our hearts beating in wild tandem. Being held like this, touched like this, *known* like this—it's making the place just beneath my breastbone glow with a warmth, a certainty, that wasn't there before.

"Rhys," I whisper against his hand. "Rhys, what's happening?"

"I think you know, love," he says, lips fluttering across my skin.

He turns me around in his arms to face him. He thumbs my chin, tilting my head up so I have no choice but to look him in the eye. Meeting those baby blues of his head-on after the world's most intense orgasm—God, it really is a miracle I don't melt.

He thumbs my lip. "It's a good thing, what we feel for each other. A bucket list thing, even though you may not have written this one down."

He bends his neck, his prince charming hair falling in our faces, and swallows my mouth with his. His hands are on my face. I smell the salty tang of my arousal on his fingers. It only arouses me more.

I tear at his jeans, ripping open the button, throwing what is probably a thousand-dollar belt to the floor and stepping on it. The lightness coming to life inside me won't be thwarted.

Rhys doesn't seem to mind.

"I'll take care of the jeans," he breathes. "Wrap your arms around my neck. Hold on."

I do as I'm told. He grasps the back of my thighs and lifts me onto the edge of the vanity. He ducks his head to suck on one of my nipples as he drops his jeans and shucks off his briefs. My pussy throbs, my heart working double at the sight of his dick.

I reach for him, wrapping my fingers around his swollen length. He winces when I squeeze, giving him a long, solid stroke. I'm glad we did the whole STD-test/get-on-birth-control thing at the beginning of the semester. I love being so close to him, not having to worry about condoms or pulling out or any of that stuff. We can actually enjoy bare sex because we're not idiots about it.

"Fuck me, Rhys," I say, softly. "It's my turn to give."

He looks at me from under his long, dark lashes. My stomach flips at the defenselessness, the care, in his eyes. No one's ever looked at me like this before. But I know—somehow I know—it's the look. *The* look. The one we all crave from the moment we're aware romantic love exists.

The glow inside my chest burns brighter. This man. This funny, talented, hot-as-hell man is looking at me like that. My throat tightens.

Rhys steps closer, trailing his lips over my neck. Sensation ricochets across my skin, making me pant. He guides his arm underneath my leg, placing his palm on the vanity just beside my hip. He leans forward and spreads my legs farther apart so that my knees are almost bunched up against his chest. The bulbous, slick head of his dick presses into my inner thigh. Using my hand, I guide it to my center, circling it against my clit. The first tight stirrings of another orgasm have me drawing a sharp breath.

I settle him in the cleft of my pussy, shaking with need. He's enormous, and enormously hard. Wrapping his other arm around my waist, his fingers clamped to the soft spot just beneath my ribcage, he pulls me toward him at the same time he bucks his hips. In that one swift, almost lewd movement, he sinks to the hilt inside me. Rhys curses as I cry out, tucking my hands around his neck.

I feel full to the point of stinging pain. But it's a good pain, a satisfying one. He lifts his head and meets my eyes. His nostrils flare. The muscle along his jaw jumps against his stubbly skin.

"Tell me how you want me to fuck you," he grinds out.

I feel myself stretching around him as he struggles to stay still. A light sheen of sweat covers his forehead and chest. I dig my fingers into the hair at the nape of his neck and give it a tug.

"Hard. Good."

He crushes his mouth against mine and rolls back his hips, slowly easing out of me. My clit pulses at the friction. I arch my back, pressing my nipples into his bare chest.

And then Rhys surges back inside me with a thorough, lingering thrust. It is so sweet and so shocking that the tightness in my throat seeps to my heart. His tongue is in my mouth and he holds me, helpless, against him as he swivels his hips, thrusts again and again and again, deep thrusts that make my tits bounce and my pulse thud. The slick sound of skin meeting skin echoes across the bathroom.

I cry out when he grinds his hips in a circle, his pubic bone pressing against the top of my sex. Mother of God, am I really going to come again?

I cling to him, worried I'll shatter into a million pieces if I don't. He's never been so deep before. It's never felt this good. I can't breathe, I can't move, I can't, I can't, *I can't*. He moves in and out of me with ferocious care and concentration. He grips my waist tightly, guiding my movements in time to his.

I feel wild and adored and possessed.

I feel like I'm going to cry.

"Please," I beg, even though I don't know what I'm begging for. "Rhys, please."

"I'm here," he says. "I'm yours."

He nuzzles his nose to my cheek, urging my head into the crook of his neck. His skin is hot to the touch, the musky, salty scent of it fills my head. It drives me insane.

"Love," he murmurs, kissing my temple. "Love." He kisses my forehead. "*Love.*"

He thrusts and I hold on to him and he holds me, our bodies writhing harder and harder with increasing need.

"Come for me," he whispers in my ear. "One more time. For real."

He pulls back a little, straightening in front of me. He's still inside me, but now we're looking at each other, and the hand he was leaning on is now free.

He rolls his hips again, moving slowly, oh, God, so slowly in and out of me as he watches my face. He reaches between us with his free hand to where our bodies are joined. His eyes on my face, he presses his thumb to my clit, sending a lightning strike of white-hot sensation through me.

I try to jump from his grasp but he holds me firmly in his arms. The way he's looking at me—the way he's making me feel—

Tears fill my eyes so I close them and let him take what he wants. Let him give what I need. He's still moving inside me, great, gasping thrusts, working his thumb over the tip of my sex like he knows exactly what he is doing.

And he does. He cared enough about me to learn.

It's his turn to cry out when I contract around him.

The orgasm rises through me, squeezing my heart, making my body shake. It's so intense that the tears I tried to hold back spill past my closed eyelids and drip down my face. Rhys lets out a strangled cry as he spears me with one final, achingly deep thrust. The hot pulse of his cum fills me as I milk him to devastating completeness.

His arm locks around me, so tight I can't breathe, but I don't care. He muffles his cries in my shoulder as our orgasms overtake us, my body huddled into his.

Only when the rush of blood in my ears begins to dim do I realize that Rhys is shaking.

"My turn to ask," I pant. "Are you all right?"

He scoffs, wiping a tear from my eye with the flat of his palm. "No. Definitely not all right. And I've never been better."

He searches my eyes. By now my throat is so tight I can't speak.

"This has nothing to do with the good-luck-charm bullshit," he says. "I'm asking you to stay because I want to be with you. I know the deadline to apply for the spring semester in Madrid has passed, but we'll work something out. I'll pull whatever strings I can to make it happen. Stay. Please. These past couple weeks—they've changed everything. You. Me. Us. We're having the time of our lives together, and that means something to me. I hope it means something to you too."

I look away. I'm going to start crying again.

Chapter Twenty-Five

LAURA

Friday

The joyful screams and shouts of the kids echo throughout the playground at Santa Caterina. The winter sun feels warm on my face as I watch them scurry from the slide to the monkey bars and back again, breathless with laughter. I wrap my arms around my torso and let out a sigh. What a beautiful day.

What a fucking beautiful life I get to live.

I've been walking around in a happy daze lately. The fullness inside me is so big and so delicious it almost makes me ache. The same vino tinto de la casa I've been drinking all semester is suddenly tastier, Madrid is more beautiful and interesting than ever, sleep is more satisfying, and sex—well. The sex is fucking unbelievable. So is coming for real. That's also pretty sweet.

Rhys and I still haven't figured out what to do about my schedule next semester. I do want to stay in Spain, but things are still up in the air. I've spoken with my advisor back at Meryton, and while he's cautiously optimistic, we're still waiting on the university here in Madrid to approve my paperwork. I'm three weeks past the deadline, which doesn't bode well for my prospects. But I figure if Rhys Maddox can't make something happen in Spain, no one can. I'm keeping my fingers crossed. I think I can still make it happen. I hope.

I blink, the playground materializing around me. I've been doing that lately—blissing out to the point of unconsciousness. I'll be in class, or on this playground, but my mind will be in Rhys's bedroom, reliving a kiss or caress that was especially toe-curling. It's driving the Madrileñas nuts.

"Earth to Laura," Vivian said earlier today in Art History. "Dude, I'm starting to think Rhys literally fucked your brains out. You've been a total space cadet this week."

I shrugged, a secret smile tugging at the corners of my lips. If only Viv knew.

I scan the little knots of kids scattered across the space, counting them off as I go. I'm in charge of twenty-three children, who, for the most part, are pretty well behaved. I count twelve, thirteen, twenty-two—

My heart skips a beat.

Twenty-two kids. That's it. I take a couple steps forward and count again, quickly, a chill seizing my gut as I come up with twenty-two again. There were twenty-three earlier this afternoon. I always double check to make sure everyone is there.

We're missing one.

Shit.

"Chicos!" I call in Spanish. *Chicos, please line up and count off.*

The kids complain that they counted off at the beginning of recess, but I ignore them. I swallow the panic fluttering around inside my chest and palm each kid's head as they count themselves off.

It's never a good thing when a kid goes missing from school. But it's *really* not a good thing when kids from Santa Caterina go missing. We're smack dab in the middle of a pretty dangerous neighborhood. I don't feel safe walking around as an adult capable of self-defense, and it's definitely not safe for a six-year-old kid to be wandering around, especially now that it's getting dark so early.

I reach the last little girl at the end of the line. *Veintidós*, she says in a shy, quiet voice.

Twenty-two.

I swallow, hard. Oh Jesus. I'm definitely missing one. I scan the playground again, making sure no one's hiding behind the swings or climbing the rickety tree in the far corner. Nothing. It's empty.

Everybody look around, I say, my voice trembling despite my best effort to keep calm, *make sure all your friends are here. If you are missing a friend, you need to tell me right away*.

Pilar raises her hand. *Excuse me, Miss Bennet, but Miguel is not here*.

Miguel, the kid who followed Rhys around like a lapdog after he helped him score the first goal in our game of pickup soccer last week. He's a total cutie, but also a total handful. Nuria, our program director, told me he's back at his grandparents' house after a failed stay at his mother's. Poor kid is struggling with the transition, understandably, and he's been acting out a lot at school.

"Where did he go?" I blurt in English.

As far as I know, Pilar only speaks Spanish. But she must hear the panic in my voice and know what I'm getting at, because she points a finger to the gate that leads out onto the street.

He said he was going to find his mom, she says, starting to cry. *He said he misses her a lot. I'm sorry, Miss Bennet, but he told me not to tell on him*.

I feel like I'm going to throw up. How stupid and irresponsible I was to space out on the job—now a kid's gone missing in a bad neighborhood, and it's about to get dark.

Don't move, I shout, dashing inside the school. I quickly check the bathrooms, and then I grab the first teacher I find and send him out onto the playground to watch my kids while I grab someone else and order her to inform Nuria we're missing a kid. There's a bunch of protocol around an incident like this—contacting the police, the child's parents, all that stuff—but in my panic I can't really remember what order I should be following the steps. Nuria will know, thank God.

Then I take off at a sprint, moving through the playground and out the gate. It slams shut behind me.

"Miguel!" I shout, glancing both ways down the street.

A few cars pass, people staring at me through their windshields. I probably look like a lunatic, but I don't care. I gotta find this kid. I should've picked up on the fact that he was quiet today, I should've paid him extra attention, I should've been a responsible adult and kept an eye on the kids. Shit shit shit, I suck.

I don't see him anywhere. I don't know which way to go—where would Miguel think his mom would be—left, right, nearby, far away—and for several agonizing heartbeats I just stand there, my eyes blurring.

Excuse me, I say in Spanish when I see someone approaching. *Excuse me, but have you seen a little boy? This tall, short hair, his name is Migu—no? Thank you, if you see him, please bring him back here to Santa Caterina.*

I keep trotting in that direction. There are so many places Miguel could be. I pass houses, bars, tobacco shops, newspaper stands. Cars dart past. He could've been run over. He could be in a hospital, or picked up by the police . . .

My eyes burn. My heart has expanded to fill my whole body, and it throbs in time to my panicked thoughts. I'm going to pass out. A missing child is just as huge a deal in Spain as it is the States. What the hell am I going to do?

I stop and bend over, gulping uselessly at the air like a fish out of water.

I almost jump when my phone starts to vibrate. Oh my God. Oh my God, maybe it's Nuria, maybe they found him . . . please let him be okay . . .

I dig my phone out of the front pocket of my jacket. It's Rhys. I have no idea why he'd be calling—he usually never calls this time of day—but considering so much has changed with him, and with us, in the past couple weeks, I can't say I'm surprised.

I'm relieved. I need to hear his voice. Maybe that will help me clear my head a bit so I can *think*.

I need to find Miguel.

<hr>

Rhys

I'm just about to walk into the gym at the physio's office when I ring up Laura.

William Wallace, who's come to chat with the physio about my progress, cocks a brow.

"Who ya callin', ya boaby?" he asks, running a hand down his stubble.

I have no idea what a boaby is—knowing Coach, it's some sort of special Scottish penis reference—but I'm pretty sure it's not a good thing.

"My girlfriend," I say. "Give me a few moments?"

"I haven't got all day."

"I promise it will be quick," I reply. I just want to say hello. Laura and I haven't spoken since this morning, and like the sad, hopelessly smitten chap I am, I want to hear her voice. I want to know how her day is going. I am beyond excited that she's agreed to stay in Madrid for another semester. I'm so excited, in fact, I hardly slept at all last night.

Waiting for her to pick up, I smile. I feel like I've been smiling for a week straight. My face and, weirdly enough, my ears hurt from so much smiling, but I don't give a fuck. This smile makes me feel invincible.

With Laura at my side, I am. And it's the best feeling in the world."Rhys," Laura says when she picks up. "Thank God. I need your help. I'm at Santa Caterina, and he's gone. He ran away. Miguel, that little ki—"

"What?" I blink, my smile fading at the breathless panic in her voice. "Laura, slow down, love. Tell me what happened. Miguel is missing?"

"Yes," she says. My stomach clenches. I can tell she's trying not to cry. "He had to move out of his mom's house, and we think he snuck off to go find her. I don't know what to do. One minute he was on the playground, the next he's gone. I wasn't watching, I should've been watching—I just. Rhys, I have no idea what to do. I don't know this neighborhood, I can barely speak the language."

"Take a deep breath," I say, firmly. "You're not going to get anywhere if you're panicking. You had the school call the police?"

"Yes."

"And you asked the other kids if they saw anything?"

"Yes, of course."

"Good girl," I say. "Now tell me what you know about this little guy."

I drag a hand through my hair and close my eyes as Laura talks. Apparently Miguel took off through the playground gate—the same one I used when I visited Santa Caterina last week—about five minutes ago. I close my eyes and try to remember the neighborhood there. The squat little off-licenses on corners, the shady-looking characters on the sidewalks, the loud music blaring from cars as they passed. It reminds me a lot of the neighborhood I grew up in, actually. Dense, seedy, dangerous. People came and went, kids especially. Someone was always running away from his mum or dad. I was no exception. Dad would get drunk, and I'd get beaten. I learned pretty fast to disappear when my father took the bottle of gin off the shelf.

I stopped running when I was seven. That's when he left. By then, the attendants at the petrol stations and the homeless guys in the park and the girls who swept the sidewalks in front of the grocers knew me by name, and knew where I went to hide. They'd hardly raise their heads as I ran past, chased by the invisible specter of my red-faced father.

Maybe that's why I'm such a fast runner now. All that training so early in my life gave me a cardiovascular leg up on the pitch.

The attendants and the addicts and the shop girls would always lead Mum to my hiding spot. They always knew where to find me.

Just like they'll know where to find Miguel.

My eyes fly open. I may not know Miguel's neighborhood, but I know what's it like to live there.

I know how to help find him.

I glance through the physio's glass door. William Wallace is still waiting inside, hands shoved impatiently in his pockets. I can't miss this appointment. My knee is still relatively fragile a little more than a year after tearing my ACL. The physio's been helping me build up my leg and hip strength—quads, hamstrings, glutes—to take some of the pressure off my knee and keep me from hurting it again. We've got another big match on Sunday, and I have to be in top form if we're going to win. The exercises and massage we'll do today could make all the difference in my play—it definitely has before.

"Rhys?" Laura is saying. She swallows audibly. "Rhys, are you still there? What I should do?"

I let out a long, low breath. *Fuck*. I can't miss this appointment. But I also can't let Laura try to find Miguel on her own. Not when she speaks broken Spanish at best and I know exactly how to find him. Sure, I can tell her who to look for in the neighborhood, and what to say to them. But considering how upset she is right now, there's no way she'll be able to communicate what she needs to. And she won't know what to look for like I do. What I can get done in a matter of minutes will take her hours.

I glance one last time at Coach. He's going to have my head on a spike, but what can I do? Laura needs my help, and right now there's no way my footy is going to win out over my lady.

"Stay right where you are," I tell her. "I'll be there in ten minutes."

I duck inside the building. "I've got an emergency. I'll meet you back at your office in an hour," I yell to William Wallace.

He looks none too pleased about it. I get it. I really shouldn't miss this appointment.

But my knee will be fine. I hope.

Laura trots beside me, sniffling as tears run down her face.

"I know I keep saying this, Rhys, but I'm really, really sorry. You didn't have to come. I know how important that appointment with the physio was—"

"Hey." I palm the nape of her neck, gently pressing my fingers to her skin. "Stop being so hard on yourself. Shit happens, love. And I'm happy to help—we'll find your little guy in five minutes flat, don't worry. I've got a plan."

She swallows, the sinews in her neck working against my hand. "Thank you. You're the best."

I offer her a smirk. "I know."

Our first stop is a little newspaper and tobacco stand one and a half blocks from Santa Caterina. A middle-aged woman sits neatly behind stacks of gum and cigarettes and magazines, chatting on her mobile. But then she recognizes me and—it happens sometimes—her faces goes red and she drops her phone and she bursts into tears before I even say a word.

"Oh dear," Laura murmurs.

I try my best to calm the woman down, and tell her I will come back for a proper hello and hug after we find the little boy we're looking for. Between great, gasping sobs, she says she hasn't seen him, but if we try the pet supply shop up the road a bit, we might have some luck. She says kids love to go there and see the kittens.

Laura and I race to the shop. It's a good walk, taking us into a depressingly anonymous corner of Madrid. We get lost. We ask for directions, which gets us even more lost. My feet start to hurt and so does my knee, but I keep going.

Twenty minutes later, we run into the pet supply place. I know the second we walk inside that Miguel isn't here. It's too quiet. The store is small, with three little aisles piled with bags of dog food and a couple tanks of fish. If Miguel were here, we'd be able to see him straightaway.

Laura does a mad dash about the place anyway while I head for the counter. I can tell by her increasingly manic footfalls that she's panicking again.

Excuse me, I ask the bored-looking guy behind the register. *We're looking for a little boy who's run away from the school at Santa Caterina. Have you seen him?*

The guy says he hasn't, and doesn't offer any advice as to where we should look next.

Cursing, I pull Laura out of the store and head back toward the school. We start to run up and down the streets, calling his name, stopping people to ask if they've seen him. By now Laura is practically hyperventilating. I feel horrible; I try to calm her down, but I know she won't be able to relax until we find Miguel. I get it. I wouldn't either.

Despite the chill in the air, I'm sweating a good bit. My knee's really begun to ache. After the endurance drills we did this morning in training, I knew I'd be sore. But I don't like the feel of the low, insistent throb in my knee that's making me limp a little.

I keep running, though, keep asking people if they've seen Miguel. It's going to get dark soon, and the more time that passes, the farther away this kid could be.

Now I'm starting to panic too. I almost get run over by a city bus when I try crossing the street without looking. Laura screams. I hold up my hands in apology and keep going. This neighborhood seems to go on forever. Or maybe we're in an entirely different neighborhood by now, I don't know.

"Rhys," Laura pants as we trot through a small, mostly empty park beside a metro station. "Rhys, what am I going to do if we can't find him?"

"We're going to find him, love, I promise," I say. "Are you getting tired? Should we slow down a bit?"

Laura shakes her head. "Not until we find him. Poor kid could've been taken—he could've gotten on one of those buses that almost ran you over—"

"Stop," I say. "Stop thinking like that. Just focus on finding him. He's a little kid who, like most kids, probably doesn't get out of his neighborhood very often. He's around here somewhere, and we're going to find him."

I blink the sweat out of my eyes and keep going.

Finally, after what feels like an adrenaline-induced eternity, we get a lead. A woman we stop on the sidewalk tells us to check out the little off-license, Alfonso's Liquor Store, just down the street. It's a high traffic area right near Santa Caterina, and she promises that if anyone has seen Miguel, it will be someone near that store.

We head in that direction and find a rickety building that the GPS on my phone tells me is Alfonso's. A man, gaunt and unshaven, stands on the side of the building, puffing on the stub of a cigarette. His fingernails are long and caked with grime. There's an aluminum lawn chair set up on the sidewalk beside him, and a jug of red wine that's almost empty.

The pounding of my heart slows, just a little. I like the look of this guy. He reminds me of Jake, one of the bums who lived on a bench in the park just down the street from my house. He was very friendly and had this awesome, booming belly laugh that you could hear five blocks away. He also bought my mates and me malt liquor from the petrol station, which could explain my fondness for him.

"Hola, señor," I say. "Como está?" *Hello sir, how are you?*

He smiles at Laura and me as we approach, one eye squinted shut against the smoke that curls from between his fingers. He's missing a few teeth.

Looking for someone? he asks in Spanish.

I smile back. I knew we came to the right place. *Yes,* I reply. *We're looking for a little boy, about this tall, six years old. He took off from the school just down the block here about half an hour ago. We think he might have come this way. Have you seen him?*

The man's dark brown eyes move from me to Laura. They soften.

Miguelito, he says. *That little rascal is always running loose around here.*

My chest contracts. Laura told me Miguel ran to find his parents, not to get away from them. I hope that's true. I hope he's not running from home. It's the worst sort of loneliness, that feeling. I'm not sure if it ever really goes away.

"Yes," Laura breathes. She slumps against me in relief. "Yes, that's him. Thank God."

Can you show us where he is? I ask.

The man stubs out his cigarette with the threadbare toe of his trainer.

Follow me, he says, waving his fingers at us. *We must go slowly, or he will run again. He is very skittish and does not like to be surprised. This way, it's just up the hill here.*

"Gracias," I say. "Muchas gracias, señor. Como se llama?" *Thank you very much. What is your name?*

The man glances back at me, a look of confusion in his eyes.

My name?

Yes, I reply. *Your name.*

He smiles again. *Fernando,* he says.

"Rhys," I reply, and hold out my hand.

He looks at it for a beat before he takes it in his own.

"Mucho gusto, Fernando," I say. *Nice to meet you.*

I turn to see Laura smiling at the two of us. Her eyes, still wet, glisten like pools in the late afternoon sun. Oh, that smile.

We follow Fernando's shuffle around the off-license and begin the climb up the next block. Laura grabs my hand, the same one I offered to Fernando, and gives it a quick squeeze. I squeeze back.

A few times I could swear I hear footsteps behind us. I glance back once, twice, but there's no one there. I obviously didn't tip off the paparazzi that I'd be out and about today, but that doesn't mean they're not lurking about. Often they'll wait outside the car park at our training facility and take photos of us coming and going in our cars. I don't remember seeing any earlier today, but if photographers were there, they would've seen me leave early to go to physical therapy.

Fernando stops in front of a sagging apartment building.

There are bars on the windows and a dog barks, loud and insistent. He points to a dark hall that cuts through the center of the building. I duck my head to get a better view. A narrow staircase leads up to . . . I can't tell what it leads to. It's dark in there. Really dark.

Up there, Fernando says quietly. *Third door to the left. It's his mother's old apartment. He doesn't know she left.*

"Thank you," Laura says, tearful again.

Gracias, I translate. Fernando offers us a smile, and then he begins to shuffle back down the hill. Laura's already on the bottom step, hand on the baluster.

"Wait," I say, taking her by the arm. "Let me go first. I'm worried we'll startle him if we both go up. I'll call down if I need you, all right?"

"Really?" She looks at me. "You really want to do this?"

"I do." I glance up into the darkness. "I have a pretty good idea how that little man is feeling right now. I think I can help."

Laura blinks, like she's not quite sure what to say.

"What?" I ask, grinning. "Are you surprised?"

"No," she says. "A week ago, maybe. But now? Now, I'm not surprised at all. And that's a wonderful fucking thing."

I hold a finger to my mouth in mock censure. "Love, your mouth! There are children here."

"Sorry," she says, wrinkling her nose as she grins too.

I move up the steps as quickly as I can without making too much noise. I turn on my phone's flashlight and hold it up, slowing my pace as I reach the top steps.

I hear a hiccup, followed by a sniffle, to my right.

I let out a silent breath of relief.

He's here.

"Miguel," I call out, softly. *Miguel, it's me, your friend Mister Maddox. We played soccer together last week, remember?*

The sniffling stops. My flashlight catches on a pair of little grey trainers. I point it down and see Miguel huddled against a door, no jacket, a thick green river of snot snaking from his nose. Poor little man.

I reach for him, but he backs up against the door and starts to cry.

I look down at my mobile in my hand. I turn it around, so the flashlight is pointed toward me and not him. I blink at the sudden onslaught of fluorescent light.

It's me, I try again. *Remember me, Miguel? My name is Rhys Maddox. We scored a goal together on the playground.*

Miguel sniffs. *No way, Mr. Maddox,* he says. *I scored that goal, not you. So we didn't do it together.*

I bite back a laugh. *You're right. You're a much better player than I am.*

Thank you, he replies. *I think so too.*

Would you like to play again today?

Another sniffle. *Will you be there?*

Of course.

He lets out a breath. I turn the flashlight toward him, just a little. *Okay,* he says.

And then he gets up and takes the hand I hold out to him. His fingers are sticky, probably from the snot. I smile.

I miss my mom, he says as we make our way down the stairs.

I know, I say. *She misses you too. Tell me about her.*

We walk. Miguel chats. I meet Laura's eyes over his head. She looks exhausted, and relieved, and so beautiful I can't bear it. I can't bear to keep how I feel inside any longer.

I love you, I mouth to her.

She blinks, her features moving into an expression I can't read. My heart skips a beat. Is it too soon? Am I coming on too strong? I knew telling her the things she knew I felt would be a risk. Things between us are still somewhat fragile, the university hasn't approved Laura's application to stay yet, and I know she's disappointed to miss out on the opportunity to TA for that professor she admires so much back at Meryton. She's got several very good reasons to tuck tail and run.

I don't want to give her another by making her feel weird, or pressured. I know Laura feels *something* for me, something stronger than *like*. The girl's offered to stay another semester in Spain with me, for Christ's sake. But I don't know if she's in love with me yet. Not the way I'm in love with her.

I wait for what feels like an eternity for her to say something.

Her eyes flick to her feet.

Chapter Twenty-Six

LAURA

I don't know why I'm so taken aback—I knew this was coming, Rhys almost said it that night in Olivier's drug-lord bathroom—but for several beats I just stare back at him, too dumfounded, or maybe too tired, to reply. My feet are killing me and my lungs are weirdly sore, like they're muscles I've torn working out.

Maybe I just don't have the mental or emotional capacity to process this right now. Rhys really has been Prince Charming today, charging in on his white steed (or black Lamborghini) to save his lady love from her self-afflicted distress. I never would've found Miguel without him.

I feel a lot of things for Rhys. All of them are good and strong and overwhelming, as all things Rhys-related tend to be.

I look at him. He looks at me.

I open my mouth at the exact moment Nuria's cry of relief pierces the air. I blink, realizing we're back at Santa Caterina. Teachers and cops and parents are running toward the fence, motioning us closer.

I offer Rhys a smile before the crowd swallows us. Miguel bursts into tears.

So do I.

Rhys

Later That Night

Laura collapses into the passenger seat of my car with an exhausted *oompf*. I close the door behind her and make my way to the driver's side, waving at Nuria over my shoulder as she locks up Santa Caterina for the night.

I climb into the car and take Laura's hand. She's crying a little, sniffling. She turns her head on the headrest to look at me—really look at me—for the first time since I told her I loved her.

"Thank you," she says. "For everything. You were really great tonight."

"And you're really exhausted." I pull out into the street. "But do you mind if we make a quick stop? I'd like to grab something for a friend. I promise it won't take more than five minutes."

"Not at all," Laura says. "Which friend is this?"

"Fernando," I say.

I get what I need, and a few minutes later, I climb out of the car with a bottle wrapped in brown paper in my hand and another baggie tucked beneath my arm. I glance one way down the street, then the other. It's empty. Still, the hair on the nape of my neck prickles to life.

I'm probably just being paranoid. But I feel like someone is following me. Watching me, maybe. I've felt like this all afternoon. It's a familiar enough sensation, I know it well. I usually like the attention, welcome it even. So do my sponsors. The paparazzi love catching me in the act almost as much as I love being caught.

However.

Being caught with a bottle of wine in my hand while hanging out on the street with a guy like Fernando would not be a good thing. Not for my relationships with my sponsors, not for my career, and definitely not for my club. My dad was caught in similarly compromising circumstances the night before a match, and those pictures marked the end of his football career.

Granted, I'm not an alcoholic like he was. But the press only needs to catch you doing something stupid once, and all of the sudden you've got a giant problem on your hands. The media can spin the truth however they want. They can spin it into an outright lie, easily, if it means more money for them. After all, misery is their biggest moneymaker.

I glance down the street again. Nothing but quiet, patient darkness. Yeah, I'm totally being paranoid. I'm also freezing, so the sooner I can wrap this up, the better.

Laura rolls down the window. "You okay? Want me to come with you?"

"No," I say, shaking my head. "No, it's fine. I thought— well. Never mind. I'll be right back."

Fernando is just where we left him earlier this afternoon. He's bundled in a mound of blankets and a faded red puffer coat. His spot on the sidewalk is thrown into dim relief by the light of a streetlamp. He's sitting in his chair, holding the blistered remains of a cigarette butt to his mouth.

"Rhys!" His eyes widen with recognition as I approach. *Did you find Miguelito?*

We did, I reply in Spanish. *Right where you said he'd be. Thank you very much for your help, Fernando.*

"De nada," he replies with a grin. *You're welcome.*

I hold out the bottle and the bag. *A gift, for your help today.*

You really saved our asses, and we can't thank you enough. I saw your jug was emptier earlier, so I got you some wine. Here's a bocadillo too —ham and cheese. Looked good.

Still holding the cigarette butt, Fernando reaches out slowly. He wraps his fingers around the bottle, the paper crinkling beneath his grasp. I probably shouldn't be supporting this guy's alcohol habit, but it just felt like the right thing to do. Plus, the boccadillo, or Spanish sandwich, will help soak some of the wine up. Right?

Right.

Thank you, he says. *Thank you very much, Rhys.*

I meet his eyes. *Do you have a place to stay tonight?*

Right here. He pats his chair. Dropping the cigarette, he twists off the screw top on the bottle of wine (I thought it was safe to assume the guy didn't own a corkscrew). *This is my place. Has been for years.*

I huddle further down into my coat. *But it's really cold tonight. You should go someplace that has heat.*

Fernando holds up the bottle. *This will keep me warm enough. Salud.*

Salud, I reply. It's the Spanish version of *cheers.* Laura and her girlfriends say it practically every time they have a sip of red wine.

I wait for Fernando to drink, but instead he holds the bottle out to me.

Drink with me, he says. *It would be an honor.*

I grin. With a match coming up, I shouldn't drink. But a swig or two won't hurt, and I know it will make Fernando's night.

So I take the bottle, still wrapped in paper, and hold it up. *Salud, Fernando.*

I take a quick sip. It's decent wine—the best bottle Alfonso's Liquor had—and even just drinking that little bit makes a zing of warmth move through me.

Behind me, I hear the electric *whizz* of Laura's window rolling down again.

"Are you two having fun without me?" she asks, smiling. Never in a million years did I think I'd be drinking wine on the street in a bad neighborhood, the three of us—me, Laura, Fernando—laughing together. But here we are, and I wouldn't trade this moment for the whole goddamn world.

I turn around, a shit-eating smile on my face, and hold the bottle of up.

"Salud!" I say.

And then I'm blinded by a camera flash.

The click of cameras going off fills the air as my heart plummets into an icy pit. I blink, fluorescent streaks painting the backs of my closed eyelids like graffiti. A sharp blade of pain slices through my head.

Fuck.

There, standing on the sidewalk across the street, is the lady from the newspaper stand—the one who burst into tears earlier today when Laura and I asked her if she'd seen Miguel. It appears she brought half the neighborhood with her—kids, teenage girls, old men—along with a gaggle of paparazzi. They're greedily snapping pictures of me as I stand here like a complete idiot with my dick in my hand.

Only it's not my dick I'm holding. It would be better if it were. But it's a bottle—a bottle wrapped sketchily in brown paper.

My heart stops beating altogether. *I've just been caught passing a bottle of bum wine back and forth with a nice but rough looking homeless dude.*

My father was photographed several times in similarly compromising circumstances. Those pictures put the nail in his coffin. Everyone was hoping he'd turn his game around, but when the pictures became public, he was ruined. He was finally, truly outed for the addict that he'd become. There was no saving him after that. He was dropped by the team. No one ever heard of him again, except for the occasional sob story in the tabloids.

How careful I've been up to this point to protect my image, my reputation. So goddamn careful. Years' worth of work and planning and building relationships that could be gone in the literal blink of an eye.

I take a deep breath, let it out. *Keep calm*, I tell myself. No need to panic. Not yet. I've been playing really well, paying my dues at the club. No matter how the press portrays me, no matter how they spin this, my team and my coach will know the truth. William Wallace knows I'm not an alcoholic. He won't sack me over something as small and stupid as this.

Only, being caught with a bottle in my hand the night before a match isn't small. It's big. It's a big deal. It states clearly in my endorsement contracts that my sponsors can drop me at any time for engaging in behaviors that could potentially tarnish their reputations. And this behavior the press thinks I'm engaging in right now, trolling around a bad neighborhood with a bottle in my hand—well, it definitely doesn't look good.

I swallow the panic that fills my chest and threatens to strangle me. I knew I was being followed. I was an idiot not to act on that suspicion. Not to be more careful.

Keep calm.

"What is you doing there in a street?" someone calls out in badly mangled English.

What are you doing with him? someone else says, clearly referring to Fernando.

You shouldn't be drinking before a match! You'll be following in your father's footsteps before long!

You're so handsome!

You're not as good as they say you are!

I look back at Fernando, my mind a white-hot blank. He

meets my gaze, his eyes darkening in confusion. I have no idea what to do.

"Keep breathing."

I look up at the sound of Laura's voice. She's climbed out of the car and is making her way toward me.

"Just keep breathing," she says, putting a hand on my arm. "It's going to be okay, Rhys."

My heart slows its staccato death sprint, just a bit.

The paparazzi are getting more aggressive, approaching us on the street. A couple of them call out to Laura, taunting her, and it's all I can do not to grab their cameras so I can punch them in their smug faces.

"We should really get out of here," she murmurs.

I press the bottle back into Fernando's hand.

Sorry about all this, I murmur, nodding at the growing crowd. *I have to go.*

He looks at me. *Who are you?*

Figures I would meet the only grown man in Spain who doesn't know a thing about football. Not that I blame the guy —I mean, he can't exactly flop down on the couch and watch a match or two on the weekends.

I already told you, I say. I dig my wallet out of my pocket. I don't have much cash on me, but it should be enough for a few nights at a hotel at least—or a months' supply of wine. *I'm Rhys. And this is for you. Stay warm tonight. Thank you, Fernando.*

I'm about to take my coat off so I can offer it to him, but the crowd is pressing in on us, and someone jabs an elbow into my gut, knocking the wind out of me.

"Let's go," Laura grunts, tugging me toward the car.

I loop an arm protectively across my middle. We make it a few yards before my trainer catches on a broken piece of pavement. I lurch forward, cursing as Laura struggles to help me to my feet. As if this situation could look any worse—

now I'm stumbling around like I really am pissed out of my mind.

All the while, the *click click click* of cameras surrounds us. A cigarette hangs from a nearby paparazzo's mouth. The acrid smell stings my nostrils.

"Please," I straighten as best I can. I blink, remembering to speak in Spanish. *Please, everyone, give us our privacy. I'm helping my girlfriend with the kids she's teaching at Santa Caterina, just down the street here—*

Bullshit, someone hisses. *You're here getting drunk. Just look at you! You can hardly stand up.*

Laura and I exchange a glance. Her calm confidence wavers, her eyes brightening with fear.

"We should just go," she says.

"All right," I say. I try to hold Laura close to me. I want to protect her from the crowd that presses in on us from all sides. But my ribs still ache every time I take a breath, making me double over in pain. Laura ends up holding me as we scurry for my car.

We're almost there when we stumble head first into the lady from the newspaper stand. She's obviously a fan—I mean, she cried tears of joy when she saw me—so I don't want to be rude. I'm sure she didn't mean to cause me or Laura any harm. But I'm still mad as hell that she put this little circus together, and forced me into such a shitty situation.

How did you find me? I ask her in clipped, urgent Spanish.

The woman points eagerly at my Lamborghini. *Easy enough when you're driving a big fancy car like that. I've never seen one of those before, except on TV! Khloe and Lamar used to have one, but I think theirs was white.*

Of course it'd be my own ridiculousness that screws me. Maybe Laura was on to something with that moped idea of hers. Probably much easier to blend in when you're on a tiny little motorbike, even if it *is* pink.

I nod at the paparazzi. *And them? Did you bring them with you too?*

I work at a newspaper stand, she replies with a shrug. *I have my contacts in the media.*

I give her a look.

Fine, she says at last. *I called my uncle—he owns my stand—and he called our distributor, who called one of his papers, who called their lifestyle editor, who called a couple of his photographer friends. I didn't think quite so many would come. A few of them said you left training early today.*

Laura shoves me into the car before I say something I'll regret and climbs in after me. I bring my foot down hard on the gas pedal. The tires screech as I make a sharp turn to the left. Even though we're out of sight from the crowd, I sit stiffly in my seat, afraid to so much as blink should my invisible audience snap a photo of me with my eyes closed. They'll say I looked drunk behind the wheel, half asleep.

I'm in trouble.

I know, deep down I *know*, it doesn't matter what the truth is. It's all about how the situation looks, how the story can be spun to sell more papers and get more clicks.

I almost jump when my phone starts to ring.

Laura glances at me.

I lift my hips and dig the phone out of my pocket.

It's George Cormier, my contact at the champagne company I did those billboards for. Oh, Jesus. The fact that George is calling me—I glance at the dashboard, it's a little past 9 P.M.— on a night before a match is a really, *really* bad sign.

Sponsors like playboys. They tolerate divas. But they have absolutely no use for deadbeats. They don't want the guy caught guzzling liquor on the street to be the face of their company.

Holy fuck I am going to lose my sponsors. I'm going to lose followers. If I lose those things, I'm also going to lose a lot—a *lot*—of money. This is bloody perfect timing. Mags just got into Oxford, Rachel had her baby and can't pay her bills, Mum found a house she liked in a nice neighborhood in Cardiff . . . how am I going to pay *my* bills now? My publicist will be working over time to fix this, and my agent is going to go apeshit . . .

"Who is it?" Laura asks.

"No one," I clip. "Don't worry about it."

My pulse thrums in my temples as I let the call go to voicemail. When the voicemail pops up, I listen to it.

George says he saw a post on Facebook about me that his "organization finds deeply troubling." He wants a call back ASAP.

Fuck. I am so beyond fucked.

"Rhys," Laura says. "Is everything all right?"

"It's fine," I say, putting my phone on silent before tossing it onto the dash. Of course things aren't all right, but I don't want to freak her out, not after the day she's had.

"This is all my fault," she says. "If I hadn't lost Miguel—if you hadn't come to help me—"

"Seriously." It comes out more sharply than I intend. "It's fine. It's not your fault. I'll deal with it."

Chapter Twenty-Seven

RHYS

The Next Day

I should spend the morning getting mentally prepared for today's match, but instead I spend it pacing about my flat, fielding calls from my publicist, Cristina, my agent, my coaches, and pretty much all my sponsors. I hardly slept, too preoccupied with trolling the internet for any photos from last night that may have leaked.

We've been lucky so far. Cristina managed to keep the photos out of the bigger papers and gossip sites. They've only popped up on a few personal Facebook pages and blogs, which is how my sponsors saw them.

Still. Those sponsors are more than a little concerned. The sports drink sponsor wanted to drop me straightaway, but my agent worked his negotiating magic and promised it was all just a misunderstanding. They responded by saying I'd better prove it by playing well tonight.

I'm not only worried about losing the endorsement deals I currently have. I'm also worried about losing future ones. If this story catches steam I'll be a pariah, and sponsors won't want to touch me with a ten-foot pole. I can kiss my dreams of a giant endorsement deal that would sustain me and my family forever goodbye.

By the time I board the team's flight to Seville, I'm so tired and so stressed I'm practically shaking. I need to play well tonight. If I do, it might make the story go away—good headlines replacing bad ones, that sort of thing.

I try to get some sleep, but the flight is really bumpy. Some of the lads handle it better than others. Olivier calmly reads *Harry Potter and The Cursed Child*, apparently the newest book in the series (I know, I know, you'd think he'd be reading French philosophers for all his airs, but our captain is diehard Quidditch fan—he's serious when he says he wishes it were real, and may or may not have invested six figures in a development company somewhere in Northumberland that claims to have made a flying broom prototype), while poor Fred loses his lunch all over his lap and, of course, mine too, because this day obviously hasn't been awful enough. I told him to have his barf bag ready, but the wanker swore he was fine . . . until he wasn't.

Coach is understandably angry with me about everything that happened yesterday, and spends the entire flight calling me a "small-dick clawbaw" while hanging onto the hand rests for dear life. Of course he doesn't believe the press, but the whole thing *is* an inconvenience, and a distraction for the squad besides.

Sometimes travel is the best part of this job. Other times, it's the fucking worst.

Today is one of those times.

I thought the weird feeling in my stomach was just queasiness from the flight, maybe some leftover nerves from dealing with the leaked photos. But as our rain-drenched bus pulls into the stadium, it gets worse. I try to calm down, focus on the match, but I can't. I'm in too much pain.

"You all right, Cabbage?" Fred asks as we make our way to

the locker room. We walk stiffly in our suits, still wet from all the club soda we used to clean ourselves up. My entire left leg feels tight—bad knee included—and not for the first time today do I wish I could've made it to the physio yesterday. "You look like I did twenty minutes ago."

"How's that?"

"Like you're about to vomit all over yourself."

"Maybe I'll get lucky and vomit all over you. Repay the favor."

Fred has the decency to blush. "Sorry about that. I really did think I was going to be fine. It just came up so . . . fast."

"I know. I was there," I say, trying not to wince as the knot in my stomach tightens. I feel like it's trying to tell me something. "Did you really have to eat fish for lunch?"

"I did." He grins. "Best protein on the planet."

Olivier sidles up beside me, tucking his book underneath his arm.

"How's Ron Weasley these days?" I ask.

"In trouble," Olivier replies. "Always, always in ze trouble, but Hermoine, she save 'im, every time."

"Hermoine is so badass," Fred says.

"Tell me about it," Olivier replies. He turns to me. "And you, petit chou—'ow goes your little problem with ze photographs?"

"It's fine," I lie, mostly because I don't feel like talking about it anymore.

As I go through the familiar motions of getting dressed for a match, I feel better for about three minutes. But then, as I'm lacing up my boots, the knot in my gut returns with a vengeance. Maybe it's the rain that has me feeling so off kilter? I have one of the physios take my temperature, just to be sure it's not some sort of bug, but all my vitals check out.

I'm starting to think I just have a bad feeling about tonight. Something bad is going to happen during the match.

But what can I do? I've got to play. I've got to make sure this story is replaced by the story of me slaying it tonight on the pitch.

But the superstitious footballer in me won't let it rest. It doesn't help that Laura isn't traveling with me tonight—she had to stay back in Madrid to study.

As we wait to go out on the pitch, I take a deep breath, let it out. Usually that helps, but it doesn't tonight. I look up at the muffled roar of the crowd as the lads start making their entrance in the pouring rain. I close my eyes, and pray that I'm wrong.

Laura

The bar erupts in shouts and curses when Rhys, sliding on the muddy field, loses the ball to an opposing defender for the third time tonight. My eyes are glued to the enormous television on a nearby wall. I nervously sip my beer. The taste of it turns my stomach.

I couldn't travel to Seville with Rhys because I've been working on the upcoming auction for Santa Caterina like a madwoman, first of all, and second of all I have a final on Monday. My study group is meeting up this weekend for some much-needed cramming. Even though I couldn't be at the match, I still wanted to watch the game at a bar, mostly to take my mind off what happened last night, maybe have a little fun.

But so far, with Rhys playing as badly as he is, I wouldn't exactly describe tonight as *fun*. Excruciating is probably a better word. Especially knowing that Rhys's awful performance doesn't bother anyone more than Rhys himself. My heart aches for him. This sport, these fans—it all means so much to him, and I know he thinks he's letting Madrid down.

He thinks he's letting everyone down. And no matter his assurances to the contrary, I can't help but feel that it's *my* fault he's struggling out there tonight. *I'm* the one who caused him to miss his physical therapy appointment. *I'm* to blame for the awful photographs the paparazzi took of Rhys and Fernando. Rhys would've never been at Santa Caterina—he would've never even met Fernando—if it wasn't for my own fuck-up that afternoon. Granted, the photos haven't surfaced on any of the major news or gossip outlets. Cristina, Rhys's publicist, said tonight's match is garnering so much media coverage no one's really paying attention to this little piece of chatter. But there's no doubt in my mind that the situation is distracting Rhys. It's keeping him from playing his best football.

He was only trying to do the right thing by helping me out. And now his play is suffering for it. What's that old saying? No good deed goes unpunished? It's so freaking true.

"Oh, Rhys," I murmur, swallowing the tightness in my throat. I wish I were there with him. It'd make him feel better, knowing I was there in the crowd. It'd make me feel better too, because right now I feel pretty damn awful.

"You okay there, friend?" Maddie asks. She drapes an arm across the back of my bar stool.

"Meh," I say.

"Right," she says. "I'll get you another beer."

The camera pans across the pitch after an opposing player tackles Rhys, leaving him sprawled out on the grass. Like any good footballer worth his salt, Rhys milks the moment for all it's worth. He clutches his middle and rolls around, face scrunched up in Oscar-worthy agony—agony that suddenly disappears when Fred Ohr pulls him to his feet.

Now the camera is following Rhys as he trots to the sideline. Rain pours down his face into his eyes. His wet uniform, marred by grass stains, clings uncomfortably to his body. He keeps tugging at it. He looks tired. Worn out.

Angry. Probably with himself, but I wouldn't blame him if he were angry with me too.

By the seventy minute mark, Madrid is losing badly—we're down four goals to zero. The crowd packed into the bar is angry, almost violent in their disgust for their home team. As an American, this kind of passionate fandom shocked me when I first arrived in Madrid. Spaniards are really into their football. Like, *really*. I thought American football fans back home were rabid, but they don't hold a candle to Madrileños. Their devotion to Rhys's team is nothing short of fanatical.

Around me they curse, they call Rhys names, they cast hexes on his mother. People hold their hands to their heads in bewilderment, eyes wide and wild. For the horror on their faces, you'd think half their city had just been destroyed in a terrorist bombing. I don't know whether to laugh or cry.

I chug my beer instead. Madrid—these fans—they're going to crucify Rhys tomorrow. The whole team is playing badly, but it's clear Rhys's black mood is infecting the guys he plays with. Sure, Olivier is the captain. But Rhys is the guy other players watch and draw energy from. He sets the tone for the match, whether he means to or not.

Behind me, Rachel squeezes my shoulder.

"So Rhys has one bad game," she says. "He plays, what, two hundred games a year?"

"A little less than that," I say. "Actually way less."

"Whatever. The point is, he plays fucking unbelievable football ninety-nine percent of the time. He's going to have an off game or two every once in a while. All those guys have to."

"I know," I say. "It's just so painful to watch. I feel bad for him." *I feel like it's my fault he isn't playing his best.*

At the eighty-seven minute mark, Seville shoots an errant pass that soars over the intended midfielder's head. Spotting an opportunity, Rhys makes a mad dash down the pitch. With my heart in my throat, I watch as he races an opposing defender toward the ball, the two of them neck and neck. The bar goes wild, erupting in whistles, cheers, fervent prayers to the Holy Mother.

This is it. I know this is going to be it, the game changing play.

"Come on," I shout, leaping from my stool. "Come on, Rhys!"

At the last minute, the defender takes the lead, and darts out in front of Rhys. Rhys, recognizing he's on a crash course with an enormous defender, draws up short to try and zigzag his way around him. But because the field is so wet, he ends up slipping. His left leg—oh, oh, Jesus, his bad knee—jams to the side. Half a heartbeat later, Rhys's leg goes out from under him.

My glass lands on the bar with a loud clatter, beer spewing everywhere. My palm flies to my mouth. I'm going to be sick.

He falls to the ground, the momentum of his body sending him tumbling across the pitch. Watching him succumb to the viciousness of his fall makes me feel like dying.

The camera zooms in on him when he finally comes to a stop. He rolls slowly onto his side and clutches his knee in both hands. Then he is still, deadly still, no rolling this time, no drama.

Two seconds later, he starts screaming. So do the people around me in the bar, but I don't hear them. The place between my skin and bones rushes cold. I can't think. I can't breathe. I can only feel the panic that squeezes the air and the blood and the lightness from my body.

He's hurt. His knee—the ACL he's worked so hard to rehab

—oh my God, it's all my fault, it's my fault he missed his appointment with the physical therapist—

Medics and physios rush out onto the field, surrounding Rhys. He isn't getting up. The camera shows a close-up of Olivier's face. He's crying.

Oh my God.

Chapter Twenty-Eight

RHYS

The Next Day
Madrid

I fly home that night and have an MRI first thing the next morning. The whole ordeal is so sickeningly familiar—the needle injecting blue dye into my veins, the sci-fi roar of the machine—that I can't even pretend to be friendly with the nice nurses who look after me.

Laura completely ignored my instructions to get some sleep so she could make her study group later this afternoon. She came with me to the hospital, and pressed a kiss into my cheek before I went in. As lovely as gesture as it is, I'm a bit annoyed by it. I'd like a little space to figure out how the hell I'm going to deal with this shit. My life is falling apart, and I don't want my problems making Laura fall apart too. I care for her, obviously, but I've also got a care for my family. And right now I really need to focus on keeping it together for their sake.

It feels like an eternity before I'm done and back in my clothes and out of the hospital. It's a beautiful day outside, but the ardent sun and crystal clear sky only make me that much more anxious. I don't know whether to hope for good news or resign myself to the fact that it's probably not going to be good at all. I don't know which one will help me more, or hurt less. Worry consumes me to the point that it literally makes me sweat.

What the hell am I going to do if I blew my knee out again? I'm already at risk of losing my sponsors and all the income they bring me. If I lose my football contract too, I will literally have nothing. I'll have no money, no friends, no purpose. I'll have to break the news to my family that we're back to square one. I'll be just like Dad.

I'm jittery, like I've had too much coffee. My stomach hurts, and holy hell so does my knee.

A driver is waiting for Laura and me on the corner. It's still early—just past seven—and the streets are deserted. We're heading to the team training facility, where I'll wait for the MRI results with William Wallace, a couple physios, and Olivier and Fred.

I try not to limp too badly as Laura and I make our way to the car. Cristina made sure we weren't followed to the hospital, but with such a giant story breaking, there's a chance the hospital staff took it upon themselves to tip off the press that I was here.

With my free hand I grab my mobile from my back pocket. I notice something strange right away. I have six missed calls from Cristina, three from Coach, and three more from Olivier. All this before eight AM? Surely they're not checking on me—my results won't be in for another couple of hours, and they all know that.

My heart skips a beat. Something's up. I have a sinking feeling it's got to do with those photos of Fernando and me.

"Christ," I murmur, pressing my thumb to Olivier's name.

Laura looks at me. "Everything okay?"

I'm shaking, so when I put the call through I accidentally put it on speaker. I'm too anxious to change it back.

Olivier picks up on the first ring.

"Cabbage," he breathes. "You all right?"

"Uh. Yeah, I guess so? Aside from the whole I-might've-blown-out-my-knee-again-and-ruined-my-career-forever   bit. Why? What's up?"

A pause. "You 'aven't seen it."

"Seen what?" I say.

I meet Laura's eyes. She looks scared.

"Oh, Cabbage."

"What?" I draw to a stop on the sidewalk, swallowing a wince at the bolt of pain that shoots up my leg. "Seriously, Olivier, you're starting to freak me out. What the hell is going on?"

"Ze pictures. Of you stumbling around with zat bum man. Zey 'ave been found. Zey are everywheres. Ze papers, ze internets. I am very sorry, my friend. Tell me what I can do to 'elp you. What zees animals say about you, it iz not true, not true at all. I know it iz not. But ze press, zey are your enemies now."

All the blood seems to drain from my body in a single instant, leaving me cold and light-headed. Holy. *Fuck*.

"I'll call you right back," I blurt. I hang up so I can search for the pictures on my phone, but Laura is already typing furiously on hers.

"What did you find?" I sidle up beside her and duck my head to get a closer look at her screen.

Another eternity passes while her phone loads the home page of one of Madrid's most popular, and most gossipy, newspapers.

If the pictures are here, that means they are all over the place.

The page finally appears. My eyes dart over the top story's

headline and the picture beneath it, my pulse marking an ominous beat inside my head. *No.* Please God no. My sponsors—all that money—my family—

Laura covers her mouth with her fingers. "Oh, God," she whispers. "Rhys—"

I grab the mobile from her hand. I read the headline again. It's in Spanish. Roughly translated, it says: *MADRID LOSES KEY MATCH, RHYS MADDOX'S DEMONS TO BLAME?* And then, the subtitle: *Star Player Caught Drinking Night Before Game, Insiders Say He's Following in Troubled Father's Footsteps. What this means for Madrid's league title prospects.*

The picture shows me holding up a bottle wrapped in brown paper, a shit-eating grin on my face. Fernando is beside me. He's grinning too. I tap the picture—just my bloody luck, there's a whole gallery of them—and scroll through four photos, each worse than the last. Me taking the bottle from Fernando; Fernando taking the bottle from me; Laura, holding me up while I stumble; another one of me stumbling, this time with my eyes half-open. I look wasted out of my mind, when really I was just blinded by the camera flashes.

I knew my terrible performance last night would piss a lot of people off, maybe make some headlines. But now I see that I've tripped a wire. People always whispered behind my back that I'd end up like my dad. I just didn't realize how eager they were to see me prove them right.

It's a great story to print—it's juicy and it's gossipy and it's tragic, the deadbeat drunk who let his team and his adopted country down finally getting his due, the way his father got his twenty years before. It's going to sell a ton of papers and garner millions of clicks.

Madrid fans are looking for an explanation, a way to understand our worst loss of the season. They're looking for someone to blame.

How convenient, then, that this story should surface, and

provide the perfect excuse to blame *me*. No doubt a thousand reporters and editors googled my name last night after my horrid showing at the match, searching for dirt. For something that would explain *why* I played so badly. The pictures weren't hard to find if you knew where to look.

I tug my fingers through my hair. I am such a fucking idiot. I should've known this would happen. I should've seen it coming from a mile away. I've always been careful, I've always thought about how something might look because I constantly thought about my family and everything they need and everything I want to give them.

Lately, though, I've let my guard down. And now it's come back to bite me in the ass.

I clutch the phone in my hand. Anger seeps from the center of my chest and fills my lungs, my belly, my mouth. I'm angry at myself, for letting this happen. I'm angry at the world for believing what the papers say is true.

I'm angry that I've destroyed my relationship with my sponsors. There's no doubt in my mind they'll all drop me after seeing this. They'd be stupid not to. In the blink of an eye, I just lost tens of thousands of dollars in current endorsements, and ten times that in potential future ones. It doesn't matter what I say next, if I apologize or deny the story. These images are emblazoned in the public's collective mind. This is how I'll be perceived from now on. This is who everyone thinks I am.

And who knows what my club is going to do with me. This is bad press for them too. If I did do some real damage to my knee again, and the team is on the fence about seeing me through another year of rehab, this disaster will be just the push they need to cut me and wash their hands of the Maddox men for good.

I'm losing everything. The thought of having to tell Maggie I can't afford to send her to university—the loans she'll have to take out will crush her and Mum—God, none of this was supposed to happen. This wasn't how my life was supposed to turn out. I've worked too hard. I've sacrificed too much.

This isn't fucking fair.

"It's not true," Laura says. Her voice trembles. "None of it is."

"I know that," I snap. I use every ounce of self-control to keep my voice low and even. "But what does it matter? Appearance is everything, Laura. As far as the rest of the world is concerned—everyone but you and me—as far as they're concerned, it happened. So it's bloody true."

"It's not," she says, more forcefully. She meets my eyes, squinting against the bright morning sun. "You have to tell them, Rhys. It's not true. For God's sake, you were playing soccer with a bunch of kids, not getting drunk with some strange dude on the street. You were doing a good thing. You have to explain yourself."

I step toward her. Again, a bolt of pain slices through my knee. Jesus *Christ*.

"I told you, *it doesn't fucking matter*. Haven't you listened to a word I said? The photos are everywhere. The story is out there. I'm completely screwed."

"What did Cristina say?"

"Cristina said not to speak to the press at all. If the time comes to release a statement—and I don't think it will anytime soon—then we can talk about it. Until then, we say nothing. Understand?"

Laura draws back. "Yes. Yeah, of course."

"Trust me, it'll just make things worse right now. Although I don't see how that's possible, considering things are pretty fucking bad."

"Rhys, I told you I was sorry—"

"Stop it, all right? Just stop it." I tug a hand through my

hair. My panic is getting the better of me, but now that I've let my self-control slip from my grasp, I can't get a hold of it again. I'm angry for getting angry; I'm angry that Laura is hurting too, that she thinks she's somehow responsible for this mess. I'm angry that I'm powerless to make everything okay again so she can feel better.

I'm just bloody *angry*.

"You can't give up," she says.

"I'm not giving up," I say with a scoff. "Don't you see it's already over for me? My sponsors are gone. My knee is probably gone. There's nothing I can do for my family anymore. I'm done. Washed up. Just like—"

"Don't." She meets my gaze. "Don't you dare say that. You're not like him."

"What would you know about my dad?" I burst. I'm in her face now, my heart popping around in my chest. "Nothing. You don't know anything."

The look of hurt on her face makes me even angrier.

"You don't mean that," she says. "I also know you don't mean to talk to me like this. I get you're under a lot of stress—"

I scoff again. "A lot of stress? Laura, I'm going to lose everything I have. My life is destroyed. Have you any idea how that feels?"

She looks away. After a beat, she shakes her head. "No. I don't."

I look down and shove my hands in my pockets. "Look, I'm sorry. You should probably just go. Take the car to wherever your study group is and . . . just do what you need to do."

"Rhys." The pain in her voice makes my gut contract.

"I mean it. Just go. I'll call you when I have news."

I look up. She's blinking, hard, trying not to cry.

You're being an arsehole, a voice inside my head warns. *Apologize again. Stop while you're ahead.*

But then Laura turns and climbs into the car and slams the door behind her. I close my eyes, the groan of the engine loud in my ears as the car starts moving up the street.

Maybe I really am just like my father.

Maybe I set things on fire just to watch them burn.

Chapter Twenty-Nine

LAURA

I have the driver take me back to my dorm. Tears roll down my cheeks as I watch Madrid pass by through the window, a tangle of traffic and concrete and people going about their day. I've never envied *normalcy* before—I mean, I am dating a rising soccer star who plays for one of the most famous football clubs in the world—but right now I'd give just about anything to be heading to class, or the grocery store, or the coffee shop, instead of dealing with this mess.

It feels almost too heavy to bear. Rhys's anger cut me to the bone. He's never talked to me like that. I know he's scared out of his mind and didn't mean to be such a douche, so I'm not angry with him. I'm just sad. Not until very recently did he let me in on the fact that he's basically supporting his entire extended family back in Cardiff. He's trying to care for them in a way his father never could.

Now he's staring down the barrel of losing that opportunity for good. My heart fucking hurts for him. I want to help, but I don't know how. I don't know if there's anything I can do, except be there for him if he needs me.

I need him. I love him. I can't wait to tell him how much I love him.

I grab the back of the headrest as the driver nails a sharp right. I swear to God, people in this country drive like lunatics. My stomach flips when I see a row of news vans lined up on the curb in front of my dorm building, satellite poles sticking up like unicorn horns from their roofs. A few people loiter near the front entrance of the building, phones in hand.

Oh God oh God oh God. I should've known the press would show up. They've always liked me, praising me on the red carpet and in the papers. I liked them too. But I have a feeling that's all about to change.

Please drop me off here, I say to the driver in stuttering Spanish.

Here? he asks.

Here, I say, and brace myself on the headrest again as he brakes to a sudden stop.

I put on my sunglasses. Climbing out of the taxi, I drop my phone on the sidewalk. My hand shakes as I reach down to pick it up. It's warm in the sun, but I shiver. I straighten, and look down the block at the news vans. I take another deep breath. It's too late to use the back entrance; they'll see me. I just have to push through them and not say a word. Then I can hole up in my dorm for the foreseeable future.

Reporters descend upon me like vultures on a fresh carcass. Cameras and microphones are thrust in my face. I blink at the barrage of questions, all in Spanish, my heart in my throat.

"Excuse me," I say. "Perdón."

One reporter—a good-looking guy with a swoop of dark brown hair—steps in front of me, blocking my way.

"Might I ask you a few questions about Rhys Maddox, Laura?"

It's so weird, being addressed by a total stranger like they know you. It's weird he knows my name. I guess everyone will know my name after they read the news this morning.

"No comment," I say, and keep my head down. "Please let—"

"How do you feel about Rhys's recent behavior?" the reporter asks, smoothly cutting me off. "You were there when he was caught drinking in the street the other night. Does his drinking bother you? How long has he had a drinking problem?"

Oh, Jesus, this is bad. I keep pushing, moving toward the door.

"Any word on Rhys's knee? Have you received the results from the MRI yet?" another reporter asks.

Do you know his father also had issues with drinking? one asks in Spanish.

Sweat breaks out underneath my arms. My pulse pops around in my ears, a hollow sound. I hear the door to my dorm open. *Thank God.* I dart up the steps past a tall guy with a backpack and duck through the door just before it closes.

I run to my dorm room and lock the door behind me. I close the blinds and fall onto the bed, dizzy, exhausted. I don't take off my jacket or my boots. Instead I sit very still and listen to the commotion outside my window. The reporters are shameless. They stop every student who comes and goes from the building, asking about me, what they know about Rhys and me, if they've ever seen us together.

Bile rises in my throat. My heart is pounding, making me lightheaded. For a second I think I'm going to pass out. This is bad. I don't know what to do. More than anything I want to call Rhys. He'd usually be the one to make me feel better. But he's made it clear he pretty much wants nothing to do with me right now. So, yeah.

I guess I'll call Emily. But just as I bring the phone to my ear, I hear footsteps outside my door. I freeze. There's no way the reporters followed me inside.

Is there?

I hang up and duck my head into the hall. A guy I don't recognize is hanging out by the stairwell. He's carrying a backpack, and is dressed in jeans and a jacket, very casual, very typical of students who attend my university. Still, his presents puts my teeth on edge. I don't trust him.

I go back into my room and look around. I've probably watched the *Bourne* movies one too many times, but I get the feeling someone is listening. That I'm being watched. Which is ridiculous, for a lot of reasons. The press likes me. At least I think they like me. They wouldn't invade my privacy like that, would they?

Still. I can't be too careful. Quietly, I grab my keys and my phone and a hat. I sneak down the hall—making sure the dude by the stairs doesn't see me—and I head for the back entrance to the building, where the smokers usually hang out. Thankfully the press hasn't discovered it, so no one is waiting for me in the alley. Glancing over my shoulder, I take off down a side street, careful to not make a sound as I head away from the building.

I pull the hat lower over my sunglasses. I keep walking, one block, then two, then four. I stay on busy streets where it's loud and the sidewalks are crowded. I keep an eye on my surroundings. When I'm positive that no one has followed me, I stop at a bench that overlooks a small playground. I pull my phone from my pocket.

"Laura," Emily breathes when she picks up. "Oh my God, how are you? I've been following the story here. I'm so sorry. What the hell happened?"

I push my fingers underneath my sunglasses to wipe away a tear. "Rhys is in trouble, Em. Big trouble. What the papers are saying—it's not true, but—"

"Of course it's not true. Now tell me what happened."

"So, like, you know I volunteer at an after school program —the place is called Santa Caterina?"

"I do."

"Rhys came to Santa Caterina two days ago to help me find one of my kids, Miguel—he snuck out of the playground, and I was panicking, and I called Rhys to help me find him. Rhys came right away. He was doing a good thing, Em. He was helping me out. The man in the picture, the homeless one, he helped us find the kid, and to thank him, Rhys gave him a bottle of wine and some money."

"How did the paparazzi end up there? You told me he's tipped them off in the past."

I look up as a woman in an expensive trench coat passes by. I wait until she rounds the corner to answer Em's question.

"I mean, a couple months ago, I wouldn't put it past Rhys to give the paparazzi a tip that he'd be doing some charity work—you know, so he could turn it into a photo op or whatever. But he isn't like that anymore. He definitely didn't call them—some lady who runs a newspaper stand in the neighborhood did. He wasn't drunk. He was just trying to help this homeless guy out. And because the photographers caught him giving this guy a drink, they're all saying that Rhys is a drunk, just like his father. It's so fucked up."

"His dad is an alcoholic? I didn't know that."

"I didn't either, not until about a week ago. The papers are making a field day of the fact that Rhys is predisposed to the disease. Which is true, I guess. But everything else isn't. And now all his sponsors are dropping him . . . it's a fucking mess. He's a fucking mess—"

Something taps me on my shoulder. I almost jump. My blood rushes cold. Oh, Jesus, no.

I turn around, slowly, to see the reporter with the brown hair hovering right beside me, holding up his phone.

He's recording me.

Holy shit.

He's *recording me*. That isn't allowed, is it? I don't know. This can't be happening. How the hell did this guy find me?

The way these guys can spin a story, the way they can take your words and twist them—

"What the hell!" I rise to my feet. "You can't do that! Turn it off! Turn that thing off right now, or I'll call the police."

"So," he says, ignoring my protests, "you're saying Rhys used your charity work as a way to boost his own reputation. What an awful, selfish thing for him to do, don't you think?"

I just stare at him. I know better than to talk to him. He's egging me on, trying to get a rise out of me. But I won't take the bait.

I hear Emily shouting for me on my phone. I hang up and put the phone in my pocket and start walking away. My steps are uneven, and I'm worried I'm going to trip and fall.

"Here you are," the reporter says, trotting beside me, "volunteering your time to help kids in Madrid's toughest neighborhood, and Rhys is stumbling around, getting drunk and doing drugs with hobos."

I grit my teeth. It takes every ounce of self-control not to tell this guy off. The lies he's spinning are so egregious, they make me so angry, that I press my fingernails into my palms to keep from shouting at him. Cristina said no talking to the press under any circumstances, and I'm not about to disobey her.

Then again, maybe I already have without meaning to.

Shit.

I start running. He runs after me. I hail the first cab I see and practically throw myself into the backseat. I'm shaking.

When I don't immediately say where I'm going, the driver asks. I tell him to just drive, please, just get me out of here.

He slams on the gas. Slinking low in the seat, I glance out the back window. The reporter is still on the sidewalk. He's on his phone, smiling.

My stomach turns to a block of ice. I have a really bad feeling about what just happened. I don't know if what that reporter just did is legal. I *do* know it will thicken an already juicy plot. Papers and gossip sites will pay big bucks for what he just recorded.

I call Rhys, choking back tears as I wait for him to answer.

He doesn't even say hello when he picks up.

"Laura, I told you I'd call you when the results are in."

"Rhys, that's not what I'm calling about." I swallow. "Listen, something just happened—"

"I have to go. Cristina is here, and she's waiting for me."

"But that's exactly what I'm calling you about. Are—"

"I don't have time for this right now. I'm hanging up."

"Rhys, just *listen*, please!"

"Christ, Laura, I have to go, all right? I'll call you when we're done."

He makes good on his threat and hangs up on me. My eyes swim with tears as I stare at my phone. The screen goes blank. I understand that he's on edge today, but he's really treating me like shit.

I take a deep breath. Whether or not Rhys wants to talk to me, he has to know about this. Cristina has to head it off before things get *really* bad.

I tell the driver to take me to the football club's training facility.

Rhys

I almost jump when I hear Cristina curse. She's sitting in one of the training facility's stiff pleather chairs beside me, a Blackberry clutched in one hand and an iPhone in the other. Cristina never curses. This can't be good.

"What?" I ask, the muscles in my shoulders tightening. "Cristina, what is it?"

She spears me with a look of such heated censure I lean back in my chair. "I told you Laura is not to speak to the press."

"Yeah," I say. "Of course. I told her that. She knows."

"Then why did *Nuestro Día* just post an audio clip of her saying you're a drunk on their website?"

My stomach dips.

"What?" I ask weakly.

She holds out her mobile. "Listen for yourself. Apparently this was recorded today."

I take it. My stomach dips again. I press turn up the volume and press play

I wouldn't put it past Rhys to give the paparazzi a tip that he'd be doing some charity work—you know, so he could turn it into a photo op.

Rhys is a drunk, just like his father.

All his sponsors are dropping him . . . it's a [bleep] mess. He's a [bleep] mess.

What the *what*? This doesn't make sense. Laura would never say these things about me. Yeah, I was a dick to her before. But she's not vindictive like this. The paper is obviously twisting her words.

"*Nuestro Día* is trash," I blurt.

"Exactly," Cristina replies. "That's why everyone reads it."

"It iz true," Olivier says. "Me, I read it every day."

"Me too," Fred says. "Religiously. I gotta get my Hollywood gossip somewhere."

"And get this," Cristina says with a scoff. "The article they wrote up to go with the audio says in so many words that 'Laura Bennet is much too fine—good, much too good a woman to be with a vain, troubled man like Rhys Maddox.'"

I blink. "What the fuck? They're lying. Manipulating what she said. Laura would never say shit like that about me."

"That's not the point," Cristina says, looking me in the eye. "The point is, she's making a bad situation worse. She's confirming everyone's suspicions—she's confirming the story that you're an alcoholic and a liar and a fame whore. If anyone had doubts about the story before—if anyone still believed in you—they don't anymore. They'll think it's true. You're going to lose whatever sponsors you have left. The team . . . well. This doesn't look good for them either."

"She didn't mean it." The words sound hollow even to my own ears. "She didn't want this to happen."

Cristina leans toward me. "You're not hearing me, Rhys. What do Laura's intentions matter when she destroyed you anyway? Because that's what she just did. She destroyed you. We could've worked some magic before. But now—now that your girlfriend's coming out and saying that you're a mess? Telling the world you don't have anyone in your corner anymore? Now we don't have a chance in hell. This story is not going to go away."

It's like a blow to the gut. I run a hand down my face as the realization hits me. Before Laura's lovely little sound bite, I was going to be left with very little once the smoke cleared from this awful mess. But I was still going to be left with *something*. The chance to rebuild, rebrand, come back from the dead like I did before.

Now, thanks to Laura, I'm going to be left with nothing. I'm going to be remembered as the guy who not only lost it all, but who also *deserved* to lose it, because I have a mean, black little heart, just like my dad.

Jesus Christ. *I am going to be left with nothing.*

Not a goddamn thing. No sponsors. No popular support. No good press. No friends or money or followers.

What am I going to do? What is my family going to do? I have a little in savings, but not enough to last us very long. I could sell the flat, but with the renovation I'm probably underwater. I'd sell my car, but it isn't mine—that sponsor will probably be calling soon to take it back—Aunt Kate's daughter is in the hospital with pneumonia, and Mum says Kate isn't doing well—everyone back home will hate me—how humiliating it will be, to go back to living with Mum, everyone will talk shit behind our backs—what will my fans think? Are they even my fans anymore?

Panic and anger and helplessness seep in my chest, filling me to the point of bursting. I feel wild with it, unhinged.

"You have to stay away from Laura," Cristina says. "She's toxic to us now. No matter what she says going forward, it's only going to look like she's backpedaling—like we're twisting her arm. No one'll buy it. From now on, we have to do everything, and I mean *everything*, right. You and I both know she can't help with that."

I spear a hand through my hair. I know, in my heart of hearts I know, Laura did not throw me under the bus on purpose. But she still stole from me. She stole my dreams and my purpose. She stole my chance to make things right, to do right by my family.

And that makes me very, very angry. So angry I can't bloody see straight. No one fucks with my family. I don't think Laura would ever intentionally hurt me. But she did exactly what I asked her not to do. And by doing so, she hurt my family, and that's crossing the line. Laura knew better, and yet she was careless.

I was right to think getting involved with a girl was a mistake. Laura is not my good luck charm. She is my downfall.

I will never, ever forgive myself for believing otherwise.

I look up at the sound of footsteps. It's William Wallace. His hands are shoved in his pockets, his face is grim.

"Yer girlfriend is here," he says. "Waiting at the gate. Says she's got to see you straightaway."

I look at Cristina. She shakes her head, a small, almost imperceptible motion.

I clasp my hands and rest my elbows on my thighs. I train my gaze on the speckled linoleum floor. I've never felt this low. This lonely. This *trapped*.

"Turn her away," I say, gritting my teeth. "She's not welcome here anymore."

A beat passes, and then my phone rings. It's Laura. I ignore it.

But when I sneak off to the bathroom a little while later, I listen to the voicemail she left me.

"I'll do whatever it takes, Rhys, to make this right," she says. "Whatever you need me to do, I'll do it. I love you. I'm in love with you, Rhys, and I want to be with you. Please, please don't hate me for this. I love you."

I close my eyes, cover them with my thumb and forefinger. She's finally saying it—saying she's in love with me. But I'm way too fucking angry to trust that she's telling the truth.

It doesn't matter anyway. We're done. Over.

Chapter Thirty

LAURA

I don't remember how I got to Javier's apartment.

I remember dialing Maddie's number after leaving a tearful voicemail for Rhys as the taxi sped away from the training facility. I remember telling Maddie about the press outside my dorm room, and her telling me to come to her boyfriend Javier's apartment in Malasaña, a cool neighborhood in Madrid. I gave the driver the address, and then . . .

Then I cried my eyeballs out. Rhys refused to see me. He didn't even pick up my call. I understand why he turned me away. I completely crushed everything he's worked so hard for. I trashed his image, which means I trashed his relationships with his sponsors, which means I trashed his chance to do right by his family. Rhys really is going to lose everything, and it's all my fault.

Then, after a minute, or maybe an eternity, I don't know, I'm at Javier's apartment, and Maddie is waiting for me at the door. Like the champ he is, Javier hands us each a bottle of red wine and a wine glass and disappears into his bedroom upstairs, leaving Maddie and me alone. We sit in front of a roaring fire as I cry and Maddie listens. I cry so hard I think I'm going to be sore tomorrow from it.

I must have fallen asleep at some point, because the next thing I know I wake up with a pounding headache and a dry mouth. My cheek, smeared with drool (lovely), is stuck to Javier's leather couch. It's dark and the apartment is quiet.

For half a heartbeat, I forget where I am, or why I'm here. I blink once, twice, and then it hits me so hard—the horrible-ness of it all, the disastrous game, Rhys's knee, the reporter recording me—I have the wind knocked out of me.

Rhys. He's gone. He turned me away.

A familiar warmth floods my eyes. Fear and self-loathing press in on me like they haven't in—well, since London, really. It's like I found this sense of *calm* being with Rhys lately, this sense that I have nothing to feel bad or guilty about. But now that he's gone, the guilt is back. It's horrible. I feel guilty about what happened. I feel guilty about letting Rhys down. I feel guilty about everything.

Rhys helped me believe I had more to offer the world than my looks. With him, I felt I was more than a collection of pretty body parts. I believed being anything, *doing* anything, was possible.

But now—now I feel scared and small again, like I did back at Meryton.

I reach for my phone on the floor. Maybe Rhys texted or called. Maybe there's news about his knee—although the way things are going today, I doubt that news is going to be good. My heart begins to thump.

It falls when I see that I have no texts and no missed calls. I guess part of me hoped exhaustion and anxiety were to blame for Rhys's behavior. But now I know he acted like that because he's really done with me.

I can hardly breathe for the hurt inside me. I type in my password and see I have a few new emails. Maybe—*please God, please*—Rhys emailed me. Although I don't know why, he never has before.

When I open my email, I see that I have a message from the dean at my university here in Spain. She sent it earlier today. My stomach flips. I've been waiting to hear from her about my (very late) request to stay in Madrid for another semester. I click on the message.

Thank you for your interest in our program . . . thrilled you've had such a wonderful experience . . . while we cannot accept your application for this coming semester, we welcome you to apply for next fall . . .

I let my arm fall off the side of the couch. I'd laugh if I didn't feel like bawling. It goes to show how far Rhys has fallen in the past forty-eight hours if even *he* can't make this happen. I know I'd be getting a much different email if this whole mess hadn't gone down.

Tossing my phone back on the floor, I wipe away a couple tears and sit up. I wince at how tight my pants are. I want to call Rhys, I want to hear his voice, I want him to tell me to calm the fuck down, that everything is going to be all right.

But it's not. Nothing is okay.

<hr />

Rhys

A few hours later

The results from the MRI came in earlier today. My ACL is fine; the surgeon says I just hyperextended my knee. A few weeks of rest and rehab, and I'll be back on the pitch and good as new.

Olivier and Fred clap me on the back and congratulate me. Coach sends a curse-filled prayer of thanks up to the ceiling, then disappears into his office five seconds later. It's good news. But the relief I feel is overshadowed by the anger and panic that seep through every layer of my being—blood, marrow, bone, skin—like a stain through cloth. I'm hot to the touch.

Cristina is the only one who doesn't congratulate me. Probably because she knows a healthy knee isn't going to bring my sponsors back. It isn't going to help me rebuild my reputation.

It isn't going to change the fact that Madrid could still wash their hands of me, and I'm still at risk of falling down on my family.

I curl my hands into fists. I've got to do something. The odds are stacked against me. I don't have a chance in hell, but I've still got to try. I've got to make people see I'm not the monster my father was. I want to show them it was all a misunderstanding. I want to show them I'm worthy of their trust and their respect.

But how? I run my hands through my hair. I'm tired, but I've got to think. Everything, *everything* depends on it.

A name pops into my head.

Monica Cruz. The curvy model Laura and I ate dinner with at the champagne party in London. I've known her for a couple years now, having run into her at several events in Spain. She famously does a lot of work with people grappling with drug addiction because she is a recovering addict herself.

What if I took Monica to Laura's auction for Santa Caterina? What if Monica and I and maybe the lads on the team took over the entire auction?

My chest contracts at the thought of screwing Laura out of her own event. She's worked hard on it for months now. She told me, point blank, it means a lot to her. But this would be an absolute coup for me. I could clean up my image in the press *and* show my club I'm a decent bloke, all in one fell swoop.

I'd be a total shit to do it. But I don't have much choice. If I can just convince Monica that the story isn't true . . .

"Cristina!" I say. "Cristina, can you get Monica Cruz on the phone? I have an idea."

Laura

Two days later

It's December nineteenth, which means tonight is the gala and auction to benefit Santa Caterina. Viv and Maddie graciously offered to come with me since my other date is . . . well, no longer my date, obviously.

Nuria and the team at Santa Caterina have thankfully been discreet about the whole Rhys situation over the past couple days. Nuria did ask if we can expect Rhys to still contribute to the auction—I told her I honestly didn't know—but other than that, no one's really bugged me about it. Thank God, because every time I *do* talk about it, I end up bursting into tears.

The auction is a welcome distraction, and it's always great to be with my girlfriends. But truth be told, I'd be a little more excited about raising money to buy books for my kids if I wasn't dying inside. I try to put on a brave face, I do. But every so often, when my phone pings and I check it and I see that it's not Rhys, or the girls cast sympathetic glances my way as we walk to the auction, my eyes smart and my throat closes in.

"So you haven't heard from Rhys at all," Maddie says, huddling against the cold.

"Not since he hung up on me after the interview, no," I reply. It's a little before six P.M., and while the sky is wide open, warm with the setting sun, the air has a definite bite to it. "I've tried texting him, emailing him. I've called him a couple times. Nothing. No response."

"Dick," Viv says.

"Is he coming tonight? To the auction, I mean," Maddie asks.

I shrug. "I texted him about it this morning, but haven't heard a word. He's supposed to bring a bunch of signed Madrid gear to auction off." I shrug again and look away. "Whatever."

When we reach the venue—it's a cool old greenhouse not far from my dorm—I immediately know something is wrong. A couple teachers are hauling supplies out the front door and putting them in the back of a truck waiting nearby. I notice a case of wine, some tablecloths, stacks of gilded chairs . . .

"Wait," Vivian says, drawing to a stop. "Aren't they supposed to be bringing stuff *into* the auction? Not out of it?"

"Yeah," I say. "They should be. I wonder what's going on."

When we walk inside, it's all I can do to keep my jaw from hitting the floor. I spent all of yesterday and the better part of today in this space, helping set up a hundred tables, organize hundreds of gifts, and put up hundreds of yards of black fabric to cover the walls and ceiling.

Now, the teachers and some of the catering guys are taking it all down.

What the hell?

I grab one of the teachers, another girl from the states, Sarah, who's studying abroad in Spain. "What's going on? Was the auction cancelled?"

"You didn't hear?" She wrinkles her brow.

My pulse begins to march. "Hear what?"

"I guess I just forgot to call you," she replies. "Did Rhys not tell you? I thought you guys were . . . you know. Close, I guess."

"We're not." Not anymore.

"Anyway," Sarah says. "Rhys Maddox is taking over the auction. He's hosting it—I guess he somehow got the team to pay for it all. How cool is that? Rumor has it he's even bringing some of the other guys he plays with."

"Rhys," I swallow, hard, "is taking over the auction?"

"Yes. He's hosting it at some fancy hotel—we had to change locations to fit all the media and extra guests. The team is promoting the hell out of it, and apparently close to five hundred people are coming."

A high-pitched ringing fills my ears. The saliva in my mouth thickens. I imagine this is how you feel after witnessing an explosion—dumbfounded, more than a little hurt. I blink, but the ringing doesn't stop.

Rhys is hosting the auction? *My* auction?

And the teachers at Santa Caterina forgot to call me? Me, the volunteer who's worked harder than anyone to make this auction happen. Am I really so replaceable? So forgettable?

"Apparently there's going to be a red carpet and everything," Sarah continues as she scoops up a centerpiece from a nearby table. "Totally crazy, right? Nuria is on cloud nine. With all this publicity, we're going to raise some serious dough for Santa Caterina."

I take a deep breath, let it out. "I guess I should head over there then, considering I'm the MC—"

"Oh, I suppose you can still go if you want." Nuria appears at my elbow. "But Rhys has it all taken care of all that. Apparently Olivier Seydoux is taking over your MC duties. Isn't that amazing?"

"Amazing," I say, turning away so Nuria doesn't see me blinking back tears. "Yeah. Totally."

Vivian loops her arm through mine and gives me a gentle tug. "We should get going."

"See you at the hotel!" Nuria calls after us, clapping in excitement.

The cold air stings my lungs when we hit the sidewalk. Tears blur my vision.

"I'm sorry, chica," Viv murmurs.

"We can blow the whole thing off if you want," Maddie says. "Go get hammered at a bar, flirt with hot Madrileños . . ."

I wipe away a tear with the tips of my fingers. "No, I need to be there. This just—God, it hurts."

Maddie leans in for a hug. I let her wrap her arms around my neck, the smell of her coconut shampoo filling my head as I struggle to keep it together.

Back at Meryton, I always felt *less than*. Less than pretty. Less than smart. And because I wasn't pretty and perfect and bubbling with intelligent things to share with the world, I thought I didn't deserve a place at the table. I didn't deserve anything. I was nobody.

It's clear I am nobody to Rhys, and I am nobody to Santa Caterina. I am easily replaced, easily forgotten.

In the past couple weeks, I'd started to believe I was important and deserved a place in the world.

But maybe I don't. It's clear I don't matter, least of all to the people who said they loved me most.

I am anxious as hell as the girls and I climb out of our taxi at the swanky, five-star hotel where Rhys is hosting the auction. A wave of nostalgia washes over me. I can't count the number of times I've swept into a place like this on Rhys's arm. It seems far away, like it all happened in an entirely different life.

Just off to the side, in front of a large terrace that faces the street, the red carpet is in full swing. Photographers call out to the players—I recognize Olivier and his fabulously gorgeous pop-star girlfriend—and people passing by stop to gawk, smiles on their faces.

As much as I began to loathe the whole red carpet rigma-role toward the end, it was so exciting at first. I mean, I eventually fell in love with the guy who stood beside me on that carpet. Hard to believe that guy, the one who looked after me in front of the press, the one who was kind and considerate, is the same guy who ripped my heart out.

"Hey." Maddie loops her arm through mine and pulls me close. "You sure you want to be here, chica?"

I try to swallow the lump in my throat. God, why does it make me want to cry more when people ask if I'm okay? I swear, I had it together two seconds ago.

And now I want to die.

I nod my head.

We're about to head into the lobby when we hear a sudden commotion near the red carpet. The people on the sidewalk who have stopped to watch are jumping up and down, their phones in their hands. The photographers are shouting, scrambling to get the perfect shot.

"Oh, God," Viv says under her breath.

Maddie gives my arm a tug. "Come on, Laur, let's go—"

But I'm frozen in place, my eyes glued to the beautiful couple that emerges on the red carpet. The flashes from the cameras illuminate their faces, their wide, glittering smiles.

It's Rhys.

Rhys and Monica Cruz, my supermodel girl crush-slash-northern star-slash-Oprah figure.

They are on the red carpet.

Together. Rhys is all dolled up in—what else—a ridiculous brocade tuxedo. His hand is on Monica's back. Their bodies are very close. He's smirking, that devastating quirk of his lips that still sucks the air from my lungs. She's smiling. He murmurs something in her hear, leaning on his crutches, and she throws back her head and laughs. He laughs too. They laugh together like they're old friends and have been trading jokes forever.

I feel sick.

Monica is taller than he is, but Rhys doesn't appear to mind that very much. She looks fucking amazing, like she always does. Her skin is flawless and glows with a perfectly even tan. She wears a fabulous dark green gown with even more fabulous jewelry. Her long, luscious hair falls past her shoulders in artfully loose curls. She is so glamorous, so goddamn fabulous and confident and happy.

She is everything I've tried to be. Everything I want to be. But those things feel further from my grasp than ever.

Those things were never meant for me.

The message Rhys is trying to portray by being photographed with Monica Cruz is obvious. *Forget that crazy American bitch who threw me under the bus. Who cares what she said? I've moved on to a super-hot supermodel who also happens to be awesome and a recovering drug addict so clearly I am clean, I am good, just like her.*

I never imagined heartbreak would be a physical sensation. But as I watch the two of them slay the red carpet together, and I begin to understand that everything Rhys promised me was a lie, my heart is cleaved in two. My breastbone buckles.

"Laur," Maddie murmurs, giving me another tug.

This time I let her lead me inside the hotel.

I make sure to stay as far away as possible from Rhys and his footballer friends during the auction. I offer to help, but I'm told everything is covered. So I sit at my assigned table and pretend to drink my wine and eat my dinner. But all the while

I'm shaking with the effort to keep it together, to not break down and cry.

I watch Rhys from the corner of my eye. He's schmoozier than ever, smiling and slapping backs like his world—*our* world—isn't on fire. Seeing him fake it so well while I sit here and shake stokes my hurt to new heights.

Why did he string me along all this time, why did he indulge my bucket-list mania, if all he really cares about are his career, his reputation, his image?

It *hurts*. This hurts. Recognizing that he lied to me—recognizing I am not beautiful enough and perfect enough for him—really freaking hurts.

I head home in two days, and I need to pack, but the bulk of my stuff is at Rhys's place. I thought I'd have a chance to grab it when we talked things out, but it's obvious that's never going to happen. He's done with me. He doesn't want to see me ever again. Which makes tonight the perfect opportunity to go over there and clean out my side of the closet, because Rhys is out and about with his new supermodel friend.

I'll spare him the sight of my ugly face and uglier body. I never deserved a place in his perfect universe. I was an idiot to ever believe I did.

Chapter Thirty-One

RHYS

I play the part of the buoyant, benevolent host with aplomb. The auction is a huge success. Taking it over was a gamble, yes. But everyone—the press, the club, the world—is looking at me anyway right now. I figured why not take advantage of that attention and use it to start cleaning up my image? Heaven knows I've got a lot of work to do.

But all the while I'm thinking about Laura. I steal glances at her throughout the evening. For weeks now, she's been lit up, flush with life, eyes happy and laughing. But tonight—tonight she looks drawn. Sad. It's almost like she's gone back to being the deeply unhappy girl she was on the plane to London.

I've got to speak with her. I've got to see her. It's killing me, having to wait until the auction is over—having to wait until I can have a private moment, out of the press's watchful eye—to talk to her.

I woke up this morning more than determined than ever to keep freezing Laura out. The club, and Coach, took the good news about my knee really, really well. Yes, they are not thrilled about the media maelstrom surrounding the photos, but the team has plenty of experience with the press and know how easily the truth can get twisted. So Cristina conferred with William Wallace about my idea with Monica Cruz and Laura's auction, and a couple hours later I got the happy news that they were in. The club would throw money at a charity to save a player they still believed in.

My relief was enormous, but short-lived. A couple hours after that, *Nuestro Día* released the entire recording of Laura's "interview" at Cristina's insistence. I told everyone I didn't care, I told them I was done with Laura. But as soon as I hung up the phone with William Wallace, I listened to the recording.

My stomach dropped about ten stories. It was obvious in the first fifteen seconds that Laura was being recorded without her consent. She didn't talk to the press. She was talking to Emily on the phone, and had the misfortune of being followed by a reporter with zero journalistic integrity.

I wanted to call Laura. I wanted to apologize, to grovel. But I couldn't. The wheels were already in motion for the charity auction to happen—the auction was going to make me look good in front of the press. The club is paying a pretty penny for the hotel and for Monica to attend with me. I couldn't go back on the team, on William Wallace. I needed this image boost, and so did my team. I couldn't let the lads down, and I certainly couldn't blow off Monica, Madrid's darling.

And what could I possibly say to Laura if I called her? "Hello Laura, I'm so sorry I took your event hostage without telling you, and, oh, I'm also sorry I'm taking a model as my date, I promise it doesn't mean anything but I really need to look good for the press, and I wouldn't look good enough with you."

I'd look like a total ass. I know Laura did nothing wrong.

She doesn't deserve to be treated like this. But it is too late to make it right.

I hope I can make it right tonight. As soon as I get Monica in a cab, I'm going to find Laura to plead my case. I don't know where she might be or who she's with. But even if I have to strangle that guy Javier with a guitar string, I am going to find Laura, and I am going to make things right.

"Everything all right?" Monica asks as we're heading out of the hotel.

I blink. Even in the darkness her painted lips still burn red, the color of a ripe cherry. "Of course. I hope you enjoyed yourself?"

She smiles, bats her eyelashes. "I did, very much. The invitation was unexpected, but I'm glad I could make it. It's not every day I get to walk the red carpet with the one of the world's best footy players."

"It's not everyday I get to walk it with the world's loveliest supermodel," I reply. I struggle not to wince at the terrible line—seriously, it's a curse—but Monica only smiles harder, a flirty thing.

I dig my wallet out of my pocket and grab a five Euro note. I hand it to the doorman with a request for a taxi. I've got to get Monica out of here, quickly, so I can be on my way. I'm practically shaking with impatience. I have so much to say, so much to put right. I don't want Laura to hurt anymore.

Monica crosses one leg over the other and leans toward me. She's waiting for me to ask her out for a drink, a smoke, a fuck. The taxi pulls up. I let out a sigh of relief. If I leave here now, I can be at Laura's in twenty minutes.

I open the door.

"So," she says, pausing on the curb, "would you like to get a cup of coffee or something? I had a very nice time tonight, and I am not ready to go home."

The way she looks at me—confidently, playfully—makes me think Monica Cruz very rarely gets turned down.

But supermodels aren't everyone's thing. I hate to be rude, but I have got to go.

"Listen, Monica"—I blink at a sudden barrage of flashes. I start, blinded, and grab onto the taxi door for support. Shouts echo across the hotel entrance, and then we are surrounded by a gaggle of photographers. The paparazzi found us.

Shit.

Going home together tonight? one of them shouts in Spanish.

Everyone in Spain will love this, another says. *Madrid's sweetheart and Madrid's bad boy, falling in love!*

"Looks like we've been followed," Monica says, a smile on her lips.

"Bloody hell," I grunt. I can't very well turn down Madrid's sweetheart in front of the press—and, by extension, in front of all of Spain. They'll hate me for it.

But if I do take her home . . . they'll absolutely love me.

"Okay then," I say, sliding into the taxi beside Monica. "Looks like we're going to my flat."

The paparazzi follow us all the way to my building. My mind races as I try to come up with a way to get out of this mess so I can go see Laura.

I got nothing.

I run a hand through my hair.

Shit.

Laura

I grab a couple trash bags from Rhys's giant, gleaming kitchen—a kitchen I've never seen him use—and head for the bedroom. Tears, hot and fat, dot my clothes as I take them off their hangers and shove them into the bags.

So this is how it ends, I think. A story in the tabloids and a couple of trash bags full of my shit.

I should've seen it coming. I knew, I just *knew*, Rhys and I were doomed from the start. Who did I think I was, dating a professional soccer player with a Welsh accent and an angry heart? I'm just a normal girl from Philadelphia with a carb-and-cheese phobia who likes to read. I have no place in Rhys's world. I don't belong in his stratosphere.

I don't deserve a place there. Not only am I not pretty enough or skinny enough. It's obvious I'm not brave enough, not confident or smart or free enough. Not like Monica Cruz is.

I clean out my drawer in the bathroom. I dump my tooth-brush and a bunch of nasty hair ties in the trash. I look at the mirror above Rhys's sink. My heart twists, tears at the pale, swollen face looking back at me. God, I'm ugly.

I'm miserable. I am a miserable fucking person, just like I was back at Meryton. I haven't changed one bit, and I probably never will.

I'm tying up the last of the trash bags when I hear the front door open, followed by a trill of female laughter. My blood runs cold. Rhys is supposed to be out with Monica Cruz.

Unless, of course, he decided to bring Monica Cruz home.

I gotta get out of here, stat.

I grab the bags and head out of the bedroom. I try to keep my head down, but even so I somehow manage to meet eyes with Rhys as he strides into the kitchen.

He draws to a sudden, almost comical stop, like he's been hit in the chest by a bullet. One of his crutches falls to the floor. His blue eyes somehow manage to go wide and contract all at once.

He looks so good in his tux, his hair pulled back from his face. Good enough to be on the cover of a magazine.

I was insane to ever think he'd end up with someone like me.

"Hey," he says.

"Hey," I reply. "Don't worry, I'm on my way out."

His eyes move to my bags. He looks back up at me, his handsome features tightening in distress. Disbelief.

"You're giving up on me?" he asks, leaning precipitously on his one remaining crutch. "You're leaving?"

I look away. "Come on, Rhys. We were over before we started."

Monica appears in the kitchen behind him. She draws up short when she sees me, her perfectly painted smile fading.

God, why does she have to be even prettier in real life than she is on the cover of *Vogue*? Her loveliness is blinding.

I look at the two of them together, both celebrities, both stunning specimens of the human species, both glamorous as fuck. And here I am in my tent-like black cocktail dress holding trash bags full of other tent-like clothes.

He brought her home with him. He chose her.

The worst part of it is *I get it*. I get why he chose her over me. I'd choose her too. I would choose someone else, someone better than I am. The two of them—they know what they want from life, and they are fighting for it fearlessly. They are brave, they are free, they are healthy and confident.

They are both far, far superior to me. Miserable old me. I am not pretty or perfect. Worse, I am a coward. I am ashamed—of my body, of my life, everything.

I hate myself.

All the hang-ups and self hate I tried so hard to let go of close in on me, squeezing my lungs, making it difficult to breathe.

This is all my fault. I'm the one to blame for this mess. I overreached, and I got burned.

Monica glances at Rhys, then she calmly but quickly disappears from the kitchen, murmuring something about "freshening up."

My face contracts and tears blur my vision. I want to be angry, I want to rage at him, but I can't. This hurts too much. I want to fucking crawl into a hole and die there.

"I'm sorry," I say, and duck out of the room.

I make my way down the hallway, pulse thumping in my ears as I pass now-familiar landmarks: Rhys's laundry basket, the tray on the narrow hall table where he keeps his keys and his wallet, his shoes lined up by the door.

I hoist the bags over my shoulder and open the door. I only have twelve steps to the elevator, then it's three floors down and I'll be out of this building, out of Rhys's life, out of this vortex of pain.

I hear Rhys's uneven footsteps behind me, heavy and hurried. From the sound of it, he's still on one crutch. "Laura," Rhys calls after me.

I don't respond. Instead I pick up the pace. It doesn't matter if he chases me, if he begs me to stay. I am not good enough for him. I don't deserve him, I can't handle him. I'm only going to mess this up.

I'm a miserable person who will only make him miserable too.

"Jesus Christ, Laura, wait," he says.

"I didn't mean to interfere with your night," I say. I feel smaller by the minute.

I reach for the elevator button, but Rhys beats me to it, slamming his palm against silver placard on the wall. The motion is so violent, so sudden, I flinch.

"Please stop," I say. I huddle against the elevator doors,

away from him. Tears are spilling out of my eyes now, spilling everywhere, there's no stopping them.

He looks at me, eyes full, wounded.

"I didn't"—he pauses—"I didn't mean to scare you, Laura."

"Congratulations," I say, nodding in the direction of his apartment. "She is beautiful."

"Who, Monica?"

"Yes," I say.

"I don't want Monica."

I look at him. "Well it's obvious you don't want me. And I get it, Rhys. I totally get it. I wouldn't want me either. You probably just forgot to text me about our relationship being over, and I *get it*. I don't belong in your life or your world. I never did."

Rhys's brow furrows. "What? What the hell are you even talking about—?"

"I'll be out of your hair in four minutes," I say, slumping against the elevator after I press the button. Exhaustion settles over me, heavy and hard. I've tried to be a better Laura—a freer one—but I failed miserably at it.

I scoff, the sound more than a little hysterical. I'm just so beat down, I don't know what else to do.

"You think this is funny?" Rhys asks. "Laura, you're breaking my fucking heart. Hearing you talk like this . . . I hate it. I hate to hear you say those things about yourself. They are absolutely not true."

He reaches out like he wants to thumb away a tear, but I move away from his touch. I'm shaking now.

"Please don't," I whisper. "I made a mistake. A stupid mistake. I feel so bad about everything. I just—I just want you to be happy, Rhys, but you will never be happy with me."

The elevator dings behind me and the doors slide open. I don't move.

"Wait," Rhys pleads. "Laura, wait, just give me a minute."

He swallows audibly. When he speaks again, his voice is tight, like he's struggling not to cry. "So you never believed in yourself? You never believed you could change?"

"Maybe I did, once upon a time." I shrug. The elevator doors close behind me. "But now? Now it's pretty clear I am who I am, no matter how hard I try to be something better. I should've never involved you in any of this. I'm sorry."

"Did you ever believe in me?" he asks, softly. "Everything I told you, everything we've done together on your bucket list —none of that gave you any faith in me?"

I inhale. My chest feels hollowed out, sore. "None of it worked, did it? So no. I guess not."

"Wait," he says. His voice is gravelly now. He must be crying, but I can't look at him. I can't deal with how my betrayal has devastated him. "This whole time—ever since London—you've been waiting for me to fuck up?"

Pain lights up my gut, my head, my eyes. "Yes. I don't know. I guess I have."

"Laura," he says. "What the fuck? You're killing me right now."

"You're just . . . you're the most superficial person on the planet!" I cry. "You and your cars and your private jets and your shopping sprees—you're fucking ridiculous, Rhys. You fooled me into thinking you were a decent human being, but now I see that you're full of shit. All you care about is money. You're so hung up on your *stuff*."

Rhys cocks his head to the side. "Oh, am I, *princess*? What about you? I know you've bought a whole new wardrobe since we got back from London, and most of it came from expensive places."

"I didn't buy a lot," I say. I'm choking on the pain now. "I paid for it on my own, so why do you care? I'm not some deranged cleat chaser who's after you for your money."

"I care because you're accusing me of being so hung up on my money, but you don't get that you are too. And don't tell me you paid for it—I know you used daddy's credit card for that stuff."

"That is none of your business."

"It is when you're saying I could never live life as an ordinary person like you, even though we both know you've got quite the privileged existence. There's nothing ordinary about staying at a five-star hotel on your first night in Madrid. There's nothing ordinary about living in your boyfriend's six-figure flat. If anyone's full of shit, it's you, doing this bucket list thing while still treating yourself to all this superficial shite. The whole thing is so ridiculous, you're lucky I don't laugh in your face."

His words—these horrible, horrible words—they would've made liberated Laura angry. But they don't.

They make me cry.

"Laugh in my face? Isn't that what you did tonight by bringing a model to an event you stole from me? Isn't that what you've been doing this whole time, stringing me along, making me believe what I said and what I felt mattered, when really all that matters to you is . . . well, you?"

The heat in his eyes contracts into something like pain. We've become toxic people—the kind who stab each other just to see who can bleed the most.

Rhys

I'm horrified.

I'm horrified that she never believed in me.

But I'm absolutely devastated that she no longer believes in herself *because of me*. Because of what I did to her, she is insecure, she hates herself. Because of me, she's morphed back to square one. All the work she's done, all the things we said and did together—I erased it in a single stroke.

No wonder she's hurting.

Truth be told, I wanted to hurt her, I wanted her to hurt the same way I hurt seeing my carefully controlled life go up in flames. I was not prepared, however, for how horrible it'd be making her feel this way. She's in serious pain. So am I. I struggle not to take her face in my hands, not to wipe away her tears and tell her I'm sorry, tell her: I love you, I love you, I've always loved you.

But I'm hurting too. This is beyond repair.

We are beyond repair.

I turn my head away from her. "The rumors you started will haunt me for the rest of my life. When I play a bad match, or I'm photographed doing something stupid, I'm going to have to work twice as hard to clear my name. In the end, that's all I've got, Laura—all I have is my name. And you totally trashed it, and now my family is going to suffer. So many people depend on me. I don't think you understand—"

"I don't." Tears stream down her throat. "But that doesn't mean I don't care, Rhys."

Her eyelashes clump together, small rivulets of mascara marring the skin beneath her eyes. The only person I hate more than Laura Bennet right now is myself. What kind of monster makes a girl cry like this?

"Whether or not you care, the damage is done," I say, struggling against my own tears. "I confided in you, Laura. I told you things about my family I never told anyone else. I thought I could trust you. I thought you understood. But you were careless, and that kills me."

"I said I'm sorry," she says, straightening. "It was an accident, Rhys. A stupid mistake. I would never betray you on purpose. Knowing I'm responsible for everything that happened—*that* kills *me*. What's done is done. It's obvious I don't deserve you. I never did."

I scoff. "Maybe you're right, *love*."

The second the words are out of my mouth I regret them. It's the most vile, most hurtful thing I could possibly say to Laura. But I said it, it's done, we're done. We're really done.

Laura straightens her shoulders, like the blow I just landed knocked her confidence back into place. She bends down and grabs her trash bags.

"Maybe that's true, and maybe it isn't," she says, quietly. "I know you think you just want to do right by your family. But I wonder how much longer you can keep pretending."

"Keep pretending what?"

She meets my gaze. "That what you want doesn't matter."

I roll my eyes, even as her words pierce my heart like an arrow. I hit the elevator button. "Are you done? Monica's waiting."

The elevator doors open. Laura moves through them, shoulders slumped. My heart thumps in my chest, an ominous, painful reminder of the hateful things I said and did. It's too late to take them back.

Laura turns inside the elevator and looks at me one last time. She takes a breath, her lips part.

Then the doors slide shut, and she's gone.

Chapter *Thirty-Two*

LAURA

The Next Day

I set the last stack of neatly folded clothes into the enormous suitcase laid out on my bed. A semester's worth of work and memories, reduced to a fifty-pound bag. There's my new jeans, the ones in the bigger size; a manila folder filled with all the essays I wrote for my classes; and then there's a Madrid home jersey, number 5, a signature scrawled in Sharpie marker on the top right shoulder.

Rhys's signature. Rhys's jersey.

I wipe away the tears that spill from my swollen eyes. I know healing a broken heart takes time, but I'm already impatient for this grieving period to be over. I'm morbidly exhausted, for one thing. For another, maybe Rhys isn't worth crying over. He was such an asshole last night. I'm still trying to wrap my head around some of the awful things he said to me. Part of me believes the guy who said those things wasn't Rhys. The Rhys I knew and loved would've never pushed me down. But then part of me believes I deserved every word.

I grab the jersey and toss it in the trash. It's just a reminder of how stupid I was to ever think I belonged in his world. I'm not blazing with confidence and happiness, like Monica Cruz. I never will be. I gave my bucket list the old college try, but it didn't work. I feel more insecure and more unhappy than ever.

I just suck.

I plop into my chair and rub my eyes. God they're sore from all the crying. I wonder if it's late enough to go to bed. It's got to be close to eight by now. At least I *hope* it's close to eight. I just want this day—this semester—to be over.

It's a depressing feeling.

I take a deep breath, let it out. I need to snap out of it. It requires a lot of energy, beating yourself up like this. Energy I need to save for the trip back home.

My phone dings—a text—just as I reach for it. My stomach flips. I hate myself for admitting this, but I can't help but hope that it's Rhys. Maybe he's feeling as miserable as I am—

I pick up my phone. It's a group text from Maddie. She sent it to me, Viv, and Rachel.

Mujeres. It's our last nite together in Spain. Throw your shit in a suitcase, then let's tear it up 1 more time. Meet at Atico? Wear your drinking pants.

I let my head fall back. The last freaking thing I feel like doing right now is getting dressed up and going to our favorite discoteca, Ático. I want to lick my wounds in private. I've had a rough couple days, and the temptation to wallow in self-pity while listening to sad Coldplay songs is too strong to resist.

Sorry ladies, I text back. *Don't think I'll make it. Thx for the invite tho.*

Rachel responds right away.

Fuck that noise. Laura, you are coming out. Don't make me come to your dorm and drag you out. You know I will.

This makes me laugh.

Its our last nite, Maddie adds. *Don't let that dbag idiot with the manbun ruin it! You know you will regret not coming.*

I bite my lip.

I have an early flight, I text.

Viv responds. *You can sleep it off on the plane. That's what 9 hr flights are for.*

I laugh again. After the heaviness of the past week, it feels good to contemplate something other than my impending doom. Plus, a glass (and by that I mean a pitcher) of red wine sangria *does* sound delightful.

Pleeeeeaaassseee, Rachel texts.

I was starting to think this semester was a total bust—I was starting to think that absolutely nothing good came out of it—but I was wrong.

I was wrong because in my self-pity stupor, I forgot about the Madrileñas. I guess because I've always had a boyfriend, I haven't had many close girlfriends. Em was pretty much the only one until I came to Spain. But that changed when I met Maddie and Viv and Rachel. They've been by my side all semester long. They've laughed and cried and danced with me, and have been there for me when no one else was.

They love me like a sister. So, yeah, I may be going back to Philly with a broken heart and a shattered ego. But I'll be going back with three new best friends. In my book, that's a giant win.

All right, I text, *you guys wore me down. Where shall we meet? And what is everyone wearing besides drinking pants?*

I stand up and wipe my eyes one last time. Enough of all this wallowing, this self hatred. Yeah, things didn't work out with Rhys, but that doesn't necessarily mean I am a total waste of life. Rhys may not love me, but my friends do. I don't deserve to be treated like shit just because I'm not perfect.

I'm not perfect. But I'm fun, damn it, and I deserve to be loved.

I'm worth it.

I am going to be the girl I always wanted to be, come hell or high water.

And that girl would go out with her friends on her last night abroad.

So I wash my face and put on some eyeliner. I dig my heels out of my suitcase and get dressed in jeans and a sparkly top. I catch a glimpse of myself in the bathroom mirror. I look . . . mehhhhh. Not amazing. Thankfully Spaniards like their bars dark and their discotecas even darker.

But you know what? I feel all right. I feel pretty stoked, actually, and pretty lucky too. I get to go out in Madrid with my best friends one last time.

I miss Rhys like crazy. I feel like I'm walking around with a hole, a physical, burned-out hole, in my chest. But learning to love myself means loving my mistakes too. I may really, really miss Rhys—God, I can hardly breathe I miss him so much—but I refuse to let what a guy thinks of me define my entire existence.

I'm done with him. Which means I can begin working on *me*.

Rhys

That Day

I may be on crutches, but I make it a point to be seen at training on Thursday morning. It's our last session before we all head home for the holidays. I want the news crews and the owners and most of all the lads to see that despite the maelstrom that's followed me the past few days, I'm still Rhys

Maddox. I'm still here, I'm still going to do right by everyone. I try to wave to the cameras and smile with the lads.

But it's more of a struggle than ever.

I can't shake feeling that Laura is right, I can't keep pretending I'm happy to live my life according to the expectations of my family, my team, my sponsors.

I felt so fucking *alive* with her. Now that she's gone, I'm dead inside.

But I've got to move on. A few sponsors decided to stick with me, and in an effort to show them that I'm more responsible and dedicated than ever, I'm back to my usual regime of eat, work, sleep, repeat. I'm basically back to the career-obsessed person I was before Laura's bucket list took over my life. I said I didn't have time for a girl before, but now I *really* don't have time. My life is literally on the line. I can't chase after Laura. What if we end up having a fight in public? I can't risk another blow to the fragile relationships I have with my sponsors and my squad.

I mean, what would the headlines be if the press knew I was back together with Laura? *Idiot Maddox Dumps Madrid's Sweetheart for Unpredictable American Who Called Him an Alcoholic?* Okay, that's a ridiculous headline, but still. I can't risk it.

I wait for all the good attention I'm getting to lift my spirits, like it usually does. I adore being adored. Or I used to, because it meant I wasn't my father, it meant I could give Mags and Mum everything they ever wanted but thought they could never have.

But I feel worse. Much, much worse, knowing I've got Spain's love—well, sort of—but not Laura's. Knowing that adoration came at such a high price. The way she looked at me in the elevator . . .

I hate myself for bringing her so low.

Practice ends, and I hobble toward our training facility as the other lads jog past me. I catch Olivier moving toward me from the corner of my eye. I up my pace. I'm not in the mood for whatever ridiculous shit he's in the mood to expound upon. Now, more than ever, I need to stay focused, stay positive, so I can recover as quickly as possible and be an asset to my club.

But Olivier will not be thwarted, per usual. He slows to an elegant stop beside me, running a palm over his bald head to wipe away a sheen of sweat.

"Petit Chou, and how iz ze bum heart—oh, I mean—bum *knee* today?"

I slant him a glare and grunt. "It hurts."

He holds his hands behind his back and nods sagely. God, he can be annoying. Who does he think he is? Gandalf? Or that other wizard from Harry Potter—Dumbledoo?

"'ave you 'eard from Laura?"

I roll my eyes. "I have no idea what you just said."

"Stop playing zat game, it iz very stupid, just like you," he replies. "What you did wiz zat model girl at ze auction, it was 'orrible! Just 'orrible. I know you do not love 'er. You love your little duck, Laura. You miss 'er, I know you, and I know your heart. I see you do not sleep, you do not eat. You look very bad."

"Thanks," I say. "That's just what I needed to hear after banging up my knee and being embarrassed in front of the entire world. You're the fucking best, Olivier."

He shrugs. "Ze truth, it 'urts sometimes. I do not want to see you 'urting, my dear friend. I am sorry my words, zey can be mean, but I only say zees zings because I want to see you 'appy. Laura made you 'appy. And now, wizout 'er, you are not 'appy."

"You're actually quite miserable," Fred says.

I jump at the sound of his voice. He's one step behind us, his thick blond hair stuck to the sweat on his forehead, his hands on his hips as he looks down at me.

"Why do you keep *doing* that?" I growl.

"Doing what?" he says.

"Appearing out of nowhere like James goddamn Bond. For someone so big, you move *really* quietly."

Fred shrugs. "It's a gift."

"No it's not."

"Anyway," Olivier says. "Laura loves you, yes? The 'eart and soul of you, not your moneys or your fame or your pretty hair."

My anger softens, just the tiniest bit. I slow down. God, I'm tired.

When the hell did I get so tired?

"I get what you're saying, Olivier. And I don't disagree. But you realize I can't take your advice about Laura loving me for me seriously when you're a guy who seduces pop stars in his bathroom waterfall," I say.

It's Olivier's turn to shrug. "I play around for a bit, 'ave much fun wiz all ze ladies of ze earth. But soon, I look for love. And when I do, I find a girl just like your little duck. Brave. Strong. Very fun, full of life."

I blink. "I know. She's—Laura is all of those things. All of them. But she's gone and I can't focus on this right now. I need to lie low, I need to get better so I'm not cut from the squad. I need to make the few sponsors I have left happy. The media circus around Laura and me has finally died down, and stirring that up again could be the nail in my coffin. I've got to think about my family—they need so much bloody help . . ."

Olivier arches a brow. "You can still 'elp your family, Cabbage, wizout zem taking over your lifes. What you try to do for zem is very noble, but it is 'urting you, it 'urts your 'appiness. I meet your mummy. I see she is very nice lady. She only ask that her son be 'appy. Give your mummy and your family what you can. But when you put all your energies into

313

saving *zeir* lives, you have no energies to enjoy *your* life. Do I make sense to you?"

My heart turns over in my chest. What Olivier is saying makes perfect sense. It's such a difficult thing to let go of, living every moment in the hope of making life better for the people I love.

But when did it become my job to kill myself to do that? When did I start sacrificing my own happiness so they could have theirs? I don't know when I lost the freedom to seek out my own life and my own happiness, but Laura gave that freedom back to me. She made me see what I thought I wanted—to show my family I wasn't my father by providing for them in a way he never could—had nothing at all to do with what I really want. And that is to be free to be *me*, to live in the moment and enjoy my life.

Things I only did when I was with Laura.

Living like this—living solely to provide for my family—isn't right. But damn it, how on earth could I make things right without losing my sponsors, my place on the squad? And after our fight, Laura would never in a million years take me back.

"You do make sense." I look out over the pitch, squinting against the early afternoon sun. "I was happy when I was with Laura. I really was. But the fight we had last night . . . I said some things. Bad things. I hope she forgets them, and forgets me, and moves on . . ."

My eyes burn at the thought of Laura being with someone else. I look away so the lads don't see. *It's just the sun*, I assure myself. *It's making my eyes water.*

But my heart—my heart tells me I'm full of it.

"I have to move on too," I manage. "It's not meant to be. Trust me, even if I tried, she'd never take me back. And this morning, Cristina assured my sponsors—"

"Bullshit," Fred says. "You can make it happen, Cabbage.

You have to try, at least. She turned your life, and your game, around. You owe her that much."

I start to move more quickly. "She's leaving tomorrow and she's not coming back."

I should be relieved Laura's leaving so soon. Being gone will also help the media maelstrom to blow over a bit more quickly. If I cared more about my career than I did about her, this would be good news. I should be feeling good about it all.

"Follow 'er," Olivier says, holding open the door for me. "Go to America and get 'er back. Forgive 'er. Make 'er yours. It is very clear to me your 'ead—and your game—will not be okay until you make 'er yours. Go after 'er. Now. There iz not one moment to spare."

My knee starts to throb. My anger returns with a vengeance. Anger at Olivier. At myself. It's too late. I'm too late.

"What part of 'it's not meant to be' don't you understand?" I ask. "We're done, Olivier. I'm fucking done with her."

Chapter Thirty-Three

RHYS

My flat is quiet when I hobble through the door. I used to like the quiet. I thought it was an essential part of my routine. I couldn't sleep if there was so much as a leaky faucet disrupting the silence, the *drip drip drip* keeping me up, keeping me from getting the ten hours of sleep I thought I needed to feel rested for training the next day. It would drive me absolutely bonkers.

Now the silence feels oppressive. It's a reminder that my flat is empty.

It's a reminder that Laura isn't here anymore.

I hobble to the kitchen and open the fridge. My chef left a bit of the usual—boiled chicken, some cauliflower—but even though I'm starving, the thought of eating that flavorless tosh depresses me beyond words. Instinctively, I dig into my pocket for my mobile, thinking I'll call Laura, maybe ask her to meet me for some deliciously unhealthy tapas at this place down the street we've been wanting to try . . .

I blink, remembering I can't call Laura. I pushed her away for good.

For a second I can't breathe, knowing I'll never try that restaurant with her. I'll never do anything with her again.

I busy myself scouring the kitchen for something else, anything else, opening drawers, digging through cabinets. It hits me that I don't know my way around my own bloody flat. I paid a good bit of money to renovate the place. I thought Mum might come to live with me for a bit when Maggie went off to Oxford, and I wanted it to be cushy and luxurious in a way our house back in Cardiff never was. I wanted to impress her.

I slam a drawer shut and splay my hands on the countertop. Sure, all the marble and the furniture and the fancy appliances are impressive. Mum will probably love it.

But what does that matter if I don't feel at all at home here? If it will never feel like home as long as Laura is somewhere else.

I lean into my hands as regret chokes me. It hits me, knocking the wind from my gut like a rogue pass gone wrong.

Christ have mercy, I've cocked up. There's no way I can live here without Laura. I don't want to. I don't want to anything without Laura. She's home, and I am completely lost without her.

The quiet presses in on me. Yes, Laura helped make a mess of my life. I'm out most of my sponsors and money. I don't know what will become of me. I don't know when I'll be back on the pitch, or if I'll be any good once I'm there.

But I do know that no matter what happens next—good, bad, or ugly—I'll be okay, happy, even, as long as Laura is with me.

I am scared out of my mind that I've lost her. I used to think that falling for a girl would distract me from my first and only love—footy. But Olivier was right (of course). Falling in love with Laura has focused me. It's not only made me a better player, it's made me a better man. A man who is worlds better than my father, anyway.

I've been so scared for so long that I'd follow in his footsteps. But with Laura, I'm not scared anymore. I like who I am with her. I love how she makes me feel. I know I'll never end up like Dad if I'm with her because she makes me happy. Dad was never happy. He never found his happily ever after.

For a while I thought maybe I didn't deserve to find mine either.

But I have. And I'll be damned if I let it go without a fight.

I grab my phone, glancing at the time. *Shit*. I hope it's not too late. Transatlantic flights usually take off earlier in the day, meaning I don't have much time to do what I need to do and intercept Laura before she takes off tomorrow morning.

I immediately start searching for names, numbers, anything that will help me make the wild idea that just popped into my head happen. It's got to work.

I've got to get my girl back.

Laura

The Next Morning

The taxi screeches to a halt in front of the terminal. I swallow the bile in my throat. I mean, yeah, I'm hung over as hell, which isn't helping matters. But it's still a miracle I made it here in one piece because every time you step into a taxi in this city, you're taking your life into your hands. I won't miss almost dying everyday, that's for sure.

The Madrileñas and I did our last night in Spain right. Less than three hours ago, I was on the dance floor at Ático practicing my sprinkler move while Rachel shimmied up against me. I giggle at the memory. I love those girls and I'm going to miss them. Maddie and Vivian are staying in Madrid for another semester, so we won't all be back at Meryton until next fall. I kinda don't know what I'm going to do with myself next semester. With Em still in London, and no boyfriend to speak of, I'm going to be on my own for the first time in literally forever.

I blink back tears as I help the driver dig my luggage out of the trunk. I felt better about the whole Rhys situation while I was dancing the night away, but this morning my sadness and ire have returned full force. I miss him. I hate myself even more for missing him. My heart feels tender and sore, and I know it's going to feel this way for a long time.

Offering the driver a watery smile, I hand him a tip and start rolling my bags toward the wall of glass doors on the other side of the sidewalk. This airport is huge and anonymous, so different from the homey airport I'd fly in and out of with Rhys. Man, I was spoiled.

I tuck my chin into my jacket. It's chilly this morning, clear and cold, and my breath swirls around me in an uneven cloud.

I slow my stride as I approach the doors, waiting for them to open. I stop short at the sound of squealing tires, followed by distant shouts.

I glance over my shoulder. A giant bus pulls up to the curb, its shocks hissing as the driver lowers it to allow passengers to get on and off. I look around, but all I see are a couple taxis and a limo.

My foolish heart skips a beat. There's no way Rhys came to say goodbye. I wonder how long it would take before I stop looking for him.

I still watch with bated breath as the limo driver opens the door. It can't be. It can't—

My heart sinks at the sight of an older couple, maybe my parents' age, climbing out of the limo. Definitely not Rhys.

Swallowing, I shake my head. I'm being stupid. Rhys isn't coming. He's done with me, told me in so many words he never wants to lay eyes on my fugly face again.

I need to go or I'm going to miss my flight.

I head through the doors and make my way to the ticket counter. It's still early, so the airport isn't crazy yet, but I still have to wait in line before I can see an agent. Standing there, my pulse finally starting to slow, my exhaustion hits me like a ton of bricks. As much as I'm dreading going back to Philly— I mean, I'm not even excited about Christmas—I am looking forward to getting on the plane and enjoying a nice, nine-hour nap. I wonder if they'll serve breakfast on the flight . . .

When it's finally my turn, I hand the agent my passport. Even though I greet him in Spanish, my gringo accent must be worse than ever, because he immediately starts speaking to me in English. It's a relief, sure, but also kind of a bummer. I won't be speaking much Spanish back in Philadelphia. I probably won't be coming back to Spain for a long, long time.

The agent hands me my ticket and checks my bag. It's a little over the weight limit, so I have to empty some of the stuff into my carry-on before he'll take it.

The security line takes forever. Long, bright rectangles of yellow morning light pierce my eyes and warm my legs. I inhale the sharp smell of freshly brewed espresso. It makes my head hurt. I sway on my feet, certain I'm going to die if I don't get some sleep soon. My bag is heavy. My feet are heavy. Everything feels heavy. It's like the universe is weighing me down, willing my body to remain right where it is.

I miss him. I don't want to leave.

I start to cry as I approach the security lady. This cry is different from all the others I've had in the past few days. Those were loud, Oscar-worthy cries where I hyperventilated myself into a numb stupor. This cry is quiet, mainly just big, fat tears that come one after the other. I wipe them away with the edge of my passport. It's the resignation cry—the cry that comes when you realize it's really over, whatever you hoped for isn't going to happen.

The semester is done. I'm at the airport. My flight leaves in less than an hour. Rhys is not here. He's not coming.

We are really over.

The security lady looks at me as I hand her my passport and sighs, like she's seen a thousand crying girls like me and is seriously annoyed by the whole thing. I don't blame her.

"Laura!"

I blink at the sound of my name. My vision is blurry, so I can't really see anything. But I recognize that voice—

"Laura! Oh, oh thank God, I thought I'd missed you."

I blink again at the sound of hurried footsteps. Someone is running, getting closer. Through my haze of tears I see a figure approaching, a weird little blob on the top of his head. *Man bun.*

It's a man bun.

My heart seizes. I'm blinking wildly now, dragging my fingertips across my eyes in an attempt to clear them. For a split second I do.

My eyes land on another pair of eyes. Blue eyes. I recognize them.

It's Rhys.

Chapter Thirty-Four

RHYS

The moped emits a high-pitched whine as I gun it. I brace myself for a surge of speed, but instead I get a slow, steady progression to about fifty kilometers an hour. I let out a howl of frustration.

At this rate, I'm never going to get to the airport on time.

Ahead of me, Olivier impatiently revs the engine of his Bentley. He sticks his arm out the window, motioning for me to speed up. I motion back, something that I hope communicates: "I can't speed up, so just do your bloody job and clear the road for me so I can make it to the airport in time to intercept Laura before she boards her flight and I can grovel and beg and cry if need be so she'll take me back."

Olivier must get the message because he slows down. On the passenger side, Fred waves cars past our sad little parade. It's early, but with the approaching holiday, the road to the airport is an absolute zoo. More than once I fear for my life. The wind is freezing, and this moped thing is not for the faint-hearted.

A couple people pull up beside me and honk their horns, laughing at the guy riding a pink moped as they pass. I think of Laura—I'm always thinking of Laura—so I flick them the bird. As our version of the bird is the two-fingered V, it feels a little funny at first. Then, as people stop laughing, it starts feeling pretty great.

Laura would be proud. I love that girl.

My heart is pounding, an insistent, panicked beat. I'm going to make it to the airport with hardly any time to spare. Despite offering them thousands of euros and my firstborn child, the moped rental place refused to open any earlier than eight A.M. this morning. By the time I filled out all the paperwork and got gassed up, I had less than fifteen minutes to reach Laura.

I've got to make it. I can't let her get on that plane without letting her know how I feel.

Without trying to apologize for being a complete and utter jackass.

When we finally pull up to the terminal, I'm dizzy with impatience. I had to keep my leg straight during the drive on account of my bum knee, but I only half succeeded and now my entire body is lit up with pain. I thought I'd just toss the moped in Olivier's trunk and drive it to the airport, but we tried and it didn't fit. Plus Olivier wasn't all that keen on a pink moped dinging up his brand new Bentley.

I park the moped at the curb, ignoring the no parking signs that are posted all over the place. Olivier and Fred whip out of the car. I duck out of my helmet and hang it on the handlebar.

"On pain of death," I say, tossing the moped keys to Olivier, "do not move from this spot."

The keys land in his palm with a merry little jingle. "Of course, little Cabbage. I will not fail you in zis."

"Fred, you're coming with me."

I don't wait for him to follow, and I don't grab my crutches either. They'll just slow me down. I hobble as fast as

I can into the airport, terrified that I'm too late, that she's already gone. I frantically search the ticket counters, even though she wouldn't be here, not unless she was going to miss her flight.

I grab the front of Fred's jacket and point to the terminals at the other end of the building. "You go over there and see if you find her—her gate number wasn't available last I checked. Call me straightaway if you do. My mobile is on, all right?"

"All right," Fred says, nodding solemnly. "We'll find her, Cabbage, I know we will."

He takes off and so do I. I head for the security line that disappears into a wide hallway a little ways ahead.

A few people stare as I pass by—I know that stare, they're recognizing me—but I don't care. I've got to find Laura.

My heart falls as I scan the people waiting in the security lines. I don't see her anywhere. I look for her long hair, probably tied up in a messy knot at the crown of her head. I look for her proud shoulders, the familiar slope of her neck. I'd recognize her anywhere.

"Please," I murmur to myself as I look, and look, and keep looking. "Please be here. Please please please."

Yes, I can buy a ticket and go through security myself if Laura is already at her gate. But by the time I do all that, she'll already have boarded. I can text her now, I can try calling when she lands, but I know she'll ignore me. It's what I deserve.

This is my only shot. My only chance to make things right before she's gone forever.

Then I see her.

I catch a glimpse of her face, an inch of an enormous black puffer jacket.

It's her.

Jesus Christ, it's Laura. She's at the very front of the line, handing her passport over to the security people.

I start running. My knee is on fucking fire, but I keep running.

"Laura!" I shout.

She turns to face me. She's crying.

Laura

Ohmigod. Oh my *freaking* God.

Rhys's eyes look tired, scared, blue as ever. And hopeful. He looks at me with hope, like he's about to ask me something.

I don't know if that look makes me feel relieved or angry or sad. But I'm suddenly overwhelmed.

I start to shake. *What do I do, what do I do,* what do I say to the guy who ripped my heart out but still looks at me like *that*?

"Rhys," I manage. My voice is high and tight. "What's going on? What are you doing here?"

"I messed up," he says.

I swallow. "No kidding."

His cheeks burn pink. "I messed up bad, Laura. I regret everything I've done in the past few days. I hurt you. I intentionally hurt you, I was totally selfish and totally stupid, and I wish I could take that back. But I can't, and I'm sorry. I'm so fu—" he glances at the people around us. "I'm just really, really sorry. I don't expect you to forgive me. It's only what I deserve after the way I treated you. I know you'd never throw me under the bus on purpose, but I was too angry and too scared to get past that. What happened was awful, but it's nothing we—me—I—it's nothing I can't work to fix. You're my best friend, and I love you. I am *in* love with you."

Beside me, the security lady lets out another sigh, this one less annoyed, a bit more swoony. The woman behind me fans herself. I glance at the people still waiting in line, worried they'll be pissed that I'm holding them up. But everyone is watching us with naked interest. I guess everyone loves a bit of drama, especially when it includes Rhys Maddox the football star and his cute little man bun.

God, it's cute. But that doesn't change anything. That doesn't change the fact that he betrayed me. The things he did and said were incredibly hurtful. How can I ever trust him after everything that happened?

I blink. "Thank you. I appreciate that. I, um . . . appreciate what you're trying to do here, Rhys. But I've got to go—I don't have time—"

"Don't." He steps toward me. The urgency of the movement brings goosebumps to my skin. I can't tell if they're the good kind or the bad kind yet. "Don't just leave like this. I've got a moped waiting out front—a pink one, no less—and a thousand apologies I'd like to make to you."

I draw back. "You drove a pink moped here?"

"I did. That tour of the city you always wanted to do—I'd like to take you. Show you around town."

"That's sweet," I say. And it is. It's very sweet. But it's too little too late.

Rhys must know what I'm thinking, because his eyes darken with hurt.

"Please," he says.

"I've got to go," I say. "I'm holding up the line."

"Laura."

"I'm sorry."

"Don't be sorry. Be with me, love."

I scoff. "Your lines—they're worse than ever."

"They're absolute rubbish. Stay."

"I can't."

He reaches for my face, tucking his shoulders, but I step

back, heart bursting. If I don't get out of here ASAP, I'm going to lose it. I need to make my flight.

I take my passport from the security agent.

"I'm sorry," I repeat. "Goodbye, Rhys."

Before I can second guess myself, I turn and start winding through the maze of the security line.

"Laura," Rhys calls after me. "Please . . . please don't do this. Don't walk away from me."

But I keep walking. People are staring now, and I'm crying, but I keep moving. I can't look back. There's nothing left for me here.

<hr />

Rhys

"Fred!" I huff into my mobile as I rush through the airport. "Fred, meet me at the ticket counter. I have to buy a ticket."

"A ticket? To where?"

"Anywhere. Doesn't matter. I just need to get through security. I found Laura, but she's already heading to her gate. Hurry!"

"I'm on it. I'll get on line and hold a spot for you, Cabbage. Take it easy on that knee."

By now I'm practically hopping around on one leg, but I don't care. I keep hopping. I probably look like a lunatic, and it's only a matter of time before I scare someone enough to call the cops. Hopefully that won't happen before I get to Laura again.

I almost collapse in relief when I see Fred at the front of the line at the ticket counter. He grimaces when I sidle up beside him.

"It's going to be expensive," he says. "With the holidays, almost everything is sold out."

I look at the ticketing agent. "How expensive?"

"Very," she says. "For one ticket, probably close to a thousand euros, depending on where you'd like to go."

"Anything available on flight 1811 to Philly?"

Her fingers fly over the keyboard. "I'm sorry, but that flight is completely sold out."

I dig my card out of my wallet and hand it to her. "Fine. I'll take two tickets to any flight departing from terminal 1."

"Two tickets?" Fred shoots me a look.

"Yeah. You're coming with me. If only so you can carry my corpse back to Olivier's car after Laura publicly rejects me again and I die a thousand fiery deaths. Come on, let's go."

The security line has somehow tripled in size since Laura made her way through it ten minutes ago. I shove what cash I have into the hands of the people waiting in line, murmuring my apologies, and then I get on my knees—literally get on my bloody knees like the desperate Romeo I am—and beg the woman checking passports to let us through. I know I've got her five seconds in, but she still makes me beg for a solid two minutes while she fights a smile.

I tell her, and everyone else in line, the whole sordid story. Holding my clasped hands up to her face, I finish with a tearful, "You saw how beautiful she was. How proud. I don't deserve her, but you've got to let me through so I can try to make things right. Please. In the name of love, let me through!"

She lets me through. The entire area—people waiting in line, security guards, a pilot, and some flight attendants waiting on the priority lane—erupts in applause. I bow my head, thanking them, and then Fred and I make a run for it.

Luckily, people let us skip them in the X-ray line too. Even then, it feels like it takes forever. We emerge into the giant terminal, Fred glancing in one direction, then the other.

"You know what gate she's at, right?"

I glance at the screens on the far wall. "I do. This way. Hurry!"

By now I'm sweating, breathing hard to keep up with Fred's long stride. I'm terrified that we're too late. I'm terrified that if we're not too late, Laura will just walk away from me again.

What the fuck am I going to do then?

I try not to think about it as I push through the pain and the people on my way to the gate.

"What are you going to say to her?" Fred asks, trotting beside me. "How are you going to convince her not to reject you so you don't die all those deaths?"

I shake my head. "Honestly? Haven't got a clue. I'll think of something. I hope."

"You will." Fred puts a hand on my shoulder and cracks a grin. "Just no more pick up lines, all right? They're awkward for everyone."

My grin catches as a bolt of pain moves through my leg. I draw up, clenching my teeth.

"You all right, Cabbage?"

"No," I grind out. "Let's go."

"You sure?"

"I'm sure. Go."

We round a bend and arrive at the gate. My heart stops beating altogether when I see that the gate is empty.

Completely, entirely empty.

"What the hell?" Fred says. "You sure this is the right gate?"

"I'm sure. I just checked the monitor as we passed." I look around, hoping to find someone to ask. "Shit. Shit shit shit."

I nab the first flight attendant I can find. She tells me there's been a last minute gate change, and that the plane heading to Philly is now at a different gate.

A gate that's all the way across the terminal.

I hang my head. My knee is on fire. I don't know if I can make it.

"Climb on." Fred turns his back to me.

I stare at him. "What?"

"Climb on my back. You'll never get there in time with that knee. I'll carry you."

I grit my teeth again. Then I climb onto his back. "I suppose we're doing this, then. Let's go!"

We start to hustle back through the terminal as I'm bobbing on Fred's back. People are really staring now. Just a little farther. I can make it a little farther . . .

We finally make it to Laura's gate. People are lined up and boarding. My stomach flips. If she's already on the plane, I'm screwed. I leap off Fred's back, landing on my good leg with a wince, and immediately hobble into the fray.

I draw up in front of her as she's bending down to get her bag.

Her hazel eyes, red from crying, go wide when she straightens and sees me.

"Rhys? What the hell? How did you—?"

"Tickets," I gasp. "I bought a ticket."

Laura searches my face for a beat, like she's not quite sure what to make of me, not sure what to make of all this.

"You're too much," she says at last.

"I know. Can't be helped, I'm afraid."

"You didn't have to do"—she looks me up and down —"whatever this is. I'm getting on that plane. I'm going home."

I duck my head so that I'm looking into her eyes. "Just hear me out, all right?"

She folds her arms across her chest. She looks away. "You're wasting your breath."

"You're going home," I say. "But I can't. I won't. Not

unless you're there. Because you are home. Laura, you're home to me."

I take a step forward. She takes a step back. I glance over my shoulder at Fred, who's pretending not to listen a few feet away. He nods, encouraging me, urging me to keep trying.

"I'm home to you?" Laura asks, her voice wavering. "But you made me feel like I wasn't . . . I don't know, good enough, or glamorous enough, to belong in your life. You said as much yourself. And the model, Monica—"

"I wanted to push you away. I was just using Monica to get back at you. That was fucked up, Laura. I'm sorry. Nothing— I mean *nothing*—happened between us. She's a nice enough girl, but she's not you. I'm sorry. I'm so sorry, Laura."

"That hurt," she says. "A lot."

"I know. And I don't expect you to believe me. But I do intend to grovel as long and as hard as I must to prove you're *the* girl. The only one. You'll always come first."

Laura shakes her head. "I'll never come first. We both know that. I'll always come after your career and your sponsors. You're terrified everyone will think you'll turn into your dad . . ."

"Not true," I say. "Well, that was true, not too long ago. But Laura—Laura, you made me see things differently. You turned a light on inside my head and made me see how bloody miserable I've been, putting all that stuff first."

The gate attendant comes over the loudspeaker, calling for group two to board. Even though Laura makes no move to go, I reach out and gently curl my fingers around her forearm.

She doesn't pull away.

"I understand you don't want to believe me," I continue. "But I'm here, aren't I? I'm making a fool of myself for you. I'll always make a fool of myself for you because you've shown me what I truly want."

"And what's that?"

"Doing the stuff on your bucket list—learning to live in the moment with you—you taught me that I want to be free."

"You want to be free," she says with a scoff. "Really?"

"Free from what everyone else needs. From what they think. I'm finally free to be myself because of you. *You* did that, love. We were both so caught up in appearances, in making everyone else happy. Then you took your stand, and pursued your bucket list in earnest, and you were intent to prove there was more to life than that. And you did. You proved it to yourself, and you proved it to me."

Laura

I close my eyes. Rhys is killing me, saying these things. He's saying what I've wanted to believe about myself all along—I am more than just a pretty face. I've got more to offer than that.

Life is about so much more than that.

His hand on my arm is warm.

"I'm proud of you," Rhys says. "Whether or not you get on that plane right now, I want you to know that. I'm proud of you, and I'm so fucking in love with who you are and what your soul is made of, I'm not sure I'll ever get over you."

"Get over me?" I say, my voice cracking. "Rhys, I don't know if I'll ever get over *you*."

He looks at me, really *looks*, a look that is so heated and so pleading it rearranges my insides. "Then don't. Stay with me. I told Mum that I won't be home for Christmas—I'm hoping I might invite myself to Philadelphia? I've got a plane waiting, just for us. I thought we might do the moped tour first, of course . . ."

I keep looking at him. I don't even know what to say. I

LESSONS IN LETTING GO

must be dreaming. This is a freaking dream come true. Rhys is making all my dreams come true.

And for the first time, I don't want to think about whether or not if I deserve the happiness bubbling up inside me. I don't want to wonder if I worked hard enough for it or if it's a fluke.

I just want to enjoy it. Live it. Share it with Rhys.

He clears his throat. "As I see my little speech didn't win you over, perhaps a pick up line might do the trick? I know how much you love those."

I bite my lip. "Whatcha got?"

"That outfit you're wearing—was it on sale?"

"No. Why?"

"Because it should be one hundred percent off."

I laugh. I can't help it. I laugh, a giggly, relieved thing, and Rhys does too.

"Wow," I say. "Wow, that was your worst one yet."

He wiggles his brows. "Bloody awful, isn't it?"

"Cabbage, really, that was terrible. I'm embarrassed for you," Fred says, peeking over Rhys's shoulder.

I give him a little wave. "Hi, Fred."

"Hello, Laura. Lovely speech, though, don't you agree?"

"Very lovely." I turn my gaze back to Rhys. "So lovely I'm considering kissing the shit out of him right now."

Rhys's eyes light up. His grip on me tightens, just a bit. "Really?"

I take a deep breath and let it out. My heart still feels sore, but it's a different kind of sore now. It's the good kind. The kind that lets me know it's alive. It may not be altogether well, but it's still beating.

It's beating for Rhys.

"Really," I say. "I freaking love you."

And then I drop my bag and I curl my arms around Rhys's neck and I maul him with the most delicious make-up kiss ever. I pour everything into this kiss, my relief and my happiness and my disbelief this is really *happening*. I am becoming the girl I've always wanted to be, and the guy by my side is the kind of man I've always wanted to be with. We found each other, and in so doing, we found ourselves. Or maybe it's the other way around, I can't tell. It's such a mess, our history. Such a lovely mess.

I pull back at the sound of applause. Blushing, I grin shyly at the people waiting in line to board who are cheering us on. A few guys hold up their phones, and an older man puts his fingers in his mouth and whistles.

I glance at Rhys. For half a heartbeat, I wonder if he'll turn away, run. The old Rhys would've hated being caught making a fool of himself.

Instead, he takes my face in his hands and presses his lips to mine. The kiss is slow, deep, showy, putting on a show for our little audience, marking me, claiming me, telling the world he is mine and I am his.

Behind us, Fred politely clears his throat.

"So I, um, hate to interrupt," he says. "But I'm worried your, uh, moped will get towed soon if we don't get moving."

I look at Rhys. "So you really did get the moped?"

"Of course. Couldn't let you finish your semester without doing the tour. I promised you we'd do it." He grabs my hand. "Shall we?"

Before I know what's happening, Rhys is climbing onto Fred's back, and then the three—well, technically two I guess —the two of us are walking.

We pass the security lady. Her face breaks out into a huge smile as we pass.

Inside my chest, fireworks explode.

I draw up short when we walk out the main entrance. There, pulled up to the curb and surrounded by a small mob of angry-looking security officers, is a moped painted the softest, girliest shade of pink. Beside it, Olivier leans against a gleaming black Bentley, flipping his keys nonchalantly like he isn't about to be arrested by airport cops for egregious illegal parking.

He smiles when he sees us. "Ah, ze lovers! I am very 'appy to see you together once more! Zis, it is a Christmas miracle."

"Well," Fred grunts, setting Rhys on his feet, "I certainly got my workout in today."

"Ah, but you 'ave more workouts to do zis day, non, wiz your lady friend Rachel?" Olivier says with a wink.

"Wait, *wait* a second." I blink. "Fred, are you and Rachel—?"

Fred's face turns bright red. "It's—I—she—I'm helping her find, uh, an internship," he stammers.

"An internship," Rhys says with a smile. "So that's what the kids are calling it these days. Interesting."

He hobbles over to the moped and holds out a pink helmet. "Ready, love?"

"Yes," I say, letting Olivier take my bag before I duck into the helmet.

I climb onto the moped behind Rhys. He guides my arms around his waist.

"Hold on tight," he says.

I lean my cheek against his broad back, inhale his scent. "Like I'd ever let you go, fancy pants," I say.

Rhys guns the moped. Our bodies surge forward and for a second the bike leans precipitously to the side. My heart jumps to my throat. Oh dear, maybe this wasn't the best idea . . .

Just when I'm sure we're about to plummet to our deaths, Rhys turns and rights the moped. To my gigantic relief, we take off, a bit wobbly at first. But once we're on the highway, we hit our stride. People honk, laughing, as they pass the two of us chugging along in the slow lane.

I laugh too. I squeeze Rhys, pulling him close. If I could somehow curl his body into mine, it wouldn't be close enough. He is my happily ever after, a wonderful thing. But even better than that, he's my I'm-so-happy-*right-now*-I-could-burst. Every moment I have with him gets better and better. I'm so freaking happy to be with him, to laugh with him, to experience anything and everything with him. Living in the moment with Rhys has been the biggest joyride ever. Especially when you're experiencing that joyride on a powder pink moped during a beautiful morning in Madrid.

If that's not happiness, I don't know what is.

THE END

EPILOGUE

Rhys

January – One Month Later
Madrid, Spain

I palm the door closed behind Laura, trapping her against it. I hover my mouth an inch above hers. She smells sweet, like red wine and the cinnamon sugar that coated the churros we ate. In the space of a single heartbeat I am hard as a fucking rock and wild with need. You'd think after three weeks of non-stop sex, I'd need a break already. But I can't get enough of her.

I can't believe she's with me. Lucky bastard indeed. We spent this afternoon like we spend every afternoon we both have free—laughing, eating, exploring. Madrid is a whole new city when I see it with Laura. Today we took guitar lessons, and then we went to see Laura's favorite Goya paintings at the Prado Museum. It's stuff I never would've done before—stuff I would've never thought was worth my time—but I must admit I adored every minute of it.

"Tell me, love," I say, running my nose up the length of her neck. "Are you glad you came back to Spain?"

Laura's breath catches. "I mean. I haven't been able to really walk right since I got back. But besides that . . ."

I look up to see her grinning at me. My heart swells. "I'd say I'm sorry. But I'm not. I love you."

"*I* love *you*," she says.

I press a kiss into the hollow just beneath her ear. "And how might I love you this afternoon? On the kitchen counter, perhaps? The sofa? Oooh, what about the tub?"

"Shower," she pants. "I'd like to wash after running around all afternoon."

My lips twitch. "Sounds lovely."

I follow her into my bedroom, watching as she shrugs out of her jacket, pulls her sweater over her head, unbuttons her jeans. She leaves a trail of clothes in her wake. I add to the pile, tugging at my clothes with impatient fingers.

Laura flicks the lights on in the bathroom and throws me a heated look over her shoulder.

"Hurry up," she teases. "I want you. Now."

Tripping out of my briefs, I dart into the bathroom and open the shower door. I turn on the water. The tip of my dick grazes the knob and I grit my teeth. If I'm not careful I'll blow my load before Laura comes.

And Laura's got to come first.

"Ready, love?" I ask, ducking out of the shower.

She grins. "Are you ready to work your hot footballer magic?"

I hold out my hand. "I am indeed."

Laura takes my hand. The steam from the shower starts to fill the bathroom, surrounding us.

She squares her shoulders, moving into my caress as I pull her against me into the shower. I always thought I was a tits (and tambourine, obviously) guy, but I've got to say my favorite part of Laura is her shoulders. I love the constellation of freckles that dot her skin here. I love how proud and strong they are, her shoulders, the architecture of her bones and her bravery absolutely beautiful.

My dick leaps at the sight of her naked tits.

Okay. Maybe I'm a shoulders *and* tits and tambourine guy.

I run my finger down the furrow of her spine. I cup one of her breasts with my free hand, plucking her nipple between my thumb and forefinger.

The steam gathers on her skin, covering it in a fine, almost pearlescent sheen.

"Rhys." Her arm darts out. She clutches my shoulder, using it to support her weight. Her eyes flutter shut. "Oh, Rhys."

And then I'm taking her face in my hands and bringing my mouth down on hers and backing her underneath the showerhead, my dick grazing her belly as I press my body to hers.

The water stings because it's a little too hot, but it feels right. It feels like it should hurt, like it should be almost too intense to handle.

"This okay?" I ask.

"Yeah," she says. She reaches down between us and wraps her fingers around my throbbing cock. "You okay?"

"Please." My voice is strained. "Please don't do that, love, or I'm going to come in about two seconds. I want you to come first."

"Oh—okay," she says, but before she removes her fingers the little minx swirls the pad of her thumb over the head of my cock.

My knees almost buckle.

"Fuck." I catch her hand. "You're making it really, really difficult to be a gentleman tonight."

Before she can torture me any further, I reach behind her for the soap and work up a lather.

I set the soap down, lather running down my arms, and

step back to face Laura. I watch her face as I work my hands in lazy circles across her body, paying particular attention to her breasts and nipples. Her mouth falls open, she closes her eyes, and rests her forehead on my chest. Rivulets of water soak her hair and run down my torso. I'm hot and bothered but I have her, thank God, I have her.

My heart works double. She trusts me, she's opening up to me, and that's the biggest fucking turn-on ever. I want to worship this girl.

I *am* going to worship her.

She arches into my touch. Steam swirls around us, catching the light, diffracting it into a soft glow. My hands move lower, lower.

Lower.

I slip a hand between her thighs. Her eyes fly open as the first knuckle of my thumb meets with her clit. She digs her teeth into my pec as I drag my hand back and forth. We're both slippery, wet as fuck, and I have to close my eyes to keep from coming on the spot. It's so hot in here it's hard to breathe.

"That," she moans, "feels *so* good."

I swallow, hard.

I hook a finger inside her, pressing the heel of my palm to that spot she likes so much. With that hand I guide her to the wall, teasing her mouth with mine as we move. She lets out a hiss when her back meets with the tile.

"Rhys," she says, lips tangling with mine as she speaks. "Oh, Rhys, *yes.*"

I fall to one knee, then the other, trailing my mouth down the soft slope of Laura's belly. With my free hand I grasp her thigh, as slippery and hot as her cunt, my fingers gliding up to her hip. I guide her leg over my shoulder, spreading her wide just as my lips meet with her pubic hair. The citrus scent of my soap, mingled with the delicious scent of her arousal, fills my head.

"Oh, Jesus," she says. She stays put against the wall, but her hips roll back from my probing mouth. Her instinct is to run; this is uncomfortable for her. She's trying to fight it, I know she is, but it's not easy. "What about your knee—"

"My knee is fine." And it really is, thanks to the hours I've put in at PT.

I pull my finger out of her, gently, and grasp both her hips in my hands. I look up at her from my perch two centimeters from her pussy. I want to taste her so badly it's making me dizzy.

Using my thumbs, I open her folds, baring her center to me. My dick swells to porn-star proportions at the sight of the deep, slick reds, the dusky pinks, the swollen nub at the top of her cunt.

Oh Jesus is right. I've never seen anything more beautiful.

I wait for Laura to hesitate—she's still a little self-conscious—but to my delight, she curls into my movements, opening to me without a second thought.

I dip my head and lick her, back to front, the heat of her arousal almost singeing my tongue. She tastes like Laura. Like laughter and wine and earth. She cries out when I work my tongue in a lazy circle around her clit, nicking her with my teeth. She begins to roll her hips against my mouth, and I can't help but smile when she digs her hands into my hair, urging me closer, wanting more of what I'm giving her.

I guide my tongue into the center of her slit, and she cries out again. Her legs begin to shake, she's not far off. I almost curse.

Her pussy swells around my tongue, and she's full-out riding my mouth now, her head thrown back, skin glowingly wet. I press my tongue to her clit, and then—

And *then*.

Laura comes. The weight of her body bears down on my hands and she clutches my shoulders for support and her cunt contracts. I keep my mouth on her as she comes, kissing her cunt as she cries out, and digs her fingernails into my skin. She collapses against me.

Rising to my feet, I curl her against me, holding her as the shockwaves continue to rack her body. My dick is so hard it hurts.

But I want to hold her. I want to be there for her as she comes down.

Maybe I need her to hold me too. Because having her like this, being a part of that joy of hers I fucking love, is making me feel unsteady again. Like I can't tell up from down, left from right, where I end and she begins.

After a beat, Laura turns her head, noses my breastbone, and laughs.

It's relieved laughter, and giggly laughter, and happy laughter. All those things. Things she just felt with me.

"Really?" I say in mock offense. "After the very real orgasm I just gave you, you're going to laugh at me?"

"I'm not laughing at you," she says, burrowing into my arms and wrinkling her nose. I kiss it. She's adorable. "I don't know why I'm laughing, actually. I just feel so . . . good, I guess. That—what you just did, holy moly—*that* felt good."

Her eyes blink open, slowly, sated and warm, and that tear in my chest—the one I felt that night in London when I left her—it bursts open, blood and joy and *holy fuck I am so in love with this girl* flooding my chest.

I laugh too, powerless against the joy that fills me up. And then I slip inside her, and the world goes quiet again, save for the soft sound of our bodies coming together again and again and again.

Laura

I sit on the edge of Rhys's giant, fluffy bed and towel off my wet hair. My legs are still shaking from our little shower session, and I don't trust myself to remain upright. We've been going at it like bunnies ever since we got back to Madrid at the beginning of January. It's like we can't get enough of each other.

It's freaking wonderful.

Rhys emerges from the bathroom, wearing a pair of his football shorts and nothing else. They hang low on his hips, revealing his chiseled torso, his rock-hard chest, the tattoos that cover his skin. I blink. Even after all this time, I have to make sure Rhys isn't a mirage, that this isn't a dream. He is that beautiful. Heat flares between my legs.

Jesus, is he *ever* going to stop turning me on?

He offers me a shy smile, his cheeks flushed. *I can't believe you are mine*, I silently say to him. I can't believe after everything we've been through, we ended up together.

We ended up happy.

"Do you have any homework you need to do?" he asks.

I grin at his concern. While we never got anywhere with the university I attended last semester in Madrid, I ended up enrolling in another program at an even better school in the city—one that is more accommodating to last minute applications. I'm taking some pretty great classes with even better professors. To be honest, I like it better than Meryton. The best part is, all my credits transfer, so I won't fall behind on my graduation plans even if I decide to stay here next year too.

Which, considering how great things are, is probably going to happen.

"I actually finished everything last night," I reply. "Thanks for asking, though."

"Of course—can't let the GPA part of your new bucket list slip."

"You're cute, you know that?"

"I do." He smirks. "So. Since you don't have any homework, would you like to watch that documentary you were talking about?" he asks. "I was going to cut up a bit of cheese, maybe put out some crisps to snack on."

I bite my lip. "Fuck yeah I would."

"Excellent."

I grab my phone from the nightstand. "Just let me call my mom real quick—she's dying to know how you felt being back on the pitch."

Rhys made his post-injury debut at training yesterday. So far, so good. He says his knee feels better than ever.

I hit the button on the side of my phone. The screen blinks to life.

My stomach drops. I have three missed calls from Emily, along with half a dozen texts.

Pls call me

Need to talk to you

Laura, I think Luke is cheating on me. Just had big fight and we broke up. Pls call me

Oh my God.

"Holy shit," I say. "Holy *shit*."

"What is it?" Rhys calls from the kitchen.

"Emily and Luke broke up!"

"What?" Rhys reappears at the bedroom door. "That's awful news. But I *did* think there was something slimy about that bloke."

Rhys met Luke when he came home with me for Christmas break. While Rhys loved pretty much all my other friends, he never really warmed up to Em's boyfriend.

"Yeah, but . . . he's *Luke*. He and Em, are, like, basically one person at this point. They've been together forever."

Em picks up on the first ring. She's crying so hard that for several beats she can hardly speak.

She's a total freaking mess.

"Emily," I say. "Em, take a deep breath. Tell me what happened."

"Luke. Luke, he . . . I guess he's been cheating on me for years, basically since we started dating. I got an email from this girl . . . she said they'd been hooking up. She said he'd hooked up with other girls too. I confronted him, he said he didn't do it, but then I shoved the evidence in his face. He said . . . oh my God, Laur. What am I going to do?"

I blink. I don't know what she should do. This is awful. So awful and so unlike the Luke I know, I'm not sure what to say.

I meet Rhys's eyes. He nods at me, encouraging me to encourage Em.

"It's going to be all right," I say.

"No it's not," she says. "Oh, God, how did I not—hey, Laur, do you mind holding on a minute? Kit is calling."

"Kit?" I ask. "I thought you still hated Kit."

"I do, it's just—ugh, it's hard to explain. Give me a sec."

I pull my legs up onto the bed and stretch them out in front of me. My head spins as I wait for Emily to come back. What in the world is going on? Why would Luke cheat on her?

And why is Kit calling her in the middle of all this drama?

"Hey," Em finally says. "Sorry about that. Listen, can I call you later? I gotta go."

"Gotta go? Go where? Are you meeting up with Kit?"

She pauses. Lets out a breath. "You promise not to judge?"

"Judge what? Emily, what's going on?"

"It's complicated. I'm going to meet Kit—he's taking me out for a pint. Can I call you later?"

"Um. As long as you promise to explain why Kit is taking you out for a drink after you just found out your boyfriend, who is basically your husband, is cheating on you. No offense, Em, but this makes, like, absolutely no sense to me."

"I know," she says. "It makes no sense to me either. And I still hate Kit, I just . . . look, I'll call you, okay? I'll explain everything."

"You promise?"

"I promise."

She hangs up. I drop my phone on the bed.

What the hell just happened?

"Everything all right?" Rhys asks, softly.

I shake my head. "I'm not sure, to be completely honest. She's leaving to get a pint with Kit the Prince."

"Kit the Prince? But that makes no sense."

"I know, right? Something weird is going on with them. Really weird."

"You think they're . . . you know. Hooking up?"

"No," I say. "At least I don't think so. Em is—was—way too in love with Luke. Although I do think she has a crush on Kit."

Rhys shrugs. "She'll fill you in eventually. In the meantime, shall we start that movie? I admit I'm curious about the history of wine."

"No you're not," I say, grinning.

He shrugs again. "Whether I am or not, you've got five seconds to get out of that bed before I join you. And we both know we'll never get around to the documentary if that happens."

We spend the rest of the afternoon curled up on the couch, polishing off a whole block of Manchego and a handful of documentaries I've wanted to watch. It's pretty tame, yeah.

But it's also pure bliss.

Thank you so much for reading Lessons in Letting Go! Rachel + Fred's story is up next in Lessons in Losing It (Study Abroad #4). Flip the page for a juicy excerpt!

LESSONS IN LOSING IT EXCERPT

Fred

"You've been a really good friend to me," I say softly. "What can I do to return the favor?"

When Rachel turns to look at me, her eyes are dark. Saucy.

"You can fuck me," she says.

My pulse hiccups. "I was going to do that anyway. But if you've got a lot on your mind—if you need some time—"

"I don't need time." Her hand falls out of her hair. "I need you to have sex with me. Now. Fred, please. Last night, I felt so—I don't know. Amazing. I want to feel like that again. Get out of my head for a little, you know?"

I look at her. She looks back at me.

I nail the first turn I can. We're somewhere in the old town, Madrid's medieval quarter where the streets are narrow, quiet, a labyrinth of cobblestones and shadows.

Perfect.

It's loud driving over the cobbles, but I don't slow down. I take a left, then a right, working my way farther into the labyrinth. It gets quieter. Darker.

I pull into an alley and, seeing that no one's around, throw the car into park and turn it off.

"Get in the back," I murmur, unbuckling my seatbelt.

"Wait," Rachel says. "Are we—the sex—are we going to do it here?"

"You said you wanted me to fuck you. Now." I look up at her. "So that's what I'm going to do."

"But we're in public!" She gestures out the windshield, a smile of disbelief breaking out on her face. "Someone will see us—"

"No they won't," I say. "But it could make things a bit more exciting, yeah?"

"I didn't know you were an exhibitionist."

"I'm not. I just want to repay the favor, remember?"

She looks at me for a beat. Then another. "You're fucking excellent, Fred. You know that?"

"I do. Get in the back."

"Okay." She takes a deep breath. "Okay."

Rachel unbuckles her belt and, putting a hand on my shoulder, climbs into the backseat. I'm too big to manage the same maneuver, so I turn off the car and get out. Glancing around one last time, I open the car door and slide onto the back bench beside Rachel.

It's dark back here, the only light coming from a nearby window. I can just make out Rachel's face. She's breathing hard. Looking at me with parted lips. Her dark eyes aren't wet anymore, but I hope—I think—she's wet somewhere else.

Her eyes flick to my mouth. She runs her tongue along her bottom lip.

This girl. *This fucking girl.*

I reach for her, putting my hands on her neck. Her head falls back when I bring my mouth down on hers. I lean into her and her hands go to my chest. I drink her in, opening her to me with my tongue. She kisses me back, hard, her breath coming hot and fast against my face. She tastes clean, like water, a hint of gum.

I'm hard in the space of a single heartbeat. My dick throbs against the crotch of my jeans, seeking her tight heat. Seeking release. Christ, I've been dying for this all day. Dying for her.

Her hands are on my face now, and she's climbing on top of me, straddling my lap. The front slit in her dress falls to the side, revealing the top of her thigh.

I groan when she settles her weight on me. I curl my fingers around her waist, slide them to her hips, and I guide them in a slow, grinding circle against my dick. She gasps. Bites my lip.

She's got her arms around my neck now, moving against me in a steady grind. My dick is throbbing. I lift my hips, just a little, roll against her.

I reach around her neck and gather her hair in my fingers, pulling it across her back to drape it over one shoulder. This leaves one side of her throat completely revealed— completely vulnerable. I sink my teeth into the soft skin there, gently sucking it until she cries out.

"Fred," she moans. "Oh, please. *Please*."

With my other hand I tug her dress up her thighs. Reach between her legs.

I pull back when I encounter the thin lacy strap of a thong.

It's soaking wet.

I meet her gaze. "Oh my God, Rachel."

"All day," she pants, closing her eyes. "I've been wet like this all day, thinking about you."

I swallow, hard. I knew Rachel and I had chemistry. I didn't know our attraction would go this deep. Would haunt both of us like this.

I'm so fucking turned on it hurts.

"My jeans," I grunt. "Unbutton them."

**Thank you so much for reading Lessons in Letting Go!
Rachel + Fred's story is up next in Lessons in Losing It
(Study Abroad #4).**

Thank you for reading LESSONS IN LETTING GO—I hope you laughed, you cried, you got turned on by the sassy bits. If you got *especially* turned on, please consider leaving a review. I very much appreciate reviews, as they help readers find new authors like me!

Book #4 in the Study Abroad series—Lessons in Losing It (Study Abroad #4), Rachel and Fred's story —is available now for FREE in Kindle Unlimited Check out the next few pages for a super sexy excerpt. I hope you enjoy it!

I'd love to stay in touch—here are a few ways to reach me:

- **Check out Jessica Peterson's City Girls, my reader group on Facebook for giveaways, serious discussions of seriously hot guys, and more**
- Follow my not-so-glamorous life as a romance author on Instagram @JessicaPAuthor
- Follow me on Goodreads
- Follow me on Bookbub
- Like my Facebook Author Page
- Drop me a line at jessicapauthor@jessicapeterson.com

Dear Reader,

Thank you very much for picking up LESSONS IN LETTING GO. I've wanted to write a football/soccer hero for a long time. When I studied abroad in Spain, my girlfriends and I were a little obsessed with the Eurotastic superstars who played for Madrid's famous club de fútbol. David Beckham was playing in Madrid back then, and I fantasized about running into him at the grocery store or in the park (of course he'd immediately fall head over heels in love with me).

The David Beckham-becoming-obsessed-with-me bit never happened, but I knew one day I'd love to write a story where it did. I don't play "footy"—like Laura, I went to soccer camp once and cried the whole time, no joke—but I am totally intrigued by the culture surrounding European football. I remember the athletes were practically revered as gods in Spain. I went to a match when I studied there, and being in that stadium was like nothing I have ever experienced. It was loud and raucous and fun as hell. Revisiting that night while writing this book was such a blast.

Laura's battle with perfectionism is also something I experienced in college. Looking back, I see now I lost so much time and energy to the treadmill during those four precious years —energy I should've spent having more fun, getting to know my professors, and doing more interesting things. I really, really wish I hadn't been so focused on appearances, on "playing perfect." Laura gets this while she's still in college (I'm jealous). It took me well into my twenties to recognize what an idiot I was, and how much I missed out on. I'm trying to make up for it now.

A big thanks to my editor, Kristin Anders, for her genius (and tough) edits; to my cover artist, Noelle Pierce of Selestiele Designs, who also provided invaluable feedback on the first draft of this book; to my formatters, the Formatting Fairies; and to Marie Force, for sharing as much as she does with newbie indie authors like me.

And thanks especially to you, for taking a chance on a new author. I sincerely hope you enjoyed Laura and Rhys's twisty —and smokin' hot—path to happily ever after!

Besitos,
   Jessica

PS—I love it when authors include a playlist of songs that inspired them while writing a book, so thought I'd do the same. Here are the jams I listened to on repeat while I wrote Rhys and Laura's story. Check 'em out—they're all available on iTunes:

"Underdressed", Vérité
   "What Do You Mean", Justin Bieber (sorry not sorry)
   "Distraction", RAYE
   "Superficial Love", Ruth B.
   "sHe", Zayn
   "Too Good", Drake feat. Rhianna (LOVE ME SOME DRAKE AND RIRI!)
   "Fill the Void", Stwo feat. Amir Obe & Daniel Caesar
   "Temptations", PARTYNEXTDOOR
   "Waves", Miguel feat. Travis Scott
   "All Night", Beyoncé
   "Heavenly Father", Bon Iver

ALSO BY JESSICA PETERSON

THE SEX & BONDS SERIES

An outrageously sexy series of romcoms set in the high stakes world of Wall Street.

The Dealmaker (Sex & Bonds #1)

The Troublemaker (Sex & Bonds #2)

THE NORTH CAROLINA HIGHLANDS SERIES

Beards. Bonfires. Boning.

Southern Seducer (NC Highlands #1)

Southern Hotshot (NC Highlands #2)

Southern Sinner (NC Highlands #3)

Southern Playboy (NC Highlands #4)

Southern Bombshell (NC Highlands #5)

THE CHARLESTON HEAT SERIES

The Weather's Not the Only Thing Steamy Down South.

Southern Charmer (Charleston Heat #1)

Southern Player (Charleston Heat #2)

Southern Gentleman (Charleston Heat #3)

Southern Heartbreaker (Charleston Heat #4)

THE THORNE MONARCHS SERIES

Royal. Ridiculously Hot. Totally Off Limits...

Royal Ruin (Thorne Monarchs #1)

Royal Rebel (Thorne Monarchs #2)

Royal Rogue (Thorne Monarchs #3)

THE STUDY ABROAD SERIES

Studying Abroad Just Got a Whole Lot Sexier.

A Series of Sexy Interconnected Standalone Romances

ABOUT THE AUTHOR

Jessica Peterson writes romance with heat, humor, and heart. Heroes with hot accents are her specialty. When she's not writing, she can be found bellying up to a bar in the south's best restaurants with her husband Ben, reading books with her adorable daughter Gracie, or snuggling up with her 70-pound lap dog, Martha.

A Carolina girl at heart, she fantasizes about splitting her time between Charleston and Asheville, but currently lives in Charlotte, NC. You can check out her books at www.jessicapeterson.com.